Crashing STREAMS OF CHANGE

Crashing STREAMS OF CHANGE

MOULTON AUGUSTUS MAYERS

CITIOFBOOKS, INC.
3736 Eubank NE Suite A1
Albuquerque, NM 87111-3579
www.citiofbooks.com
Hotline: 1 (877) 389-2759
Fax: 1 (505) 930-7244

Ordering Information:
Quantity sales. Special discounts are available on quantity purchases by corporations, associations, and others. For details, contact the publisher at the address above.

Printed in the United States of America.

ISBN-13:   Softcover   978-1-960952-35-6
                eBook   978-1-960952-34-9

Library of Congress Control Number: 2023910190

CONTENTS

Dedication

It is with heartfelt love and impassioned devotion that I dedicate this most searchful and profound book to my dear, dear wife, Shelley, who has been with me through the thick and the thin. Oh, love, like an old friend; it just wouldn't leave you alone. And how wonderful it is to have a friend indeed. Friends, like flies around molasses; most fly away after the factory goes to sleep: The others remain and build new ones. Friends, as many as reliable people whom you just know would be there in the brume. Oh, my darling girl, Shelley! As pretty as a star and as warm as a fireplace. Love, like a flaming meteorite; it flew six trillion miles and landed right in our bosom.

ACKNOWLEDGEMENT

The realization of being called to the august station of literary work is a delightful experience indeed, and being set aflame with writing talent's burning candle, on the inside of you, is a life awash with zeal's flaming light. Waking up one day and realizing that you have been called to society's astral circles of brilliant writers has been truly a difficult thought to assimilate. The blazing fire of writing has always burned in my heart, and in that vein; I have always been inspired and prodded to write. When the time did finally come for me to realize that long elusive dream; I plunged into it with all the fire, and ardor, and enthusiasm that had long been boiling in my soul. The delightsome journey of writing this book—with all of its beautiful twists and turns and flaming moments—has been a very inspiring engagement and useful experience.

Its myriads of humorous episodes, delightful scenes, and heartwarming moments will fill its uncounted readers' hearts with many smiles, chuckles, and giggles. Moreover, this very lively, provocative presentation will do something else: It will infuse your hearts with unforgettable memories and leave you with a lot to think about for a very long time!

Although the actual writing of this book was a piquantly pleasant experience, filled with stirring moments and strong laughs; its overall preparation was quite arduous and toilsome. The spiny, thorny sandpapering process of proofreading, varnishing, and polishing this book's pages was a massive and Herculean task that should not be undertaken by the faint of heart. This marvelous literary production would not have been possible without my wife Shelley-Ann Mayers' profound sense of understanding of the toilful rigor of penning a book of this caliber.

Moreover, much of this book's scrubbing and polishing may be directly attributed to Shelley's unweariable effort in helping me to produce this flaming and most wonderful piece of art. Her unwearying endeavor with the book's clean-up process has been a most charming and meaningful contribution to this mammoth literary production. Additionally, the Internet's numerous and versatile forums have also been a powerful and useful instrumentation in helping me to assemble the multitude of ingredients needed to execute this most interesting and intriguing task. I have also been inspired by a few impassioned writers, in particular, Mr. Mark Levine's *The Fine Print of Self-Publication* has been quite instrumental in putting this together.

The Introduction

ave ever wondered why people read books and seem to be in a never-ending search for some obscure treasure? Is life itself a mystical search for some lost connection in the past—does the world seem like a search for some hidden treasure? If you've been besieged by these rather harrowing and compelling questions and are still looking for these answers; you will, most certainly, find them in the pages of this book. Life is a hidden treasure that only gives you so much time to find it; but once you find that priceless pearl, it changes your life forever. Have you ever wondered why some people seem ever so happy and fulfilled, and others are grumpy and unhappy all the time—why? If these questions have never bothered you and you are happy with your business-as-usual life, do not read this book: It is written to people who are puzzled by life's strange and often confusing quirks that leave them wondering, why?

However, if these questions have burned within, and intrigued you; and you've been curious about life's meaning and how it is all going to play out, this book encapsulates all the answers and treasures for which you've been searching. Have you ever wondered why things end and people deceive themselves and others? Yes, if you would take this book and read it very carefully; you would find virtually all the answers for which you've been searching all your life: You would also find that this is a book like practically none other, and you would wonder, "What is the origin of all this fresh information—where did this writer learn all of this? To which university did he go? And the truth is that he went to the same university to which you went but asked different types of questions and lingered in that zone of inquiry until the answers came.

This presentation is a very lively, entertaining, and arrestingly delightsome work of art; although its contents are somewhat controversial, it is a refreshingly promethean love story, with tremendous entertainment value. Its superb blend of sassy entertainment and poignant controversy forces its readers to re-evaluate their perception of life as they have always known it. In this regard, it is important to understand that this is not a Christian book per se, but rather a matter-of-fact presentation of truth from the sprawling library of nature and the colorless mind and eyes of true science. Forasmuch as the book treats the issue of truth and meaning, it does embody a decidedly religious flavor; however, it is not necessarily a religious book: It is written to a universal audience that is tired of the stuffy and rampant lies that are so cavalierly told in society today and wants a more meaningful reality.

The sheer strength and Turneresque beauty of its poetry are extremely inspiring and uplifting. If you read this book with an open mind, detached from contemporary society's frothy biases vanities; you will discover a new and refreshingly delightful world of freedom, passion, dynamism, and a flaming splash of new colors and beauty. A realistic, new adult fictional genre; the book is a riveting, matter-of-fact look into the dusky cave of the human experience on the earth: It would make you laugh like crazy, cry like a baby, and rethink the way you see the world forever. Written to a broad audience with a clear, academic bent; the book is a splendid read, with many episodes that you would remember for a very long time. This seemingly wonderful commentary does not come close to doing this book the justice that it really deserves; for the materials presented in it are so profoundly meaningful, refreshingly different, and positively life-changing!

This book, in plain language, is a game changer and a new way to look at the world; and oh, what a novel perspective that is! The book's radical objectives are as follows: First, it endeavors provide readers with clean, refreshing, and dramatic entertainment in the context of unvarnished truth; although the materials are interesting and sparklingly delightful, they are also very informational and thought-provoking. Inasmuch as this author delights in provoking people to think for themselves; he has presented fresh, provocative ideas which he believes would jar his readers to start thinking for themselves. His reason for doing this is not necessarily to get his readers to agree with him; but rather to inspire them to initiate fruitful, constructive, pragmatic dialogue on the subject. This book is the first in a series of five fictional monographs that are squarely intended to instruct and challenge societal perception about how the world really works.

Secondly, this book endeavors to expose the rank lies and senseless gaps in society about human existence in the world. Although the ideas presented are exotic, different, and somewhat obscure; their everyday value is rock-sold, explosively provocative, and life -changing. The ideas contained in this book represent a uniquely different angle at which to view the world: It is a sick, confused, pathetic institution of human society on the earth, with hidden secrets scattered everywhere. They explain the root of all human problems, conundrums, and woes and offer tenable scientific solutions; specifically showing you how the world works and how to win and succeed without following the false model that it presents to mankind.

Thirdly, the book strives to amplify and dramatize the fact that, because the human system in the world is false, even the noblest of societal institutions cannot be trusted; and the reason for this is that human institutions are woven from the same fabric of falsehood, out of which earthly life itself is knitted. As has been stated before, this ideological twist is unique and challengingly unfamiliar; however, this writer strongly encourages those who find the materials disturbing to open their own eyes and begin to see and think for themselves.

Hence, this is where objective, unbiased observation becomes so handy and valuable. You need to understand that the world trains and socializes you to only think a certain way—the wrong, false way: All this book's author asks of you, his critics—and he knows that there will be a shrivel of you— is to observe the world as objective spectators or unbiased scientists and see what you find. If you are honest about things, you will reach some of the same conclusions to which this writer has arrived because that is merely the way truth works—objective observations, analyzed by people with no hidden agendas nor axes to grind.

And fourthly, this book desires to accentuate the value of patience and true love in a world where these virtues and values have faded and have become virtually extinct. The book parodies the tremendous importance of patience and truth in human relationships, through a grotesquely difficult relationship framework in which the participants are merely thrown together like stones in a storm. This book's matrix encapsulates a flaming love story; and, in the writer's signature style of throwing things together and making them work, he chooses two of the least likely persons to be successful in an intimate relationship.

The story's stars are Simeon, an Orthodox Jew, and Vanetta, an African American woman. The two billionaires are madly in love with each other; but, for some reason or other, they cannot get along: After several unruly brawls and close calls with the law, they mutually agreed that they needed to turn over a new leaf. The agreement to which they arrived had three major elements: First, they agreed to work harder on themselves and to say "I am sorry" with greater sincerity and regularity; secondly, they agreed to a tournament of forgiveness, whereupon they would cultivate a keener sensitivity to one another's "set-off buttons"; and thirdly, they agreed to help each other out by reminding one another of his part of the deal, and, in this regard, they kept squeaky clean records of each other's behavior.

The upshot of all this was that they worked hard on themselves; and, in the end, love triumphed. This remarkable couple, as different as light and darkness, vowed to make their love work—and it did in grand style! Though their interests and cultures were radically different; though they got off to a very rough, shaky start; they worked hard on their difficult relationship and turned it into a superb, enviable model of heterosexual love. The dramatic turn of things attracted worldwide attention and turned their formerly troubled relationship into a royal wedding that doubled its venue's urban population (the City of Ajaccio, Corsica, France).

This poetic narrative reflects elements of a novel but maintains a clear poetic idiom; although, here and there, the poetry appears to get lost in the author's hard-hitting, matter of fact delivery of controversial information and smooth, delightful prose; the book's strong poetic idiom stands out pretty conspicuously throughout its entirety. And this is not the boring, insulse, meaningless poetry to which contemporary society has become so accustomed: These are powerful paragraphs packed with the pure juice of excitement, humor, pizzazz, gusto, and undiluted reading pleasure. It is unfortunate that the raw vivacity, ebullience, and piquancy that ought to be in poetry and prose today are quite often not there.

This splendid, dazzling, and pulseful blend of poetry and novel forever expunges any concerns about readers becoming bored and falling asleep. You will not find any of that in this lively, fast-paced, dramatically exciting presentation. In spite of the unusual nature of the material covered in this book; most people who read it with a clear conscience and an open, objective mind; would probably read it more than once. Despite the author's sharp disagreement with contemporary global society's power brokers' bias against Christianity's tried and tested traditions, he has delivered an explosively humorous and refreshingly promethean poem. This jarringly hilarious narrative yields a bellyful of laughs and a mind filled with fresh, sparkling ideas that would leave its objective readers with something to think about for a very long time! Read it; it's a gleaming bundle of giggles and a flaming glass of joy!

A WORD TO CONCERNED SCIENTISTS

As a scientist himself, this writer pulls absolutely no bones in unscreening the flagrant deception and lies told by modern science today. Throughout the book; he has, again and again, poignantly demonstrated how the false, polluted, atheistic machine of modern science has hoodwinked and deceived the global community with its flawed philosophy of plain sophistry and lies. These venal, vulpine scientists have taken pure conjecture and speculation about nature and presented them as unvarnished, unimpeachable truths and laws. They slide a hand, contending that religion (the Bible) and science are mutually exclusive because no one can prove God's existence.

At the same time, they advance big bang and evolution theories—which are themselves purely conjectural notions—as the essence of natural laws in operation. The fossil records and all of nature's archives and libraries have not yielded any consistent train of evidence to support either of these theories; in this regard, they should be merely viewed as speculative, conceptual instruments. These contraptions have been cunningly manipulated to support modern scientists' atheistic cause and to look, and sound, like immaculate truth. To the contrary, Cambrian-explosion fossils; the White Cliffs of Dover; huge, out of place erratics in Europe; strange occurrences in sedimentary rocks; presence of Carbon in Precambrian rocks;

painful missing links in the evolutionary chain; and a host of other elements of scientific curiosity dispute the evolutionary claim.

They boldly contradict these conjectural ploys of atheistic modern science and convincingly support the claims of design in the universe. The isotopic elements of Carbonate rocks, of all apatite deposits, contain Carbonate rock deposits from the Precambrian Aldan Shield; Precambrian rocks are the oldest rock deposits in nature. If evolution is true, carbon deposits should not be present in these old rocks from time immemorial; again, the science is just not there to support the evolutionary claims. Atheistic modern science's blind faith in finding missing links, which clearly are not anywhere in nature, underscores the absurdity of these crooked scholars and their in-your-face bias against the Bible and plain scientific evidence in nature that supports design. Any evidence for evolution is merely cooked because it is just not there.

Modern science's senseless quarrel with the Bible gives it away and suggests that it is, itself, a powerful, false, occult religious empire in the world. Look at how corrupt and sick the United States has become since it has abandoned Christianity. With shooting sprees almost every day, one wonders who these so-called brainiacs think they are fooling; look at the mess into which they have turned the United States! These dangerous social engineers almost entirely advocate an amoral, atheistic worldview that is conspicuously free of any biblical leanings. Now, they ask for it—they have it; they now have to contend with shooting sprees as regularly as they breathe. That betrays the true intent of modern science and its United Nations: To create a worldwide religious empire that expunges all traces of Christianity and sanity from the public square.

These smart boys hide behind the bushes of evolution and big bang theories' billions of years to cover up their satanic, occult leanings and to bamboozle an unsuspecting public about their dark, sinister agenda in the world. And they have been able to get away with this sort of thing because no one has been watching that closely and connecting the dots. Now, the curtains have been pulled on these unethical academic villains; and their hiding place has been uncovered and demolished in the turbulent storm of objective scientific inquiry. It is important to understand that this book was not written against the many earnest, sincere scientists out there—genuine scholars who've been gaffed by the idea that modern science is the bible of truth and ultimate answer to all human problems, as so many scientists would have you believe.

Rather, it merely alludes to modern science in order to illustrate and underscore the incontrovertible fact that the world, which you think you know so well, is not what you think it is: It is a titanic system of falsehood and deceit. After very circumspect observation of numerous streams of earthly systems, this writer has come to the conclusion that the system of reality in this world, that we assume to be so well-meaning in its operation, is anything but well-intentioned: It is flatly false. And, to this writer's strange surprise, not only is this world system false; there is also a powerful machine of guile that has been designed to overtly cover up that which is true and what is really happening in this world. In this regard, the world itself is a strange booby trap.

Additionally, it is very interesting to notice that this same writer; who appears to be so decidedly Christian in his ideological worldview; has written scathing, devastating pieces against the false, gimmick-ridden Christian Church in America. This clearly indicates that he is colorless, objective, and unbiased in his undisguised effort to get down to the bottom of truth in this world. Though he may seem, and sound, like a Bible-thumping Christian; he is merely a detached scientist in hot pursuit of the plain truth that is clearly written on the parchment of nature. The ultimate fact here is that unvarnished, unpolluted Christianity and objective, unbiased science are the only two reliable custodians and mouthpieces of truth in the world; true science does not contradict the Bible: It supports it. True science is unbiased: It reflects the two clearly visible systems of operation in the world and would proceed to investigate them in a colorless, matter-of-fact way.

Objective scientific observation reflects the fact that much of what is called modern science today is really the work of an obscure, false religion; working diligently to discredit Christianity and to cover up clearly discernible, highly visible truth. The false religion of modern science is really the dark side of the two systems of good and evil in the world: Real science does not contradict the Bible; it is the polluted kind that has been stained by this false religion and secret societal program that does. Thus, because these two systems of operation have been tarnished by the stains of corruption, greed, and foul play; they are no longer tenable, trustworthy societal institutions that can deliver the goods of objective assessment of nature and respectable, reliable, and professional conduct to a world floundering in chaos.

In this regard, they both must be brought to the carpet and spanked for their naughty, unruly behavior in the world. But who would bring them to the carpet of correction—the corrupt government machine in the world or the crooked backslidden preacher? Modern scientists cannot prove their revered theories of evolution and big bang: They were not there at the beginning to ascertain and verify the speculative remarks that they are passing off today as truth. These theories are entirely conjectural: They cannot, and have not, been proven. Their advocates were not there, at the beginning of things, to verify that what they are saying actually happened; moreover, they cannot find any consistent train of hard, raw scientific evidence in the yawning library of nature today to substantiate their claims without a lot of gimmicks.

They rely on sophisticated mathematical and computer models to back up their speculative hypotheses; but it is the same story all over again—they are using mathematics and computers to hide behind the bushes of the lies that they cannot prove in the plain, open glass case of nature. And, in the process, all they have created is a sprawling, troublesome, false religion that does not work. It has predisposed the global community to an atheistic worldview that is calamity-driven and flush with woes; as we see today, the world is jammed with confusion and trouble: Who created all of this? —modern science.

On the other side of the ledger, the phony Christian Church in America has transmogrified Christianity into a get-rich-quick gimmick that leaves society unchanged, confused, and messed up and takes everybody to hell with it. Now, we see all kinds of people rushing to reality television dating programs to find the answer for which they've been looking: Loose women; meeting men for the first time and engaging in intimate behavior with them, as if they've known those men all their lives; throw their honor away. And just as quickly as they got intimate with these dashing bachelors, they are rejected two or three weeks down the road.

Their swank lover boy, the debonair bachelor fails to give them a rose; even after they've served themselves on a silver platter to these spruce, pert bachelors. And if they get pregnant, when they get back to the bachelor who pumped the fertile seed into them, all he tells them is this: That is not my problem; see to that for yourself. We got together and had some fun, but your pregnancy is your business— not mine. In the wake of the hard reality facing these lonely women in our extremely violent and weird society, they view their situation as having absolutely no other choice than to abort the baby. It's a strange, false world of fast living; fast sex; fast rejection; fast suicide; and moving on to the next side. Nobody seems to have any time to wait for anything anymore. This writer is fully cognizant that his views are not mainstream but are rather abstract, obscure, and out of tune with things in a twisted, shadowy world—a world of falsehood, guile, and injustice.

However, he is willing to present what he, as a conscientious scientist, knows is true. These sober remarks are not conjectures, cooked up in the mind of some crack-pot scientist: There is unassailable evidence to support the solemn, sober remarks enunciated on this sacred parchment of truth. This writer is poised and ready to treat all the unfavorable remarks from his shrivel of critics: He is equally ready to welcome those favorable comments from people who've removed the blinders and masks that modern science's false religion has strapped around their faces. They behold the plain, unvarnished truth about the false, biased system of reality in the world. They understand that the world is an illusion and is filled with booby traps and lies that well-meaning people hear and believe every day.

THE PROLOGUE

Have you ever wondered why so many of the world's population are poor—why are so many people poor in a world that is so richly stocked with resources of all kinds? Is the world changing in a negative way like you have never seen before; and if so, why all this flurry of change so suddenly? Is the mystery of the world being revealed to a lost, confused people right before their eyes? According to an old Roman adage, *Satium satis, satium visti*: The only thing that doesn't change is change itself; and according to Heraclitus, the only constant in the world is change. The dramatic change that we see in the world today contains a jarring message to which few of its ultra- perverted people are taking heed.

As you can see, this book is one unlike virtually any other; it is a treasure trove of knowledge and wisdom, with benefits beyond your wildest dreams; and so, what are some of those benefits? This is one in a series of five books that will be followed by somewhere around seventy-one more, and it is richly stocked with life-changing benefits: it will make you laugh, and cry, and will change your life in the direction that you've always wanted but never knew how to pull it off. These golden benefits are revealed in a stream of secrets that deliver the inside scoop on the workings on the real world in which you live. Life, success, and happiness are encapsulated in the capsule of elusive, evasive secrets that are interconnected and hidden in plain view.

So, what are these benefits that this book delivers? The secret to success and happiness is the fact that the world itself is a secret, and that secret is contained in the pages of this book and the other seventy something books that I have written. Most people fail in life because they do not understand the world's Machiavellian workings, and this is the case because they are naïve and take the world at face value. Trapped in an interminable flurry of activities, they never take time to think for themselves; and so, their inner eyes never open wide enough to see what is going on around them.: You need to understand your environment's contents.

One of life's most powerful secrets is that all people are born talented, educated, rich, and successful—they just don't know it or don't know where to find these resources, even though they are right there in their world: That information is hidden from them because of the way they were born; they have to be pointed to their purpose in this world; and sometimes, not even they themselves can find it. This book and the many others that I've written contain the recondite secrets of life, success, and happiness. I urge you not to read these books if you want to continue living a vain, mediocre, and meaningless life; but if you are appetent to find *the real you* for whom you've been searching all your life, I vehemently urge and implore you to read this and the other books that I've written: they are richly supplied with profound revelations and beautiful secrets of the universe.

Have you ever wondered why most people in the world are poor and unhappy? People are poor and unhappy for one reason: They misinterpret and misunderstand the world's workings: They've been fooled by the cruel architects who've erected this world's superstructure and system of guile and deception by which it functions. If you are sick and tired of living a hopeless and meaningless life, do not just read this book; this is merely the foundational primer of the broader internalization program of reality, which is treated in all the other books. In addition to this book, you should ransack the world's bookstores and read all the others that I've written; for all of life's secrets are scattered throughout their pages. These are the secrets that have allowed me to have been able to write so many books—and I'm not done yet.

The Book's Essence

This revolutionary volume's principal goal is to demonstrate the cause of the rapid changes transpiring in the world today and the real facts behind these highly destructive trends and changes that currently confront society. The content is delivered in a gripping fictional presentation that captures the rawness and frightening reality of the times around the world. The world's current moral collapse is fictionalized in a dramatic love story, involving two top university professors who met at a pond in the Jerusalem Botanical Gardens. Simeon Auckner; a quantum algebraist; and his fiancée, Vanetta Firne; an astrophysicist; met there in Jerusalem and had to work through a slew of moral issues in a rapidly changing world.

They had to deal with the jarring changes in the world and put a scientific spin on what was happening around them; though the climate change pretext seems logical, many other things were happing that had nothing whatsoever to do with climate change. Although the world's climate is unquestionably changing, the poignant growth of savage criminals and callous psychopaths hardly have anything to do with climate change—do they? Here the book poignantly demonstrates twenty-first-century- man's shallow and hollow understanding of reality and his blind willingness and profound hypocrisy to call things other than what they are.

Man's flagrant abuse of the natural order of things has engendered a volley of unnatural changes in the world, wreaking massive destruction on the human race worldwide. Much of this unnatural destruction of the human cosmos is reflected in run-away global moral decay that twenty-first- century man calls the Transhumanism

Revolution or the New Scientific Revolution. All the taboos have been broken, and the world was—and still is—drowning in a squalid sea of perversion of all kinds. Sex perversion is the order of the day, and a substantial portion of the world's population now flatly rejects the conventional framework and context in which sex is executed. It is a time of dramatic change; social scientists grope in the moral darkness, ardently looking for pragmatic explanations for the jarring moral decay and the seemingly unexplainable changes in human society today.

False Handling of the Abortion Dispute
At the same time, society has bifurcated into two clearly defined moral and spiritual camps: Iconoclasts and traditionalists. The iconoclasts were often very liberal and bluntly rejected any notion of a monotheistic God; they were the societal engineers and political architects who had been running society's show for the longest while. However, as things waxed darker and rawer, it became rather evident to society that something was wrong; just as how many people, looking at the societal landscape today, are waking up to the fact that something is wrong: The world is just not what it used to be, and things are heading in the wrong direction. Suddenly, many people did not embrace the glib, naturalistic explanation of reality anymore; over time, people began to reject the notion that the universe created itself—it just didn't sit well with them anymore because it left too many unanswered questions.

Many people became increasingly confused and frustrated with the No-God universe model and all the frustrating views associated with it; for example, iconoclasts cavalierly advocated abortion for all unwanted babies. However, many women became confused: They did not understand why men were allowed to impregnate women, abandon them, and get away with all that Scot free. The laws, about men's obligations to the women whom they impregnated, were on the books; but in a chauvinistic, misogynistic world; those laws were largely ignored. Because of the loose application of the laws, most women aborted their babies; driving another wedge into society and creating a wider and wider chasm between the two sides. Naturally, these babies aborted are human beings; and they cried out to God form the womb. In the course of time, hundreds of millions of babies were aborted; and they cried out from the womb.

God heard their cry and responded; as a result, society began to break up into pieces: Hundreds of rivers and thousands of lakes began to dry up; floods and sink holes began to devour whole neighborhoods; atmospheric rivers, storm surges, brutal tornadoes, and baneful hurricanes began to increase exponentially; crushing sophisticated communities to pieces.

They folded whole communities like pieces of paper and scattered them over the land like trash. People went to sleep in million-dollar homes, only to be washed away into the sea by the next morning: Many woke up in the sea, stark exhausted and worn out—oh, how sad! Man's wickedness is catching up with him, and he is calling it *climate change*: Oh, what a farce, what a burlesque!

Oh, my; is the world ending right before man's eyes; and he is calling that climate change? What a dramatic new age of change into which we've been wheeled! What an age of change, where things are called different names. Storms, from the blue, wash away virtually everything in their path—what a world of change and endless chaos! Nations are distressed; people are losing their minds in a world in which they have not even a clue about what is going on. There is distress of nations with perplexity; the sea and the waves are forever roaring and smashing human communities to shreds.

Nature's Insanity in a World Gone Mad
Many went to sleep rich and woke up in battered homes; their roofs torn from the top, and the upper floor filled with water. Yet lost,

confused mankind calls God's punishment for his sinful, evil deeds, *climate change* in the new age where a fish is called a refrigerator, and a tree is called a house. Hey, can we set the record straight and just call things what they are? Brand-new homes, staggering like a tree in a storm, are violently avulsed; their rafters are torn to shreds, and the windows are unhooked and dashed a thousand miles away! Oh, what fury, what wrath nature is displaying here, in the wake of man's wickedness in the world!

Folks, all that is not just climate change; there is a message in that somewhere there, warning mankind to turn around and disassemble his baby-killing and sex perversion machinery in the world; and forasmuch as man has not read the cryptogrammatic message in these violent storms, they've waxed more violent and even more savage. The secrets of life, success, and happiness have been violated; and instead of things getting better, they've waxed worse. And sad to say, many grand, aristocratic homes have been reduced to rubble. large rivers; like the Mississippi, the Arkansas, and the Ohio Rivers; have been reduced to a creek. Their flow has been vastly reduced; interrupting regional economies, divesting farmers of invaluable water supply, drying up aqueducts in dozens of cities, and robbing them of life-giving water. Many cities in the United States are on the verge of running out of water.

What is so curious here is that these liberal democracies of the world are the atheistic systems, leading the world down the precipice of moral decay. The shocking perversion fad of more and more people, opting for sex with dogs, is sickening. Have you: Have ever heard anything like this in your life before? Are these savage and doomful storms that we see today conveying a cryptogrammatic message to lost, confused man? On many of these brazen blogs, women have abandoned the normal use of men and have moved on to sleeping, and having sex, with dogs; saying that no one can do it to you like a dog. Now, that is new and atrociously extreme and perverted: Many mothers, lost in the fog, make several children for their boys.

The proud amoral political bosses, in these liberal democracies, bluntly reject the idea of God and morality; and I need not say that these are the same societies with the highest levels of moral decay and suicide in the world. These amoral bosses are the iconoclasts that promote a dystopian culture, replete with lawlessness and chaos of every imaginable kind. In the course of time, society did become tired of this kind of lawlessness and false political power play. People became tired of these corrupt political bosses' false power play; they got sick and tired of these iconoclasts' sour, shallow, lame, and hellish ideas and began to reject their oversimplified view of the universe and society.

Many began to open their eyes for themselves and see for the first time; this created a tremendous amount of pressure on the amoral iconoclasts, sparking a fresh scientific revolution.

This forced iconoclasts into discussion with traditionalists; many of these ideological gatherings were held at various convention centers and in hotel conference rooms around the world. One of the principal goals of these conferences and symposiums was to decelerate the moral decay and to extract the world from the chasm into which it had fallen. However, slowing down the moral decay and vulgar carousing on sidewalks and in the middle of the street was easier said than done. The world had gotten accustomed to moral decay, public nudity, and public sex; it was very difficult to turn around this shocking tide of moral looseness that had devoured the whole world. Man had forgotten God and his sacred writing, just like we see today: Everything is upside-down.

Man's Flagrant Departure from Natural Order

Quite to the contrary, it was at these gatherings to slow down the moral decay process and turn it around, where the full-scale of moral decay was displayed. This was quite poignantly disported at the Mishconet Convention Center, there in Jerusalem. Every imaginable kind of perversion was on display: These were not necessarily people who lived in Jerusalem. The one; held at the Pan Am Convention Center, in Vancouver, the year before, was just as lurid and shocking. and shocking. There was a stirring Gay Pride celebration not far away from the convention center; there were zoophiles, expressing their pride.

This involved both men and women who had developed intimate relations with a variety of animals.

Moreover, dozens of mother-son and father-daughter couples were there, sharing their romantic experience with the brash, colorful crowd that displayed strange and variegate quirks; and certainly, it is not appropriate to discuss here all the many colors that were displayed right there in the streets. Although, under normal circumstances, these public erotic displays were illegal; society had outgrown those relict laws, and people were merely told, "If you don't like what is going on here, simply move somewhere else. We are not going to change for you." simply move somewhere else.; we are not going to change for you."

Against this backdrop, public nudity and other forms of perversion had become widely accepted in that societal environment. The public environment had waxed highly dystopian, and shame and disgrace had become almost non-existent. It was a world like no other; the traditional view of the world had changed dramatically. Though many people had rejected the view of the self-created universe; having become seasoned and shameless *amorals* and vulgarians, just as many did not embrace the Christian worldview. These viewed themselves as transhumanists; however, over time, the tide began to change; and people became weary of living at the subhuman level of having sex in plain view. Many women became tired of being penetrated by dogs and foxes, and many died in the process of being humped by dogs with long, oversized phalluses.

On seeing how sordid and subhuman the free-sex movement had made society, with thousands committing suicide every day; people began to change again and to go back to the Christian worldview. They reopened up to the creation point of view, going back to the Aristotelian Perspective *of whatever is always was*: Everything in the world was designed and created by a universal creator. The sweeping changes that transpired in this wave were referred to as the New Scientific Revolution; efforts were made to link this to the Transhumanism Revolution, but they failed, as this became increasingly linked to the creation worldview. People simply got tired of living wrong and decided to go back the normal way of life that they used to know; and besides, the number of suicides and crimes committed were shockingly high.

 Over time, they realized that the perverted lifestyle just did not deliver anymore. They wanted reality—not fairy tales. Lies can only work for a certain time until you forget the first lie that you told. Merely saying that God does not exist and deliberately living contrary to the natural order of things are inherent lies to your own self, and those lies add up over time in a shortened life span; deformed babies; and dying, having sex with dogs. Lies just don't work; they fade after a while, leaving you stark naked in the cold. You look around nowadays and see how chaotic the world has become: The chaos in the world today is not by accident; it is the result of man's flagrant violation of natural order and living below his natural station in the world.

A fish cannot live on land, like human beings, because it is not an amphibian, designed to live like that: Fishes live in the sea, and man lives on land; that is the divine design for the world. When God's creation attempts to foil that design and create its own system, chaos is the result. In a similar vein, man cannot live in a perverted way and expect things to work well for him. Look at the chaos in the world; there is more to it than mere climate change, and anyone with a clear conscience would agree. The world has become way too perverted, too unclean, too vile, and too false to function in the manner in which God had originally designed it.

What ss so interesting here is that all the perversion and vileness that we see in the world today emanated from man's boredom with the world around him that does not make any sense—and it does not make sense because man was never meant to live to please himself. Just as how woman was made for man; man was made to serve and worship God. Once his existence wanders away from that context; boredom, confusion, and unhappiness result; and human society becomes confused, vile, perverted, upside-down and wrecked. And this has happened all through history again, and again, and again. It is nothing new; The same confused societies that you see today existed in the past just, before their end came as they opened up to humanism and liberalism.

CHAPTER 1

THE RISE OF SCIENTIFIC ARISTOCRACY

The New Scientific Revolution was in full swing, and the world had changed forever; global politics had assumed a new cast, and the spirit of science was everywhere. Though old money and dirty politics were still around, new rules appeared on the scene: A titanic faculty of academics, largely composed of scientists, appeared from nowhere; more and more, scientists began calling the shots on just about everything, everywhere. And oh, how the tide of things in the world had changed; many sought fresh answers: They wanted practical explanations for the status quo and real answers from their politicians—and breaking with the old, they wanted those explanations and answers right away.

Loud, empty political promises no longer satisfied the world's teaming masses; billions, lost on planet earth's yawning shores and famished of meaning, wanted more. They no longer allowed evolution's empty claims and dirty politics to represent them— they wanted a more rational, systematic understanding of terrestrial existence. Evolution's gaping gaps and traditional politics' blank merry-go-round had lost ground; people just wanted more from a system that they felt had betrayed them for years, and isn't that just as how today's corrupt politicians have wheedled and hoodwinked the whole world? The strident, hollow grind of everyday life and things' vapid tone bothered many people; and they bluntly refused to settle for the way things used to be—they clamored for change.

And like a fierce swarm of locusts, fresh scientists began appearing on the scene; the dashing, new boys on the block had many answers that grabbed the people's minds: Their new epistemological spin on things seemed to go further than their predecessors' oversimplified evolutionary claims. Their logical, systematic analysis of the universe's origin was new and interesting; and their unique model of human origin and existence created a storm of controversy. Fierce quarrels and ugly fights erupted among the ranks of scientists.

Though the wheel of change was turning fast, status-quo scientists put up a fierce fight; but oh, their loud, empty clanging was no match for the new boys' shower of dollars. And what a shrivel of critics that these visceral discussions generated for the old guard: The classical evolutionary perspective began to be keenly and exquisitely scrutinized; suddenly, evolution began to be viewed as rogue science and inappropriate public policy.

Old-school scientists were seen as rank traitors of the traditional societal order; and so, the squabbling and wrangling continued to grow between the two power blocks. But though evolutionists balked at the design concept of the universe's origin, they could not ignore its exponents' growing popularity and swollen bank accounts. Many theological scientists and design theorists had amassed huge financial empires: Design scientists' prodigious wealth accumulation began to flurry, not a few naturalists; for their alarming amassment of wealth began to define science's very meaning in the world. Yea, it began to define the meaning, the goal, and the role of science in a novel kind of world; it was a new, refreshed, and enlightened world populated by millions who suddenly could see.

As a result, evolution theory's very existence began to be viewed at the new, dashing scholars' mercy. These rich, splashy boys poured billions of dollars into the promotion of their cause: They built sprawling multiversities, sophisticated research centers, and geoponic institutes. They erected large oceanariums, scientific libraries, State-of-the-art laboratories and science-promoting museums: This magnificent and dazzling array of scientific facilities was constructed all over the world. All this trenchant political and ideological activism engendered rapid scientific and political change; the rise of the scientific aristocracy put a brand-new face on objective scientific inquiry, understanding of government, and the entire political process.

Crashing Streams of Thought

The old school of thought was out; and the new school was wheeled in, front and center; and what a world of change it brought with it: Oh, what a storm of change it engendered! Two groups of scientists emerged in this rapidly unfolding world of flux and dynamism, and they were as different as trees in a rainforest and human faces on the earth: The two scientific camps included atheistic naturalists and design scientists, and there were significant philosophical differences within these individual groups. Three distinct philosophical views were propounded by naturalistic scientists: The classical evolutionists were the first group of naturalists in this arrangement and nasty fight.

These scholars espoused the big bang theory and progressive evolution; they advocated a progressive development, from a single cell to the human pinnacle that we see today. The Herculean task to find and prove this bottom-up evolution in the fossil records was quite a problem, and it was a formidable one which these evolutionists— and evolutionists as a whole—had not been able to solve. Somehow or other, the parts did not fit; the model had (and still has) acute missing-link issues. The second group of naturalists, quantum evolutionists, adopted a sager view of things. Forasmuch as all evolutionists had been unable to show concrete proof of their claims, the quantum evolutionists tried to skirt the issue regarding lack of transitional forms in the fossil records—and this was pretty wise on their part; but again, they ran into the same problem. They argued that the evolutionary changes occurred very rapidly, over short time periods; and, for that reason, there should be no transitional forms in the fossil record library.

The problem with this view was that it destroyed the entire notion of scientific theory and of evolution itself: The basis of science is objectivity, raw evidence, and colorless observational analysis. The upshot of all this was that, if no transitional forms of evolutionary changes existed, then evolution had never transpired anywhere on the earth, as the fossil records revealed. If the gloves do not fit, you cannot convict; therefore, you have to acquit the accused. With no concrete evidence to prove their case, they could not find their way in the fog. Evolution is a blunt, bold-faced lie: Men would just rather believe that it is true; accordingly, the quantum-leap boys of evolution had no grounds on which to stand. The third group of scholars in this atheistic camp were ufological scientists: These smart boys bluntly rejected evolution as a tenable tool of scientific inquiry. In their plain rejection of evolution, they adopted the idea of design in the universe.

They contended that, due to the sheer complexity and size of the universe; evolution—as presented by their colleagues—was, at best, a naïve view of things; rather, they believed that the universe was designed by UFOs, billions of years ago. And, as the story goes; very heated, contentious dog fights erupted among these scholars. Accordingly, there was no small squabbling and infighting among these terribly misled human beings; every man highly valued his point of view and fought fiercely to defend it. Their rank disunity and litigious attitude threw them out of favor with the new societal public: secular science quickly evolved into a system of intrigue, betrayal, and mudslinging; and though they all held tenaciously to the fundamentally atheistic view of things; in reality, they seemed to argue and disagree incandescently on just about anything else.

On the argument's other side, theological scientists also held strikingly different views—obviously, their views were palpably different from those of naturalistic scientists; but even within this camp, these scientists also disagreed along ideological lines. Two broad groups evolved and conducted fierce debates within the design science camp: Theological scientists maintained a strict design scientific view of things. They contended that the universe was assembled by the very knuckles of God himself; they dismissed the notion of any evidence of evolution being in the spin of things. These theological scientists contended that the earth was quite young—per their quantum algebraic analysis, the earth was less than forty thousand years old.

They passionately affirmed that proof of God's existence is just about everywhere one looks; they stated that houses of worship's universal existence indicate something beyond—it indicates a divine presence beyond the shallow naturalism that one saw in the world. Furthermore, they posited that the existence of good and evil offers no other plausible explanation—their presence offers no other rational explanation than that of God's existence itself. In their view, the good-evil dichotomy is the purest manifestation of the Bible's essence in the world; they viewed it as the paragon of the Bible's living reality and evidence of the God-devil duality which we see in the confused world of man. The secularists' inability to furnish concrete explanations for this dichotomy spoke volumes; it betrayed their radical opposition to glaring, unvarnished truth revealed in nature about the epistemology of the human story.

These theorists argued that shunning bare facts in nature undressed naturalists' biases against Christianity, and their biased stance uncurtained the false religion of modern science in the world; it rendered them traitors of truth and capsized the ship of naturalism in the world. Design scientists adopted a more moderate view of things, with more focus on precision; they strongly emphasized mathematical quantification in their understanding of things. Per their perspective, the universe is old; and evolution is part of the creation process. According to them, evolution is still transpiring and will continue to do so indefinitely. They, and would continue doing so indefinitely. They, nonetheless, pointed out the broad machinery of design, clearly visible in nature; a system which modernists, naturalists, and secular humanists utterly ignore.

And though they disagreed on the finer points of a strict Biblical account of things, their fundamentally cohesive argument of a universal government system began to stick. The idea of a loving, monotheistic God began to resonate in society's sprawling mart. Despite the luculent differences within the two individual groups of scholars, it was rather remarkable to notice the giant strides which design theorists had made. Who could have ever thought of a day when both views would be taught together? That day had finally come when creation science was held on par with evolution; the new boys on the block had routed old-school evolutionists in every public debate. Secularists, time and time again, dropped the ball when it came to concrete evidence; yea, they fumbled and fell when asked to give tangible evidence to prove their cause.

No transitional forms were on hand to validate their passionate point of view, and the Cambrian explosion was the final nail in the coffin of their lame argument. These public debates revealed no living proof of evolution within recent or distant times; all the fossil records revealed no such occurrences ever happening anywhere on the earth: In each public debate, the evolutionists fell flat on their faces These public debates debunked and exposed the inherent weaknesses of evolution; the fossil records were empty and devoid of any trace of evolution on the earth; yea, they were as empty as an abandoned castle, far removed from human habitation. Evolution theory is a school of scientific thought that leaves its exponents ever searching;

and the passionate search leaves them in a world where the pearl is entirely incorporeal. It is as if one is looking for a mummy in a high-end Manhattan clothing store!

There were several other arguments that flat out destroyed evolution as a tenable theory: The crude microscopes used in Darwin's day furnished incomplete information on cells. According to Dr. Behe; in his book, ***Darwin's Black Box***; evolution is not tenable; per this avant-garde scientist, Darwin's conclusions are out of step with reality. In Darwin's day, the available scientific tools were very crude and primitive: They were not as advanced as the highly sophisticated electronic microscopes of today; accordingly, they could not accurately photograph the cell, the simplest unit of life; therefore, they could not map the entirety of the cell's eerie, mind-boggling complexity. Today's sophisticated, precision microscopes reveal the entirety of the cell's structure.

Per Dr. Behe, in order for the cell to function at all; all of its parts must be in place. In this regard, the entire machine of the cell must have been assembled at the same time; and if this shrewd observation is tenable, evolution is, at best, a naïve hoax. The reality here is that all of the cell's components must be in place for it to function; this is not some cooked up fact: this is scientifically testable information. There is no evidence that the extremely convoluted components of a cell ever evolved; the cell's sheer complexity and baffling efficiency of chore execution are just too much. According to contemporary biological scientists, more than one billion biochemical reactions occur in a single cell per second: That amounts to more than thirty-seven billion trillion biochemical reactions occurring in a heathy human body every second!

This suggests that, merely on the basis of the tremendous efficiency with which the body works, man should never grow old and fade away; Thus, aging is itself a biological miracle. In view of this mind-boggling information, there is just no way, in this world or another, that the single cell could have ever evolved—yea, there's no way it could have evolved to the complex biological machines of today! The trillions of biochemical reactions per second within the body tell the whole story; there is no way that such a complex machine could have evolved on its own. It takes *a hell of a lot* of faith to believe something as absurd and grotesque as that, but this is the sort of crap that secularists are asking sane people to believe.

It takes a whole lot more faith to believe that than to believe in the obvious—the universe was designed by a superhuman designer, beyond the realm of man's mind. Behe's irreversible complexity theory reveals Darwin's hasty, unscientific conclusions; it lights a flickering candle in a strange, uncanny world bedimmed by Darwin. This fatal blow to evolution should shut even Steven Hawkins' mouth forever. These were the visceral issues that were cantankerously debated in academia's halls; and so, things began to open up for the creationistic perspective about cosmic reality; for he who owned the ruby coins owned the world itself. And oh, the new boys—the dashing billionaires of scientific aristocracy were shaking things up everywhere.

Oh, see the world, blossoming with the sprightly new boys of design science on the block; they travelled the sunny skies in colorful jets that moved as fast as the speed of light! And for the first time, after hundreds of years of evolution theory's hegemony; design science's voice began to be heard and received everywhere with great respect; yea, the throttled, muffled voice of truth finally began to break forth in the world. And there were many whose ears had heard enough of lies' blank, empty explanations; the teeming masses had waxed hungrier and hungrier for a radically novel view of things: They had outgrown the hollow, empty paradigms of naturalism and secularism.

The Decline of Evolution Science

Life's end, in the shabby junkyard of sand, began to bother not a few folks; the raucous meaninglessness of life impelled many to burrow into the archives of truth—yea, life's clanging emptiness and cosmic vacuity pushed many people over the edge. The alarming incidence of drug addiction, divorce, and suicide kept psychiatrists busy; this puzzling swarm of societal maladies befuddled the authorities and kept them working around the clock: They could not understand this startling outbreak of societal ills. These bizarre, surreal deviations from societal norms left many sociologists puzzled; they wondered what had gone wrong in an otherwise smooth-working, hedonic world. Lost in a maze of doom and gloom, they scratched their heads for feasible solutions: For months, they scratched their heads for rational answers to the puzzling conundrums; but they could not find any logical reasons why sane erudites brashly ended their lives.

They just could not unlock the mystery behind the long stream of inexplicable tragedies: Floundering in a churning fog of strange conundrums, they wondered and wondered; and, as if the very hand of Providence had drawn the curtains on the fate of naturalism; one thing after another went wrong for the religious boys of atheism and evolution. For some strange reason, they did not get an equal piece of the scientific aristocracy pie. The dashing boys of design science and theological episteme had outscored them; yea, they had outscored the secularists in points, in the race up the socioeconomic ladder; and for every twenty design scientists who became billionaires in that world of flux, there was one secular scientist who became a millionaire. And oh, the ill blood it bred! Why did these great minds produce such different results in the same economic milieu?

The cause of this jarring disparity was a profound mystery in that world of academia: For one thing, the splashy boys of secularism and evolution tended to be more profligate; their lubricous lifestyle and liberal, amoral bent beclouded their moral conscience. and forasmuch as liberal secularists tended to adopt a more morally relative lifestyle, they did not give much thought to those things that really mattered to design scientists; and where moral rules did not apply, progress and prosperity were often quite scant. Those who broke nature's laws often paid a steeper price than they had in mind; and when the laws were cavalierly and brashly violated by empty, hollow people; nature often brusquely removed the light of sight from the minds of its violators. And the rugged father of lies rushed in like a flood and filled their souls with darkness; and oh, lost in the moiling mist of all that booming noise and confusion; their steps were often misdirected and took them to a host of false destinations.

So many things got misplaced and lost in that seething, crazy world of darkness—oh, that frenzied, chaotic world of confusion, vanity, intrigue, and empty, maddening noises! Who came to their rescue when things went wrong, as they so often did? For whatever reason, the secularists were outstripped by Christianity's polished boys: Powerful infighting among evolutionists helped to bring the curtains down; and when things went wrong, so many other things went haywire as well. With a sharp revulsion in public attitudes towards science, and in particular, evolution, the ardent children of the faith deemed it necessary to defend their sacred religion; accordingly, they brought the controversy into the bold, broad mirror of public view. They conducted fierce, fiery debates with various elements from the design science camp: These high-stakes debates conferred much honor on those who participated in them; and when the secularists seemed to have performed well, it was like a quasi-promotion.

They got to hobnob with some of the day's brightest academic stars and richest men, and this tended to foster a nasty sociopolitical climate among many evolutionists. Infighting among secularists to defend their sacred religion of naturalism was fierce: Their mad rush for a spot in the world's public view engendered revolting squabbles; these shockingly ugly skirmishes over public debate representation spotlighted other things. Yea, they jarringly exposed the darker side of things that dampened public mood. A powerful mud-slinging machine was put in motion; and oh, the damage it did! Sophisticated, erudite men who belonged to society's astral circles began losing it; repulsive name calling and belittling of their colleagues became quite rife.

They made slanderous remarks against their peers and leaked classified data to the press; their venenous in-fighting and titanic scandal machine revealed the wrong side of things. Horrible arguments, replete with strife, pitted one faction against the other; and quite often, these overheated arguments unveiled nasty under-the-table cover ups. For example, there were numerous disagreements among evolution scholars; some of these very heated disputes represented real issues of academic integrity. Massive areas of scholarly work, favoring a design model, were often summarily trashed; this was a survival game and any port in a storm.

Email files that deviated from the classical evolution point of view were merely ruined: These repulsively ugly cover-ups left many objective viewers wondering what else was hidden from public view; consequently, many began to scowl upon the idea of evolution. And that was not all: There were more embarrassing cover-ups and shocking discoveries. An archaeological dig in China uncovered a strange fossil that lit up the scientific world; and oh, how the Darwinists rushed to the scene to claim their golden trophy: Oh, see how the secularists viewed this part bird, part dinosaur fossil as their missing link. Scores of scientists, clad in enthusiasm, reveled in the glory of the golden moment; and what a gleaming glass case of proof of the evolution model it was supposed to be!

The darling discovery was viewed as the much-craved missing link so long sought for; Darwinists proclaimed it as an unanswerable transitional form between one specie and another. But oh, after all the tests had been done, it was just another disappointment—and what a crushing disappointment it was for the Darwinists of the scientific world! Careful examination of the fossil revealed that it was merely the fusion of two species; somehow or other, fate had brought two distinct animals into a very fatal collision. A deadly accident, I might add, which had nothing to do with Darwin's Theory of Evolution. It was just another instance of desperate erudites trying to fabricate evidence that wasn't there: Oh, what a difficult task it has been for them! It was as if they were trying to carry water in baskets!

How piteous and pathetic it has been for those who've created the false religion of modern science: What crushing disappointments and bruised feelings that they've had to endure! Oh, how lost could misguided people become in their frenzied effort to hide the truth! But oh, the truth, the truth—no one can cover it up! It is a sponge ball that does not sink—and never will. Oh, empty, wretched hearts of men; behold the sponge ball of the truth, gazing at you. Oh, behold that bold, colorful ball of the truth; ever floating and gleaming in the water. And though earth's dashing power brokers have hired submersibles to sink that ball; it just wouldn't disappear from their bold, glaring view; forever staring them in the face. Oh, that beautiful fruit of truth is forever there, gazing vain man smack in the face. When will he open his eyes?

Oh, when will he open his eyes and behold the plain truth? When will man gaze upon that which is so glaringly written on the parchment of nature? But instead, on and on he goes; trying to find that which has never been there: Oh, what a blank, laborious search for gold among a brash heap of stones! When will the Darwinists, and secularists, and atheists open their eyes and see the truth? Oh, the blind vision of the human race—so many eyes, so little sight; what a tenebrous mystery in which lost people are trapped!

The False Religion of Modern Science

Modern man is lost in the yawning museum of nature, so full of plainly written directions. Though the truth is etched on every stone, yet man's mental opacity obstructs his view of things: He stares into the glaring mirror of truth, and is blinded in the process. But oh, the Darwinists, and the secularists, and the brilliant scientists would not stop there: They just kept right on digging, and excavating, and hoping for that which is not there. And the fraud of evolution went— and continues to go—on even further; this time, it was the Piltdown man. This skull fragment of an apparent ape man was discovered early in the twentieth century; and, as usual, this was another trophy, made of rubies, for the Darwinists. They celebrated the victory of this major discovery, and spirits ran high.

However, it was not too long after that scientific dating technique uncovered the great hoax: What an elaborate scam that was perpetrated by the fraud-ridden scientific community! And yet, these frenetically desperate fraud technicians would not cease in their moil: They would not halt the senseless grind for evidence that cannot be found anywhere. These crass religious zealots and bigoted pansophists would not halt the senseless search for links that are not there; from there; they then introduced the peppered moth to substantiate the religion of evolution. In a book, **How Now Shall We Live**, a Darwinist discussed the behavior of moths. Per this scientist, moths changed their colors in order to adjust to their environment; and this he postulated was evidence of Darwin's Theory of Natural Selection.

When all the facts were in; the so-called evidence, used as proof of evolution, was just another hoax. Yea, when the truth emerged from the scientific world's darkroom of lies and cover-ups, the evidence was faked by a biologist who had glued dead moths to trees. How much more fraud, propaganda, and falsehood must be shoved down the public's throat before it wakes up? What must be done here to stop this crass type of fraud? When will the public wake up and see the irreparable damage that evolution has done? Look at how violent, sick, and psychopathic their godless society has become—it has literally blown up in their face. How many young, impressionable minds have been imbued with this poisonous lie of smashing and grabbing things that do not belong to them—is this evolution for the fittest guide?

And to make things even worse, many desperate Darwinists have jumped off a cliff: As was mentioned earlier—and this does merit repeating—some Darwinists got desperate. Upon realizing that nature's yawning museum revealed no evidence of transitional forms, many Darwinists began subscribing to the misleading view of Punctual Equilibrium. According to these particular naturalists, the transitional changes occurred very rapidly; in fact, according to them, these occurrences were so rapid; that they left no trace on the scroll of nature. Here is a case where supposedly unbiased, objective scientists are changing science's nature and telling plain lies. They hate the Bible and the Christian worldview; they don't want it to be true because they know what that truth means for them—and I get that; but why do such educated people have to resort to lies?

Look at how they've messed up the world, turning it into a camp of psychopaths and demon-possessed folks. Have you seen the world recently? If they insist that these transitional forms transpired quite rapidly, there should be evidence somewhere—shouldn't there? In plain geological language, the evidence should be etched somewhere in nature; and this is so because rapid changes in geologic time often amount to millions of years. Evidently, had these transitional changes occurred; they would be visible somewhere. And so, the punctual equilibrium scientists have either gone mad or are plain drunk. They know scientific facts cannot be established without repeated, raw evidence; and so, now they have gone from science to the establishment of a secular religion.

And this is so because they are basing their model on the incorporeal evidence of faith. But this is exactly what they have been doing all along and lying to the public. Hiding behind the caliginous veil of science, they have established a sprawling religion—one that requires billions of years with no objective scientist observing the vain show. Oh, they've built a prodigious religious multiversity around the entire world; and, beneath the mendacious umbrage of scientific inquiry, what a lie they've told! they've poisoned the minds of our children with the religion of naturalism. Oh, they've corrupted our children with atheism, secularism, and moral relativism; and oh, the intrigue, the falsehood, the professional dishonesty, the cover ups…oh, my!

Fresh Classroom Laws

See how far they've gone to destroy our values, to ruin our morals, and to turn our world up-side down: See how far they've gone to transmute our world into a moral sty; see how they've transmogrified our world of beauty into a howling jungle of chaos. And yes, by this time, the public had had enough—the people had heard enough; yea, they had had enough of evolutionists' missing links, cover ups, and fraudulent practices. With evolution virtually on life support and a new stream of moral laws in the classroom, the Darwinists' gig was over; they had lost their unprecedented power in the classroom: Their unscholarly books, slammed by the media, became the laughing stock of the times.

Oh, the lusty, lively buffoonery of their publications in the sardonic mart of society; how quickly change took root in a world of crashing streams of change and opinions. And oh, the wonder and amazement of yesterday's lofty pillars; hewn to the ground! The gleaming temples and palaces of yesteryear's places of honor had been demolished; dashed to pieces in the flaring storm of change which had come so quickly! Oh, false religion, thou swine that wore white shirts and ties, where art thou today? You've been tossed into the trash like an automobile, violently thrown in a storm; see the furor of the growling, groaning storm of change in a world so filled with whim. The moral sty of the world was frenziedly being cleansed of the fetid spume of falsehood, and those who had poisoned the hearts of the little ones with the fraud of evolution—yea, those who had turned their classrooms into quaint churches had finally been judged!

The meteoric stream of new laws virtually wiped the classroom's slate clean, and the harsh penalties for proselytizing in a classroom setting sent a crystal-clear message: The repulsive, loathsome felony carried a maximum punishment of fifteen years in jail. No longer were secular humanist priests allowed to peddle their wares in the classroom; irresponsible comments' wanton use about life's sacred origin was a serious matter. And oh, the sacerdotal system of professors who bluntly thrashed Christianity—oh, the fire that burned the hem of their garments could light the whole world aflame. And what a serious felony that such a misdeed turned out to be for so many preachers! The priestly system of professors bluntly thrashing Christianity was outlawed, and trashing the innocent Christian religion in a classroom carried stiff prison terms; those who tried to use their podiums as pulpits of naturalism were summarily jailed.

Oh, how things had changed: What a great change that had come upon the world! And those who dared to violate this noble, sacred law were stuffed into dark, musty prisons; oh, the thick, heavy darkness of these horrible tiny prison cells drove not a few stark mad. And what a new day it was: The pendulum had swung all the way to the other side; and things went back to normal, as they were before Lyle, and Hutton, and Darwin. In addition, funding for evolution research rapidly began to dry up; driving many out of work; accordingly, naturalistic scholars of that ideological persuasion fled the classroom in droves. And, for their own safety and economic security, they lied to all prospective employers.

Many of these former academic stars were glad to scoop up pedestrian, entry-level jobs; and those who remained in the classroom quickly understood the beautiful art of disguise. They bluntly refused to play politics and fool around with their survival. Oh, what a change that had come upon the earth: Oh, what long overdue judgment of wrong was now due! All the chickens had come home to roast; and oh, what a dainty meal that was! The world had gotten tired of secularism's blank, empty, stuffy answers to life's puzzles; and the frightening, unnerving societal trends of destructive behavior did not help either. The skyrocketing rate of alcoholism and obesity; the unrestrained growth of anarchy; the rapid increase in drug addiction, teen pregnancy, and the ever-growing suicide rate; the spiraling scourge of violence and the burgeoning growth of divorce jarred the world!

Oh, the swift, rushing stream of social maladies ruffled all the feathers in society. It sent politicians scrambling and fluttering about the world, looking for answers; and eyes, formerly blinded by the veil of falsehood, suddenly flickered open. Secularism's rank inability to furnish tenable solutions soured the world it once mocked; suddenly, the whole world began to see the truth about the fairy tale of evolution. Glib, politically correct answers, with no teeth, no longer worked in that world of bloom; and oh, what a tragedy that had befallen such a mighty kingdom of false knowledge! The great, titanic kingdom of Babylon had fallen: Yea, it had fallen flat on the ground; and all of its gleaming, glorious palaces had now been turned to mere rubble and dust.

They lay strewn across the face of the earth like fallen trees, hewn in a mighty storm: Oh, the wreckage of such a powerful kingdom was a picturesque view of a faded age; and there it was, for the whole world to see—the ghost that had led the whole earth astray. Oh, cruel phantom of Darwinism, how hast thou plagued the earth with the thorn of lies; how hast thou poisoned men's hearts against the Almighty Government of the universe! With thy mouth full of lies and sand, you've filled men's hearts with vanity's husks and straws; you've polluted the hearts of the earth's misguided children with lies' empty promises. Oh, what irreparable damage you've done to the sprawling kingdom of earthly life. You've constructed a titanic technocracy, run by amoral technicians, sheared of truth. Oh, crass, brash technicians of the Darwinian Age; why hast thou polluted the earth with so much vileness?

Why hast thou corrupted the innocent children of the earth with thy false teaching? You've poisoned their hearts against the untarnished beauty of truth, reason, and soberness: You've filled the earth with the poisonous, destructive words of falsehood and intrigue; you've ripped the Holy Writ from the hearts of men and women, and pelted it into the sea. Oh, crass, cruel cowards of evolution; you've hidden truth's golden light from the earth's wandering lambs: Oh, the little lambs, just learning to run and gambol over the tawny pasture of earthly life; you've been tricked by the cunning ones. They've used the classroom as their pulpit to disseminate the empty lies of fraud; Yea, they've utilized thy podium to promulgate and promote that which is abominable.

And oh, thy loathsome diatribe and frenzied, angry tirade against the Christian religion—what irreparable damage you have done to the very unhappy children of the earth! Oh, how hast thy irresponsible conduct ripped and ruined the delicate fabric of human society: Children, raised in fatherless homes, have turned into wild beasts; capsizing society's ship. Lost in the smoke of a false reality, they grope in the darkness of a bogus socialization. And like powerful waves pounding vehemently against the iron reefs of the sea, they've vented all that pent-up rage upon society's social engineering institutions: Schools, under siege by young criminals, looked like war zones after the storm had passed. Young school children, wielding combat armament, fired into screaming crowds:

Oh, the howling fire of AK Forty-Seven and Bush Master Rifles poured into the air like rain; children and adults, slaughtered like animals in a storm, screamed with the shriek of death. And when the storm was gone, the shredded parts of human remains were everywhere, scattered like leaves in a strong autumn shaking! The lost lives had been immolated to the gods of falsehood, vanity, and human folly. The religious doctrines of secular humanism and naturalism were never inculpated; yea, these false religious doctrines were never prosecuted for these senseless tragedies: They continued to be taught as sacrosanct truths to the sacred flock of innocence. Evolution's amoral system of analysis created a society where morals were irrelevant; And the negligible, exiguous presence of moral teaching created a shitload of troubles.

The endless sanguinary stream of school shootings and fallen heroes left society on edge; everyone agreed that there was a problem: No one seemed to know what it was. No one even had a clue about the origin and cause of those terrible kinds of problems. If anyone dared to suggest that the false, amoral teaching of evolution and the worldwide homosexual rebellion against God was the problem; he was either pronounced insane or summarily hanged on the nearest tree in the city. And so, false science's sacred cow of evolution turned out to be a barbarous butcher; Yea, a serial killer who maimed and killed for fun, hiding behind college professors' aprons and people's sexuality! But who would ever believe that sort of nonsense?

Whose eyes are that wide open? No one is that awake in society's sleepy camp of epicureans, whose religion is fun. The clarion cry is: Let us eat, drink, and have a good time; for tomorrow, we die. How noble and pragmatic that that ideological notion appears to be on the surface! But just beneath the shallow veneer of all that trash were dangerous social engineers—well educated men and women who worked laboriously to capsize the ship of Christianity and society. Oh, those malicious social engineers, dressed in the sacerdotal garb of good manners—those mischievous knit wits conducted a dark underworld of wonder and mischief; these impassioned religious nuts worked on society from behind their glass masks. Yea, they operated in a quaint, arcane world of mischief, intrigue, and betrayal of society; and like skilled cooks in a school cafeteria, these spin doctors framed the world they desired.

And, in that dark world of wonder and intrigue; they spun a society no one ever thought possible: Oh, they created a social world that fitted into their naturalistic ideology—yea, a society that snugly fitted into their secular religion like exquisitely chosen gloves! These are the ax-grinding social engineers who run our educational institutions today; these are the suckers who lie to you in election campaigns, promising you so much change. Oh, they promised you so many things that not even God himself would, and could, deliver—even God himself would not fulfill those empty, lofty promises under any circumstances.

But once they were elected, they brashly pushed through their own dark agendas; and by the time they were done with your vote, you didn't even know your own name. Far removed from the ordinary course of things, so many strange things happened: Yea, one thing after another seemed to go wrong right before your eyes; and you had to pinch yourself to see if you were still in the land of the living. These are the shockingly ugly types of games that these crass power brokers play. And when the Sophoclean news broke about the Virginia Tech massacre, people merely threw their mouths open and wondered what had happened there; the questions poured like smoke from a chimney—and they came from everywhere: How could this happen in the United States? Who are we and what have we become?

What have we become? Well, we've been teaching Darwinism and evolution in our schools; moral rules and human life were of very little significance in that naturalistic world. And so it was, one violent rampage after another in the frightened square of public life; here, a quiet workplace went amok; after a shower of AK 47 bullets, tears gushed like rain: There, shoot out with the police had shut down the entire neighborhood for two days! The people's faces, like blustery clouds, scowled with the long frown of disbelief: Their deep, booming, brawling cries sounded like cannons going off in the distance; they stuffed the air with the funereal sounds of sorrow and behave as if there would be no tomorrow! In a few minutes, their entire world had come crashing down; vaporized in a flash! All the beauty of their world had been lost within the twinkling of an eye!

Not far away, a bank was being held up by brawny young men discharged from prison the previous day; and a thousand miles away, a university campus was being transmuted into a war field. Why has society been turned into a howling jungle of wild beasts? Why, why, why, why? Suddenly, a sane society is filled with psychopaths, sheared of respect for human life. And so it was: The world finally woke up and saw who the real wild beasts were, and many tossed themselves into the wash that had swollen a day or two earlier. Everyone was still entitled to his own religious beliefs and moral convictions, but no one had the right to arbitrarily shove his religion down the throat of a classroom; that felony carried a maximum penalty of fifteen years in a state penitentiary.

And so, finally, the world began to awake from its long slumber of the evolution hoax; oh, the fairy tales, the fairy tales of evolution, naturalism, and secular humanism! The hegemony of that unholy trinity slipped into the picturesque eclipse of oblivion. And oh, heavens, what a wonderful world that unfolded thereafter; so filled with jolly folks. Truth resumed its rightful place smack at the podium of every classroom in the world; the cryptic veil of mystery, barbarism, and surrealism faded from the sunny skies above. The bloated coffers of scholars who wielded the staff of truth waxed even larger; and oh, the strength of pure money—what a fine job it did in cleaning up the world! Behold the earth, its cheeks gleaming with the bright blush of truth and the sane smile of joy.

Young men grew up in a world with such sacred respect for the law and human life; pregnant women raised children with their young, burly husbands right at their sides. Now, what had happened all of a sudden? What was the trigger of all this change? Nature's laws of respect for truth and authority were now in full force and control again; truth was taught in the classrooms of the world, and violators were severely punished.

Evolution was taught merely as a speculative theory of science— and that was all; no one, in his right mind, tried to mix conjecture and speculation with scientific truth. There was nothing else added, and there was nothing more—nothing else, nothing more! Prayer and Bible reading were reincorporated into the educational process; and oh, the keen, jarring, dramatic change that transpired was groundbreaking indeed. All the boiling, crazy, violent rampages on school campuses had ceased forever: Children ran and gadded about the place like a frisky litter of puppies; and oh, all of a sudden; so many things became virtually useless—so many things!

Prison cells, once jammed with young felons, now lay idle and practically empty; death-row wards; once throttled with violent, sadomasochistic murderers; now looked like inviolate chapels, far removed from the stain of human blood. Public schools, brisk with the business of educating young people, ran quite smoothly. Gone was all the mayhem, and confusion, and disorder associated with naturalism's lies. All the school fights were over, and all the sadistic and barbarous knifings came to a sudden end: The strident shrieks and cacophonous cries of violence were gone—and gone forever. The surreal calm that overshadowed the world of that day was rather picturesque and intriguing; many just could not believe their ears and eyes; however, whatever they thought did not matter anymore: Things had changed, and a new world had appeared.

CHAPTER 2

Oops, Here She Comes

Oh, how quickly and dramatically things had changed; the flame of change was everywhere. What a different place the world had become—so much change, in such a short time! The stain of bloodshed had faded from the halls of educational institutions, and the beautiful spirit of goodwill and brotherhood imbued the air just about everywhere. Oh, see the people's happy, lusty cheeks; painted with the gleam of joy and bloom. Their gleeful faces, like pungent Christmas lights, flamed with the glow of gladness. School yards and quads, filled with the chirp of cheer, roared with the boon of bloom! The world; splattered with gladness, pulse, and thrill; seemed like a wonderland.

Laughter rang like bells from the joyous voices of effervescent young people; and oh, what beautiful environments had been created for feeding the human mind; and the light of change was seen on every mound, hillock, knoll, and mountain. It seemed like springtime everywhere: The sallow, faded cheeks had all vanished. Even the wind's touch upon the cheeks was softer and more refreshing and beautiful; the shrubs that clad the far-flung hills looked like verdurous flowers in daylight's bloom. and their cheerful, pretty dance steps created a delightful showroom in the outdoors. Oh, the beautiful, piquant whistling of the wind filled so many hearts with joy and cheer.

And what a glorious boom time it was for those who had erected huge financial empires; what a wonderful and marvelous time it was for the earth's dashing empire builders! They had amassed sprawling kingdoms that wandered all the way across the earth; these giant financial empires, created by design scientists, raised eyebrows everywhere! Among the billionaires were the Firnes, the Sustifanis, the Hasslebecks, the Scrubbs, the Melons, the Jacksons, and the Omous; see how rich these pert, debonair boys of pen and ink had become in such a short time. The Age of Divine Design Scienc bristled with bloom, abundance, and amplitude.

The Firnes' Footprint in a Changing World

Many had thrown all their life's earnings into cheap real estate in that dreaded recession; they bought up houses for nickels on the dollar at the height of the last economic crisis. Doom and gloom were everywhere: Many mocked, and jeered, and scoffed at these boys: Yea, they bantered and laughed them to scorn and wondered whether they were insane; suddenly, the downward train of property values came to a screeching halt; and things began to turn around as if the hand of Jesus had been waved over the world. Oh, home values' feverish appreciation sent the world into a frenzied buying scramble; and, as if the splashy design science boys had been in prayer for forty days and forty nights—the rude scramble of the buying frenzy was nothing short of an interruption of nature.

Folks who had bought homes for nickels on the dollar became billionaires overnight; homes, bought for eighteen thousand dollars, were now selling for a half of a million! The Firnes' Global Enterprises' seventy-five hundred homes netted thirty billion dollars. Oh, the vicissitudes of life! Today, you are a pauper; tomorrow, you are filthy rich. But the Firnes were never poor; and their sprawling, opulent mansions earned them a mint. Oh, the booms and busts of life—they come and go like trains at a crowded subway station;

yea, they come and go—today, it is a flourishing boom; tomorrow, it is a savage bust! And those with eyes to see and who heeded history's strange lessons raked in billions! Homes moved around like Christmas toys on a rack at a busy up-scale suburban mall; things changed hands as fast as objects moving around in a tornado.

The smart design science boys had built up considerable wealth from the last recession; by then, most of them had amassed millions of dollars and were ready for the next bust. They understood the cycle and waited in the wings for cheap properties to come again; and when the tide came in again, they bought up thousands of inexpensive properties; then suddenly, things began to turn around; and well, these boys became filthy wealthy. Oh, the real estate balloon swelled and swelled, inflating their bank accounts' size. These sage scholars toted stacks of money, as high as small hills, to the nearest banks! And what a wealthy class of people they had become in that world of dollars and cents; in addition to the real estate bonanza, many scholars had established consulting firms.

Thriving consulting operations became noisy money machines that added to their wealth; and many shrewd, sagacious billionaires charged exorbitant fees for their services. Some business consulting firms charged as much as five thousand dollars an hour! And, forasmuch as many of their clients became rich overnight, that was a small fee to pay. Many of their rich clients, on the down low, dished out a fortune to save their marriages; the clients of these dashing boys of design science paid the fees with great pleasure. The dirty-rich Firne Family had developed a bustling worldwide real estate empire: They had built sprawling real estate consulting offices on all habitable continents; they had also built grocery chains in Australia, New Zealand, Britain, and Argentina. See the Firnes: Their global footprint had become a trademark in the world of business.

These filthy-rich billionaires had commanded great respect around the world, and their *swarthy* skin color had become as immaterial as cars passing by on the streets! The picturesque Firne footprint had been firmly placed everywhere around the world. Not a few, yea, many business tycoons had come to view their word as good as gold! The Firne Consulting Firms in South America and Australia were enormously successful; these busy, brawling, sprawling financial machines operated virtually around the clock. Clients lined up in long lines that stretched across, and snaked around, several blocks; and, on average, these powerful money machines netted in the billions of dollars—each of these financial monstrosities netted in excess of seven billion dollars per year. And when all the cash from real estate, banks, and grocery chains were added up; the total revenue was somewhere around five hundred and fifty billion dollars per year!

All that money was generated just from those operations in South America and Australia. The Firne Global Enterprises' annual revenue was around one and a half trillion dollars! And these pert, savvy boys were not at all finished with the business world. Dr. Mildren Firne was a brilliant academician and had earned two doctorate degrees; earlier in his life, he earned a Ph.D. in urban architecture and design in the United States. He waxed into a world-class urbanologist and architectural design specialist; his expertise was widely sought around the world, and he was always on the go. His urbanology consulting practice had more than one hundred offices around the world; and oh, what colossal success he had achieved in that sparsely pursued field of science.

He had a business consulting practice with one hundred offices and ten thousand employees! But the stress of absenteeism from his beautiful wife began to flurry his family life; and though he had built lavishly furnished mansions and palaces on several continents, he was still on the go all the time: All this began to tear the fabric of his family life. And though he did not completely withdraw from the business of urban design, he began to delegate authority to people in the astral circles of his consulting operation. And, within four or so years, Dr. Mildren Firne had finished a doctorate in brain science: He still operated the business consulting monstrosity by delegation of authority; but most of his time was spent on building a small neurological practice in Los Angeles. He expended much energy and passion on this work that he valued so highly.

And, with the passion of Fred Hoyle, Dr. Firne began to write books on brain science; and oh, his pulchritudinous wife, Dr. Margolyn Thorn-Firne, was just as prolific a writer. They had worked feverishly and passionately to dethrone the evil religion of naturalism; the couple held brawling, sprawling town hall meetings and conventions around the world. The new laws that forbad professors from proselytizing in classrooms had just taken effect. And oh, how tirelessly they had worked to engender this dramatic change; how unwearyingly they had labored to inspire this sensational victory for science! Those who had cavalierly lied in the classroom about man's origin were silenced forever; big money had worked laboriously to ensure truth's landslide victory over naturalism, and the false religions of Secular Humanism and Evolution Theory had met their match.

Victory had come at last for those normal people who believed in the laws of order; oh, see the streets, flooded with music and dancing: Behold the people's alacritous faces! Behold the sprawling, brawling streets like loud, cacophonous dance halls of joy; oh, the joyous, triumphant people; clad in blazing, fiery colors of glory and victory: See the gleaming stentorian streets, ablaze with the flaming fire of excitement; the streets of the earth lit up like long, serpentine galaxies; blazing in the night. Oh, see those prismatic rivers of light, gushing with the glow of glee and gleam; See how they bristled with the bloom of victory's blush and flush—oh, the revelrous spirit of victory and its electric, carnivalesque scenes in the streets! The surging pulse of truth and change imbued the people's hearts with the light of joy: Victory's pulsating flame flared and flickered from every cheek like candles in the wind.

Behold the gleaming faces of the people, encased in the starry glow of pretty smiles. They are dancing; they are jumping; and they are shouting; "Down with naturalism: Away with evolution theory and secular humanism, and fill the world with truth." And amidst all this brash and glorious jubilation, the kings of the earth became excited; oh, see the powerful billionaires who had torn down the temple of Evolution: Behold the omnipotent billionaires of design science whose bare hands had done the job. Their gleaming chariots, as fast as the speed of light, roared like atomic bombs across the earth: Yea, they flared like a powerful storm in the distance; glorifying the truth.

Their Godwit jets, as glorious as fulgent stars, stuffed the air with the roar of triumph; big money released shoals of vapor-writing jets across the skies of the earth; and oh, what a dazzling, magnificent show of power they demonstrated in the air: The truth had finally been liberated from the tenebrous caves of naturalistic classrooms. Oh, the wanton, impudent proselytizing of evolution scientists had ceased forever! The Holy Writ's meek and gentle spirit was finally liberated from falsehood's cave, and the Christian God had been summarily resurrected from the dark castle of oblivion. And so, the mighty kings of the earth splashed about the heavens like flying automobiles—yea, they splashed across the earth like a sports car; racing through a puddle of water.

Oh, let the heavens roar with the mighty glory, pomp, and pageantry of pure truth; and let the golden children of truth be born in a world filled with life and soberness: Oh, let the fierce mongrels of falsehood and vanity bow before the progeny of truth. And it was against this glorious backdrop that a miraculous birth was recorded; the Firnes had amassed hundreds of billions of dollars and had established businesses all over the world. Their charming brand and staggering wealth had become household names and icons of success; their three children were treated with great royalty wherever their jets landed. They were the day's royalty and flew virtually all over the world. The boys were very handsome and buffed, and many ladies around the world tossed their intimate attire at them.

Her Sudden, Mysterious Appearance

Amadyn, Arnold, and Sasha had gone to the most prestigious schools in the world; and with multiple Ph.Ds, their expertise was widely sought around the world. They all had global television programs that promoted their parents' impassioned cause. Incidentally, Dr. Firne had always wanted more children; but his wife did not bear him anymore. Thus, they had become used to the idea of three children and no more: They were finished with raising children. One miscarriage and years of attempts to have more children were enough; however, presumably, nature was not finished with them. The dashingly colorful couple had been celebrating the defeat of the Evolution religion: They were on a swing tour around the world, promoting their brand-new books; they had just conducted a loud, brash, cacophonous victory rally in St. Johns, Antigua, in the Caribbean.

They had also conducted meetings at the St. John's Polytechnic University, in Antigua: Their gleaming design science auditorium there was jammed with die-hard celebrants; they had had a magnificent book-signing assembly in Antigua's capital city of St. John's. Upon completion of the book signing there, their Godwit jet flew nonstop from St. Johns, Antigua, to Auckland, New Zealand, a distance of 14,078 square kilometers, covering a timespan of twenty-one hours and six minutes. The streets were throttled with passionately joyous, revelrous celebrants: They were headed to the sprawling Auckland Convention Center where the Firnes were to promote their books. Dr. Margolyn Thorne-Firne, a prolific academician, had just finished two monographs: ***Psychopathic Behavior, a Societal Thorn;*** and ***Biorhythm Analysis, a Gem in Employers' Hands***. And her erudite husband, Mildren Firne, had also written a new book—his provocative monograph, ***Understanding the Genetic Clock***, had stirred quite a buzz around the world.

And even before their lively book signing tour had ended, the books went out of print. Their publishers, besieged with orders, were swamped with work; and though they worked around the clock, within days, all the copies were gone. Millions of copies were sold within minutes; and oh, the buzz they stirred in the world. The fabulously successful science professors had just wrapped up a full day of celebration. The city of Auckland was stirred with the buzz of the Firnes' presence; they had visited the Auckland Star University and held talks with officials there. The carnivalesque Auckland streets, strewn with trash, had begun to cool off; the action and excitement had moved to the psychedelic Auckland Convention Center.

And oh, the stirring enthusiasm that Dr. Firne's new book had generated! Excitement swarmed in the air like a seething fog, roaming in the dusk of nightfall. His revolutionary work, ***Understanding the Genetic Clock***, was the talk of the hour; folks; crazy about living a long, healthy life; worked up quite a stir there in Auckland. Fresh research in cells' genetic behavior promised, at least, one hundred and twenty years! Folks, excited about their new lease on life, could not remain quiet in the auditorium. Dr. Firne, engulfed in a thick cloud of enthusiasts, was overwhelmed by the stir. Oh, people; wangling their way through the blithe, frenzied crowd; crushed upon him: They pressed against the humanitarian billionaire, besieging him for autographs.

His wife Margolyn, lost in the swirling smoke of vain passion, chatted with colleagues a few feet away from the crush. Many of her fellow professors had read her books and were quite excited as well; she was just being congratulated by her long-time friend, Rosslyn Molluck. Her friend, Dr. Molluck, had already read both monographs and was bristling with excitement when; suddenly, Dr. Margolyn Firne began experiencing strong abdominal spasms and cramps. Her body began shaking violently like a tree, spinning and whirling in a storm; and, in the smoke of the unlooked-for emergency, she, too, was crushed by the crowd. Within minutes, medical emergency vehicles had rushed to the scene; whereupon she was whisked away to a state-of-the-art private Auckland hospital!

Shortly afterwards, the tests results indicated that Mrs. Firne had been pregnant—and it was confirmed that the emergency was not, in any way, a miscarriage. According to the thrilled and baffled gynecologists, the cryptic pregnancy had gone its full term: The plump, pretty Margolyn Firne; for whatever reason; was not aware of the pregnancy's existence. The whole world was in shock; and her doctor, Dr. Scrubbs; went briefly into a trance. The Sir Winston Churchill Medical Facility, at which she was treated, was swamped; it was as if the whole city of Auckland wanted to catch a glimpse of the eleven-pound baby girl.

Dr. Firne could not believe that such a revered dream had come to pass; yea, he could not believe his ears and eyes when he heard, and saw, his pretty baby girl. Quaint, colorful caravans; winding around the hospital; had blocked traffic for miles: These die-hard epicureans gladly welcomed the new stir in the beautiful Auckland area. They snaked around the up-scale suburban Auckland hospital and stuffed its hallways! Those who could not get in jammed the medical facility's switchboard with phone calls. They waved branches, flowers, and flags; clamoring to see the world's new princess. In the meantime, the mystery pregnancy had made news around the world; televised programs in Jerusalem hailed the birth as *The Queen of the New Science Era.*

Hoboes in the streets of Jerusalem clapped their hands; singing, "Mary has come again. The mother of Jesus has revisited the Earth: She has come to proclaim a new era—the Virgin Mary has come to announce the onrush of a new cycle of earth history." Oh, see the parched, dusty ground; listen to the howling, angry noise of the wind. See the drunks on the streets; their faces powdered with the dusky fog of dust. Oh, hear the squealing noise of the wind, like a neighing horse; galloping on a race track. And oh, see the dust it kicked into the air; showering the crowded streets with sandy rain. Behold the powdery cheeks of the scampering crowds, scurrying across the intersection.

Brisk, ecstatic open-market shoppers in the Antiguan capital of St. Johns wept for joy; many bellowed in the streets," Why didn't it happen here among us: Why over there? They've brought us so much hope, and joy, and excitement. Why didn't it happen here?" Londoners, lost in shock and bewilderment, camped out in parks and slept in the open air. In New Delhi, Hindus and Buddhists celebrated for days in the streets, honoring the birth of a new princess. They claimed that the child's secret birth was a sign and wonder to a wicked world, drowning in darkness. And so, just about everywhere in the world; someone had something to say about it. The tenebrous mystery of Mrs. Firne's pregnancy filled the world with joy and wonder; she'd had an active menstrual cycle all through this unfathomable pregnancy: She led a very active and vigorous life throughout the entirety of this strange period.

Mrs. Firne taught all her classes at the university with flair as she had always done; she went swimming, bowling, dancing, and had spent much time on the golf course with her husband. Absolutely nothing out of the ordinary was observed by her or her doctor; Though she claimed that she'd felt periodic cramps and spasms in her abdomen and had had jittery feelings in her stomach from time to time, she had not had the slightest idea that she was carrying their fifth child.

And oh, the joy and ecstasy that filled Dr. Firnes heart! He wished it were a twin, but he thanked the Christian God for being so kind to him and handing him such a gem. Yea, he thanked the God of heaven for realizing a long-treasured dream. His eleven-pound baby flooded his heart with unspeakable joy!

And oh, the obscure birth's highlights were the quickness with which it transpired; the cramps and spasms came on very suddenly, strongly, and noticeably. And within minutes of the university professor's arrival at the hospital, she gave birth to an eleven-pound baby girl: And oh, she was as pretty as a star! Oh, see her pulchritudinous cheeks, encased in a beautiful smile that lit up the room with bloom! The rest of the Firne Family was shocked, embarrassed, and jubilant about the birth. The pretty baby girl's sudden appearance in the world spanned the gamut of emotions; her brothers and sister were extremely happy at hearing the outlandishly joyous news. At first, its strange jocularity sounded like abstract jazz music to their ears: Their mother loved Luis Armstrong's Jazz, and played it just about every day.

The gynecologist, who delivered the baby, Dr. Marlene Scrubbs, was herself a prophetess. And she spoke very kind words over the beautiful eleven-pound baby girl; Dr. Scrubbs called the cute, little angel "Vanetta Roslyn Firne" and kissed her cheeks. Within hours, the Firnes were back in the United States at their sprawling Malibu Ranch; they could have stayed at their beautiful palatial summer cottage in Auckland; but rather, they chose to return to the United States as quickly as possible. They had to take care of immigration matters and dual citizenship issues at once. A flashflood of emails, congratulatory cards, and monetary gifts swept the Malibu Mansion; accordingly, the residential campus staff was overwhelmed with a frenzied flurry of tasks.

A Rhapsodic Baby Dedication

The fifteen hard-working residential campus employees were hired to do clerical work: Much of their work had to do with preparing the Firnes' books for publication; suddenly, the work was so intense; fresh temporary assistance had to be hired. There were thousands of emails, congratulatory cards, and heart-warming letters to the Firnes; oh, there were hundreds of barrels and parcels with childcare supplies to last for a thousand years! And there were also stacks and stacks of monetary gifts. Story-hungry photographers and impassioned newsmen smothered the scene; Die-hard tabloid writers swarmed around like bees whose hives had been disturbed. They swooped down upon the place like hungry quails in search of food; oh, they rabidly scoured the scene; gobbling up the stirring, dainty story like hot cakes.

The refreshingly delightful story remained on worldwide television for weeks! Millions, glued to their television screens, watched the numerous telecasts about it. Oh, hear the fairy tale news story; welcoming Vanetta Roslyn Firne into the World. Listen to that magnificent tale told by a million different voices! It was as if the whole world had been expecting Vanetta—and she finally came; and oh, the massive groundswell of gladness that swept the earth! And after all its many twists and turns; some put her birthplace in Brussels, Belgium. Pretty pictures of the adorable princess flashed on every television screen in the world; oh, see how tellurians loved pretty, little Vanetta and carried her picture everywhere!

And in the fullness of time, the ceremonial proceedings of baby dedication had come. Dr. Chapellson, Ph.D. Systematic Theology and Theological Science, was the presiding minister: The hush-hush event drew people from as far away as Wellington and Jericho. The Upper Room Tabernacle's sprawling auditorium was jammed with die-hard fans, and although every effort was made to conceal the sacred event from the moiling mob; somehow or other, word had leaked out about the upcoming, very high-profile ceremony. And Firne enthusiasts flocked the area and swarmed around the church like bees.

The picturesque scene of helicopters, swirling around the church, moved many to tears; and, forasmuch as the *Big Wigs* were allowed in first, parking was a nightmare! Posh, expensive automobiles; the cost of a luxury yacht; were everywhere. These svelte, glistening sports cars spilled into the surrounding neighborhood; and mammoth crowds, as large as a carnival parade, milled about the streets. The heavy police presence frightened away the faint-hearted and trimmed the crush; oh, the colorful, picturesque scene brought tears to the eyes of so many people. Many even tried to compare the quaint circumstances of Vanetta's life with that of Christ!

And, although the entire baby dedication was carried on worldwide television; not a few people could afford to miss a glimpse of this magnificent event! And, within the rather commodious church auditorium was quite another spectacle. It seemed as if the entire global society's astral circles were convened for the ceremony; and the credentials read out were quite impressive and exalted, to say the least. The pretty baby princess, as charming as a specially designed doll, smiled with everyone: Her soft cheeks; painted with the flame of bloom, beauty, and innocence; warmed many hearts. Her adorable, chubby countenance; awash with beauty, boon, bloom, and blush; radiated much glister, gentleness, and kindness.

Behold her jet black, curly hair; fluttering in the gentle breeze of the moment and painting the atmosphere with glister and happiness. And her beautiful smile, as dainty as a Camellia flower, brightened everyone's cheeks with appreciation, merriment, and pulse. Oh, her father, her father, Dr. Firne; how proud, and blitheful, and rapturous he looked and was! How brightly the glorious beams of joy and gladness radiated from his cheeks; and the baby's brothers and sister all sat around, soaking up the glory of the moment: See how joyously and excitedly they looked on! What a magnificent and most unforgettable scene that had been created there; the colorful audience, brushed with the polish of gleam, and beauty, glowed with glee. What a happy and glorious scene that was, and Dr. Firne was the happiness man in the world, there.

Vanetta's Arrival on the Scene

Oh, see how the many joyful faces, abloom with blush, radiated beneath the chandelier lights; see how excitedly and jubilantly they waved and wafted kisses at the little princess! Distinguished guests, from all over the world, filed into the cavernous, gleeful auditorium; and, beaming with joy, they gingerly sauntered down the aisle and cheerfully sat down. They were the who's who among the world's eminent scholars, and statesmen, and financiers; and like a picturesque bouquet of flowers, eight godparents gathered around the baby. Dr. Chapellson; himself, a godparent; waved the beautiful princess before the audience: He then lifted her into the air and said, "Name this beautiful angel, smiling at us all;" whereupon Dr. Firne cheerfully said, "Her name is Vanetta Roslyn Firne, a most adorable gift from God."

Flush with pride, he smiled; and the audience broke out with a volley of applause. Some screamed, "Vanetta Roslyn Firne, the golden flower of the morning!" Others whistled with ardor and excitement, throwing polychromatic pompoms and confetti in the air. The roaring noise spilled from the altar all the way into the brawling streets. Noisy automobiles, whirring through the streets, tooted their horns at the joyous crowd; and then, the time had come for all the godparents to present their gifts to the princess. And oh, what a moving, delightsome scene that was to see the many gifts presented. Dr. Chapellson, the presiding minister, handed Dr. Firne a check for the baby: The check for one hundred and seventy-five thousand Euros was the best he could do; yea, it was the least that he could do for his wonderful, beloved goddaughter.

And he recommended that the money be invested into stocks and bonds for her college education; and that, if the broker had all his ducks in a row, things should work out quite well! By the time his beloved godchild was eighteen years old, she should strike it rich; and, by that time, the money should grow to more than one hundred million Euros! The crowd went crazy; screaming, applauding, and tossing flowers and pompoms in the air; Then godparent number two; Dr. Hasslebeck, Ph.D., Nuclear Physics; stepped up to the podium: You could hear a pin drop anywhere in the graceful, gaping, awestruck auditorium. He said, "Well, Good morning, most distinguished ladies and gentlemen. What an honor! I'm thrilled to be here at this most auspicious and momentous occasion of my god baby's dedication.

The gracious God of heaven has blessed us again with this most beautiful princess, and to her I present this precious wedding gift before you all: She is such a bundle of gladness. My wife and I flew to Florence, Italy, to purchase this most treasured wedding band; and the cheerful, gracious sales clerk let us have it for just one million Euros!" And with that, Dr. Hasslebeck leaned over and kissed his goddaughter's pretty cheeks; he softly touched her hair and ambled away, waving at the blithesome audience. Dr. Hasslebeck was quickly followed by Dr. Omou, Ph.D. in Neurology and Mathematics. He said, "Ladies and gentlemen, be it known to you this day, that this, my godchild, is a star; and she deserves all the best that life has to offer to someone of her exalted station. and without further ado, I present to her a stock account for three million Euros to her!"

The antsy audience remained very quiet as godparent number four stepped to the podium; the electrified audience, inoculated with awe and shock, sat there as if they were numb. Dr. Sustifani; Ph.D., Atomic

Energy and Mathematics; handed Dr. Firne a check: The five-million Euro gift was a jaw-dropping stunner that jarred the benumbed audience! He explained to the flabbergasted folks that he and his wife Roslyn had been praying for that; they had been childless and had always thought of having a goddaughter. He affirmed that Vanetta was a direct answer to their prayers from the God of heaven; he wanted the money to be put into stocks and bonds toward the purchase of a yacht, and specified that this luxury motorboat was to be a special wedding gift for his godbaby! He said that they had already begun to pray for his goddaughter's carefully chosen husband.

As Dr. Sustifani walked away; a dashingly sprightly couple strutted up to the altar: Dr. Gonzalez; Ph.D., geomagnetism; beckoned with his hands and spoke zealously to the audience: His voice spilled much glee on the rabid cheeks of the joyous guests. The distinguished Barcelona Spanish scientist explained how happy and honored he was to witness such an unexpected birth and delightsome Christening. He regarded the moment as a most unforgettable and momentous experience in his life; his radiant wife Anahi, dripping with beauty and charm, handed Dr. Firne a deed! They had bought a seventy-five-acre ranch for their pungent, beloved goddaughter: They had already built a magnificent summer cottage to be in the Firnes' custody! As they gaily walked away from the podium, godparent number six presented his gift. Dr. Molluck; Ph.D., Mathematics and Econometrics professor; hailed from Auckland, New Zealand: Larger than life itself and with a big smile on his face, he also presented a deed to the Firnes.

This generous Auckland University professor was also a very filthy-rich businessman; he had known Dr. Firne for a very long time and had managed their business in Auckland. The deed he presented them was for a five-hundred-acre farm just outside Auckland, New Zealand—and indeed, that was over the top; but these were the world's billionaires and scientific aristocrats of the day! As he quickly walked away, godparent number seven scurried onto the stage with a smile. Dr. Gutierrez; Ph.D., Geodetic Science; was a young, brilliant scientist from Buenos Aires: He had just come into the ranks of the global scientific aristocracy, attaining billionaire status. And he had amassed a tremendous amount of wealth in the commodities market! His five million-Euro-gift for Vanetta's wedding band was merely a drop in the bucket; his young, pretty, very wealthy wife, Elizabeth, also welcomed the idea of a godchild.

And finally, Dr. Zonakh; Ph.D., Physics, from Canberra, Australia; came to the podium. Inoculated with cheer, thrill, and pulse; He greeted the minister, kissed the baby, and said: "Oh, most gracious and wonderful gaggle of academicians, scientists, and others here today; it is indeed a distinct honor to be here in your presence and to witness this marvelous miracle. I am so piquantly delighted and beside myself to be this beautiful princess' godfather—I am so happy to be a part of this mysterious miracle; her college education is paid in full. She will attend the prestigious Canberra Polytechnic University in Australia; the arrangements have already been made, even as the hand of time has already begun to tick. Her three-million-Euro stock account has already been put into motion."

And with that last presentation, Dr. Chapellson blessed the pretty princess again; whereupon the assembly was quickly dispersed, thus ending the glorious and awesome ceremony and leaving the parting audience with many things about which to talk for the next million years! The area, bristling with police, looked like a New York City peak-hour traffic jam; but, alas, all the motorists were quite cordial and urbane in their disposition. The snarled traffic was gradually dissolved; and oh, what a wonderful day it was! The unclogging of the traffic arteries soon enabled the chariots to move more smoothly. Many left the quaint gathering; holding their breath, sighing, and blushing: They had never seen anything as weird and extravagant as what they had just witnessed in that Malibu church; many wondered how, in the world, a child could be given such outlandish wedding gifts.

Oh, the child, not far removed from the womb, was so quickly introduced to the adult world. Pelted into the uncanny cave of adulthood like a green fruit, plucked in the fury of a tempest; the baby princess was summarily brought into the foggy castle of holy matrimony. The gifts were varied, numerous, and extravagant; and they'd be around for a long time. Oh, the exquisite foresight of obsessively and frenetically delighted godparents; they flooded their goddaughter with gifts beyond anyone's wildest dreams! They turned a little baby girl—a mere infant—into a multibillionaire, even before she could understand what was going on around her. The little infant baby, looking around and smiling, had not even the slightest clue of what was going on around her! This thrillful angel of God had already been introduced to, and made friends with, the world; and the whole world was abuzz with her amazing appearance.

Trying to Make Sense of It All

How on earth could a mere christening ceremony turn an infant into a dashing billionaire overnight? How could a baby dedication make such a darling little angel so filthy rich right on the spot! The discourse of three Upper Room Tabernacle members brought things into sharper perspective; Lucile Gompers, church clerk, and Elizabeth Jefferson, church secretary, were quite upset. These two church members were highly discombobulated about the baby dedication; but Mrs. Richards, a Malibu school teacher, put them in their place—and they did not like it: They were highly upset.

Mrs. Gompers: Good heavens; well, well; we've seen some very strange things today! Haven't we, girl? And you look so sassy in your glamorous, new garment.

Mrs. Jefferson: But oh, my dear; I know that my new dress is not what's on your mind: You are befuddled and lost by all that Babylonian display of generosity; you have never seen so much money passed in an ordinary church service in your life! —have you?

Mrs. Gompers: But you see, my friend; that baby dedication was anything but ordinary: Five helicopters panted overhead like giant waterfalls, over towering and tumbling over steep cliffs—that was quite a sight to behold. The five panting helicopters overhead and all the people, standing in the streets and cheering, created a most beautiful scene: They were excited, too! That little New Zealander is indeed a celebrity from birth—she just has it! And girl, did you see those handsome billionaires, as flashy as Michael Jackson and as rich as a bank vault?

Mrs. Jefferson: Yes, I saw the handsome gentlemen; but the show was not about them; it was about this nifty, dashing little girl who got all of the attention and the money—and I was so mad, too; I should have put my hands on some of that money!

Mrs. Richards: What do you mean by saying that the show was not about them: It was about this bratty, little girl—and you were so mad? You ought to be ashamed of yourself for saying that. Of course, the show was not about them: It was about Vanetta, the beautiful, little baby who was being Christened; and to refer to her as a nifty, little brat is reprehensible! The handsome gentlemen who were there were there for Vanetta—not for you, ladies. They were the ones who donated all the big bucks.

Mrs. Gompers: Well, those were some fine gentlemen! And Dr. Gutierrez, the Buenos Aires billionaire; just looked like a dashing bachelor. But oh, his wife is ten times as rich as he! Who are these filthy rich folks? I've never heard of scientists with all that kind of money. My God! Who are they? They must be professional bank robbers and drug pushers in their countries because only those people who usually have that kind of money. I tell you what: I'd spread my legs, wide open, for any of those dashing tycoons; girl, I'd carry on as if I'm crazy. I'd tell you what: One dance with me, and they'd never go back to their wives again. I'd be filthy rich!

Mrs. Jefferson: Well, there is not enough dope in the world to make that kind of money: You have to cut down all the trees in the world and package their leaves in huge bundles; and then, you are going to dose up the whole world with drugs and cheap sex, like only you can give to sell all those big stacks of dope!

Mrs. Gompers: But you know what; I will send Dr. Molluck an email, thanking him for his generosity; I'm sure that some of all that money will make its way into our church—we need it, too. And I will ask Dr. Molluck if he needs a maid or someone to sweep up his yard: I'm simply just wasting my time, working for pennies here; it just does not cut it here anymore. Perhaps, if Dr. Molluck hires me as his yard girl; I will be able to make a decent living, working for him.

Mrs. Richards: And, may be, if his wife takes ill; you will fill in for her, too hah? Yea, if Dr. Molluck's wife gets sick; you will make things all right there, hah? You see, that is what's wrong with you people—you shallow hypocrites: You do not really know the Lord; all you know to do is to play games.

You are so mercenary and epicure, you would sell your soul to the devil if you could! You are so *da gone* greedy, selfish, and full of evil; you should work in hell instead: You sound like witches who wear sheep's garments in the Lord's House. You see, my friends; money is not everything: You two should be praising the Lord. You should be giving him glory for his magnificent display of the divine power that he has displayed here today; oh, how mightily he has showcased his love and power at that glorious baby dedication; he has turned a little infant girl into an instant billionaire, right before our eyes!

Come on, ladies, what we have just witnessed is nothing short of a miracle. And what he has done for Little Pumpa, he certainly would do for the church secretary: How dare you talk like a whore like that—a flat out hooker, right on the heels of such a heavenly display! Are you saved? Do you know Jesus, the savior of the whole world? Shame on you, prattling like a downright slut right on the heels of such divine power! These men are the design scientists who have debunked the theory of evolution: These wonderful scholars have changed the course of human history forever; they are our heroes. We, of the Christian community, must be proud of them.

Mrs. Gompers: What does their being our heroes have to do with anything? Once a gold digger, always a gold digger; and I certainly know some gold when I see it: My mamma was a gold digger; I am a gold digger; and I will always be a gold digger.

Mrs. Richards: Oh, slutty woman, how dare you insult the Lord Jesus and talk like that! The God of heaven has blessed these erudite men beyond their wildest imagination: They're the richest men in the world, and they have displayed much generosity before us there today; yea, they've shown much kindness and love to our baby princess, Vanetta, there in that lowly church. And here you are, talking like a prostitute, eagerly in search of "your own Johns."

This is so shockingly disgusting—you all need to repent and seek help now: You two need to repent now before the earth opens up and swallows us all; yes, you all must call upon the Lord before it is too late for both of you. You work for the Church and ought to have a higher sense of reverence for the things that belong to God, rather than lusting after the gentlemen who've blessed this little girl. Well, I am absolutely shocked at your behaving like seasoned whores.

Mrs. Gompers: Well, you are hitching a ride from me and talking crazy like that to me in my car! You must be out your *da gone* mind, addressing me in that tone of voice: How dare you call me a whore and hooker in my own "fk"ing car: You must be crazy! One *hood rat* must know another; you "f"ing woman with a little paint on your skin.

Mrs. Jefferson: Be careful, girl; you are about to drive this car over that cliff. Perhaps, Mrs. Richards' voice is the voice of God because your body is jerking. You are beginning to shake violently: Stop this car and let me out—you are losing it!

Mrs. Richards: What are you doing, Lucille? Do you want to kill us all? Have you lost your mind? I know that you can handle this automobile much better than that! I've seen you drive before, and you are a brilliant chauffeur.

Mrs. Jefferson: Don't worry; she's not having an epileptic seizure: She'll be all right. She shakes like that when she is very angry: She goes into spasms, and she is now very angry with both of us because she has a phobia for the truth. We are too mercenary and greedy— we attach far too much value to material things: What we have overlooked here is that this little girl did not ask for any of this; it was merely freely given to her. She is just a little, innocent infant—an angel from heaven! She does not even know what, in the world, is going on around her and really doesn't care; she merely smiled and waved her tiny hands at the exuberantly applauding audience.

We should be happy to have witnessed such a magnificent display of God's power; and besides all of this, these billionaires have taken this infant as their own. Their generous giving reflects the loving heart of God, who has smiled upon this child; love and giving love are all that Jesus knows to do: those are the only things in his heart. Jesus does not know, or have anything else, to give to the human race: He gave himself; yea, his life for all the greed, selfishness, whoredom, and sin in this world. Watch *The Passion of the Christ*: You'll see the staggering price that Jesus paid for us all for all of us!

These noble men see Vanetta as their own baby, and they are investing in her right now; and besides, what is one million Euros to these filthy rich giants of science? They are the societal architects who are designing a new world order for all of us—a fresh global political machine, sheared of the garbage and alloy of evolution. And we must applaud the wonderful work that these noble men are doing in the world; and who knows—Vanetta's mysterious birth might be a sign from heaven itself. Don't you think that these brilliant men have already thought all of that through? They are grooming Vanetta for a major role in that fast-approaching world government; they have even already selected her bridal accouterments.

What a message: What a straight message that they are sending to the naturalists and secularists! "We are building a new world order; this child would help us in the engineering process of it." Yes, Mrs. Richards; you've been my son's science teacher—and a good one, too! I repent for our senseless gossip against the eye-popping display of God's power there today. And I am sure that Mrs. Gompers would agree with both of us.

Mr. Richards: And sometimes, bruising words need to be spoken to get folks' attention; especially folks who've gone off the deep end, acting way out of character.

Mrs. Jefferson: As highly visible folks of our church, we have to set the proper example: We are the leaders of Upper Room Tabernacle of Faith. We ought to be good examples—yea, we ought to be the finest example of Christian love and integrity in the world. Our pastor, Dr. Chapellson, also an eminent scientist, has been a good example to us:

How dare we smear his name with hood rats, hookers, and whores on the streets!

Mrs. Gompers: Thank you, Mrs. Richards for standing up to us and telling us the truth; we have embarrassed and stained the beauty of Vanetta's day with the smudge of soot. we owe our dear princess Vanetta an apology for our careless, irresponsible comments; and from this day forth, I vowed to turn my life around and live for the cause of Christ. I repudiate embracing the idea of being a gold digger and a plain old slut: I am no gold digger—I am saved.

And I owe it all to Mrs. Richards' integrity and to our precious little princess, Vanetta: Oh, how easy it is to stray from the golden path of righteousness, truth, and integrity! The war that Christian soldiers fight every day is fiercer than World War One's trench warfare, and this is the reason that men have found it right in their own eyes to deny and reject the truth. Good heavens, it is so easy to follow the broad, evil path of this world's way of doing things.

All one has to do is merely that which comes naturally and pleases him—and no one else! But you see, this is the basic principle of the Satanic Bible—just do as *you* wish. You do not have to please anyone else but yourself; and oh, it is so easy to fall into that trap! But that Satanic piece of advice always leads one into the formidable and unhallowed trenches of destruction; it is never long before he finds himself in that detestable trash can of failure, defeat, and ruin. Thank you, Mrs. Richards for standing up to me.

CHAPTER 3

EARLY CHILDHOOD YEARS

Oh, the wonderful children of the world; they loved Vanetta with all their hearts: She was their golden idol in a world where so much was fake and meaningless; these beautiful children had finally found someone with whom they could identify. They loved the little princess so much, they hung her picture everywhere in their homes; and whenever she was on television, they crowded around their screens and stared. Oh, see how they gazed at this beautiful little princess, doing all sorts of things! See how they loved little Vanetta and endearingly referred to her as "Little Pumpa." The frisky children of the world affectionately called her Little Pumpa! Oh, Little Pumpa, Queen of the Morning, painted with the blush of daylight's beauty.

See her eyes, as bold as golf balls; and her face, as pretty as a burning star! Her hair as fine and soft as silk, and as flowing and beautiful as a pristine stream! Oh, behold her soft, pretty, dimpled cheeks; abloom with the blaze of beauty. Behold her sweet, tiny, kissable lips; brushed with the incarnadine light of strawberries. And oh, who could resist admiring the scarlet paint of her dashingly delightful cheeks!

See her nose, as sharp as a spear and as straight as a rod; that dainty flower of cheer: Oh, how exquisitely well nature had placed it upon her high, golden dimpled cheeks. And when the incomparable "Little Pumpa" smiled, the whole world smiled back at her. Oh, what a fiery and adorable little girl this beautiful princess had become! What ineffable joy and unbounding cheer that she had brought her proud, wealthy parents; and when she affectionately said, "Daddy, Daddy;" Dr. Firne's heart would leap for joy. Oh, the joy that her dazzling smile and soft, tender kisses brought to this great billionaire's heart; her soft, gentle, tiny hands upon his bristly visage filled his world with the pulse of gladness.

And good heavens, how quickly she stepped away from crawling upon the ground! Suddenly, she stood up; held on to the table; smiled gleefully; and began to step off the floor. And like a tender tree, shooting from the ground; she quickly learned to walk. What pride, and joy, and thrill, and cheer that she brought to the hearts of her entire family! They were so delighted and enraptured about her growth, they all wept for joy! And, full of love and pride, as if they could not wait upon the ticking hand of time; they quickly began to train her mind to the sound and beauty of music.

First, it was the piano; and then she was introduced to the saxophone and guitar: Time began to take her to greater and greater heights; and oh, the joy she brought everyone. And within a few years, she began to whip up concerts in the neighborhood; oh, the alacrity and jubilation of her brawling, cheering audiences! It was as if she had been trained from birth to play Luis Armstrong's Jazz; Her music began to sound just like that which her mom had been enjoying for years. All through her mysterious pregnancy, Margolyn had been listening to jazz music; oh, how she loved Luis Armstrong and the beautiful, soothing sound of his trumpet. Behold Vanetta Roslyn Firne, the child phenom of music and dance; see how she dazzled her audiences with music cooked up in heaven. She was a talented music and dance star; she was so charming and beautiful, everybody loved her and supported her thrilling and electrifying musical concerts. Vanetta was quite a pulseful package of talent and entertainment.

The Child Phenom: A Dashing Cosmopolite

The five-year old child prodigy learned to play the violin and drums on her own: No one had taught her to play these abstract musical instruments. One day, everyone looked around; and there she was, playing the violin; and then, Vanetta was playing the drums all by herself—what a child! The little princess danced, and sang, and entertained just about everyone; and as if trained from birth to be a politician; she began giving speeches. By the age of seven, Vanetta had won virtually every major pageant in the area; and how easy it was to think that favoritism had earned her that distinction. It had absolutely nothing to do with her royal status: She was just pretty and clean.

Vanetta was just very talented. In fact, she was judged more strictly, rigorously, and stringently than her peers; the standard of judgment used to evaluate her performance was unfair to her. She was judged on a higher standard than all her peers—and she won every time! Even though many of her peers were very good, she outshone their brilliance. In performance after performance, Vanetta outdid her rivals—and triumphed! She possessed talent way beyond her years: Oh, the joy she brought to so many. The joy and delight she brought to so many hearts were way beyond measure! See how she warmed the hearts of the world's teeming masses. They were so proud of their *Little Pumpa*: She seemed to have grown up so quickly! She dazzled the hearts of the world's children and served as their role model. The pretty, little girl grew up smack in the flaming light of world attention and had achieved worldwide popularity.

And then the tug of war began: Godparents began fussing over her summer vacation. "Well, we are having her over for summer; no, we are having her over for summer." Often, Vanetta had to make the choice; and she almost invariably chose Barcelona. She loved Spain and Auckland, New Zealand: Oh, she loved her godfather,

Dr. Molluck. And by that time, her palatial summer cottage in Barcelona was already a bank vault: Dr. Gonzalez, bent on turning the property into a money machine, leased it to rich folks; he leased the summer cottage out to a company that handled vacations for the rich. And the rich and famous worldwide vacationed there all because of Little Pumpa. The seventy-five-acre ranch was put to commercial agriculture—and it bloomed; it became very prosperous and attracted visitors from all over the world. The Firne Agribusiness Farm produced olives, grapes, plums, peaches, and apricots: Things began to happen in the financial arena almost immediately for the child billionaire!

The Vanetta Firne Agricultural Enterprises netted about forty million Euros per year. The commercial agricultural ranch canned fruits and meat and bottled expensive wines; and by age ten, Vanetta had already become an agricultural tycoon in Europe. She was flown from one European city to another in her own private jet; red carpets were laid out for her every arrival. And oh, how the people adored her. And as her wealth began to accumulate in the world, she waxed more and more famous; and this child had not lifted a finger to produce the financial empire created for her. There were rapidly growing stock accounts and exploding commercial ventures; it seemed like wealth sprang from just about everywhere for this darling societal icon. But the tug of war continued: Her Auckland Farm Operations dwarfed that in Europe. Of course, her farm there was seven times the size of her ranch in Europe; and accordingly, its commercial output was far greater than its European counterpart.

The Beauty of Childhood

The young billionaire loved the glorious city of Auckland, imbued with the breath of beauty; see its dashingly delightful landscape, ornately painted with the flame of splendor. The wide, open ocean softly danced at her feet like leaves fluttering in a quiet waft; its virtually mute waves, as tacit as dawn's quiet roar, gently splashed about the shore! See how they lathered the sheeny, glistening, white sand with that gentle romantic touch; they flickered and blazed across the soft sponge of the shore like pretty candles. See the glistening lights that leaped ever so pungently from the dancing froth on the sea; behold the golden beauty of the waves, painted with the light of freshly fallen snow. And oh, the dancers, the stunningly delightful dancers, clad in the garb of gleam! See the flitting waves; like pretty flowers that danced in the refreshing breath of the wind: Oh, see how they climb into the vaporous air like tiny, picturesque butterflies; and Vanetta Firne, that adorable New Zealander, reveled in all the grace and charm of Auckland.

Vanetta: Daddy, Daddy; Auckland is a pictorial castle, carved out of the beautiful sand that surrounds it: Oh, Auckland, chiseled from the iron face of granite with the bare hand of nothing; oh, Daddy, what a magnificent palace this breathtaking city of Auckland is!

Dr. Molluck: But Vanetta, I was there last year with you in beautiful Barcelona, Spain: Do you remember how much you said that Barcelona was the prettiest city in the world? And now that you are here with us, you are giving Auckland that same wonderful distinction; you are saying that Auckland is a palace, carved from the sand by the hand of no man: Would you please make up your mind, my precious little one? What is your favorite city in the world, Vanetta? —there can only be one!

Vanetta: Well, well, Daddy; I don't really know: The world is such a beautiful place! The geologic structure of the earth is an esthetic masterpiece: It is a glorious showcase. I love all the beautiful cities in which all my handsome, generous daddies live; I love Buenos Aires, and Ibadan, and Lagos, and Barcelona—and Daddy, I love Auckland, too. I love them all, Daddy! But truly, truly; I say to you, Daddy; Auckland is the best. I love Barcelona: it's very pretty there, and the water has so many delightful colors: Sometimes, it looks green; sometimes, it's green and blue; and sometimes, it's just blue. And the quaint-looking boats that spangle the shore are so heartwarming: Daddy takes us way out in the ocean for beautiful boat rides among the splashing waves. And it's nice, and pretty, and just enjoyable: Wow, wow, wow; Barcelona is the bomb! But Daddy, it's not the bomb like Auckland because my special friend lives here.

Dr. Molluck: And who might that special friend be; my darling goddaughter, Vanetta? —you are very popular around the world and have many friends.

Vanetta: Of course, you, Daddy; didn't you know that you were my special, special friend, too! I'm stunned that, after all this time, you do not know who I am. Of course, you; Daddy: Didn't you know that you are my special, special friend! I am surprised that you are so slow to catch on: You get all the tickles and softest kisses. But you know, my other daddies get them, too—you just get so many more than they. I love Australia, but it's so hot there: It is sunny, and parched, and dry, and dull; but I love my daddy in Brisbane—he takes me to those large amusement parks there. and oh, Daddy, there are children there like flies: They are everywhere on the rides. They love my pretty jazz music, especially when I am playing the saxophone; and I like giving it to them, too. When I'm done, they cheer and roar like crazy! Oh, Daddy; what a wonderful place this world is! The world is the bomb, too; hah, Daddy? Who made this big, old, beautiful world? I don't believe it made itself—did it?

Dr. Molluck: Well, my dear daughter; why do you ask me all these questions? —you sound like a police officer, investigating a crime, only that the crime is that of knowing more about the world. You have an extremely curious mind!

Vanetta: Well, you see, Daddy; don't you know why? It is because you are my favorite dad! I want my favorite dad to satisfy all my curiosities about this big, old, beautiful world! Did you ask your daddy a lot of questions when you were my age, Daddy? And if you did, did he answer you every time? Come on, Daddy; let us talk! Remember: We are very, very good friends; and we like each other— don't we, Dad?

Dr. Molluck: Well, Vanetta; Dr. Firne told me that you were a chatterbox: I really see what he meant now; and yes, I like you, too. You are my darling girl, and I will answer all your questions: Ask me all those questions again!—Go ahead, ask me!

Vanetta: Well, well, well; Daddy: You've forgotten my questions that quickly! I did not know that my daddy's mind was changeable and rambling; let us remain on the topic at issue and thrash it out until we are done—okay.

Dr. Molluck: No, no, no, no, no; I just want to see if you have forgotten them: Dr. Gutierrez and I were talking about you, and he said that you were a genius!

Vanetta: Who is a genius, Daddy? I know a genius is a very intelligent person: His IQ is off the chart! Isn't it, Dad? I guess that I am a genius, hah, Daddy? I am very smart! Well, back to my questions—did you ask your dad many questions about the world when you were my age?

Dr. Molluck: Yes, my child; I did, and he answered all of them, too! He must have been very brilliant; or may be, your questions were not that difficult at all, hah, Vanny?

Vanetta: Wow, that was some father you had there; And he did not get bored! He was a chatterbox like me, too, Daddy? He must have been some kind of guy! What did you ask him, Dr. Molluck? Did you ask him who made the world?

Dr. Molluck: Why did you call me Dr. Molluck? You never said that before! I was so pleasantly surprised when you called me by my professional name.

Vanetta: Well, Dad; you said that I was your best friend, remember?—you said it, Dad! And you are very smart too: I wanted you to know that I knew who you really are? You are Dr. Molluck: You have a Ph.D. degree in economics and another in mathematics. Dr. Molluck, Dr. Molluck! I am Dr. Firne, Ph.D. in astrophysics.

Dr. Molluck: Wow, my girl; who taught you all of this stuff? Where did you learn all of this so soon? I am shocked; you have a Ph.D. in astrophysics!

Vanetta: Yes, Dr. Molluck; I was born with it, remember: I am very smart, you know! I've been reading books since I was two years old; Dr. Gonzalez taught me to read: He is very smart, too; his doctorates are in physics and geomagnetism—wow, and this has to do with the earth's magnetic field, doesn't it?

Dr. Molluck: Well, Vanetta; you seem to know just as much as I do; you don't need answers from my simple mind: I need to learn from you. Talk to your father and teach him a thing or two: You've talked to your mother about this!

Vanetta: Well, Dad; let us go back to square one: You are my godfather. I am your child, and we both have a lot of money; don't we, Daddy? I hate those secularists, and naturalists, and evolutionists with a passion!

Dr. Molluck: Well, my dear little girl; that is not nice to hate people in such a fog; the world is filled with foggy people who are wandering deeper and deeper in their fog of confusion. Thus, they have been misguided and lost in the fog.

Vanetta: But Daddy, Daddy; they hate those things which we cherish ever so dearly: They frown upon our God—our great, great God; and they hate him, too, hah Daddy? Now Daddy, that is too bad; such brilliant men like Fred Hoyle and Peter Gould; oh, these astonishingly bright paleontologists who ought to be glorifying God—they find themselves locked in a titanic battle against the marvelous one of heaven. Shame on them—how could they have come to such ridiculous conclusions! The Cambrian Explosion is the smoke that has blinded their minds and eyes—I am so little, compared to you, Dad; and even I know that God created the world: I feel it right here in my brain and stomach; I feel God in the center of my being.

These people who reject God must live in a smokestack, hah, Dad? Yea, it is the scorching smoke that has blinded their crazy minds; and their foolish thoughts must have sent them insane. These are the mongrels whose bark has stuffed the world with angry, crazy noises; their guileful, malicious sermons on evolution have poisoned man's mind against God. Oh, what a shame, what a disgrace: They've turned the world upside down! They've proselytized everywhere and poisoned the water of earthly life: Oh, that I can put my hands on them; I will pray for them that they will see the truth. And when I am done, I will invite them over to dinner and give them some money.

Dr. Molluck: Some money! No, you will throw them in jail for lying to the human race; they are liars and Trojan Horses that have conspired to deceive the human race.

Vanetta: No Daddy, it's not them who lied to the human race: It is the prince of lies. It is the devil who deceives the spirits of men and tries to turn them against God; and even Steven Hawkins, that genius from Great Britain, has been deceived.

Dr. Molluck: Oh, Vanny, Vanny; I am afraid of you: You know more than all of us. I will have to do some extensive research in order to hobnob with you next time; you are a walking university library that few would ever recognize—you are a genius! Oh, behold the encyclopedia of Vanetta Molluck; give me five again, girl. You are the bomb; I've learned so much from you today: I am stuffed. You've filled my mind with all sorts of new and refreshing information about the world; you ask me questions about things that you seem to already know. I am just blown away by the depth of your knowledge and understanding of things; you ought to be a college professor at the prestigious Christchurch University. I am so proud of my girl, Vanetta Roslyn Firne-Molluck: You are larger than life! You are blessed with genius, knowledge, and wisdom.

Vanetta: Don't worry, Dad; I will teach you everything that you will need to know; remember Dad: I am smart; and you are, too. Together, we can change the world. Oh, all my daddies are the bomb! And we have a lot of money, too; hah, Daddy? We can buy up all the universities in the world and kick evolution out of our schools. Yea, Daddy; come on, come on; give me five: Let's go get *um*, Daddy!

Sharing the Young Intellectual Phenom

And yes, it was stuff like that which caused Vanetta's godparents to squabble over her. But alas; they were intelligent, sophisticated, rich folks; imbued with urbanity. In fact, they were far too sophisticated to engage in malice and falling out; but this was not to say that the tug of war was not fierce and sharp at times. They did work things out, and the pretty girl travelled the world like only a billionaire can. And within a few years, she was speaking seven languages quite fluently; occasionally, her godparents would team up to have her in their presence; and it happened once every eight summer vacations; for there were eight godparents. each would have her once every eight years. Because of the length of time involved, some godparents opted to have her during spring break instead. Her stay with them was much shorter, but they didn't mind at all. They had to team up and visit each other's homes in order to share the pretty princess.

And oh, she showered all her parents with so much love and pretty giggles and tickles! She was always a powerful dynamo that suffused her parents' homes with vivacity; she entertained them with piquant tickles and blithesome moments of music and dancing; she often held concerts for her beloved parents and would tell them to dance and applaud. Wherever she went, whenever she was in town; her fans came from everywhere! No one could have ever asked for a more delightsome childhood than Vanetta's, and where, on earth, were the Firnes during this child's guardianship struggle? They were right there, smack in the midst of all of it; and they, too, shared her at times: Yes, of course; Vanetta spent most of her time with her biological parents. But the love, nurturing, and camaraderie among her godparents were so rich and great; they all felt somewhat the same way about their beautiful and adorable child prodigy.

And oh, what a marvelous time it was to see the pretty girl grow up in the eyes of a gazing world. She literally grew up smack in the eyes of flashing cameras and splashing photographs; but, despite all the spectacular success of Vanetta's life, things were not always bright: Life had not always been this way for this wonderful, highly celebrated family; they had undergone great struggles, and life's vicissitudes were not always kind to them. Dr. Firnes' bout with depression and alcoholism had almost ripped his marriage to shreds; and the early onset of mid-life crisis almost sent his wife stark mad, but she was strong. Long, intense psychological therapy and sustained prayer and fasting had to be done—the process was ugly and messy at times, but Dr. Firnes' faith brought her through that. Things are quite often not what they seem to be, especially when folks are so wealthy! They went through a period of great struggle, and trouble, and gossipers' mumble jumble; but alas, the crane of love can pull anyone from the quicksand of life's messy storms.

And in the case of the Firnes, it yanked them from way down in the bowels of doom! This courageous family overcame it all with flying colors, and look how far they've come! So, if you are going through a time of hardship and struggle, reach for your sixth sense; faith is your sixth sense: It has great virtue—and will carry you a very long way.

Earthly life's problems are caused by the terrible lies that either we or others tell; and lies are like a train whose station is teetering over a precipitous cliff. Cliffs, oh cliffs; they are everywhere: They warn the wise to avoid the rim of danger. Some are sheer and jagged, dropping thousands of feet below on rocks as sharp as a spear. Others are gentler, reflecting rolling waves of less acute danger; they are forever there. And those who tell lies are like unskilled drivers, unable to negotiate dangerous curves. Oh, see the verdant meadow of life, speckled with falsehood's colorful train stations! And, as if that is not enough; the world itself turns out to be one of those dreaded trains stations.

Oh, the strange train station of life, flush with so many unwilling passengers. We must live by exemplifying truth and always endeavoring to know where it is. Truth, oh truth; so elusive, so exiguous: Finding that priceless pearl is the essence of life. And so it was, the Firnes had pulled themselves from a host of life's nasty quagmires; they no longer went from city to city, toting new publications around the world. Now, their books flew off the shelves of sprawling bookstores like combat fighter jets! And oh, what a wonderful life they had built for themselves and for their golden eggs. After a while, the cloud of struggle had been expunged from their world's flaming skies; the beautiful princess had been born into a treasured legacy of chastity and loyalty; chastity and loyalty were among the pretty colors that painted their noble linage. Oh, the glorious paint of virtue; how quickly it has wilted from our world of faded morals; see our unbuttoned age of twisted values and mildewed morals of no value to so many.

However, this was not so in the case for the Firnes: They had established a legacy of virtue; yea, they had set in stone a legacy of chaste, loyal, durable marriages that lasted for life! And that august, sublime legacy chased and scampered behind their distinguished progeny. Firne after Firne came into; and enjoyed; wonderful, lasting marriages: Yes, a long, virtually endless cycle of fulfilling marriages followed their descendants; and more importantly, they themselves got to witness this flowery unfolding of their children's wonderful marriages. Yea, they saw the beautiful blossoming of this noble inheritance in their own children. And oh, the joy they felt in the ever-winding stream of marriages they witnessed; oh, the unvarnished glee they felt at seeing their own values and virtues flower in the splendid garden of their offspring—and how proud they must have been at seeing that!

The virtues and values that they treasured so dearly did not fade with their passing years; and the magnificent transmission of these golden pearls slowed the hand of time; oh, see how slowly and gracefully they aged in the picturesque hourglass of time; but their huge stash of cash went a long way to make all that graceful aging possible. Oh, the flaming flower garden of riches and the favors it grants to the fortunate; yea, the fortunate with a brawling shower of dollars to spend as they see fit! See how the glorious and filthy rich Firne Family had the whole world on a string; and with state-of-the-art Godwit jets that flew at the speed of light, they virtually owned the earth. However, despite their command of the airways, they maintained a tight-knit family circle. They knew the exact source of their riches and remained little in their own eyes; however, many who'd gotten wealthy during the economic downturn's rebound had swollen like a blimp. They waxed proud and beside themselves, behaving as if they owned the world.

With their chests as high as a mountain and their heads lifted high in the air, they began looking down on others with disdain; however, because such pride does not work in the real world, such attitude did not last either. It was not long before many of these vain fellers had lost virtually all that wealth that they had acquired from their stock and real-estate investments during the rebound from the economy's downturn. Their economic understanding of things was correct. but they could not handle the new wealth that had come to them; and they spent much of that money in pleasure, instead of using their new wealth to become even richer than they had become. Running dozens of women and spending their money foolishly, many of the new dashing boys on the block, with all that new wealth, did not hold up—they lost it all. However, those who belonged to the World Scientific Aristocratic Club waxed even richer and began using their wealth to influence public policy and to advance the truth of Divine Science in the world.

CHAPTER 4

THE LATE CHILDHOOD YEARS

The golden seraphic crown of the Firne Family line blazed before the eyes of the whole world; it retained its gleam and luster for such a very long time and kept people talking. Oh, the stirring, poignant tale of Vanetta Roslyn Firne was one of thrill and beauty; her handsome love story has painted many a cheek with beam, and bloom, and beauty. Oh, Vanetta, Vanetta, Vanetta; the youngest child of the celebrated Firne Family: See the pulchritudinous Vanetta, the cosmopolitan princess and the world's prettiest girl! Oh, gaze at Vanetta, as rich as a ruby mine; as bright as a solar flare; and as pretty as a star. Behold the lovely, flaming young lady; as beaming as a bright bouquet of flowers.

Oh, the dashing Vanetta, as athletic and venatic as her mother's earlier years. Vanetta grew into a tall, sleek, svelte, pretty young girl filled with verve and vivacity; her florid, unsullied cheeks and stately stature caught not a few eyes. Behold the lovely young lady, as pretty as a tanager and as nimble as a falling star; ever so frisky and energetic, she exhibited the restless energy of a rushing stream. And oh, under the ever-watchful eyes of the whole world; see how quickly she bloomed: Look how quickly she leaped from the ground of childhood into the tree of maturity; oh, how rapidly she moved from crawling on the ground to leaping on galloping horses!

And in the quaint museum of our world, everything changes and takes on another form; but oh, good heavens; some things change so fast—their speed is almost breathless! Oh, see how quickly she raced through those delicate years of childhood: The young, pretty princess grew by leaps and bounds and acted far beyond her years; she sprang from the tender, tenuous twig of a toddler to the giant stature of a teenager. And oh, she did it so swiftly; it certainly seemed like another Haley's Comet appearance! And peeping at adulthood in her early teens, her giant stature dwarfed her parents: Yea, just at the age of thirteen; she began to make her parents look like Lilliputians. And while Amadyn and Arnold were busily occupied with their own scientific research, Mrs. Firnes' early love for hunting began to effloresce in her daughter like wild flowers.

She had cleverly slipped out of the limelight of world attention as she began to grow up; and in her late childhood years, she became very unsociable, shy, and cloistral: She would withdraw from her family members and spend long hours far into the woods. Vanetta then developed a passion for hunting wild animals during that obscure period; she had almost become a hermit, preferring the wild's barren beauty to all that luxury and popularity. Vanetta had gotten accustomed to the pomp and pageantry of Western aristocracy; and, perhaps, she had gotten tired of it all: She wanted something that was different. She was born in the spotlight with both silver and golden spoons in her mouth; she had been the center of worldwide attention for virtually all her life. All she had known and had gotten used to was the grandest and best of life; she had been exposed to the best of what global scientific aristocracy had to offer.

Her father's sprawling financial empire frequently took her around the world in a flash; but somewhere along the line, Vanetta got tired of all the lights and cameras; and she slowly began to retreat into a life of hermitage in the backwoods of the wilds. She wanted something that was novel and unique, yet simple and free from all the flare and flash:

Oh, see Vanetta, as tall as a tree; as strong as an ox; and as brave as fortune itself! She virtually lived in the fields, throwing javelins and perfecting her skills in archery; she carried sharp, frightful bows and arrows just about everywhere she went. She also became a masterly gunner, bringing big game back home for dinner; and sometimes she would haul her mother, Margolyn, and father, Mildren, with her. She loved the wilds and spent much time hunting and being alone: It was rather strange; and her parents were quite concerned about her obscure, masculine behavior.

Ever so often, she would take them with her to enjoy the mystic beauty of the wilds; they went hunting deep into the howling, dusky bowels of the woods. And they would always return with horse-drawn carriages full of fresh meat; they toted back to the house game fowls, rabbits, deer, and a host of other animals. And though the rich stock of meat lasted for months at a time; those avid hunters, impregnated with boundless passion for thrill, kept going back; yea, they went back again, and again, and again, enjoying the thrill of the wilds. And though danger was never far away, they did not seem to mind at all; often, they would give so much meat away; it could feed the city's poor for a full year! A few times, Amadyn ventured out with them and brought back tall stories; he spoke of hideous, grotesque lions; roaring and rumbling about the tent at night.

What on earth drove wealthy people from the warmth and luxury of their opulent homes? What sent folks from their splendorous mansions into the shadowy womb of the woods? Was the thrill of uncertainty and living on the edge worth all the risks involved? Why would billionaires leave their home's comfort to spend time with wild beasts? Oh, the world, so fraught with meaninglessness; so replete with rich empty people! Sometimes, even the wealthiest of folks feel the grinding emptiness of stuffed wallets; or, perhaps, the world is filled with people who live from one adrenalin rush to another; and, somehow or other, this question bothered other members of the Firne

Family. Vanetta answered that very question as Arnold delved into the murky matter himself: As he peered into the mystical reaches of his family's mind to make sense of it all; he could not understand why his sophisticated family went and slept in the wilds.

It really bothered him, and again and again he would ask himself the same question: Why do Daddy and Mommy go out there in the wilds with that wild girl of the woods? Again and again, Arnold pried into the tenebrous cave of his family's weird ethos; and he would say to his sister, "What do you find so exciting out there? Tell me, brave girl: What virtue is there deep in the dark, uncanny bowels of the woods?" And Vanetta, his sister, would merely chuckle; "Ardor, thrill, passion, and enthusiasm!" And though he saw his family's hunting obsession as a weird, disturbing dysfunction; Amadyn, Vanetta, and Sasha simply saw it as plain diversion and gust for life. But, alas, like a dazzling Argentine cloud shaft in the pictorial cavern of nightfall; its brilliant beauty, so stunning and stirring, yet so brief and fugacious—Vanetta's obsession with hunting and evading civilized society soon swooned.

The wilds' exotic shagginess and brash beauty no longer furnished that thrill she sought; and like the fleeting beauty of a flower, it all began to wither in the stain of familiarity: Yea, her strange passion for the wilds soon faded into the picturesque eclipse of the past; suddenly, all the colors of her interests began to change. And oh, what a change! New interests began to develop as the thrill for the wilds ebbed and quickly wilted; her hunting craze and getting away from human civilization came to a crashing halt. It quickly gave way to a voracious craving for knowledge, books, and academic interests; moreover, a more sociable personality began to crystallize as she entered her late teen years. And slowly but surely; that strong, colorful interest in boys began to appear: The quaint unkemptness and rude beauty of the wilds furnished her thrill for a while; but like the evanescent freshness of falling snow, it soon wilted and vanished away—perhaps, it no longer brought her the adrenalin rush and fun that it did in earlier years.

A Brash Bevy of Swains

Vanetta's womanhood blossomed like a pretty donation flower, clad in bloom and beauty; and, as if some mystical clock had orchestrated and coordinated her psychobiological life; things began happening just about where they ought to as if wired to some quaint timer. The social and psychological changes and patterns appeared right on schedule; the jarring switch from the wild, adventurous girl to a dashing, urbane lady was quite striking. And slowly but surely, Vanetta returned to the world attention spotlight; the sudden shower of phone calls and the male voices' salience was a stirring spectacle. And then, the boys began to pound down the iron door of her innocence's resistance; they were there at just about her every turn, trying to jar loose the bolt of her resistance. And that was quite another change that took her world by storm; the bloomy, flowery lights of her early years of dating were interesting and intriguing.

Oh, see her handsome swains; their arms as stout as a tree trunk and as strong as a crane: They hailed from very wealthy families with Swiss accounts as large as some countries' entire budget! And there they were, splattered around her like autumn's fallen leaves; their svelte, gleaming cars; the cost of a suburban mansion; flared with grace and bloom! And what was it about this sleek, willowy, glamorous lady that caught so many eyes? The world was replete with young, pretty girls whose bosoms were as high as a knoll; yea, their bosomy chests; as firm as a ripe cantaloupe; were as cold as ice! Oh, how unfortunate and disconsolate some of the world's most brilliant stars are; even some of nature's most desirable and well-advertised wares go unsold. The hard, cold bosoms of so many pretty ladies remained untouched by the hand of amor.

Such voluptuous gifts from Providence remained unwrapped by a stroke of misfortune; and in the cosmic courtroom of justice, filled with the grimaced cheeks of angry women; these acheful cases' noble judge must have been a dashingly handsome man himself. But so it is in the world; for one reason or other, things just are not fair: Some people wind up on the wrong side of the track, fighting a war they did not start. Who would bring them justice in a world where so little of it was left? Who would comfort them in that raging storm of unhappiness in their world? Certainly, not Vanetta's innumerable suitors whose eyes flared upon her golden cheeks. Oh, see Vanetta's swains holding on to her with the grip of Hercules' hands; her vertiginous mind rendered her hands as slick as city streets after a rainstorm.

And like a beautiful tanager, flaming in the bold, giant mirror of the public's eyes; she bruised the hearts of many swains, head over heels, in love with her. And the pretty princess of the earth played with the feelings of all sorts of men; the brawny, burly suitors who threw themselves at her were thrown away as trash. And oh, what a landfill of castaways that she had created of so many good men! Suitor after suitor who tried their hand at her found themselves in her sprawling trash can; and oh, the joy she got from playing with the sensitive feelings of genuine suitors. Their hearts were smack in the right place: they meant well and ardently desired her. But he who held and kept the hand of the beautiful princess had to be a very special man, for the overtures poured in from around the world—faxes, emails, phone calls, and letters: Every big shot's son in the world wanted the flaming princess' hand in holy matrimony.

Their parents, as rich as King Solomon, tossed gold in the streets like dice—yea, they tossed golden coins in the streets like dice on a spinning casino wheel. They hoped for a chance in a million that their sons would be the swain of choice; oh, the wanton spillage of ruby coins, pelted into the hollow boom of the wind! Many asked for her hand in marriage and tossed splendiferous offers on the table; but alas, Vanetta wrapped them around her fingers and tossed them behind her back; yea, she pelted them into the howling tempest of her own fluxionality and vanity. But oh, she was so young and unready for the strange tempests of life's distractions. And though she went out on umpteen dates with not a few big shots of world aristocracy, she left these sour men with broken hearts and poisoned lives—oh, what a trash heap that all these suitors and swains had become!

What a picturesque rubbish heap she had left behind from these empty, shallow dates. But haughtiness and superciliousness are the earliest signs of impending ruin: The Law of Sowing and Reaping is always working, even when we are not aware of it. And in Vanetta's case, that retributive law was at work; lurking in the wings: eventually, when it struck; it struck Vanetta as if it were a bedazzling bolt of lightning. But the trig, natty, flashy swains just kept on coming; one, after another, after another. The long, seemingly interminable stream of suitors was a moving showcase of dash; and Vanetta, caught in the rushing tide of male admiration, soaked it all up. Though many of the exciting and zealous suitors were cast away from her presence, they were quite thrilled and happy to have been a part of the royal selection process.

Enamored with the Smile of Ruin

But alas, alas; all that changed when the man of dash came on the scene—it all changed! He was rugged and brash, yet swish and natty; he was hairy with flashing eye lashes—he winked often below bushy eye brows and smiled over pretty snow-white teeth. His quaint, pungent comeliness and wild, brash manners ensorcelled Vanetta's heart! Thoroughly trained in amoristic matters and with a mouth full of romantic sentiments; Vanetta was fair game for this svelte suitor who trapped her in his web of words. And though she was able to wrap all those other suitors around her fingers like a string; suddenly, in the twinkling of an eye; all that changed when Anush entered her world. The lambent, flickering flame in Anush's eyes caught fire in Vanetta's soul!

Oh, the playful bird of caprice had lacerated the emotions of strong, husky men; behold the picturesque stream of brawny bodybuilders whom Vanetta had cast away. The colorful stream of trash that she left behind was a stirring showcase of wonder; oh, see the strong, brawny men she left behind; still so happy that they even had a chance. Their muscles, the size of a beam in the Empire State Building, could uproot trees; behold all these strong, handsome giants who had failed to woo the Princess of Malibu. But oh, how quickly all that changed when the new dashing boy appeared on the block. Oh, see Anush again; his soft, curly hair felt like silk between Cleopatra's lubricous fingers; his streaming eyes, like a flashing Hawaiian river of fire, lit Vanetta's face with delight. His gleaming, glossy smile painted the Malibu Princess' cheeks with the flame of love; that intriguing glow of his smile, as bright as a Lilly's bloom, lit the lamp of her life.

Oh Anush, Anush; see his cluttered, bushy eyebrows like vines climbing on a fence! Behold his pungent eye lashes that flashed and flickered a thousand times a minute, and each flicker was accompanied with a flaming smile that painted her face with glee. See his chic, pert moustache; as pictorial as a tarn in the glistening flame of daylight; look at his piquant, exotic countenance; speckled with bristly strands of silk. His quaint, bushy hair style made him look like a dashing man from the wilds; and his lips, as scarlet as a strawberry, looked as soft as the Queen of Sheba's breasts. Oh, how strange and awkward life can be sometimes—how unfathomed and inexplicable! There they were—husky, burly swains; as strong as an ox, tossing themselves at her feet: Only to be pelted away in the whirring noise of the wind of caprice's whim. And, then came Anush; the swain with the flame of a mighty rushing river of fire! And though the flaming flower of love seemed beyond the price of rubies, Anush's skillful training in matters of love was too much for the golden princess.

And within weeks, Vanetta was asking him to be her lover forever; Oh, what a spell that was: Anush ensorcelled the young, pretty princess with dash! Per the ***Auckland Gazette*** editorial, the world's child princess had come of age and found love in the strangest of places. The editorial's headline was entitled; *Oops, here, he Comes; a Handsome Jewish Boy!*   And other world newspaper editorials were also filled with the love story's fire and liveliness; the world raved at the dashing, new relationship between the two lovers. Though speculation about a betrothal was vaguely mentioned here and there, most tellurians merely saw the relationship as a spring bloom that would soon burn off.

They saw marriage as a sociological behavior more suitable for seasoned adults; in fact, they saw marriage among young, inexperienced adults as a ruinous train wreck. And, not a few, truly with Vanetta's interests at heart, wished ruin upon the relationship; they wanted Vanetta to thoroughly educate herself, come into true adulthood, and be trained for a powerful position in the coming world government. They still saw her as the pretty, little princess whom they've always known; and, as far as they were concerned, she'd never grown up and had become her own woman. Many said that Vanetta was way too young to take trifles like these so seriously; she had not received formal education at a royal school to prepare her for life. The world, at large, felt that she was ill-prepared for life's challenges and complexities; nonetheless, the juicy story travelled as fast as light and kept many a dinner table talking.

The buzz around the world was the pretty princess' new choice of the week; alas, she had had so many around her; even her dad, Dr. Firne, had begun to worry: "My child, Vanetta, is too young for this dangerous stream of dates with boys. My heart weeps at caprice's mistreatment of my daughter; she is just too young for this: She must obey me and follow my instructions, especially in matters of love. I have chosen a splendid wife and life partner—and I did not rush into it either. My darling wife Margolyn was not chosen from among a thousand flashing flames; she came to me with prayer, and fasting, and waiting on the hand of Providence. My wayward daughter must cease flirting with disaster, and she must do it right away: I cannot stand this worrying matter; it's driving nuts!"

Accordingly, Vanetta was put on a strict curfew that lasted almost a year. Unfortunately, by then; the dashing Anush had already stolen her heart from her bosom. Dr. Firne, her father, did everything that he could to pluck Anush from Vanetta's heart; all was of no avail; the letters, emails, and phone calls kept on coming. Oh, the gift, that special gift he had to steal the hearts of society's high-profile ladies! And when he was done with Vanetta, she was head over heels in love with him; but this was his talent to gaff the souls of love's priceless pearls and spellbind them. And, in the spirit of a swank, skillful amorist; he swept Vanetta right off her feet. And just when she had felt ensconced in the snug, colorful tent of his love; he dropped her like a heavy mallet fallen from a thousand miles; she was damaged. And oh, what seemingly irreparable damage that must have been done! Crushed by the crane of despair and hurt, Vanetta coiled into the shell of hermitage; the lusty shock of betrayal jarred loosed the iron bolt of her self-assurance.

Downcast by Love's Betrayal

Lost in the angry waves of betrayal's agony, her eyes dripped with the dew of sorrow; her quaint eclipse in solitude's cave filled uncounted pages of stirring poetic lines. She must have needed a gushing river of ink to pen such moving pages of poetry; oh, the stirring lines of her poetry ushered in a fresh focus in the halls of literature. But, alas; when passion's flaming, florid flower suddenly fades from one's view; the painful, bleeding gash of betrayal's knife always seems so irreparable. And her own stirring poetic lines graphically depicted the boiling anguish she felt. Oh, how her heartfelt poetry reflected the searing agony deep within her soul.

Vanetta: Oh, that all the saline waters of the ocean would rush into my soul! Oh, that all the towering billows of the moiling sea would come crashing down upon me. The lethal poison of passion's betrayal has brought me so much delirium; the whole world seems to me like a cosmic gyre, whirling a trillion miles per second! And when vertigo's madness and dizzyingly disgusting feelings appear to wear off; the harsh, exquisite pain of love's poisonous sting just becomes so insufferable. Caprice, thou child of mischief and vanity; you've filled my soul with hot sand; oh, caprice; thou colorful, deceptive bag of hot air; you've gaffed the child of love. Betrayal, oh, betrayal; thou villain of trust, thou mischievous child of caprice and guile: thou art a pregnancy of sourness and pain that I must carry to the end; thou art that noble crucible endured for the seraphic beauty of faithfulness in love. Where is man's deceptive faithfulness? It is whirled in the wind.

Oh, the words; the kind, gracious, beautiful counsel of Beverly Hills' finest therapists—the wonderful sentiments of Malibu's best psychologist brought me so much comfort. Oh, those well-meaning words of Los Angeles' most brilliant counselors: See how hard they all tried to bring solace and comfort to a heart jilted by false love; but the shallow words of all these children of wisdom are but clattery noises—yea, all their beautiful words are but a sounding brass and a tinkling symbol. Oh, these clattery noises and stuffy factory fumes in the churning fog of my soul! And, as sorrow's stream gushes through the tear ducts of my soul's scarlet windows; it seems as if my pregnancy of chagrin and anguish will never end. But, alas; the bright, saffrony flower of hope splashes pretty beams of light before me; oh, my eyes behold the beauty of that light; flaring the unlighted chasm of my soul. And suddenly, the flare of gladness and the flame of joy extinguish all the gloom of betrayal's dark, blustery clouds.

But oh; the scoffing, sardonic flashbacks of love's fugacious moments with him—they are the cruel, mischievous children of the past who banter, jeer, and mock me; see those fiendish, little children who jape and gibe me into anguish's pouring rain. Oh, love's happy, pretty moments of the past; so filled with stale, blank promises: Those scruffy, cynical brats who've jeered and sneered at me; laughing me to scorn. And like sharp, tiny arrows; they are the painful thoughts that bruise my soul. Oh, the sour pregnancy of love's brutal betrayal: what exquisite pain it inflicts on me! Oh, love that seemed so real; it gleamed the refreshing bloom of freshly fallen snow. And like the refulgent sheen of a long, sleek limousine; love seemed as if it were there; then suddenly, it plunged over that steep cliff; violently pelting all its passengers away.

Oh, how cruel and sad, how capricious and savage love that once seemed so real can be; and oh, how that phony love with Anush hurt the very heart that kept me breathing: Oh, how its gleam and glitter seemed like all the wonderful things I had come to love. Long, blooming limousines streaming around the Malibu Mansion's serpentine streets! Its picturesque beauty seemed like Auckland's magnificent harbor with all its toys of joy; but, alas; it was just a fairy tale, hatched in the mind of an impressionable little girl. Yea, a little girl who'd had so much attention; she could not detect the real fool.

And oh, what a jarring, lusty shock that that crushing experience was for Vanetta Firne! Anush's betrayal of the young global princess was a major crucible of her early adult life; the gaping gash remained a pictorial scar on the radiant cheeks of her soul. And though time healed no wounds, it did camouflage the unsightly scar of that gash; eventually, time's slipped moments did soothe all the pain from that senseless gash. The horrid, scoffing flashbacks that mirrored betrayal's agony began to subside; yea, the terrible memories that poignantly painted the painful past began to swoon.

They began to sink deep beneath the memory bank of the young princess' soul: The prismatic flowers of humor and laughter beamed, and bloomed, and boomed again; yea, her florid, gaily lighted cheeks were once again a piquant bouquet of pretty smiles; but all her many romantic adventures that left a stream of broken people abruptly ended. The long, Argentine stream of suitors; obsessed with her beauty; rapidly dried up. Oh, what an abrupt end to which her dashing amorous adventures came; suddenly, her flaming tent of vanity was ripped to pieces and blown to the ground; yea, it was ripped to shreds in the violent storm of life's quaint quirks and unfair dealings.

See that once glorious tent of sham love, wrecked in the foul tempest of human whim: Oh, that angry, termagant tempest of flux and caprice; so blurred by the fog of folly! See the ever-fading coat of caprice, fluttering like a broken kite fallen to the ground: Behold the florid light of whim—as pretty as a falling star; as strange as a midnight fog. And even Dido, the Queen of Carthage, perished in the searing smoke of love's vagary: Caprice, oh, caprice; thou fool with a golden spoon in thy mouth, look what you've done! See what irreparable damage you've wrought upon beauty's naïve, innocent handmaid; the indelible scars of Anush's fake love remained on the cheeks of Vanetta's soul. And yes, the exotic band aid of time's passage did soften the brash fall of her pride; and oh, what a beautiful and flaming flower that bloomed from the debris of defeat!

Though the ugly scars of irresponsible romantic adventures were hardly ever expunged; Vanetta's brash, ebullient energy painted them with the glaze of gleam and glee. And, by the time Anush had recognized the egregiousness of his blunder; Vanetta had long vacated the unlighted cave of hermitage in which she'd been pelted. She awoke from her long incarceration of hermitage and wept bitterly for the last time. And suddenly, it was gone—Anush and all his flair, and swank, and dash were gone; and new, colorful poetry began streaming from her mind and pen. Oh, the glorious lines of exalted words that her soul uttered on the parchment of joy!

And like a florid robin, speckled with magnificent colors, Vanetta flew from that cave. Her long streaming hair, as soft as silk, dropped on her buttocks again; and her French fragrances, the cost of a mink coat, tinctured the air with vivacity again. The long, sour moments of lost love faded into pretty thoughts and gleaming smiles; oh, the pale cast of betrayal's tristful frown swooned into sprightly, lightsome giggles. The viscous stain of sham love was expunged by the flaming bloom of fresh swains—new ones, burly and strong—they came from everywhere to mend all the broken parts; but by the time they had gotten there, there was not a crack or crevice left unsealed. Youth had paid an exorbitant price for its rank folly and brash, irresponsible actions; youthful love's vitreous jar of joy had been shattered by the wanton wind of temerity.

New life had begun to spring up again; and oh, what beauty that followed: The polychromatic robes of glamor and swank painted exclusive ballrooms again. Oh, the adorable, youthful princess; as pretty as Cleopatra; raised eyebrows again! See Vanetta, that splashy, cosmopolitan girl; lighting the halls of glamor with grace. Her beautiful smile, as refreshing as splashing waterfalls, warmed so many hearts. Yes, the dainty, vernal beauty of her cheeks warmed even the hearts of the mafia! And where was all that beauty in the dusky prison house of betrayal's pain? Who had concealed that golden paint from the world's searching, streaming eyes? Where had she hidden it during all that time of dolor, and anguish, and chagrin?

Alas, the young princess' impeccable beauty had never gone anywhere—it was merely left uncared for in the dark, dingy hall of infatuation's chat with reality. It was just left unattended in order to appear stale, and old, and worthless; but it was always there—yea, right there beneath all that false perception of self. And so, it is with people who allow others to put a value on their worth! Those who see themselves as fluttering straws in the wind often see others that way, too. A fair lady in a fool's arms is like a gleaming, golden chain around a pig's neck; and though Anush's parents were rich Jews, they were not scientific aristocrats.

CHAPTER 5

QUIETING THE STORM

As the saying goes, time heals all wounds; and it did work wonders for Vanetta. In time, all her pain had evaporated; and a fresh garden of life sprang from the wound; all that ebullient energy resurged, and the old Vanetta returned with a vengeance. Bubbling with fresh life and vivacity like the effervescent spurts of a geyser; the young, graceful princess waxed brighter and more beautiful than she ever was. But oh, how cautious and circumspect she had become in matters of love and war! And, after triumphing in uncounted pageants; it was time to leave home for college: The pain had now shifted from daughter's past to parents' thorn in the boring empty nest. How would Dr. Firne and his wife Margolyn handle their daughter's sudden departure? They had doted upon her for so long, she was virtually all they had in that mansion; They took her everywhere: She was their pride, joy, and pretty flower.

And when she was hurting, Dr. Firne had threatened Anush's parents with law suits; things were settled under the table, and huge sums of money changed hands. Vanetta begged her father to restrain his wrath and not rip the Lablums to pieces; and though they were rich, they were not as filthy rich as this scientific aristocrat. In the aftermath of a flood of apologetic emails and an under the table settlement; the storm of fury quieted down at the Firnes' Mansion in the pricey Los Angeles suburb. The ***Pretoria Times*** called aristocratic science's big stick approach "troubling": The ***Columbo Breeze*** in Sri

Lanka dismissed Dr. Firne's ire as paternal and measured. Per that newspaper's staff writer, Jao Mooney, things are not what they used to be. The world has become a complicated place that is hostile to raising wholesome children. Parents are raising children in a world throttled with pedophiles and psychopaths.

They do have a moral obligation to protect their children by whatever means available to them: And where so much is at stake; the record must, by all means, be set straight. Mr. Mooney saw nothing wrong with Dr. Firne's legal action on his daughter's behalf; in this case, every father has a moral obligation to protect his daughter's innocence. And, in a world of impudent wolves; that obligation becomes all the more urgent. And every scruffy hand of guile that violates a child's innocence should be broken in pieces: These stern words sparked heated debates in uncounted cities around the world. These town hall meetings attempted to address teen sexuality and child molestation issues. Oh, the incandescent emotions that were sparked in these cantankerous discussions! Emotions, as strong as a tsunami, poured forth like superheated lava into the fluid air.

False Socialization

The loud town hall meetings were colorful showcases of societal decline and confusion; oh, the powerful emotions that poured from these impassioned, rowdy gatherings. Tempers flared like a storm raging in the distance, and so little was accomplished; and, at the end of the day, so many issues remained confused and unresolved. In more general terms, the matter reflected the issue of purity's absence among the youth: Oh, how protective and irrational parents had been about their children's well-being! The delicate, uncomfortable issue of sexuality among children was a ticking time bomb, unfortunately, most parents had been puzzled and confused about this matter; they were not adept at treating this very complex, exquisite moral problem; and, quite often, frustrated parents would burst into anger when the topic came up.

Parents' coy attitude, regarding their children's sexual behavior, had not helped either: Their evasive proclivity regarding their children's knowledge and practice of sex and their naïve disposition about their children's understanding of sex and its cost have created a host of societal problems. All these irresponsible attitudes have helped to obfuscate the whole issue of sex among young people; accordingly, they wound up getting false, dangerous, and destructive education on this issue; thus creating a range of societal problems. A host of corrupt, misleading sources; churning in society; led young people astray: Few parents tackled this thorny moral problem head on with any measure of success.

In a rapidly changing world where sex had become such a loaded, provocative issue; many parents treated this very delicate topic with denial, evasion, and emotionality. Unable to handle the thorny issue, they acted as if it did not exist. They often burst into flames when their daughters told them that they were pregnant: Their angry frustration, bottled up for years, poured out like water from a geyser; suddenly, they were faced with the ghost that they had stuffed behind the veil of things for years; yea, that ghost of moral confusion and their own failures had even driven some mad. They were not sure what to do with a sexually active teenager who thought like an adult. And often, society's various socialization agencies cringed from the contentious issue; except for the public school system, these powerful societal agencies skirted the matter.

They had quailed from tackling this spiny moral matter in a pragmatic, efficacious way; and ultraconservative families, not sure how to treat the matter, simply left it alone. In the process, rapid societal decay ensued; and sexual problems got way out of hand. And, in that quaint, unbuttoned age of picturesque societal decay and moral lawlessness;

public schools stoked the fire by giving a blind green light to teen sex's ruinous effects! Many brazenly distributed condoms to children as young as five years old. This rank irresponsible behavior among the educational bureaucracy was unfortunate; this shockingly abominable, cavalier attitude about teen sex was odiously disgusting. It is true that public school officials could not be inculpated for the teen sex epidemic; however, the lascivious, libidinous atmosphere around many schools stoked the fire; and no concrete measures were taken to slow the tide of moral chaos in these situations. More was to be done to decelerate the pace of ruinous sexual behavior among teens; there ought to have been a carefully coordinated societal effort to stem the ruinous tide.

The powerful atomic bomb of promiscuity among teens began to rip society to shreds; and forasmuch as morality, for all practical purposes, had been abolished in the West; no one seemed to have had any qualms about teenagers' destructive participation in sex. More importantly, no one had the guts to simply tell young people the truth about sex: The cantankerous matter had been treated as a golden coin concealed in a landmine. Oh, the exorbitant societal cost of little children gallivanting in dangerous places! So many lives have been ripped to shreds in a wanton world where so few seem to care; and in a world drunk with the booze of moral insanity, no one treats these matters. Public school officials, aware of irresponsible parents' folly, merely look the other way! What an unhealthy moral climate that all this had fostered in a world of empty noises: Oh, see what a lewd, lecherous moral environment had been created around these schools.

The unwieldy chains of false caution and political correctness had handcuffed the truth; accordingly, public educational institutions were transmogrified into moral ghost towns. Why would children respect adults who had removed all their moral boundaries? They allowed children to live like adults and do whatever seemed right in their own eyes. Oh, the poisonous words of profanity, once forbidden speech in hallowed classrooms; profanity, a dashing fad on school campuses, now gushes forth like a flushing toilet; oh, the moral mayhem that has overtaken the West and its brawling shower of woes; young girls, raised as harlots, habitually spoke and acted like hookers working the block. Their mouths, as foul and filthy as a toilet, were filled with profane, poisonous words; and boys, sheared of the virtue of moral training, treated girls like whores and hookers; yea, they perceived them as worthless prostitutes, always looking for their own Johns. Shackled by the rusty chains of restraint from child abuse, parents felt lost in a mist—oh, they felt lost in the swirling cosmic fog of despair, chagrin, consternation, and ruin.

Many parents, lost in the smoke of moral confusion, sexually abused their own children; and this was the dark, poisonous smokestack in which tomorrow's leaders were raised. Though that impassioned science-driven world worked the town hall meetings like mules, not much change transpired in parents' perception of treating sexuality in children. The town hall meetings flung the door of mystery and intrigue about teen sex wide open; they revealed the rank failure of rogue societal institutions that have betrayed everyone. The family, the church, public education, and government—they had all betrayed society: That society had betrayed itself; it bought a one-way ticket to its own demise's crash site. The town hall meetings were a rank failure due to parents' resistance to change; parents, lost in the mist of naivety and conservatism, repeatedly dropped the ball.

And by virtue of abolishing tried-and-tested Christian morals, values, and traditions; the West today has unwittingly purchased a one-way ticket to the crash site of its own doom. The Christian Church in America, as impure as a harlot, merely overate and looked on; but who would ever blame the priesthood of evolution science and false Christianity? Who would inculpate these revered institutions for society's fast-approaching doom? Alas, somebody had to pay for the chaos that amorality and moral relativism have bred.

Oh, the exorbitant cost that America must pay for its social engineers' terrible missteps! With morality's abolition, the inevitable doom of American society was a stark certainty; that was a very troubling reality that should have kept all sane Americans up at night. It should have kept them up at night, wondering how they got into that mess and how they would get out of it; but instead, America got smug and distracted by pop culture's drama: It dispossessed itself of all that really matters. Would they ever be able to extricate themselves from the dark clouds that are forming? They've been outplayed by evil and have lost it all.

Their society has been tricked by the bad shepherd and is dealing with problems that it cannot solve. Homes, shattered by flying bullets on school grounds, were never the same again; young criminals, wielding combat ammunition, turned schoolyards into war zones. The people shunned the truth and shoved it far away on the other side of things: That which was politically incorrect was out of step with the obscure fads of the day. And oh, what an extortionate price that so many paid for others' irresponsible behavior! America is filled with axe-grinding social engineers with dangerous hidden agendas; but in a world ruled by scientific aristocracy, children were the pearls of the earth; and playboys who ignored Big Money's wrath often found themselves on the wrong side of things, with more than they could handle. They learned that the world belongs to the rich, especially those with old money.

Rich men, wielding bloated wallets like big sticks, were often a terror to them; and oh, what powerful lessons that those young, dashing playboys had to learn—those who drove cars had to be aware of exclusive parking lots off limits to them. They also had to be aware of the enormous price tag for violating such sacred territory; and when the lots were new; the fines were so steep, no one could afford a violation. See chastity's tender twig, bruised by the knuckles of playboys' thoughtless words; and when dashing pimps' careless, irresponsible words crossed the line in the media; what a storm of woes into which they found themselves, fighting for their very lives! Oh, behold the husky, brawny hand of Hercules with an axe the size of a tree trunk; see Dr. Firne, as rich as a ruby mine; and as protective as a lioness of her cubs. How did he amass all that wealth? He was not only a genius; he was also a man of faith.

A Father's Golden Role

Oh, society's playboys, they are found in every age and in every country of the world; and they were particularly numerous in the Los Angeles area, in Dr. Firne's heyday. There were parking lots all over town, but the few exclusive ones were off limits—yea, they were off limits to those natty, spiffy playboys who carelessly parked their cars. Many seemed unaware of the steep fines for violating those exclusive parking lots, and those who were drunk on their way in hardly ever made it out alive and intact. Playboys had to respect the royal quarters of those who moved in society's astral circles;They had to treat them with the utmost respect, veneration, reverence, and deference. They had to revere society's scientific aristocrats because they lived in their world.

And when Anush made careless, lewd comments to the media about Vannetta Firne; he had crossed the line and parked his dashing sports car in an exclusive parking lot. He and the television networks that aired the salacious piece had violated sacred territory; and oh, what an exorbitant price that Anush and his journalistic entourage paid. What steep fines they paid for staining the sacrosanct character of people with money! Oh, the power of *old money*—as strong as a storm; as useful as a roof over one's head. And so, all the bruises of fake love's gaff faded away with the passage of time; and like a scroll, whirled away in the wind, Anush's folly and caprice faded out of view. The silly prank slipped into the chasm of the past and never surfaced again, but Anush learned a great lesson about living in this world of fake and sham; thus, Dr. Firne was vindicated for the soilure of his beloved daughter's character. Things are hardly ever what they seemed to be, no matter how innocent they may look; and a princess, even drunk on a sidewalk, is still the beloved daughter of the king. If you ever wish to lend a helping hand, be sure that your hand is as soft as sponge.

Alas, the angry king is the father of the beautiful princess, lying on the bare sidewalk. Though he may be very distempered with his daughter for soiling his royal crown, he still deeply loves her and would push away a mountain to protect her. The false wandering of youth's missteps often leads even royal subjects astray. And like so many of us, they too sow their own wild oats into sin's fertile garden; and, in time; those hardy and robust seeds of vanity, caprice, and folly sprout forth and turn into a mountain of troubles. They yield a bountiful harvest for the royal subjects who've so carelessly sown them; and though the king may not be pleased with his child's sordid deeds, the great love of a father for his children is forever lodged in the recesses of his soul.

Yes, his child's harvest of wild oats may have plagued and polluted his royal throne; the umbrous veil of shame and disgrace may have soiled his palace's ornate beauty. oh, the hardy weeds of disobedience may have eclipsed his kingdom's former glory; but the fact that blood is thicker than water, his heart is forever soft towards his daughter. And as soon as she is ready to return to the palace, the king's arms will be wide open; his outstretched arms will be there to meet and greet her with unequivocal pardon. And though Vanetta may have transgressed her father's stern rules about dating, he still wanted her every decision to be replete with fulfillment and success. and yes, he was furious about Anush's careless, irresponsible comments to the media; yes, he viewed talking about his daughter to the media as senseless gossip.

And indeed, it was unwise gossip that was met with the fiercest of wrath; for all the television stations that had aired the scandalous remarks were shut down! Slapped with wrathful lawsuits that required massive amounts of financial resources, many of these television stations opted to go off the air rather than fight Goliath. Although a flood of emails inundated the Malibu Mansion's staff about the matter; Dr. Firne was in no mood for apologies, for the damage had already been done. And from his point of view, his daughter's character had been almost irreparably damaged; accordingly, more than a dozen television stations were summarily shut down! Call it "the big stick approach" or whatsoever you want, money calls the shots; and when the reputation of a globally celebrated princess is at stake, the shots fired are as loud as an atomic bomb and can be heard a from thousand miles away!

Anush's parents, the Lablums, were lucky and hurried to the bargaining table; as the story goes, they dished out one-third of their earthly possessions to settle the case: The eerie, under-the-table deal netted in excess of forty million dollars. On realizing their close call with utter ruin; they walked away saying, "Thank you, Jesus; we could have lost all of our earthly possessions: at least, we still have most of it left." And with that, Anush escaped some stiff prison time and millions of dollars in damages for saying that he sodomized the king's daughter: The Firnes were as angry as a wasp about Anush's careless, irresponsible remarks concerning their daughter. And indeed, the sleazy, vexatious remarks were ireful and vexing indeed; Dr. Firne was willing to blow his financial empire to fix things.

According to the Auckland Gazette, the Lablums Narrowly Escaped a Train Wreck

Anush's father, the driver, must have had much experience negotiating these dangerous curves; and, essentially; these mighty legal maneuvers formally cleared Vannetta's name. As part of the settlement, Anush had agreed to renounce all his remarks about the matter; he had to go on worldwide television and publicly renounce his irresponsible remarks; he had bragged about taking Vannetta down and sodomizing all his former girlfriends. These careless, bumptious remarks set off a firestorm of public outrage around the world: Vannetta's father, Dr. Firne, pledged one half of his financial empire to clean things up; he vowed to tear the Lablums to pieces and start afresh with a world without them. And with the full support of the International Media, he went ahead full speed; yea, the colorful billionaire set out to make a point and to expunge the cloud of shame from around his daughter.

Vannetta cried like a baby to her father, saying that there was never any intimacy; she affirmed repeatedly that Anush wanted her to make secret withdrawals from her accounts: When she insisted that withdrawals could only be made by her father Dr. Firne, Anush began threatening to walk away: She cried and finally decided to end it all. Upon realizing what had happened, Anush tried to get back in where he was; he began calling Vannetta late at night and trying to recapture her lost love. She was so hurt, she went into hermitage and abandoned the light of day for some time: When the telephone records were carefully examined, they all agreed with her story; the Lablums, sensing imminent doom, rushed to the Malibu Mansion to settle the matter. Soiling the character of a global scientific aristocrat would have been a major problem—yea, a major problem for the Lablums! And oh, how happy they were to settle things!

 Tearful apologies and a sizable chunk of their earthly possessions took care of business. Per_the *London Wave*, "More is needed to protect the sanctity of scientific aristocracy; folks who are barely making it have too much access to scientific aristocracy's might. And when the children of mongrels hobnob with the brilliant stars of royalty; far too many things go wrong in the world. New laws are needed to protect science; for cheap, legal settlements cannot undo the irreparable damage done by mongrels." And though some liberal media outlets blasted the *London Wave's Editorial* as arrogant, the vast majority of global newspapers strongly favored that newspaper's position. They argued that fathers were the spiritual anchor and backbone of any sober society—they had an unforfeitable right to protect and defend their children's character. Per the *St. John's Times* in Antigua, "Those voices that condone shame lack the strength of moral courage: No one has the right to stain a princess' character with libel.

The shockingly disgusting idea of smudging and soiling a princess' character is out of line; Anush's scandalous, libelous remarks to the press are painful blows below the belt; and for that type of behavior, there is really no pardon in the books—none whatsoever. A princess is a princess, and no one has the right to stain and defame her golden name." Oh, the spiritual authority of fathers and their overwhelmingly powerful place in society! They've become the faded colors which today's society spurn and scorn. And oh, how unfortunate it has been for children who've been raised without a dad; behold dad; that iron post that holds the roof over the heads of his beautiful family. See that glorious scepter of strength whose voice is as the sound of many waters; oh, see how he welds all the seemingly disconnected cogs into one unified whole.

He is the master of the morning and the evening in the glorious castle of his home; his presence paints his children's cheeks with the flame of beauty and delight. He diffuses the thick, dark smoke of petty quarrels and expunges the fog of malice; he is his children's charming, adorable king; his lap is filled with tiny tots. They gambol like little lambs around the table and scream, "Daddy, I love you". Where did all that golden beauty of family life go? Who stole it all from us? Our fathers have taken a long walk into the woods and have been lost—and lost forever. Yea, society's fathers have been lost in the swirling smoke of change and moral decay. Who will pluck these scared pearls from the smokestack of societal decline?

Oh, see the spinning, whirring kite of moral decay; so colorful and so destructive! Who will bring back those bright bouquets of flowers around the dinner table?

A place where whole families gathered together, prayed, ate, talked, and laughed—see the gleaming cheeks of whole families, as pretty as a nosegay painted with beauty. And yes, there were problems that had to be solved and differences to be ironed out—no one ran from the noble responsibilities and duties of parenthood and family life. They were all shouldered with a profound sense of responsibility, pride, and nobleness. Families bowed their heads in prayer and sought the one true God for divine counsel: No one—absolutely no one sought refuge in violence, suicide, and pornography. And, of course, that was a time when people, not only prayed around dinner tables; they made it a point to pray at school as well: Prayer meant something to everyone.

Reading the Bible was an essential component of every-day American life; but oh, society's pert visionaries could not stand the idea of children praying to a holy God. These evil social engineers and venal power brokers had other ideas in mind; they pushed the antichristian religions of secularism, hedonism, naturalism, folly, and tolerance. Oh, they pushed these atheistic religious systems with all their might; and, as things continued to deteriorate, other strains of vice were introduced!

The Resulting Flood of Moral Decay

Violent, pornographic movies flooded the public arena with the rage of a tsunami; and America, enticed by the guileful gremlins of lust, tossed marriage into the sea. Witches and warlocks quickly filled the gaping chasm excavated by Christianity's eclipse; and, in no time, the roof of American society rapidly began to cave in and collapse. The dashing boys in the pulpit, clad in the garb of guile, invented new theologies; and within a decade or so, American society's moral superstructure began to wobble. Within a year of the removal of prayer and Bible reading from the public-school arena, violent crimes jumped nineteen hundred percent; schools were turned into war zones. Young criminals, armed with combat rifles, began shooting into school yards: The false religions of evolution, secularism, and naturalism had changed things forever.

The American society was transmogrified into a quaint, brawling slaughterhouse; serial killers and psychopaths, once a rarity, blossomed into ordinary news coverage. These grotesque, shockingly despicable spectacles became ordinary news materials; and today, these horrid atrocities have become such ordinary evening news stories; no one raises eyebrows at these endless, odious crime reports anymore—and no one seems to know exactly what has spawned all this shocking societal mayhem. Oh, no one dares to inculpate evolution or witchcraft for these appallingly disgusting woes: He would be branded as a fool for his thoughtless, irresponsible comments. And though the mystical veil of intrigue and secrecy has been gradually removed, few seem to have the "guts" to place the blame for society's woes where it belongs.

School officials, sheared of moral convictions, treat young people like seasoned adults; the entire array of sexual paraphernalia is as available to them as oxygen in the air. And, naturally, those students who practice abstinence are viewed as queers and drolls; the subtle command to be sexually active, regardless of orientation, is everywhere. These strong, tacit messages to become sexually active come at you every day: They are as ubiquitous as human problems and as powerful as an atomic bomb; no one wears the mask of shame or even seems to lose face any more about them. This is a brand-new age of any type of sex with anyone, at anytime, anywhere just for fun; and oh, the doomful effects of this frenzied sex craze have driven society stark mad. The whirlpool of sexual partners has been poisoned by the swishing hemlock of lust. In Washington DC, one out of every five women now carries the dreaded HIV virus.

This shockingly sick sexual frenzy has rendered the sacred act of sex as cheap as dirt; I mean, who wants to say no to a good meal of sex served up in a hot, few sassy moments! Very few pass up a quick meal of physical intimacy, dished out in a few hot minutes: The slam bam thank you ma'am prototype has become the norm for so many people now. But oh, at what price! What a staggering moral price that society has paid for all of this! Oh, what an exorbitant moral bill society has absorbed for its blunt betrayal and violation of nature's laws. But this is where evolution, secularism, and naturalism have taken human society; they have cast the universe's one true God into the rat-infested dustbin of scorn. And, in so doing, they have incarcerated themselves in the calaboose of societal doom; and that thralldom is itself a quaint electric chamber; carrying them away, one by one. All the morals of human decency have been summarily trashed and tossed into the wind.

This was the reason that men of moral conviction like Dr. Firne had to be applauded; though battered by the callous storms of life, he had withstood all its horrid crucibles. And now; like pert, frisky children; flickering about the brawling schoolyard; The scientific world's first couple began toiling over the earth's sprawling vineyard. They cranked out one best seller after another and created a global publication machine; their books, snapped up like hot cakes, were enjoyed all over the world. Sprawling bookstores, from Paris to Valparaiso and from Auckland to Johannesburg—yea, major book stores from all over the world carried the Firnes' masterpieces.

Their insightful ideas had a tremendous impact upon the world's young minds; and things really began to happen for the Firnes: Treasures flowed from all directions. On the heels of the recession, the real estate market turned around—the market began to appreciate;

and, within a few months; it brought them a bonanza! Suddenly, Dr. Firne had powerful money machines working for him all over the world: He had paid his dues; and all his ships had waded ashore, laden with treasures; yea, all his ships had finally come ashore, overcharged with fortune's distant treasures. In addition, he had had a few bumper-crop years on Wall Street, with high net stock returns.

Everything seemed to have come together for this real estate tycoon; treasures gushed from everywhere, and nothing seemed to have gotten in the way. And certainly, this dashingly successful billionaire had the world at his fingertips; but there was one small matter of which he had to take care—his daughter's farewell: She was at the threshold of a major rite of passage into the murky world of college life. And, for the first time, Dr. Firne had to tell his beloved daughter Vanetta good bye; she was going off to college in Australia; and oh, how hard it was for both of them!

CHAPTER 6

A QUAINT FAREWELL

And like a colorful stream of sign posts on an important journey, far away from home; the Anush misstep quickly vanished out of view as fresh things appeared on the horizon. The whole world seemed to be a different place—and oh, how different it became! The old blunders of the past seemed like faded knolls, scarfed in the blanket of a fog. Everything was new now; yea, so new, it was as if the future was paved with gold; new types of suitors fished around. Her friends were different and more mature now. The wild parties ceased; and the restless, termagant horse of youth had been tamed. Yea, it had been tamed by vanity's close calls with ruin and doom of her character.

Vanetta's cloistral moments in the cavern of hermitage were a strange classroom lesson; the obscure instructor of folly taught her some of life's most unforgettable lessons. But the mist of love's agony had lifted, and the invaluable lessons had been learned; alas, the time had come for the beautiful lady to move on to the next phase of life. She had to move away from home and go to the uttermost parts of the earth; yea, she went to school off the beaten track into the distant reaches of the earth.

And like the Queen of Sheba, she left the palace she had always known and went away—far away into the distant reaches of the world, where godparents swarmed for her arrival. But she had to leave Mom and Dad at home to cry all by themselves in her absence; and night after night, they cried themselves to sleep to expunge her face from their view. And oh, the love that they had showered upon her; it was as if she had never grown up: Yea, it was as if Vanetta had remained the beautiful "Little Twit" that they had known.

Oh pretty "Little Twit", as lovely as a tanager; as frisky as a gamboling lamb. Yea, see "Little Pumpa", as larksome as a gallivanting lamb about the green meadow! In her parents' eyes, she had never grown beyond that pretty doll baby they had cuddled. Oh, the flaming little princess upon whom they had showered so much love. She was their last child; and suddenly, she was plucked from their bosom of love and warmth—yes, she was suddenly extracted from the plushy playpen of their golden arms of affection.

The tender *paps* that nursed and nourished her life now lay abandoned and useless: A lachrymose farewell party was thrown for her departure to Australia; and now, a few new suitors were on hand to share in the tearful moments with her family; these were more or less male friends who had developed an interest in her. Her parents, richly equipped with Godwit Jets, were prepared to follow her wherever she went; however; they realized that the time had come for the umbilical cord to be severed. And oh, the tears that gushed from the faucet of their eyes could fill Lake Baikal! Dr. Firne became very distraught about his youngest child's departure to college, she was his last child and the gleaming cynosure of his beautiful world of opulence.

Vanetta had met a long, heartfelt need and yearning which he had had for many years; and when she was born, it was as if a sprawling ruby mine was freely given to him. Vanetta's birth was like a strange fairy tale: It happened so quickly and unexpectedly; and after reveling in her presence for seventeen years, it was as if the dream was lost. He retreated into the dusk of solitude and said very little to anyone for hours on end; this went on for a few days, prompting Vanetta to suspend her college plans. Upon the suspension of her plans to attend Canberra Polytechnic University, Australia; Dr. Waugh, sociology professor from World Academy, Brisbane, flew into Malibu. By the time he got there, Dr. Firne was up and alert and doing quite well; nonetheless, he still exhibited much frustration and anxiety over his daughter's leaving.

.

A Good Friend's Consolation

The real estate tycoon and brain surgeon was overwhelmed with stress and chagrin; he discoursed with his long-time friend, Dr. Waugh, about the perils of college life:

Dr. Firne (Ph.D., Architectonics and Neurology)**:** Oh, the shower of grief in my heart! My soul is sick with uncertainty—the unpredictability of my daughter leaving home: My little girl, my youngest child is going off to college; and I do not know what to do. I can't live without my child at my side: This adjustment is much more than I had thought. She has been with us for the past seventeen years and has lit out world with enthusiasm; my child is going off to college to be taught by professors whom I do not know; suddenly, she is brashly plucked from us like green fruits, snapped in a storm. My heart is full of dolor and glumness at my daughter's fast-approaching departure: Why must I be divested of that gleaming, golden fruit of my joy and happiness?

My daughter wandered into my world when I had forgotten about having any more children—my wife's womb was barren and unable to bear the fruit of another golden princess; I had virtually given up on that long elusive dream of bringing more children into the world. Suddenly, the most unexpected miracle that I could have ever anticipated was right there: I was minding my own business, doing a thrilling book signing in Auckland, New Zealand; when, all of a sudden, The glorious God of heaven handed me my dream of a lifetime! I was smitten and filled to the brim with joy; it seemed as if she would be around forever.

Just as quickly as she came into our world, she has to abandon this desolate, empty nest; and it hurts—oh, it hurts so much to be rent from my "Little Pumpa's graceful presence. But alas, I must release you, Vanetta, my dear child, to go into the world—yea, I must release you to go into the world and find yourself, far away from us; for the role that we must play in your life has run its course: We must release you now to go into the distant reaches of the earth to carve out a career for yourself.

It is time for you to move on to the next phase of your wonderful world of beauty: That glorious world of beauty and adventure is patiently awaiting you out there; and we shall always be there with a multitude of counselors to cheer our daughter on. Oh, these sour moments, like stale grapes, are so nauseatingly unpalatable and unsavory; only the God of heaven knows the pain I feel at my loving daughter's departure.

Dr. Waugh: And oh, my friend, I certainly understand your pain and frustration; it is the pain of every loving father for his child, leaving him and going into a demon-possessed world that is riddled with so much uncertainty and spiritual darkness, and it hurts.

Dr. Firne: I knew that one day she would have to go off to college; but now, it's so hard! And though I can fly her to Canberra on our own Godwit Jet, I would not do it—I knew that it would be too difficult to say goodbye to our beautiful "Little Pumpa".

Dr. Waugh (Ph.D. Sociology; World University, Brisbane): Oh, farewell, farewell; farewell, thou splendidly painted bird, spangled with so many colorful lights. Oh, farewell; thou beautiful, lightsome Nightingale assembled without wings to fly; though you must fly far, far away so soon; your wings are so weak and heavy. Oh, how hard it is to say goodbye, and though we design the reality in the world today; though we've created a classroom atmosphere where evolution can no longer mock God; we are still leery about sending our children into these darkened halls taught by naturalists.

Dr. Firne: But we are completely in control of the sociopolitical situation, aren't we? We are the earth's new owners; atheistic science and ancient religion are now evicted.

Dr. Waugh: Yes, Dr. Firne, we are in control of the political situation; but you know—these folks are the brazen mongrels of hell and would proselytize at the drop of a hat! These godless, religious nuts are not afraid to disassemble the chariot of society—oh, these odious bigots would not bat an eye to overturn the carriage of truth and turn things upside down: This is what they do—they are atheists, anarchists, and amoralists. Dr. Firne, when my daughter, Jeanette, went to World Academy in Colombo, Sri Lanka; my wife Marlene and I had similar sentiments and were also quite tearful about it.

Dr. Firne: I remember the stark frustration that you and Marlene endured at that time; life can be frustrating at times; and sometimes, we have to relinquish those most valuable appendages—and it makes absolutely no sense whatsoever. How can I live without my *Little Pumpa.*

Dr. Waugh: We were very impressed with the rank and prestige of that institution: That Sri Lankan University has one of the most prestigious medical schools in the world. We wept and prayed night and day that God would lead and protect our daughter; in a world that is so replete with liars and truth distorters, one must be very concerned. After all, she is your child; going out into a world where many professors are rank liars and often rape their students right in their office—or even in the classroom: Some professors even recruit female students into prostitution—and you know that young girls can be insecure and vulnerable to this new appeal of sex; these corrupt professors would distort the truth at the drop of a bucket just to insert their own poisonous views.

These are the traitors who have poisoned the world with the arsenic of evolution; these callous amoralists have polluted a whole generation with their atheistic sentiments. They have absolutely no concern for your child's religious beliefs: They simply push theirs; and when they are done with your child, she would not even know her own name.

Dr. Firne: But Dr. Waugh, that type of behavior is illegal and frighteningly sad. Do you mean to tell me that all those things are happening on university campuses, and no one is doing anything to correct these clear abnormalities—have we lost our minds?

Dr. Waugh: I know; these folks do not care about the law—they are obsessed with evil: They do not care who they hurt and whose religious beliefs upon which they trample—they are there in those positions of academic stewardship to pollute society with atheism and witchcraft. That is why they are there, and if you do not protect your child's right not to hear that; they will pollute and poison her mind and worldview with all that utter garbage that they believe.

Dr. Firne: Yes, the lines are drawn in the sand: Christians who carelessly cross it are ruined; but sadly enough, they are crossing it every day and are wrecked by the wrecking crew of the spiritual darkness that is sweeping the world today. Many Christian couples claim that their sex lives are no longer fulfilling; they want something else—they want variety and have opened themselves to the moral atrocity and ridiculous travesty of spousal swapping, exchanging their wives for other men's wives in order to mine the kicks of swinging—Oh, God, help us: The Christian Church has lost its mind, Dr. Waugh.

Dr. Waugh: And that is why you must exercise the utmost caution in protecting your child—you must do whatever you can to shield your daughter from these dangerous atheists. They are cognizant that what they are saying is not true, but they have much faith that it is; therefore, they present it as if it is true to the blind, mindless masses of society. And in the process; that gross, crass lie becomes viewed as if it were a sacred tenet; that is the way these heartless secularists and brazen naturalists do business: They play ball with the truth; using the dry, empty husk of evolution and naturalism; they cook the truth and callously shove venomous doses of it down our children's throats.

Dr. Firne: Parents have lost control of the educational process; they've become rugged and careless, and this has turned the classroom into a war zone. Unfortunately, many parents are not incensed that devil-worshipping professors are teaching their children atheism and recruiting these gullible young people into prostitution.

Dr. Waugh: Well, there is nothing new about that: That has been going on for years! And it would not be so bad if they had only polluted themselves with that sort of stuff: They pollute and poison the whole society with that and make us look like rank fools. But you see, Dr. Firne; this is exactly what they've set out to do—destroy our children; they do not want a Christological worldview presented in the classroom: It is poison to them: They do not want any trace of Christianity in their world of amorality—it gets in their way! For it is the perfect antidote of their inane evolutionary perspective; it sinks their ship. Earlier debates that drew upon the Cambrian explosion have debunked evolution; That view, as a tenable scientific perspective, is stone dead—and we are bent on removing from our presence.

Dr. Firne: But you see, Dr. Waugh; the world is filled with hard-nosed naturalists: They would do anything to advance the cause of a broken theory—they loathe truth!

Dr. Waugh: Right on, give it up, brother; I know exactly about what you are talking: You have that right to protect your daughter's heart from the moral sewage of false teaching. The world already knows that evolution is a lie cooked up in the bowels of hell itself; the whole world knows that naturalism is a pretext and cover for modern science's false religion of atheism. But these crass, impudent naturalists just do not care about good science—they are liars! These wretched suckers are good liars who are obsessed with darkness and sex perversion; they are merely interested in pushing the pointless religions of evolution and secularism on our children.

Dr. Firne: And do you know where all that trash is going? It is a powerful pollutant; it is going smack into my daughter's mind, and soul, and heart; turning her into a zombie.

Dr. Waugh: And that, Dr. Firne, concerns me greatly because I have other children: My daughter has made it through the system, but I have other impressionable children. Professors talk that crap all day in class, societally engineering folk's children with that mess; but suddenly, when the Biblical model is brought upon the screen of scientific inquiry; it is confusing religion with science. This is the sort of bias to which they seem blind. So, of course, sending your daughter to university in Australia is not a picnic in the park—there is quite a lot involved.

Dr. Firne: Dr. Waugh, we are the only ones who can look after our children in this world; Hard-nosed, atheistic professors would not look after them; they are swindling suckers.

Dr. Waugh: And yes, Dr. Firne, I truly understand the emotional ravages of letting go now; but there is no need to worry; there are scores of scientific aristocrats in Australia: These attorneys have created a national network of paid employees to treat this matter. Rogue professors are aware of the steep consequences for violating this ethical principle: Proselytizing in the classroom is absolutely against the law and carries stiff penalties; steep fines and lengthy prison terms are enough to keep these propagandists at bay.

Dr. Firne: I thank my God for the stream of victories that out camp has racked up recently; at least, it has given our side a decided edge in this internecine battle against evil's minions and those who hate the truth.

Dr. Waugh: These dark henchmen of the false religion of modern science are diehards; however, they know the law and the Herculean might of global scientific aristocracy. Despite these safeguards in place, though, many parents still have concerns and are greatly stressed over this matter.

Dr. Firne: Well, Dr. Waugh, your visit could not have come at a more opportune time; we have been immensely refreshed and regaled, and the Chardonnay was superb: Your beautiful words of wisdom have helped a friend who so desperately needed them. We have seen the type of damage and destruction that careless college attendance does; oh, the destructive influence of evolution on the impressionable minds of young people: They would turn your children into lesbians and homosexuals at the drop of a hat! That is what they do; you cannot afford to blindly send your child to college today: Their iniquitous, slimy frat houses would turn your daughter into Mary Magdalene. Their darkened Halloween halls, flush with witches, would spin your daughter's head around a thousand times! This is the stygian world that naturalism has spun, out of the darkness of lies, for all of us.

Dr. Waugh: And at the end of the day, we cannot win this war without our Supreme God; he is the anchor of our souls: We are fighting a titanic battle against dangerous human beings. And while the professors themselves may not be directly involved in these crass activities—while they themselves may not directly promote these obscure, devilish types of behaviors; they create the shadowy environment in which these dastardly activities and behaviors thrive. And this is the sort of thing that these darkened environments do to people's children: You absolutely cannot afford to send your children to any and any kind of university out there today; no parent, in his right mind, can afford to entrust his children to these naturalistic cynics.

Dr. Firne: Dr. Waugh, I am cognizant of the risks associated with releasing my daughter in this kind of environment—I've been psyching myself up for this moment for the past seventeen years of my child's life; and I am, by no means, minifying the dangers connected with releasing a child to college; I am aware of the risks. The prince of this world has a well-trained battalion of atheistic professors in the university system out there: They are out there in full force to distort and pervert your children with all kinds of evil inventions.

Dr. Waugh: I'm aware of Dr. Larry's situation and what befell his daughter in Cape Town: She was raped in the girls' restroom, on the second floor of Clarence Hall, in broad daylight; and per school statistics, one in five girls on that campus is raped while in college there. Dr. Firne, these maniacs and psychopaths are out there to inflict maximum harm to others: They are out there to turn your children into moral zombies that you, yourself, would not even be able to recognize them; and like a vacuum system, they suck your innocent children into their darkened world.

Dr. Firne: It is comforting to be fully aware of these risks and dangers in a lawless world; we, as parents, do have someone to whom we can talk about all these wretched concerns.

Dr. Waugh: And when they are done with the virgin that you've raised in your home—when these dark, slick suckers are done with your kids; you would not even be able to recognize them: Dr. Firne, they turn your children into odious moral zombies, bold lesbians, and smooth-talking call girls.

Dr. Firne: Oh, Dr. Waugh, I'll throw my empire away in attorney's fees to ruin such a one. We, of the scientific aristocratic class, belong to the God who designed the universe—our children must be taught that as standard scientific law: They must be taught the truth. Anything else must be presented as merely conjecture and speculation—nothing else: Any attempt to brainwash my child with evolution would fetch a hefty lawsuit from me; and when I am done with that professor, he would not even know his own name. That is the way it is, and this is the way I want it—nothing less, nothing more.

Dr. Waugh: Although the tide is changing, we cannot sit idly by and let bygones be bygones; we must engage in trenchant sociopolitical and ideological activism to push our cause and to push back against these nefarious patterns and trends in world society today.

Dr. Firne: Yes, Dr. Waugh; evil reigns when good people sit by and simply do nothing; and we have scored mammoth victories, about which we are proud, over the past two years. Evolution and naturalism are losing the war; they are no longer tenable scientific models; they are merely fairy tale ideas of scientists who refuse to see design everywhere in nature. They are the views of those who overlook the broad machinery of design in the universe; these are the misguided people who have turned the West into a mess—an utter mess. And I tell you, none of them seem to care.

A Stirring and Glorious Flight

And so, the long discourse of his daughter's rite of passage eventually came to an end; Dr. Firne cheered up and began enjoying his distinguished friends who had come over; they talked, and laughed, and hobnobbed in the sprawling, palatial guest room. The exquisitely prepared curried goat and turkey were favorites at the dining table; the finger-licking good meal was like the icing on the cake of a most memorable day; and Amadyn, Arnold, and their wives were on hand to wish their sister, Vannetta, all the best. Oh, what a quaint farewell it was. Some were dancing and wafting kisses to her; some were crying, weeping, and bawling: Others were drinking, and singing, and having a time!

Then suddenly, an orchid Austin Martin Sports Utility Vehicle pulled up at the gate; three burly bodybuilders leaped out the automobile and began loading it with suitcases. They were laughing and cracking funny jokes about their dates the previous night. One of the strongmen, Mr. Stutes, talked about taking his new girlfriend to the movies; he told his peers that they had gone to see the new James Bond Movie, *Casino Royal*. He said that his girlfriend, Helen Baker, had met him on a website two months earlier; one of the other gentlemen, Mr. Scrubbs, talked about a guilt-ridden affair that he was having.

Suddenly, the gloriously garbed princess; arrayed in fine linen; debouched from the crowd; her cheeks, as soft as the powder of freshly fallen snow, flared with the flame of blush, flush, and flash. Oh, behold the gorgeously attired flame; her eyes as bright as a gleaming stream—see the resplendent star of her smile that glowed so brightly from the burning lamp of her soul; see her long, flowing, glossy hair; falling on her buttocks like vines veiling a fence. And oh, her rubicund cheeks; with such soft, pretty dimples; smiled with the world. See her lusty, scarlet lips; as dainty as strawberries, beaming with the bloom of blush; oh, those luscious brightly painted lips, peeled across glistening teeth as white as snow!

See the fulgent beauty of a dazzling princess, illuminating the candle-lit evening; suddenly, a crowd was formed from virtually nowhere, crushing her for autographs. And then, the radiant princess climbed into the gleaming carriage and was whisked away. About eleven miles away, her Godwit Jet was oiled and thoroughly inspected; yea, the state-of-the-art luxury jet plane was exquisitely checked for that long trip to Australia. The often slumberous eight-thousand-mile journey was but a stone's throw away; the magnificent aircraft, built by Sustifani Aviation in Italy, was one of the fastest in the world! It consumed the journey in record time.

The brisk flight, rather routine, lasted anywhere from two and a half to three hours! The luxury jet plane was fully equipped with computers and a wide range of modern amenities; it had a beautiful office, a delightful dining room, and a sumptuously furnished bedroom; all the palatial trappings of life at home were present on this marvelous aircraft. Accompanied by her brothers Arnold and Amadyn, Vanetta felt quite at home. Hors d'oeuvres and roast turkey were served with rice, French bread, and Chardonnay. The cost of the wines served was easily a middle-income American's annual earnings, and dainty Champaign was also on hand to slake the die-hard epicureans' thirst.

Oh, the jazz, the music of Miles Davis and Luis Armstrong, blared deep into the sky; see the cheerful, merry Firnes; talking and laughing as if they were at home! The Godwit Jet's ride, as smooth as ice, made everything so simple and relaxing; equipped with sophisticated sonar devices, it revealed all the wonders of the deep! Measuring and mapping the ocean floor's entire profile, its screen lit up the night. Oh, see the swarthy froth of the deep, like a caliginous jungle in a lost world. Yea, an obscure world that was once there; but mysteriously disappeared somewhere!

Oh, hear the boiling billows, forever roaming across the far-flung reaches of the sea; and the streaming, golden fruit of daylight; scarfed with dusk; lay far behind the clouds. The ever-whirling, wailing ocean howled in the distance, in the sacred bowels of night; oh, how the restless, roaring ocean bawled in huge, foaming, billowing heaps. And like a titanic churning factory, working around the clock, the sea's mystery—oh, the sprawling, brawling, foaming mystique of the sea remained just that: A mystery.

Oh, how the weird, obscure creatures that appeared on the screen jarred and confused the thoughts of the pretty lady. And here and there, she would turn and look away from the quaint, hideous sights; and her brothers would scream, "No Vanny, no; wait a minute— just look at this one!" And when she had had enough of the ocean's mysterious bowels, she walked away. She went into the gleaming office and began to pen the most stirring of poetic lines:

Yes, all the world's oceans have crashed down upon me. Oh, see how they rushed in; they came upon me like the flying debris, spawned by an atomic bomb's detonation. And I did not... oh, I did not run from the calamity which I had so painstakingly created; I stayed there and courted that handsome, dashing, gallant knight of disaster; and I was so brave and bold to face the flaring storm that howled against my life. I stood there in the bowels of agony, but destiny's Herculean arms withstood the storm; and, with the voice of crashing streams of wonder; I spoke to the storm, and it retreated. And then, suddenly; I felt that destiny had fought for me and pushed me out the way: Yea, the brawny, Samsonian hands of destiny pushed me out the way of danger; and the roaring, howling, swirling tempest retreated back into the bowels of calm.

Oh, the might of Providence, so prodigious and incredible; so wonderful and kind. And from that sprawling, cavernous cave of self-defeat; I debouched with triumph. And behold, I am triumphant forever: I am she who was lost and is now found. My whole world has come to my rescue; and oh, what a rescue mission this has been! Behold the world at my fingertips and all the things that I have ever needed and wanted; but alas, alas; the stooge of youth has been a dear friend and a splendid teacher. Oh, what a great teacher of life's priceless lessons that youth's folly has been to me! It is so unfortunate that someone from the palace of earthly life has had to learn this way; no one should have to learn life's poignant lessons through folly's dumb errors; but alas, I did.

I went, I looked, I erred, and I learned some very precious lessons. Oh, what beautiful and priceless lessons that life's golden classroom has taught me. The old, stale words of subterfuge are gone now; new stars are forming in my world: New voices are heard on the telephone line of the future, and everything will be just fine. Oh, Australia, Australia; thou land of powder and dust; thou shore of simmering froth; Australia, thou golden gardens, brushed with the paint of elegance and splendor—here I come to learn and be among your warm, amicable, amiable, and lovely people.

Oh Australia, Australia; here I come with my heart in my hand, gently handing it to you; and with so many family members here, I cannot but triumph and move on in life. Oh, the world and all its pomp and pageantry patiently await destiny's child. Yea, see how the many servants await destiny's glamor girl of love and wonder; But amidst all that glory and fanfare which I behold before my beaming eyes. I shall never let the stain of pride and arrogance get the better part of me again: I am the transubstantiation of earthly dust into the gleaming temple of a princess; I must, and will, never forget the very essence of all telluric glory: humility. Vanity is that endless stream of change that takes us up and brings us down again!

And while she penned all those golden poetic lines, the nimble jet; screaming, roaring, and barking like an angry jackal in the night; whirred into Australian airspace: It dashed, darted, and zoomed over Newcastle like a flaming meteorite! and within minutes, this most magnificent air machine zipped into Canberra like a rocket. Flying at top speed of twenty-seven hundred miles per hour, Godwit zoomed into Canberra; Yea, it whirred into the soft, caliginous foam of the glorious city; shrouded in the frothy spume of a fog. Curried mutton, exquisitely cooked, was the last meal served on the swift Godwit aircraft.

These highly skilled cooks, consummately trained in Paris, greatly deserved their reward; their daintily prepared sushi, roast turkey, and curried mutton filled the trip with fun and gust. They kept everyone licking his fingers and mouth for the most part of the journey; and oh, what a plump reward they received from the golden mistress of wealth. Each of the seven cooks received a whopping tip of nine hundred euros! Awash with delight, they effusively and exuberantly thanked Vanetta for the gifts that she had bestowed upon them; they wished her a wonderful stay in Australia and a marvelous life at Canberra Poly. It was such a charming good bye.

Within minutes of their Canberra arrival, the unloading team was already on hand; seven husky men, as strong as an ox, scurried to remove the luggage from the plane. Their arms, as big as an average adult's thighs, looked like quaint inflated tires; these burly, brawny men; as strong as Hercules, could lift a sports utility vehicle into the air. Wearing chic beanies and pert overalls, they looked like strongmen from Pluto; these dashing, jaunty bodybuilders smiled with all the glory and beauty of daylight. Oh, see how strong they were: They lifted up huge boxes and tossed them around like toys! Within minutes, they had removed all of Vanetta's luggage from the aircraft; and the cheerful, bountiful hand of generosity was not unkind towards these men either.

Judging from the glee in their smiles, they must have been given a million euros! And oh, how cheerfully and gladsomely they shook hands with the Firne children. They must not have ever earned so much cash in such short time in their whole lives! But that was just another perk of working in society's astral circles of aristocracy. To those very thankful bodybuilders, their tip was a plump, handsome reward—and to them, Miss Firnes' generosity went way over the top: It was utterly incredible! It was a plump boon that painted their cheeks with joy and gladness. They couldn't believe that a client could have ever been so kind and generous to them.

A Most Unforgettable Weekend

And by the time that they had brusquely driven off in their gleaming taupe Ford Bronco; a sleek, scarlet Aston Martin limousine pulled up; two fine gentlemen alighted from it. Dr. Zonakh and his son Gershom quickly wrapped Vanetta into their arms, kissed her on the cheek, and motioned her into their automobile.

Dr. Zonakh: Oh Vanny, Vanny; welcome to Australia; welcome to our marvelous world here down under! It has been quite a while since we last saw you here in Australia; and oh, how you've grown! How was your trip? We've been here all evening awaiting your long-anticipated arrival.

Vanetta: And oh, Daddy, you and my brother Gershom look so absolutely well! He looks just like you; it is so amazingly delightful to see my Australian family.

Dr. Zonakh: And you, look how much you've grown since you were last here four years ago! I spoke with your dad this morning, and he has taken your rite of passage very hard; I told him that I understood the thorny difficulty of letting go a last child.

Vanetta: Oh Daddy, my daddy spoke so graciously about you and said to say *hello*; he said that you would see him around your dinner table in exactly one month's time. Daddy said that he went hunting with you in Maragle State Forest for Brumbies' meat.

Dr. Zonakh: Well, I will tell you something: That is a feller who really loves Malibu: I spoke to him briefly earlier, and he appeared to have been in very fines of spirits: He seemed to have put the worst of your farewell behind him—that is so wonderful! He was upbeat and quite jovial and cordial. He said that I would see him soon and that he knew that his daughter was in very good hands and with Australia's best. Gershom, my son, get the napkins from the car; our baby girl is here—oh, such joyous tears; she'll be with us for the next seven years—wow, we've won the jackpot! You all will be having your beloved California sister for a good while!

Gersham: Oh, Daddy, Daddy; see how Vanny cries for her beloved Los Angeles family! Though she longed to be with us, she'd miss her Malibu family there in California.

Vanetta: I am not crying because of my family in Los Angeles; my brothers are here—I am weeping for joy—the joy of seeing both of you again. You bring me so much joy: I longed to be with my family here in Brisbane again! I'll see Mom, and how is she doing?

Gershom: And oh, my dear sister, Vanny; we are so happy to see you again: It has been such a long time since we last saw you—we missed you so very much!

Dr. Zonakh: Cecelia, Paulette, and Patsy have been over our house quite often; they have not ceased to inquire about you: They wanted to know how you were doing. Paulette was ecstatic when she heard that you were coming—she kept bugging us; unfortunately, at the last moment; all those young ladies had to leave the country. They have all gone to further their studies at prestigious universities in Europe: Cecelia and Patsy have gone to Oxford; Paulette is studying medicine in Paris, France.

Vanetta: Oh, Daddy, do you mean that my best friends are not going to be around? What am I going to do without these wonderful childhood pals—oh, how it hurts! We've had such glorious childhood days here in Australia—and oh, those girls; they were such delightful people around whom to be: I will certainly miss them!

The Firne's Welcome to Australia

Dr. Zonakh heartily embraced Vanetta's brothers and shook their hands; yea, he shook Amadyn's and Arnold's hands with the iron grip of Samson himself. And oh, how he thanked them for taking good care of his beloved goddaughter. By this time Gershom had gotten back into the svelte, gleaming Aston Martin carriage; his godsister Vanetta, his father Dr. Zonakh, and Amadyn sat in the back seat. Arnold and Gershom sat in front; and oh, all the chatterboxes began to talk; and, as he revved the Aston Martin's engine, it sounded like a jumbo jet on takeoff. Oh, within a flash, this dashing race car driver was on the Canberra Speedway; and coursing at one hundred and ten miles an hour, Arnold was frightened in his boots and inquired whether it was a suicide mission.

Dr. Zonakh, sensing that he had some real issues with Gershom's driving, comforted him; he assured Arnold that everything was all right and that he would be home soon. He said to Arnold, "Don't worry, young man; my son would not hurt you—he wouldn't hurt a fly: This is the way he drives all the time—and he drives very safely. The Island of Australia, as broad as heaven, encourages this sort of thing; and besides, my son is one of the finest race car drivers in the world! You have not seen anything yet; but he can handle the Australian Highway very well."

And within ten minutes, the nineteen-mile distance had been devoured: They were home! And like an automobile with a dozen engines, the Aston Martin pulled into the driveway. Arnold was still holding his breath as he got out the beautiful carriage; he said, "My God; good heavens—what a dash that was! Gershom, you are bad!" And though veiled beneath the thick, woolly shawl of the night's frothy curtain; the gleaming city of Canberra looked like a flaming fire in a thick, moiling fog. Flickering lights, like sprightly July Fourth fireworks, seemed to dart from everywhere. And like the flashing embers from a dazzling meteorite, crashing through the night; Canberra's colorful, pearly lights blazed from the obscure, exotic cavern of night.

Though most of the luggage had to be brought to the residence by special delivery, some of her particulars and personal belongings were brought on the street jet. And like gracious, loving brothers; Amadyn and Arnold began to unload the carriage; Dr. Zonakh and his son Gershom quickly joined in and unloaded the beautiful limousine. The four strong gentlemen, in the prime of health, took all the items into the residence. And again; as warm, loving brothers; obsessed with their sister's well-being; they promptly volunteered to help unwrap and unpack her stuff while she was away. The Zonakhs had already chartered a jet to whisk Vanetta to Brisbane for the weekend; they had also planned a huge shopping spree for this coveted member of the family.

Vanetta flew into Canberra around 10:40 in the evening and had a quick nap that night. By 7:30 the next morning, she was back on a chartered jet to Brisbane for the weekend; and oh, what a rapturous weekend that lay ahead of her: She was in for a grand time! Within forty minutes, Dr. Zonakh's Gulf Stream Jet had arrived in beautiful

Brisbane; it quickly consumed the short six-hundred-mile distance within just over half of an hour. And like a rhapsodic bevy of little children, the Zonakhs brashly rushed onto the plane; oh, the blazing zeal and passion that they expressed at seeing their wonderful god sister. They raved at seeing the beautiful princess; their eyes waxed as bright as a star!

Oh, the poignant delight that they expressed at seeing their favorite girl in the whole world. And what a pity that her stay was going to be so evanescent and episodic: what a pity! But they did not mind that at all—they were just so happy to see their gracious friend: It had been four years since they had last seen their god sister: It was time to see her again. Oh, the rapturous screams and applause when they blessed their eyes upon Vanetta; and the very moment that she alighted from the aircraft, the long weekend party began. There was singing and dancing, jumping and screaming, and laughing and talking!   The entire Zonakh gang was on hand for the weekend and had a bellyful of laughs; all of Dr. Zonakh's nine children had flown in from all over the world for the occasion.

And, as a matter of standard family policy, Dr. Zonakh had never shown any difference—no, he had never made any difference between his nine children and his godchild, Vanny. And way back from childhood, all the dear children saw Vanetta as their veritable sister; there was absolutely no confusion in that home, and there was no frown either; there was no frown about Vanetta being one of the most beautiful women in the world. They were so proud of their little sister; and oh, when they saw her this time—when they saw her, she was the bomb! Her long, streaming hair falling on her buttocks; her rubious, high cheeks; her bushy eyebrows; her piercing eye lashes, and her pungent dimples—her soft strawberry lips, as pretty as red roses; and as dainty as ripe, succulent peaches.

Her dashingly delightful smile; as pretty as a star; and as radiant as a gleaming stream; filled their world with joy and gladness! The entire weekend was a glorious jar of joy! All twenty-nine of Dr. Zonakh's children and grandchildren were there to enjoy her; they swarmed around her like bees, asking her about the many pageants she had won. The Champaign bottles went off like pungent bombs in the soft, aquatic Australian air; and the music carried on way into the night: The stream of fun went on and on. Night stretched into day and day into night again. Oh, what a glorious weekend it was. What a wonderful time they had together in that unending merry-go-round of fun; it was a weekend stuffed with amusement: they took Vanny shopping that very Saturday. And what a dashing shopping spree that was: Her godparents bought her so many things! Cash gushed like a beaming Hawaiian river of fire, flashing pretty lights into the ocean.

The Zonakh Family Celebration

Later on, that day, the entire Zonakh clan blithely gathered in the mansion's banquet hall; suddenly, a lilac Lamborghini pulled up at the Zonakhs' sidewalk: It sounded like a bomb. Dr. Molluck and his pretty wife Rosslyn alighted from the carriage, walked to the door, knocked, and waited: The house was flush with jubilation, exultance, and conviviality. "Oh, Daddy, it's Dr. Molluck and his wife", cried Gershom's graceful wife, Suzanne. "They've come to join us for the weekend's festivities! Oh, Dr. Molluck," she raved; "We are so glad to see you; we are all here: The whole world has come to Brisbane. We are trying to get as much out of her as we possibly can. She will soon be gone, and we do not know when we will see her again. She will be studying so hard!"

Jaslyn, Dr. Zonakh's wife and Rosslyn, Dr. Molluck's wife, heartily greeted each other; they hugged, kissed, and disappeared into one of the mansion's several banquet halls. Doctors Zonakh and Molluck ardently shook hands and embraced each other with zeal; the two gentlemen sat down and began vigorously discoursing about evolution's plight.

Dr. Zonakh: Well, well, well; Dr. Molluck; it's so good to see you around here! How have you been, and how goes the evolution fight: What landfill would accept it?

Dr. Molluck: Well, Dr. Zonakh; we have the dead dog in the bag: We're about to send it off to the animal shelter in Jerusalem, where it will be incinerated. Our team of attorneys is on standby to turn rogue proselytizing professors into jailbirds: We absolutely would not stand for this kind of nonsense from anyone anymore; we've also hired a brawny team of private eyes to patrol and monitor the classrooms. These covert aides would pose as students taking classes in order to monitor the situation; they will take very good notes and secretly tape record any inappropriate comments.

These documents would be handed over to our dashing, competent team of attorneys; and we will take it from there. It is high time that this evolution nonsense be stopped and be thrown into the trash; it's time that its lies be exposed and be seen for exactly what they are— lies and the problems that they cause in human society.

Dr. Zonakh: Well, it would appear as if we have nothing about which to worry this time around; we seem to have the situation fully under control: Am I looking at the correct picture here, or is there something else?

Dr. Molluck: Yes, Dr. Zonakh; you are most certainly looking at the correct picture. On an even brighter note, my wife and I heard about the celebration party here in Brisbane; it's all over the news in Auckland—Vanny is in Brisbane for the weekend; and Dr. Zonakh, you know me very well—I couldn't pass up an occasion like this one! Our girl has grown into the most beautiful young lady in the whole world; and we are so proud of her: it is indeed an honor to join in this festive celebration. We've brought a small gift with us for the beautiful lady whom we love so much.

Dr. Zonakh: You are a man of great taste; and what might that be, Dr. Molluck? You are not only a man of great taste; you are also a man of extraordinary extravagance, and nothing is small in your world of lavishness and prodigality.

Dr. Molluck: Well, we were at the car show in Wellington, and we knew she was coming: We saw an Aston Martin, MSRP: We liked it very much and flat out bought it for her; we only paid three hundred thousand euros for the beautifully designed British car, and we know that she would like it very much!

Dr. Zonakh: That girl is the luckiest young lady in the world; she has a bunch of Daddies; and to top it off, they are all filthy rich human beings who do not mind splurging on her, spending ridiculous amounts of money towards her comfort.

Dr. Molluck: Our dear daughter, Vanetta, has created a soft spot in the hearts of all of us; and for that reason, we've all spoilt her dirty with nothing but the best—she expects it! I have spent much time with our beloved goddaughter right here in Brisbane—I know her; believe me—I know what she likes. She has very polished, exquisite, and expensive taste; that young lady has walked me round and around in many sprawling shopping centers. Sometimes, my wife Rosslyn, Molluck, would joke with me; saying, "And don't forget me!" And when we went shopping as a family, with my wife and other children, nothing changed: Vanny was always the center of the show, telling us which shopping malls we ought to visit and what we need to buy.

Dr. Zonakh: And when she is with us, she always plays that beautiful Myles Davis Jazz; her fingers move as fast as light on the keyboard, and we all get into the groove of the music and dance around the house.

Dr. Molluck: Somehow or other, she never sought the spotlight; it always formed around her. My wife, Rosslyn, and all the children treated her as if she were their favorite candy: They were always lifting her up, spinning her around, kissing and licking on her cheeks; and Vanetta loved every moment of all the attention and love that her family gave her. Often when we went to the Auckland Car Show, she always loved the Aston Martins: And she would say things like; "Daddy, Mommy; let's go for a spin around the block."

World Scientific Aristocracy's Celebratory Excesses

Wow, my, my, my; listen to what these filthy-rich scientific aristocrats call small gifts; their small gifts are money that most people would not make in several life times! And, good heavens; as if that was not enough for the beautiful lady of dash—Dr. Zonakh and Dr. Molluck spoiled her some more in a shopping spree in Brisbane. They went shopping that very Saturday evening, and went back on the following day! Oh, see the Indooroopilly Shopping Center in Brisbane, abuzz with smiling shoppers; the massive structure, the largest shopping mall in Eastern Australia, was jammed.

Sprightly, sassy shoppers; as lively as a butterfly; fluttered about the multi-story unit! Nestled among a grove of trees, it looked like an oversized castle in a fine garden. Vanetta's two godfathers scoured the sprawling facility, looking for the best gifts—they searched the complex in quest of the finest gifts on hand for their goddaughter. And oh, the joy and pride they felt shopping with the world's most beautiful woman! When they were finished, they had spilled more cash into the many busy cash registers; they bought her a diamond necklace, a laptop, and a piano for eighty thousand euros.

In addition to all of that, they bought her a personal computer for fourteen thousand euros; and finally, they topped it all off with thirty thousand euros in clothes! The two scientific aristocrats had bought their goddaughter all that they felt she needed. Oh, what a magnificent weekend that was: Those who had so much just got some more. By 7:30 on Monday morning, Dr. Molluck had whisked Vanetta back to Canberra; and that glorious weekend marked the end of her days of frivolity. From that point on, she shouldered the unwieldy wheel of arduous academic moil.

Oh, the intriguing, colorful bird of passion's whims briskly flew away and did not return; yea, love's flaming robin flew away and remained in the bushes for quite some time. Vanetta buckled down to college's formidable library of books and scholarly toil; and though academic toil was not quite a royal banquet feast for the fine lady of dash; it was, by no means, grinding mental drudgery and teeth-gnashing readjustment either. And far away in another world, the pert billionaires of the day waxed richer and richer. The scientific aristocrats of the world virtually sat at the helm of authority and power; their words, as strong as the voice of thunder, carried authority everywhere on earth.

Their Godwit jets, the cost of a city block, whisked them around the globe; and oh, what sprawling financial empires that they had built upon the earth! Behold the Firne Family: See how resilient and tough they were, though battered by the cruel, whimsical storms of life; they had remained strong. Tossed and embattled by the savage winds of wrong turns and misfortunes; they stayed the course, they fought the many battles, and they triumphed. And oh, what superb role models they had become to a sour world community! They had thriven in a world battered by a storm of woes and crises; and oh, what spectacular and fabulous career success that they had had recently! The wanton storm of alcohol abuse had blown away: A new day had arrived. And good heavens, what a magnificent turn of events that had transpired in their world! They belonged to the robust, new scientific aristocracy that had stormed the earth. And how fabulously wealthy, successful, and popular they had become!

They had established garment outlets in Paris, Auckland, London, and New Delhi. Their sprawling grocery chain in Australia and New Zealand had grown nationwide; and they owned banks and significant real estate holdings around the world. Their assets' total value was somewhere around nine hundred and ninety billion euros! Oh, behold the new aristocratic class of ridiculously wealthy men of science; they hailed from the entire globe and banded together as tightly as molecules in a solid. And there were some things which they absolutely would not tolerate: Exogamy was one of those revoltingly hideous monsters that they all detested; they poisoned the minds of their children against intermarriage with mongrels. And who were mongrels? Anyone whose bank account was less than theirs!

Oh, see how fiercely they protected their assets with an exquisite team of attorneys; their children attended the finest schools in the world and sparkled like Christmas lights. Their ubiquitous presence around the world was nothing short of a political takeover of the whole earth. And when their children married, wedding ceremonies lasted for weeks on end! Oh, the sprawling, lavishly decorated five-star hotels that served as bridal venues. And like one big aristocratic family, they travelled from far and near to the site— Mayors, governors, prime ministers, presidents, and kings attended from everywhere. The entire academic aristocratic bureaucracy was always in full attendance. And oh; the brawling parties that followed these unthrifty wedding receptions were quite a stirring spectacle!

CHAPTER 7

CONQUERING UNCERTAINTY'S FOGGY WORLD

And this was the kind of world for which Vanetta was so circumspectly prepared; all the time of fun and games had come to a screeching halt: A new season had begun. It was now time to prove herself in the often murky, changeful world of college life; and oh, what a splendid job she did of doing just that: She proved herself to everyone. Her stay in Australia was a sparkling success, and she dazzled even the university president: They were stunned by her mental acuity and raw academic genius; what a star she became! Despite all that academic talent, soaring popularity, and arresting pizzaz; she remained meek and humble. Her undergraduate work at Canberra's prestigious Polytechnic University was smooth; it went by as swiftly as a comet, and there was little wriggle room for dating and connecting with the male species.

Oh, Vanetta; as bright as a blazing meteorite; impressed and ensorcelled her professors. What a refreshingly delightful two-and-a-half-year journey that was for this most graceful lady; the child prodigy had suddenly become a flashing academic star in the public's eyes. Her straight 4.0 grade point average attracted high-profile people's attention: She was called into the university President's office and flat out offered a free ride there; he, straight out, offered her a full scholarship for a doctoral program in mathematics, with the promise of a tenure-track position after receiving her doctorate there. This is the conversation that the university president had with her in his office.

Dr. Victor LaMack (President of Canberra Polytechnic University): Oh, Miss Firne; it's so nice to see you! I've heard so much about you, and those grades are very impressive—they've greatly impressed me. I've spoken to Dr. Cornwall (your quantum algebra professor), and he was very impressed with you: He said that we could not afford to lose you to Oxford or to the University of Paris, and he has forcefully recommended a full scholarship for you in quantum algebra. Ordinarily, this doctoral program should last anywhere from three and a half to five years; but we have a hunch—and are confident—that you can complete it within four years.

Miss Firne: Well, Dr. LaMack; I'm deeply honored to hear such gracious words from you; I'm just an ordinary, everyday student who happens to excel in her academic endeavors. I'm a simple person; I don't know if I can live up to all that you've said there. I always see myself as being equal to, but never better than, others; and I work hard.

Dr. LaMack: Well, Miss Firne, it shows—you are a work horse and are doing very well at our school. I'm profoundly moved by your humble response and lowly spirit; you could easily assume *the big head*; but instead, you've embraced the way of humility. You are bright and have your head on right; and we would love to have you here; as per our faculty here at Canberra Poly, you've lighted up their classrooms with joy. You are a dashingly delightful person to have here with us: we can certainly use your genius here at our school; in fact, someone in the vice chancellor's office has already suggested to us a tenured position for you—and I'm in perfect agreement with that suggestion!

Miss Firne (star mathematics student): A tenured position for me—oh, what an honor! Oh, Dr. LaMack, that is over the top—I haven't even begun the doctoral program as yet.

Dr. LaMack: Well, as of now; it is only a rumor; but your mentors are certain about it: They shower you with accolades and praise and highly recommend you to us. We've already gone about doing the paperwork on your doctoral program here at Canberra Polytechnic University; and as far as we are concerned; you are a mathematics genius—we are so proud of you. Your performance in that Miss Australia Pageant, last month, has made all of us here so happy! We do not know what to do with you; you seem to have it all together in one place; you are quite a lady: You carry a full course load and bloom so brilliantly in public life—and yet are so humble! We've never seen your kind.

Vanetta: Well, you see, Dr. LaMack; I am a scientific aristocrat: I only aim for the top—my daddy taught me to be this way; he pounded this lifestyle into my head. I want to make daddy proud of his daughter. My socialization has been a grueling and enervating one; I've been trained only to excel. It's the lifestyle of the world's scientific aristocrats, and I hate to say it in public because it casts me in the wrong light; it sounds supercilious.

Dr. LaMack: I see how your world of champions and victors works—oh, what a world! Well, I think that you've taught me something today; I'll pound that same mentality into my daughter, Ava's head so that she can pull away from the boys who hound her daily. You seem to have put it all together so well: What a remarkable person you truly are; I know your dad, Dr. Firne; we were very pleased when you chose to honor us here with your university attendance. Yea, we were so pleased when you chose to grace us with your noble presence. You could have gone to a thousand other schools, but you chose Canberra

Poly—and for that, we are quite happy and delighted to be honored with your presence. Oh, what a most remarkable lady you are!

Miss Firne: You see, Dr. LaMack; my daddy had chosen this school for me years ago: This choice was made for me even when I was a little baby; Dad selected this university for my attendance. At my christening, ridiculous gifts were given to me by all my filthy rich god parents: One of them, Dr. Zonakh, tossed in a stout stock account to take me through college. But I am glad that they had chosen this school for me; I truly like it here, and I like you, too, Dr. LaMack: You are a wonderful man who makes me feel quite at home. It seems as if I've been attending this school all my life.

Dr. LaMack: Oh, my, my, my, my; this is so extraordinary: It sounds like a fairy tale. Though it sounds like a fairy tale, it's not: It is just the extraordinary stuff of the Firne Family. Miss Firne, I know your biological father very well; he is a splendid human being: I've gone to many of his exciting town hall meetings and conferences here in Canberra; I was there, in Auckland, when your mother, Dr. Margolyn Firne, began to get dizzy and to go into spasms when she was having you; I'd never dreamed of a day like this one—and oh, what a wonderful day this has been.

Miss Firne: Dr. LaMack, you were there when I was born; oh, what a great event that was! So many people whom I've met have witnessed my mysterious birth: What a moment that was—Daddy told me that the whole world was shaken up!

.

Dr. LaMack: I am fully cognizant of the quaint circumstances surrounding your birth, and I am also aware of the titanic philosophical and religious wars that are being fought in the world today. I am not slack concerning the problem of proselytizing in classrooms; and, based on your experience here at Canberra Poly, thus far, we've handled that matter. We have a magnificent track record that honors objective, unbiased scientific research: the pedagogic methods used on this campus are blind to individual philosophical biases.

Miss Firne: My parents and I did extensive research on Australian universities' standing: This university was eclectically and exquisitely picked for reasons that I will not discuss here; however, I'm very happy for being here, and things are great, thus far.

Dr. LaMack: You're a sublimely delightful lady; your presence here is deeply treasured. We absolutely do not tolerate scientists proselytizing in any of our classrooms; the law is clear and very unequivocal; scientific proselytizing is a federal crime. No professor is allowed to state that there is no god in any of our classrooms, for that statement is an unscientific one—he has not been everywhere in the universe, so he can't say that.

Miss Firne: I'm talking about that very matter; my father is very concerned about that and other matters of moral lawlessness on Australian university campuses. My spiritual life and faith in Christ mean quite a lot to me and to my parents as well: We are deeply spiritual people; thus, these are natural concerns to us.

Dr. LaMack: And Miss Firne, I'm fully aware of what you are trying to say to me; and all that I am saying is that we, at Canberra Poly, belong to the same class as you. There are absolutely no conflicts of interest in your attending school at this university campus, and we are quite happy to have you here; I've been president of Canberra Polytechnic University for the past decade or so: I am fully aware of the legal changes that are sweeping the earth's university system today. As a matter of policy, this institution of higher learning has maintained a searching eye for the issues which you've voiced here today: Miss Firne, I am fully cognizant of the numerous abuses that transpire in classrooms: Here at Canberra Poly, we've gone overboard to protect our students' legal rights and religious concerns. We feel that students have the legal right to attend classes without being bullied into going along with patently religious ideas with which they do not agree—we are fully cognizant of this kind of professor abuse and will not tolerate it at our school, and we've had a pretty good track record thus far.

Miss Firne: Well, Dr. LaMack; I'm most delighted by your effusive show of graciousness to me; and all my daddies are so pleased with the wonderful work that you are doing here. They've spoken quite kindly of you, and several of them recommended this institution; per my Nigerian parents, the Omous, Canberra Poly is the top university in the whole world. Doctors Molluck and Gutierrez, two of my godfathers, have also raved about this school; they've been flat out impressed with you and your very distinguished faculty here. And Dr. LaMack, tell me: Were you good in mathematics when you were in school?—I'm just curious.

Dr. LaMack: Oh, yes, Miss Firne; my doctoral degree is in mechanical engineering, and my being at home with mathematics helped me out considerably. You see, oh dear, Miss Firne, the whole universe is written with the ink of mathematics: God must be a great mathematician indeed—what a world that he has created!

Miss Firne: Mathematics is a unique culture of abstract thinking: It's a gift from God. It has always fascinated me: I've always enjoyed working and toying with numbers. And studying the backgrounds of the fathers of mathematics has greatly inspired me, too; Archimedes, Gauss, Euler, and Newton have done much to advance the human race. Against that backdrop, I will begin the Quantum Algebra doctoral program in September.

Dr. LaMack: Well, it has been quite wonderful and reassuring talking with you, Miss Firne. You are so brilliant and warm-hearted;

I've truly enjoyed talking with you: Good afternoon and good bye. We shall be in touch. Good bye Miss Firne!

The Birth of a Rising Academic Star

And there it was: Vanetta's academic stardom, etched in the sand of school politics. Oh, there it was; signed with the ink of gracious words and sealed in the envelope of pretty promises. Oh, the beautiful envelope of human potential, splashed everywhere there in brilliance—the dazzling academic star's glory was splattered everywhere in the wind; and what a charming lady she was; but the dumb, inane chatterbox of the world's gossip columns used no discretion whatsoever. Before the ink dried on Vanetta's commitment to the Canberra Poly Doctoral Program; it was crassly splattered all over the world, leaving no room for human privacy.

This girl's life was not a public affair; she deserved the privacy of a human being. and the news media should not just barge in and violate this young lady's civil rights; she deserved the media's discretion in matters having to do with her personal life. It is so unfortunate today that even people in society's astral circles are not given the respect that they deserve—there's no respect for highly celebrated people's privacy! They are people—not objects. And when Dr. Firne was going to turn down the scholarship at Canberra Poly; Dr. LaMack, the university President; persuaded him not to do so. He told him that he was aware of his concerns but that his daughter would do very well at his school. Oh, the delicacy of aristocratic politics; Vanetta told her dad that she really admired Dr. LaMack and wanted to stay put—and she did.

Dr. LaMack informed him that Vanetta had done so well; she had sealed a sure deal; yea, she was, beyond doubt, the best candidate for a full tenured position at the university. And with the speed of the morning rush-hour train, Vanetta began working on things; she presented new, insightful models in quantum algebraic permutations. And, as it turned out, this beautiful young lady was teaching most of her own classes; she was so far ahead of her peers and even some of her professors. She practically taught many of her own doctoral classes, and oh, her genius—Miss Firne created some of the toughest quantum algebraic equations in class. Even her professors fumbled, here and there, in working out the practice problems that she'd created for herself; and tidings of her genius diffused over the earth as a beautiful fragrance in the wind.

As per the Calcutta Times' Editorial, "Doctoral Mathematics Wiz Stuns Professors!"

An article carried in The *Pointe A Pitre Le Vent* read *"La Candidate mathematique Doctoral a Etourdi les professes* (doctoral candidate astounds mathematics professors). And on and on the global news machine went with the epic tale of her academic greatness The celebrated Firne girl had done it again, tossed into the spotlight all anew. And, this was coming off the heels of the Miss Australia Pageant in Tasmania.

Oh, how could she shun the spotlight? She was born in the gleaming castle of stardom; she was born in a mint as high as the Empire State Building! she had lived virtually everywhere and became a citizen wherever she good well felt like; all her parents were filthy rich; all she had ever known were luxury, fame, and celebrity. No one but she could block the whirling, impetuous stream of fame that carried her; oh, the handsome, charming motorcade of success that followed her at her every turn.

Courting the Dapper Knight of Disaster

See how she had bewitched all the people in her social world with her charm and beauty; and mid-way in her doctoral mathematics program, she was befriended by a young man. This dashing gentleman, Dr. Innerko Kbergnes, already had four doctorate degrees; and when he met her, he was pursuing another doctorate in agronomical science. His four other doctorates were in mathematics, atomic science, astrophysics, and political science: He had been President of the student body for one year. He had met Miss Firne on his way out of the university's main library: This swank, dapper bachelor was about thirty-one years old and was quite well known.

Yes, he was very popular on campus and was well known for his dash and swank. He was also quite well known for dating ladies high up in society's astral circles; moreover, many believed that Dr. Kbergnes was heading for world leadership. He was just that kind of guy who could wangle his way in and out of any situation. Kbergnes was as slippery as an eel and as cunning as a fox. Dr. Kbergnes was handsome; he had dash; and he knew his way very well around campus. But there was one problem with this gentleman: He did not keep his flames for long. Many had accused him of being a sex addict: he just seemed to be that way.

And he had impregnated not a few beauty queens on the Canberra Poly Campus; somehow or other, complicated DNA test results always seem to exonerate him. The issue of free-wheeling sex maniacs was a major problem on campus. The idea of handy, comely men; feeling like master studs; turned not a few women off. Dr. Kbergnes' sexual addiction had been widely suspected and discussed. Full of charm and dash, many had wondered why this cavalier was still a bachelor; there were scores of desirable women who had an eye for Dr. Kbergnes on campus. In fact, quite a few of those women had gone with him and had become rather sour; they complained that he was too pushy and wanted too much way too soon—they did not like his aggressive behavior and could not keep up with him!

They said that Dr. Kbergnes had major trust issues and was not worth their time. For whatever reason, destiny had arranged that very eventful meeting of the two: From the very beginning, he became quite enamored with the golden princess; and oh, from the outset; Miss Firne was rather circumspect and cautious with him. Though he had requested her phone number on that very evening of their meeting, she did not give it to him until a month later: She also resisted going out with him; Miss Firne did not go out with Dr. Kbergnes until three months after she had first met him. She played it as safely as she possibly could in order not to mess up.

And this was not before discussing the entire matter with her godfathers in the area; accordingly, Miss Firne had introduced him to Dr. Molluck and Dr. Zonakh. They looked him over like a federal official inspecting bolts at an automobile factory: Though they were impressed with his many distinguished credentials; they were very leery about his intentions—he just seemed like a loose bolt to them. And, caught in the storm of a dashing bachelor's guileful world and her career goals; Vanetta had prepared herself to deal with any subterfuge that he might dish out. She had fully prepared and armed herself for any curve balls that he might throw at her; he was a great inspiration to her, and encouraged her to go on in the world of academia.

As a brilliant and passionate astrophysicist, Dr. Kbergnes was a walking computer! He discussed at length with her sophisticated computer models about the universe: He had quite advanced knowledge about the abstract physics of the universe; And oh, how he dazzled Vanetta with his utter command of cosmography. Though their long nightly intellectual discourses jarred her academic program, Vanetta did not mind because Dr. Kbergnes seemed to be a science research center himself: He was a walking computer and a superb university library all in one. But oh, what a beautiful bouquet of deceit this dazzling bachelor displayed! Suddenly, Vanetta had risen to the top of school politics at Canberra Poly.

After all, this was the same lady who had spurned political involvement earlier; her undergraduate involvement in university politics was almost zero. The lady of dash shunned the limelight in favor of focused academic progress; but gradually, especially at the graduate level; things began to change. Miss Vanetta Firne had waxed extremely popular on campus, and it became almost impossible for her immense fortune to be kept a secret. The cat got out of the bag and ran all over Canberra Polytechnic University! At first, Vanetta tried to disguise her true identity and presented fake images; but the student body soon caught on that a billionaire was in their midst. And, as her association waxed stronger with the trig, dapper student body president; she began to open up more and more, but she never had forgotten the Anush fiasco. She envisioned that she needed at least two full years before she could trust him.

And she was more than up to the task of dealing soberly and sagely with Dr. Kbergnes. In the course of time, she had risen to the ranks of Student Treasurer of the university; Vanetta's closer association with Dr. Kbergnes had become so obvious to all, it was even rumored that an imminent betrothal was high up on the horizon. Many of the campus community waited with great anticipation for the announcement; and, to many students who were not cognizant of Dr. Kbergnes' sexual addition; the relationship seemed like a superb match—the kind that was made in heaven. The two key political leaders of the university's student body were highly visible; they were seen together quite often, and seemingly appeared romantically involved.

They had led the student body into several poignant, controversial debates: They had even brought Dr. Molluck and his colleagues to debate die-hard naturalists; and from the looks of things, everything went very well: The exchanges were cordial. The amicable environment seemed to be mending important fences in the world; but Dr. Molluck and Dr. Omou had always been leery about this swank, natty chap. They constantly told Vannetta, "Be watchful, watch him, and remember who we are."

The Spoon Restaurant Fiasco

The Anush emotional gash had been healed, but old sores could be easily irritated; and at long last, Vanetta begrudgingly agreed to a date with this man at an up-scale Canberra eatery. The meal was a delectable sea food dish, topped with strawberries and plum pudding; but, for some reason or other, Vanetta did most of the eating—and she was flurried. She quizzically wondered—and even asked him, "why so little of the meal? Isn't this a very delicious dinner, Innerko? Why aren't you eating? Is there something on your mind? What is it? Could you tell me what is on your mind? I am just getting to know you, and you are raising so many red flags already. I would like to get to know you and to know what kind of fellow you really are."

Antsy and perplexed, Dr. Kbergnes responded; "Well, you see, Miss Firne; I cannot get you off my mind: You have taken over my soul—I am obsessed with you. And I have arranged for us to get together at this fabulous five-star hotel; oh, my dear, I've selected the finest hotel in Yarralumla for us to spend the night; I have made all the necessary arrangements, and we'll have a wonderful time together. Miss Firne, I have just never met a woman like you in my life: You are so awesome! I roll and toss all night on my bed like the callous, toilful, roaring, rolling waves of the sea."

Cautious and fully alert, Miss Firne stayed clear of the fog in which he was trying to encapsulate her: She was about to get up and walk away from the disappointing situation. The sophisticated suburban middle-class audience was enjoying some Louis Armstrong Jazz; the colorful gathering, mainly evening students and professional people, was quite relaxed. For some reason or other, several dozen of the guests wore bright, picturesque beanies; these florid hats, brilliantly painted in the evening bloom, flared beneath the chandelier lights. The bubbly, delighted guests; basking in the soft music; sat there enjoying the delicious food. Miss Firne was about to get up and walk away from what she thought was a terrible mistake.

The guests themselves did notice some measure of uneasiness about her; thus, they glanced occasionally in her direction. at one point, it all came to a head; Dr. Kbergnes drew closer to Vanetta, lunged at her, and fiercely grabbed at her midsection; whereupon she screamed, "Rape, rape! Police, police, police; call the police! Emergency; right now, right now! At that point, the manager intervened and promptly called the police to address the matter; within minutes, a half of a dozen squad cars arrived and surrounded Spoon Restaurant. A brawny pack of police jumped out the squad cars with guns drawn and ready for action.

A young couple, jarred and aghast at the frightening spectacle, turned into the color of milk; trembling like a leaf in an evening flaw, their green and yellow beanies fell to the ground. The young lady, Oscilla Thompson, held on to her fiancé as her body jerked spasmodically; but by then, Dr. Kbergnes had already vanished from the scene; and the man hunt was on! Police scoured the entire area, looking for the suspect, but not a trace of him turned up; and from that very unfortunate night, not a whiff of Dr. Kbergnes was seen anywhere again for years.

Hard-nosed Yarralumla police searched every building in the area, going from door to door; but somehow or other, Dr. Kbergnes had eluded their circumspect combing of the area. They gradually increased the search area, interviewing curious people—all to no avail. And though the fierce, urgent manhunt had expanded beyond

Australia's borders; not a single trace of this illusive, slippery suspect ever turned up anywhere in the world! It was rumored that the elusive convict had several wives in the Pacific Samoa area; and, in the process of his quaint obsession with polygamy, he had mastered the art of disguise: Moreover, with umpteen wives, he had become a man estranged unto himself. He had seemingly developed an uncanny knack for disguise and believable subterfuge.

And though his distinguished credentials could be substantiated anywhere in the world, his life-long fudging with the truth had virtually turned him into a villainous vagabond. And oh, how many precious hearts he must have bruised and broken into pieces; rumor also had it that he might have flown to Wellington, New Zealand: He had frequently visited that country and ranted about its lush, verdant ambiance. According to his bosom buddy Dr. Ben Scott, an eminent paleontologist at Canberra Poly; Dr. Kbergnes had married into a very wealthy family in Wellington, New Zealand. His wife, Andronica, hailed from a very wealthy family who owned a third of New Zealand!

As pretty as a button, she was loved, favored, and treasured by the world community. And by the break of day, the fierce manhunt had expanded to the world's backwoods: Newspapers around the world carried the story but protected Vanetta's identity; all the newspapers referred to her as a high-profile academic mistress at Canberra Poly. And thus, Vanetta's godparents were spared the confusion and senseless anguish. The University, shackled in chains of shock, flew its flags at half-staff.

The Canberra Poly President, Dr. Victor LaMack, was so distraught; he simply swooned: Dr. LaMack was so overwhelmed by this troubling issue; he had a nervous breakdown. Oh, the shame and shock were so insufferable; many students wept bitterly. And who could stand in all that whirling, fainéant smoke of confusion on that campus? Every effort was made to protect Miss Firne's unstained identity, character, and sanity; and the *Canberra Poly Times* glossed it over as a high-profile academic mistress. Colorful bevies of students came up to Miss Firne to console her in her time of loss; and oh, how gracious she was—she promptly forgave Dr. Kbergnes for his betrayal: Her words were quite kind and gracious about this disreputable academic genius.

A Rushing Flood of Mud

In a very tearful student body meeting two days later, Vanetta addressed the audience: She informed the student body that the rumors of their betrothal were false. Miss Firne spoke quite highly of Dr. Kbergnes, but insisted that it was just an illusion; she emphasized the fact that the perceived relationship was merely a curious charade. She had become quite close to the student body president, and they liked each other: There was no discourse about betrothal and marriage in their three-month association; she accentuated that it was unfortunate that Dr. Kbergnes had gotten himself into such a mess. She maintained that, as far as she was concerned, he was a man of great dignity and class; Vanetta affirmed that they were close friends: Nothing had progressed beyond that.

Crisis teams of behavioral scientists were dispatched to console distraught students; and towards the end of the emergency student body assembly, the format changed. And oh, what a colorful meeting that was! Quite a few high-profile people were there. The university vice president, Dr. Booth, and a host of others were present at the meeting. The student body vice president, Miss Brown; the Canberra Police Chief, Mr. Akhan; and the city's crisis unit—they were all there in attendance at the visceral assembly. The New South Wales Governor and others had also graced the school with their presence. The colorful quest-and-answer session was quite revealing, to say the least!

Fourteen Canberra Poly students, seated on the front row, had much to say about things; and though much effort was made to save face for the very prestigious university, things began to go downhill very quickly for the administration of the school. All fourteen young ladies were doctoral candidates and spoke discreditably about him. Per this fine bevy of young ladies, they had expressed great concern about Dr. Kbergnes; and, for some arcane reason, their concerns were not heeded by university officials. They just kept on raving about how intelligent this dashing Dr. Kbergnes was: He was a swish, elegant Jamaican bachelor with four earned Ph.D.'s—who could ask for more!

But there was a dark side to this dapper, jaunty gentleman from the island of Jamaica: The women testified that they had been groped repeatedly by this spruce sex addict; they said that he was very smooth and slick in sliding his hand into their bosoms, and that he had a special knack for hypnotizing his victims into his shadowy world. Oh, what a special flair that he had for luring unsuspecting women into his slimy world of lust. You are talking to Dr. Kbergnes; and before you know it, he has his hand in your bosom. And to make matters worse, he would even try to slide his hand into other places as well!

An Intriguing Interview

Of the fourteen ladies who came forward and testified about Dr. Kbergnes' shortcomings; four of them had actually gone out with him, and what they had to say spoke volumes!

Mr. Akhan (Canberra's Police Chief,): Is there anyone here who knows Dr. Kbergnes personally? Is there anyone here who'd had close ties with him and would like to speak about their intimate relationship with him? If the intimate encounters were coerced or done in a spirit of unwillingness, please make this quite clear to the audience.

Suddenly, five ladies stood up and began making insulting remarks about Dr. Kbergnes—and they were furious! A few of the women began sobbing and weeping profusely, suggesting that they might have been traumatized as a result of their intimate encounter with Dr. Kbergnes.

Mr. Akhan: One at a time please—this is a police investigation, not a vengeful tirade! Molly Peters, would you step forth to the podium please and tell us about this man.

Miss Peters: Good afternoon, ladies and gentlemen; my heart is bleeding with regret. Oh, that depraved man who has served as our student body president—what a rotter he is! He just has his way of enticing you into his shadowy world of lustful passion: I went out with that dog two nights before that disgraceful incident at the Spoon Eatery; and oh, what a villainous man he is: He enticed me into having sex with him!

On hearing what the police chief had to say, Vannetta began weeping and sobbing bitterly: She had to be summarily removed from the auditorium.

Miss Peters: The next day—the very next day—I spoke with a friend; and she told me that he had done the same thing to her. It was like she could not say *no* to him.

Chief Akhan: And what is that friend's name—we may need to talk to her as well in order to get down to the bottom of all of this.

Miss Peters: Well, I cannot tell you that: She secretly confided the matter to me. Of course, she did not envision what happened at

Spoon Restaurant a few nights ago; she told me that she could not say no to him: His psychic powers were too strong. It was as if he had hypnotized her—she said that she was burning on the inside for him. Dr. Kbergnes is a trickster—he knows all the tricks in the book about women's secrets: It is as if he has some mystical gadget with buttons that he mysteriously pushes; and once he presses that certain button, he has zapped you—you are gone for hours!

Chief Akhan: Well, Miss Peters; would you consider Dr. Kbergnes' behavior to be illegal—would you say that what happened to you in that five-star restaurant was tantamount to rape—how do you view his behavior?

Miss Peters: Absolutely not! I think that Dr. Kbergnes works with high-level trickery. And I tell you; if you do not want to be intimate with him, please do not get close to him—oh, please, do not get close to this man if you do not have those feelings for him; my advice, especially to old-fashioned women, is to avoid getting close to Dr. Kbergnes: Do not go out with him: If you do, you most certainly will be violated, and it will not be his fault: It will be all yours!

Mr. Anzel, (Governor of New South Wales): Well, it seems like we have a felon on the loose around here—we must do everything in our power to protect our students from this woman eater. And he is somewhere out there: We must intensify the manhunt in order to capture this felon; we must bring this depraved human being to justice: We must capture him, dead or alive! We cannot allow this man to continue to abuse our students; this is absolutely absurd!

Miss Peters: But Mr. Anzel, why do you call him a felon—he has not committed any crime. This man just knows and understands women's secrets—that is a special skill. If a man plays a woman like Luis Armstrong plays the trumpet, how is that his fault? If you play a woman the way Jimmy Hendrix played the guitar, how is that a crime? You are simply good at what you do, and there is nothing wrong with that whatsoever!

Dr. Booth: (Vice President, Canberra Polytechnic University): But oh, Miss Peters, you are missing a very important point here: Dr. Kbergnes is a public servant. He is a very educated man with four doctorate degrees—he is a public risk! We cannot afford to have people like Dr. Kbergnes making a fool of our students, and that is exactly what he has been doing. Oh, what a shocking shame that is! This charlatan has literally turned our educational institution into a sprawling frat house: He has violated our doctoral candidates and tarnished our noble code of ethics; this sexually addicted man is a maniac and rank felon who belongs to the penitentiary. In my opinion, unless Dr. Kbergnes is hunted down and brought to justice; there would be a whole lot of us soon spending long hours in unemployment lines.

The governor sighed and nodded his head; he was manifestly shaken by the testimonies that were delivered by these women about this woman eater, wrecking the lives of dozens of young ladies who are being deceived and beguiled by this sociopath on our university campus—we absolutely cannot have this sort of thing in our community.

Chief Akhan: And Dr. Booth, what a shame that things have come to this: Oh, what a pity that so many women are slow to report these heinously abominable crimes tormenting our society.

Dr. Booth: This perverted felon must be hunted down and captured, dead or alive! This is a university matter; and must, by all means; be handled as such; accordingly, the order is issued now for Dr. Kbergnes' immediate capture and arrest. Since that odious incident, my office has been besieged by the Federal Ethics Board.

Chief Akhan: Yes, Dr. Booth; I certainly do concur with those sentiments; however, this is a criminal investigation, and all the witnesses must give their own testimonies. Thank you, Miss Peters. Your sentiments will be very circumspectly evaluated: Would Miss Arlene Gregg step up to the podium please? Tell us your take on the matter; we would very much like to know your perception of Canberra Poly's student body president.

Miss Gregg was a Ph.D. Candidate in Geomagnetism; she entered the auditorium, weeping and wailing because of the huge injustice that had been done to her by Dr. Kbergnes: Crisis team was asked to console her for a few minutes; She continued weeping and shaking her hands wildly for about four minutes, and then she regained control of herself and of her composure. Her equanimity returned, and she was ready to speak to the august body in attendance. They all, somewhat shaken up, sat on the edge of their seats, wanting to know what had transpired between Dr. Kbergnes and Miss Gregg— she seemed so shaken up and traumatized. The atmosphere in that auditorium that afternoon was electric and surreal.

Miss Gregg's Piercing Testimony

Miss Gregg: Good evening, ladies and gentlemen; I am extremely sorry about what has transpired here at Canberra Polytechnic University: It has truly shaken our school at its foundation. I have known Dr. Kbergnes for more than two years now; he is a very polished man: He is dapper, glamorous, funny, and intensely interesting; but he can be fresh at times.

Chief Akhan: Miss Gregg, can you give us some more details about his being fresh? What exactly do you mean by saying that Dr. Kbergnes can be fresh at times?

Miss Gregg: Well, I was just about to explain myself regarding that very idea; sometimes, Dr. Kbergnes would seem to become another person and do strange things.

Chief Akhan: What sort of strange things, Miss Gregg—what exactly do you mean by strange things? Are these things too private and personal to be discussed in a public setting of this nature? We are waiting on you: Speak to us, or we can arrange a closed-door meeting with you.

Miss Gregg: Well, I am getting into that mood again about which Molly spoke; it is as if he is right here with me now, touching on me and fondling my breasts. I never understood how this ingenious man could turn a woman on and off like that: Dr. Kbergnes has turned me on and off as if he were flipping a light switch! And oh, how wonderful it felt to be touched by him! He just puts you in that mood: A mood which seemed inescapable; and every time that mood came, he was right there—he was right there, and you did not know what to do with yourself. That was the scary part: It was as if he left you dangling between heaven and earth. Dr. Kbergnes works with magical powers that undrape the garment of women; he does it in the mind and then in the body. He must be cured of these strange talents.

Chief Akhan: Miss Gregg, have you been out with Dr. Kbergnes at any time in the past? Has he deceived you into going against your wishes to satisfy his own warped desires?

Miss Gregg: Yes, I did, Mr. Akhan, and I regretted that I had gotten so close to him: I felt as if I were violated by this roguish man; he took, at least, one of us out per night. At first, I too was duped by his dashing demeanor and incredible academic credentials; At first glance, he is an unbelievably polished conversationalist and debonair gentleman. He quotes whole chapters from celebrated science textbooks and recites encyclopedias; Dr. Kbergnes rattles off very abstract computer programs as if they were nursery rhymes: Mr. Akhan, I've never met a more brilliant man than Dr. Kbergnes in all my life. I swear that he is the most ingenious scientist anywhere around today—he is awesome: There is absolutely no one as brilliant as this very strange, mysterious, and sick man.

Mr. Akhan: And you are saying that Dr. Kbergnes tricked you into going out with him; it is incredibly difficult for any level-headed young lady to detect his psychopathic illness? Miss Gregg, why do you suppose that such a brilliant man like Dr. Kbergnes is a psychopath?

Miss Gregg: The world is a funny place, and things are hardly ever what they seem to be; Dr. Kbergnes has a whole university inside of him, but a part of him is in dire disrepair. As I said before, this fellow strikes you as an urbane, refined, well-bred gentleman; his conversation is full of life, and pizzazz, and enlightenment—he is so warm and juicy. Dr. Kbergnes is any woman's man, and it is hard not to be caught in the trap of his world: You meet this fine, pert gentleman; and he dazzles you with all this knowledge and flair. But before you know it; you are hooked on his strange talent, craving for his affection!

Chief Akhan: Miss Gregg, tell me: Are you saying that Dr. Kbergnes has mystical powers? Have you ever felt tricked or hypnotized while you were in his presence.

Miss Gregg: Yes, Mr. Akhan: His presence is, itself, a hypnotic spell that binds you; he is literally able to take you far into physical intimacy without ever touching you. He has some obscure ability to tap into a woman's deepest thoughts of physical love: This ingenious man literally hacked into the computer of my deepest sexual fantasies. That is exactly what he has done to us: He met us, charmed us, and deceived dozens of us! We are like pretty birds in his romantic cage;

we have virtually become his sex slaves. I have literally gotten up at night and drove all the way on the other side of town to his house: I needed his hypnotic love and pizzazzy sex play that bad: He is a well-equipped stud with grand sexual tools that any woman, who truly enjoys sex, would crave and relish,

Chief Akhan: Oh, most distinguished governor, vice precedent, and so many others here today; I've been working in law enforcement for years—almost twenty-five years now; and I've never heard anything as disgusting, absurd, obscure, and downright weird as this! People, with this kind of expertise, must be identified, quarantined, and thoroughly retrained; they need to be removed from society, lest they spread their virulent germs to others. Can you imagine, oh Mr. Governor, the problem that we would have on our hand: Mr. President, can you fathom the trouble we would have if people like these are let loose in our beloved land of Australia? These new cases warrant brand new laws on the books to deal with these new tricksters. He is not normal; he's a child of Lucifer, and he is deadly dangerous: We can't afford to have people like him, loose on the streets.

It was a jarring moment; when the governor and the university's vice president realized what was going on; they shook their heads in stark shame and shock. It was a very unsettling and sobering environment; the testimonies were so surreal and dream-like, many pinched themselves to see if what they were witnessing was real.

Miss Gregg: Mr. Akhan, I do not know what to say: Dr. Kbergnes is a very sick man and have messed up a lot of us women.

Chief Akhan: In your opinion, Miss Gregg, do you view Dr. Kbergnes as a felon, or an incredibly talented man who understands the psychology of women and their hot spots?

Miss Gregg: Yes, he is a criminal because he has mystical powers that can rob a woman of the most valuable asset in her life—he steals a woman's right to say *no* to him. He is a criminal: He should be locked up in prison and the keys pelted far out into the sea. I will never be the same again: I cannot get this man out of my mind—it's nuts! He has turned me into a sex slave—his sex slave; this man is a power broker of evil and darkness: He is dangerous and should be removed from the sprawling mall of human society.

Chief Akhan: Thank you, thank you, Miss Gregg; you've helped us considerably: We shall thoroughly analyze all the testimonies that we've gathered here today. And could Miss Victoria Paulina Saunders come to the podium to give your testimony of what happened to you in Dr. Kbergnes' presence?

CHAPTER 8

THE REMAINDER OF THE POLICE INTERVIEW

It is pretty difficult to wrap one's mind around behaviors such as that displayed by Dr. Kbergnes on that Canberra university; after all, no academic behaves in such an odious and shabby manner. Academics are well-cultured people who do not stoop to the level of raping female college students through hypnosis and getting them to participate in behaviors that are well beyond their will. Moreover, many of these young ladies have been wheedled and wangled into on-campus prostitution; and the question that one must ask about this matter is this: How do these clearly out-of-line activities get started on university campuses, who pulls the strings behind the scenes, and who are usually involved? Obviously, it is difficult to start a prostitution ring on campus below the radar of the authorities involved—isn't it?

How does one orchestrate such a massive smut shop on a university campus without the president's or vice-president of academic affairs' awareness? Typically, what happens is that the university was never an institution of higher learning; rather, it was always a very sophisticated brothel, staffed by a flagitious secret system, and when some of the top world universities are routinely implicated in these types of behaviors, you know that the world is not what you think it is. Do you mean to tell me that the world is an illusion? No, I do not mean to tell you that the world is an illusion; the world has already told you that it is an illusion—many female students are being raped by their professors, right on campus! How clearer do you want this truth to be communicated?

Whatever might be the case, these behaviors are routinely practiced on university campuses, around the world; and, as will be seen a little further on, many college professors use their position to a great advantage; turning their female students into their second and third wives and sex toys. Moreover, many even turn their students into prostitutes, working right there, on campus, in dashing call girl rings. It is against this backdrop that criminal investigation was opened at that Australian polytechnic university; and oh, the number of publishing professors whose hands were caught in the cooky jar was absolutely amazing.

Do you mean to tell me that publishing professors participate in stuff like this—oh my: What a time! What this reflects are the surprising facts about human nature; people are not what you often think they are; but they wear the false human perception and understanding of reality to their maximum advantage, leaving society in a fog. They wear the mask and deceive the shallow people around them; therefore, it was in view of these facts that they continued the police investigation at that Australian university, some years ago. And oh, my; what an intriguing inquiry that it turned out to be!

Miss Saunders' Riveting Testimony

Miss Saunders (Doctoral Candidate, Psychiatry): I am not afraid of anyone; I've known Dr. Kbergnes for ten years now: He is flat out brilliant and smooth! I've loved and admired this fine gentleman from Kingston, Jamaica; his father was a Norwegian man who migrated to Jamaica after World War ll. He had numerous wives, both in Norway and Jamaica: He met them all young virgins; broke them into adult life, so to speak; and then abandoned them. From what I've gathered, he has a weakness: He can't stay with a woman any longer than a month and a half.

Mr. Akhan: Miss Saunders, you seem to have had an advanced relationship with him: How long have you been intimate with Dr. Kbergnes: What has it been like with him?

Miss Saunders: Mr. Akhan, let me tell the story: I will certainly get to that part of it. Zhranh must have been married about nine times; Innerko's mother, Elizabeth, was his last wife; she was a Jamaican woman of a rubicund complexion and very fair. She was a very beautiful lady and ran from Zhranh for more than three years before she finally gave in to him. And so, Innerko has had sex addiction problems all his life. I thought that he was a little strange, but he is extremely brilliant and arresting in stature; and without beating around the bushes with you and giving you a reason to ask me any more questions; I have been one of Innerko's lovers for the past two and a half years now.

Chief Akhan: Miss Saunders, did he ever bring any of his lovers to your place of residence? Has Dr. Kbergnes ever disrespected you with any of his many dozens of lovers—has he ever made you feel disrespected in any way?

Miss Saunders: No, not exactly; but he constantly mentioned new lady friends to me. At least, two new names were mentioned to me every week—and I simply got tired of it: I knew about the unnamed, high-profile academic mistress before most of you; he spoke very highly of her to me and said that he was breaking her in, so to speak. It has been difficult for me to break away from this man; and, in my view, he is a felon. He hypnotizes women, controls their thinking, uses them as if they were napkins, and then tosses them into the trash: Dr. Kbergnes has greatly harmed my life and has had me in a cage all these years. I don't know what he has done to me, but I cannot seem to leave him. It is as if he has me on a leash; I can only go so far before I go running back to him again.

Chief Akhan: Miss Saunders, do you consider Dr. Kbergnes a sour menace to society? How do you view this bizarre human being—how does he strike you?

Miss Saunders: Most definitely yes—oh, yes, he is, in the strongest sense of the word; a criminal. My, my! I want to break free from Dr. Kbergnes and his vulpine hypnotic machine of vain, empty sex addiction; but I can't seem to do so. Yes, Mr. Akhan; I feel as if I have been crassly violated by this weird, deceitful man: Other men come and ask me out all the time, but it is as if I cannot say yes to them. It is as if something has been barring and confusing my mind; and sometimes, it seems as if I'm losing my mind. I've always wanted to leave Dr. Kbergnes, but I kept holding on—he has me on a string! As I said before, it is as if I were on a leash; I kept holding on, and going back to, him; hoping that he would finally change; but he has not done so. Somehow or other, the change never came.

Chief Akhan: And why is it that he could not hypnotize this mysterious, high-profile lady? Why was he able to abuse some of the women and not the others who were around him—and even went out with him. It is rather noteworthy that he only succeeded in hypnotizing some of the women and not all with whom he went out on dates.

Miss Saunders: Well, he spoke quite highly of this high-profile lady: he prattled much about this lady's incredible wealth and power: He knew better than to try to mess with her intimate life. Dr. Kbergnes understood the cost of doing that; he'd be dead tomorrow—and he knew it! He knew her father and the circumstances around her life. This beautiful woman has a very wide social circle and a strong cosmopolitan disposition: She is a very beautiful woman with powerful connections and hitmen all over the world—and they are told to shoot at the drop of a hat and ask questions afterwards. In fact, he said to me that their association was very closely watched by special people—a thousand private eyes have been closely monitoring his every move! He told me that he was scared to play around with this high-profile lady.

Chief Akhan: And why do you suppose that this relationship was so closely monitored? Why do her parents pay so much attention to a grown lady's personal details—isn't this the age of women's liberation? What makes her so unique and special?

Miss Saunders: Well, you see; this lady belongs to the world's astral circles: She hails from world scientific aristocratic society's very top—her private eyes are everywhere! And any wrong turn on Dr. Kbergnes' part would mean the end of things for him in this world, so he knew better than to work his dirty tricks on this most graceful lady. They were watching him day and night for any wrong move on his part—they waited patiently for that iconic wrong turn on his part: He knew that if he did to her what he had done to me, he would be history—and he knew it! Thus, if he ever tries anything with this lady; he will have to run and hide for the rest of his life.

Chief Akhan: Miss Saunders, what did he do to you? Please share that with us. This is an adult audience, and I would like you to be as forthright with us as possible. We are all grown people here, trying to get into the mind of this strange psychopath.

Miss Sanders: He raped me in my dorm room and tossed my underclothes into the trash; I felt like nothing and wept for weeks. This man is a monster—a psychopath who has absolutely no regard for a woman's privacy: He violated me.

Mr. Achan: Now, tell me, Miss Saunders; if Dr. Kbergnes has you on a leash, as you've so clearly spoken; what are you doing now that he's no longer around? Are you still turning the fellers down who come up to you and ask you out?

Miss Saunders: Well, you see; I don't know that he has vanished; I would lay a wager with you that Dr. Kbergnes is still in town: The Authorities just don't know where he is—I don't know where he is. But I promise you one thing: the slightest hint I get about his whereabouts, I will inform the Authorities immediately.

Chief Akhan: Thank you, Miss Sanders; you have well-spoken on the matter. Miss Angie Baker, could you tell us about Dr. Kbergnes and his sorcerous talents?

Angie Baker's Word on the Matter

Miss Angie Baker (Doctoral Candidate, Mathematics): I thought that it was just me—I thought that I was a whore who had no morals whatsoever; but after what I have heard here today, I know that I am a lady who deserves a better life: Dr. Kbergnes did the same thing to me that he did to Miss Saunders: It is hard to discuss.

Miss Baker drew a napkin from her Hilde Palladino bag and wiped the tears from her eyes. It was so surreal and gripping, seeing a grown woman weeping in a public setting.

Chief Akhan: And Miss Baker, did you have any inkling about his hypnotic abilities—had you sensed that this man might have been a social liability, prior to getting close to him? There must have been some red flags along the way—weren't there?

Miss Baker: There were susurrations about Dr. Kbergnes' bizarre sexual addiction: The whisperings about his erotic idiosyncrasies were quite plentiful on Campus. But you know, you just cannot believe everything that you hear—and I didn't. This very heinous psychopath wandered into my life and flat out turned it upside-down; and after two abortions and one miscarriage, I feel entirely lost in the smoke of his tricks. I feel like old clothes; this man has taken away from me my very virtue—I was a virgin when I met him; I didn't know anything about men and sex: He broke me in and walked away. Many a night, I would crave him and drive twenty miles to his house to get what he had.

Chief. Akhan: Well, Miss Baker; it appears as if you were very deeply involved with him: Were you, at any time, engaged to be married to Dr. Kbergnes—did things ever get that far? How did he get that far with you: Why did you let him use you up like that?

Miss Baker: Yes, Mr. Akhan; Dr. Kbergnes once gave me a ring as a token of our betrothal: According to several of my girlfriends, he has left a litter of puppies at Canberra Poly: I feel violated by this very depraved man who has made a fool out of so many of us. He has some strange talent that makes women desire him sexually; and, in most cases, the women were the ones suggesting and initiating the intimacy with him.

The distinguished city council members blushed and wiped away tears from their eyes; they were shocked at the level of inroad that this horrible man had made into the lives of the innocent, unsuspecting young women who were genuinely looking for a male partner, and this monstrosity took advantage of them.

Chief Akhan: Do you know if he had given rings to any other of his many lovers— Are you aware of any more betrothals between Dr. Kbergnes and any other of his lovers?

Miss Baker: No, Chief Akhan; but I am aware of the absolute wreckage that he has left behind and of the destruction that he caused dozens of women; he had slammed the lives of hundreds of women, impregnating them and not looking back. Right off the bat, I can rattle off the names of two dozen women whom this nasty rat has victimized and abused; all those women have, at least, one child for Dr. Kbergnes.

Chief Akhan: And what might that absolute and damnable wreckage that this man has left behind be? Can you give us some names of women whom he has impregnated so that we can interview them after this press conference is over? It doesn't have to be in this setting; we can do that afterwards.

.

Miss Baker: Because of this vile and evil man, many students have had to drop out of school: Impregnated by this mindless beast, many of my friends now have the added burden of a child which they have to raise alone. Canberra Poly is filled with women who have been violated, not only by Dr. Kbergnes; but by a host of professors here and at the schools from which they transferred: This irresponsible type of behavior is a rank disgrace in the scientific community. Just as how many naturalists have taken upon themselves to define reality for all of us: Many—oh, so many—have taken upon themselves to make sluts out of so many of us; these so-called perverted scientists have turned many of us into high-class hookers who have abandoned life's purer moral taste.

Dr. Booth: So, Miss Baker, are you saying that there are call girl rings on this campus—on this campus, Miss Baker? Am I hearing you correctly—professors have turned our school into a high-class brothel. This is absolutely incredible!

Miss Baker: Why do you think Dr. Kbergnes was drawn to this academic institution, in the first place? These verminous perverts have redefined the classroom as a herd of harlots and molls—and I'm as mad as hell.

Dr. Booth, swollen like an inflated balloon, exploded like a bomb: "Not at this school! we will prosecute them, send them behind bars, and throw the key away."

Miss Baker: And should I mention the number of active frat houses and call girl rings on this campus, the Australian Government would shut this place down—and his has been so for years! It didn't just start today. There are plenty of loose women, attending this university, who would freely work for crooked, corrupt professors, who'd give them an A at the end of the semester—all they have to do is to work for them as prostitutes. On campus prostitution is alive and well here at Canberra Polytechnic University. If some women would have sex with dogs, you know they would freely sell their bodies for grade and money; and if you think that I'm lying, just open an investigation on prostitution on campus here: You'd be shocked at what you'd find, Dr. Booth. I've wanted something like this to happen here for quite some time."

Dr. Booth: The Australian Government will not be shutting down this blessed campus; but I tell you this: Many a rogue professor on this campus will soon be looking for another job: If they think that this revered university campus is a whorehouse, they have something coming, and it's a terrible disappointment.

Miss Baker: Mr. Vice President, they surely have it coming because they view it that way; so many professors on this campus regard it as a rank whorehouse—their whorehouse. Many professors lure female students into their sex traps in exchange for academic favors; I do not need those kinds of favors: I have performed very well in all my classes, but many of my friends have gone the way of the dogs and have belittled themselves. The number of female students who are prostitutes is absolutely shocking; morality has been thrown into the trash, not only here at Canberra Poly but all around the world. Prostitution has become extremely demotic and fashionable in our society; especially since the Great Recession of 2007.

Chief Akhan: Do you have specific names of offenders and students willing to come forward? Can you round up a few of these students who would be willing to testify against these villains?

Miss Baker: That practice is so commonplace around here, that should not be difficult. I was raped by Dr. Kbergnes and have become his sex slave. Oh, what a piteous case—a male-dominated world of scientists, flooded with perverts who distort the truth; yea, they distort the truth and teach evolution and naturalism in order to dodge moral accountability. These are the main culprits raping students on school grounds today.

Chief Akhan: What do you mean by saying that professors have turned many girls into sluts? Are you saying that they have a program that breaks students into the life of whoredom here on campus? How can naturalistic professors turn female college students into prostitutes against their will?

Miss Baker: They are amoralists and moral relativists: They believe that morals are irrelevant; thus, turning a student into their sex slave is an amoral issue. It merely serves their purpose. It's neither right nor wrong: Given the context in which it occurs, it's the pragmatic thing to do. And yes, I vehemently believe that Dr. Kbergnes should be incarcerated for life; and not only him, but all those amoral secularists who teach evolution and naturalism. My friend Phyllis Rowe told me that her chemistry professor advised her to burn her Bible—he said that it's a bunch of lies and well out of step with contemporary evolutionary thought. The next day, he raped her in his office, and she aborted the pregnancy that resulted from the forced intimacy.

Dr. Booth: Can you give me that chemistry instructor's name who told your friend that and did that naughty thing to her? He will not be working on this revered academic campus for long: I can tell you that.

Miss. Baker: My friend Helen Benpaul knows him; I'll have her call you tomorrow. Dr. Booth, that same professor made all kinds of overtures at my dear friend Helen; and before she knew it; he had violated her; forcing her to become his call girl. This is the sort of thing about which I am talking, Mr. Akhan: This must be prosecuted.

The governor, shaken by the testimonies, shook his head more than a dozen times in utter amazement; he could not believe that society had deteriorated to that extent; he was shocked and threatened to turn the campus upside-down, looking for these sex offenders.

Chief Akhan: Oh, Miss Baker, are you suggesting a prostitution probe for your school? Do you recommend that my office conduct a prostitution investigation at Canberra Poly?

After the truth about society's moral wash away had sunken into Dr. Booth's system, he just could not take it anymore and was removed from the Graham McKenzie Auditorium, with chest pains. Several other dignitaries were also quite physically and emotionally shaken; they were stunned at what was actually happening on campus.

Miss Baker: Sir, I am recommending that prostitution probes be done at all universities: The problem of prostitution frat houses on university campuses in our society is stark; and I believe that it has to do with our glib acceptance of naturalism as standard truth. Those omniscient professors who peddle evolution do not believe in right and wrong—they do not believe that frat houses and prostitution at the university level are wrong.

Chief Akhan: Miss Baker, this is a formal police investigation; can you back up your words? You are saying that professors on this campus have active call girl rings operating here? It sounds like a fairy tale to me.

Miss Baker: Mr. Akhan, I can back up whatever I've said and implicate dozens of people; they have no regard for moral principles— they simply see others as their needs' fulfillment. In their tortuous understanding of the world, that is merely something that people do; these are the axe-grinding social engineers who run this current global age of vanity. They are the odious villains who've made call girls out of so many of us; and they are our very clients: They come to our homes, use our bodies, and walk away; yea, they wipe their mouths like a dog and merely walk away as if nothing happened. And many of us are trapped in this vicious cycle, unable to escape because we live in it: These are the flagitious scoundrels who threw the Bible away to sooth their conscience; and now that the cat is out of the bag, we might as well let it all hang out here today!

Chief Akhan: But Miss Baker, don't you think that a system-wide probe is over the top? After all, this is a local matter—isn't it?

Miss Baker: Mr. Akhan, we have messed around and winked at evil far too long—if it were in my power, I would conduct a sweeping prostitution probe of all universities in Australia. At least, we must take drastic measures to deracinate the poisonous weed of prostitution here on our campus: We must not allow this venomous vine to continue spreading. We cannot ignore it anymore; we must stop it dead in its tracks—and we must do it now! I implore you, oh, Mr.

Chief of Police, to open up an investigation of call girl rings here; you'd be shocked at what your inquiry would reveal about dorm life here on campus! I know that we all have this Miss Goodie Two Shoes mentality; with our, "No, that can't be happening here." Well, I tell you; it is happening here and just about everywhere else. This is the age in which authority figures are spanked for treating wrong. When the stuff is thrown at the doorsteps, they act as if they've been ever on it.

Chief Akhan: Thank you, Miss Baker; your testimony was insightful and provocative—oh, provocative indeed. We shall look into this matter as soon as possible. And finally, Miss Eskarlen Mooney, tell us what you know about Dr. Kbergnes and about prostitution on campus here at Canberra Polly.

Miss Mooney's Shocking Testimony

Miss Mooney: (Doctoral Candidate, Atomic Science): Good afternoon, ladies and gentlemen; oh, dear people, it is an honor to be here among you to share regarding this great matter. Dr. Kbergnes has been my dear friend: I like him very much, but I've, not at all, been his lover: I've kept myself pure and have refrained from being sucked into his great vacuum of lust. I've spoken to more than forty women who've been molested by this guileful, odious man: Those women have rushed into burning buildings with him, and they've been screwed. He has taken advantage of them, and many of them were impregnated; trapped and lost in the smoke of his hypnotic machine.

Chief Akhan: Miss Mooney, you are quite an extraordinary lady: how was this possible? How, on earth, were you able to escape being physically intimate with this great charmer. From the looks of things, it appears as if he has charmed more than five hundred women!

Miss Mooney: Mr. Akhan, women were created for men; they have a natural weakness; that irrepressible tug is always there: Wise women recognize it and act accordingly. Dr. Kbergnes is quite a clever man with special talents for enticing young women: He has tried his stuff on me; but every time, I would kick his shin and slap his face; and he would stop, smile, and leave me alone. In this regard, he is not at all a felon. Some women are too *da gone* double minded, silly, and weak; and you can't be that way around a man like Dr. Kbergnes: He is a master at trapping women and working on their minds.

Mr. Akhan: Well, you are quite a capable and extraordinary woman; you've won a trophy: Such an exploit is equivalent to winning a trophy: You've excelled in quite a rapacious jungle, replete with wild animals.

Miss Mooney: He tried some of the same tactics on this high-profile lover, mentioned earlier. The Spoon Restaurant incident the other night illustrates very vividly what I am saying: His high-profile academic mistress did not allow herself to be lured into his hellish sex trap; she hollered, and screamed, and bawled vehemently; "Rape, rape; police, police, police! Emergency, emergency now!" That lady did not allow herself to be sucked into the slimy marsh of his fancy hotel sex trap: She was prepared, saw it coming, pulled her gun, and zapped him dead; he failed with her.

Mr. Akhan: Well, Miss Mooney, I must say that you are quite an extraordinary human being; your courage, pluck, mettle, and sense of self-restraint are beyond anything that I've seen or heard of before.

Miss Mooney: Thanks for the compliment, but it is just a matter of making up your mind; yes, it is just a matter of deciding and purposing in your heart not to be anyone's sex slave. Those who've wandered into the picturesque smokestack of his life have truly lost their way, and they deserved every imaginable scar that they got in his shoddy tool shop of lust. I have kept my distance from this dangerous human being, and it has paid off for me big time; I avoided being alone with him—period: I just could not afford that kind of risk and ruin. Oh, the embarrassment and stolen pride of being used and screwed by the devil was too much; Dr. Kbergnes is a very dangerous man whom every woman should avoid. I understand that he has notebooks of all his conquests and is quite a braggart; A senior professors, close to the matter, is fully aware of Dr. Kbergnes' exploitative feats. In addition, he himself has managed two call-girl rings right here on campus.

A Felon's Evasion of Arrest

And oh, what a student body assembly that that emergency gathering turned out to be! Several arrests were made, and many school officials were sacked or shuffled around; the call girl rings on the campus were smashed to pieces, and several professors were jailed. A global manhunt for Dr. Kbergnes turned up cold, and the story slowly faded away; and so, Dr. Kbergnes vanished from the view of the Canberra University Campus. Rumors swirled around of an attempted rape against a high roller on or near campus. The Canberra Gossip Mill went into high gear, filling the air with the smoke of intrigue: Some said one thing; others said another: no one knew exactly what had happened. Grapevine sources poured even more swirling smoke in the air: They claimed that Yvette La Mack, the president's daughter, was the victim in the case.

Others confidently affirmed that the rape was committed against Giggly Foster; this young lady, daughter of the South African President, was politically active. She was a prominent member of the student body and served as treasurer for some time.

According to sources close to the story, one unidentified eyewitness came forward; yes, a gentleman came forward and spoke to the Press on condition of anonymity. This gentleman was at Spoon Restaurant on that momentous evening of the assault. This university professor affirmed thatthere was never any attempted rape that evening; according to him, Spoon Restaurant was jammed with twilight romanticists. Everyone was eating, drinking, and having a good time; enjoying some Luis Armstrong Jazz. He observed that a romantic couple, wearing purple beanies, had gotten somewhat tipsy; they got carried away with the Chardonnay Wine and smooth Luis Armstrong Jazz.

He noticed that they began engaging in—well—some inappropriate behavior. And when the unidentified male counterpart brushed his hands against his lover's breasts, she jumped and screamed: "Love me more: Cuddle and caress me forever—I love it;" Whereupon the Spoon Restaurant supervisor, Jack Vaugn, got quite rattled! He jumped to his feet, sprang to the phone, and called the police; Within five minutes, the Canberra Swat Team converged on Spoon Restaurant.

They swarmed into the elegant eatery with guns drawn, fully ready for action; but by then, the two lovers had vanished into thin air as if they were phantoms. Somehow or other, they got separated; and the young lady broke off the relationship. It is alleged that she connected with another lover. The standard crime-reporting procedures were clearly followed that evening. Though a rigorous police report was made, and many students had come forward with their own stories and testimonies; none of the Spoon Restaurant clients wanted to get sullied in the slimy case.

And for that reason, all legal proceedings were dropped in the wake of the foggy details; accordingly, Dr. Kbergnes got away scot-free; but he remained at large for some time. It was alleged that insiders in the Canberra Police Division had close ties with this felon. The mathematical genius had done statistical analysis for that police department; and, as the story goes; department insiders were sympathetic towards Dr. Kbergnes. They expressed strong empathy for him and chose to look the other way in the case; rumors also swirled around Canberra Poly that Dr. Kbergnes was counseling officers, and that many of them had learned numerous occult tricks from the master himself.

It is alleged that he had taught them tricks about how to take pretty women down; criminological reports did confirm Dr. Kbergnes' involvement with that police division. His beloved students, presumably, owed him quite a debt for his priceless tutelage. With Vannetta away from the scene and all legal charges dropped against Dr. Kbergnes; within a few years of her graduation, the man of tricks was smack back on campus! The dapper, natty Dr. Kbergnes was back on campus, virtually running the show again. How could all this have happened? He had well trained the local police division; he taught many top-ranking officers how to steal the minds of beautiful women.

And what man is there who does not have a dream love symbol—a sexual fantasy? A sex symbol with whom he would like to have a fling or two for a good while. show me a man who does not have a dream sex symbol he would do anything to have—show me such a man, and I'll show you a man still in his mother's womb. Dr. Kbergnes had the police department so well trained, it owed him allegiance; its high-ranking officials gave him so much deference, it was as if they were his children! Whatever the case might have been, Dr. Kbergnes evaded arrest and triumphed; the genius of this evil man, like a canopy of fortune, thwarted some steep jail time and being put away from society for a good while.

A High-Profile Politician in the Making

And yes, the vulpine man of dark wisdom evaded at least twenty years in prison; however, within a few years; startling changes began to appear in Dr. Kbergnes' life. The swish thirty-five-year-old genius abruptly dropped out of academia: enamored with power and politics, he resigned his professorship and headed for the road. He abdicated his tenured position at the Edinburgh Polytechnic University in England; he had been working a busy schedule, trotting around the globe and giving lectures. He brusquely resigned his professorship but continued giving speeches and lectures; most of his speeches were at graduation commencement ceremonies around the world.

But before all that had transpired, sweeping moral reforms had transformed university life. Though the Spoon incident had become stale and had already begun to fade; its lingering effects had strong moral and economic implications for university campuses, but the moral clean-up was too little and too late for Dr. Samuelson and a few others. A proselytizing probe was conducted at World University in Melbourne, Australia; the probe revealed stark irregularities and violations of the new proselytizing law. Government watchdog officials ransacked professors' offices and found a gold mine; whereupon Dr. Samuelson, president of that academic institution, was deposed!

This big wig was demoted, and within weeks, sent to head a Caribbean high school; he was brashly sent to run the Kingstown Boys' High School in St. Vincent. The swift, stiff, and poignant disciplinary action caught news headlines around the world; it also caught the eyes of other university presidents who had gotten lax about the law. Many of these administrative officials received telephone calls that shattered their worlds; and oh, what poignant, gut-wrenching telephone calls those were for so many of them! But despite all these maddening changes, the Spoon incident was still fresh on campus; however, the real story was never told: It was stuffed in the colorful trash bin of illusion.

Vanetta's identity was concealed, and the real story was glossed over as merely another woman who was raped at Spoon Restaurant; Canberra Polytechnic University's dirty laundry was finally exposed and cleansed. And what titanic efforts that that institution had made to absolve itself from guilt—yea, to clear itself from the guilt and stain of corruption and dirty school politics! The fact is that Dr. Kbergnes was working at Canberra Poly, and that put the wrong spin on things.

Fixing Things and Starting Over

The entire faculty was cleansed of rogue frat-house scholars and call girl rings: The whole campus was even repainted and festooned with very costly decorations. Vanetta completed her doctoral program in quantum algebra and was now ready to move on. And oh, the yawning chasm that her departure excavated at that institution! As for the tenure-track position offered to her earlier, it was declined on the grounds of trust. Just around that time, about two months later, Vanetta's graduation was executed; and the soilure of the Canberra Polytechnic University's reputation had begun to fade.

New, stringent ethical rules were introduced to extirpate the weeds of corruption; and Canberra Polytechnic University blazed with fresh and bright glory and pomp. Dr. LaMack, a shrewd politician, executed a magnificent make-over of the school. New brains and think tanks were brought in from the uttermost reaches of the earth; some of the finest mathematicians and physicists were hired by the troubled university. They brought with them a wealth of knowledge and experience to the institution; they were all given rigorous sensitivity training regarding the new proselytizing law, and tidings of the Canberra Polytechnic University's new image went around the world.

Finally, the stain of the Spoon Restaurant attempted rape case began to wilt and fade. and even Dr. Amboozle, the current Chairman of the

Federated Earth, was brought in; he was invited to speak at Vanetta's graduation ceremony two months later. And the spiffy, trig statesman gave a stirring graduation commencement speech. His moving, impassioned speech was archived at great universities around the world:

Dr. Amboozle: It is my heart's profound desire that all the citizens of our great federal nation of the Earth succeed. Oh, gladsome, jolly children of greatness; you are the lusty fruits of the Earth: Our nation, the beautiful Federation of the Earth, is your kingdom and joy. We have consolidated all the world's kingdoms and powers into one geopolitical block; and today, the great Federation of all the Earth's principalities is a reality. The Federal State of the Earth is your nation: It is my nation; it is our nation. We have all captured the ultimate trophy of world government—and we are proud.

Our government of the Earth is a divine decree: We are the golden children of the Earth. And now that we have attained what many formerly viewed as a fairy tale; we must subdue the Earth and stock it with golden gardens replete with fruits; and you, oh joyous children of the future, are the gems and pearls of the Earth. The future eagerly awaits your brash enthusiasm and rugged determination; your courageous defiance of the impossible is the spark of a daring and most wonderful future: Oh, revered, ambitious children of the Earth, rise and run to the numerous opportunities that currently stare you in the face; embrace the present and race into the sprawling heavens of the future.

You are the golden sparks of the future. Go; light the dazzling, dynamic world of your future with the flame of zest and genius: You are young; you are strong; you are healthy; and your arms are as strong as steel! You are the stalwart, majestic pillars of tomorrow's towering skyscrapers: You are the husky, burly giants of your own destiny; flush with greatness and creativity. Fill your hearts with the burning fire of enthusiasm, determination, and greatness: Go forth, conquer, and subdue the earth and the future that belongs to you!

O what a dazzling, Periclean commencement address that was from Dr. Amboozle! It was laconic, powerful, tantalizing, and as sweet as sweet as honey: Dr. Amboozle's speech was that juicy, nectarous, and succulent fruit of promise. The speech was that superb ally to the overall moral make-over of the eminent academic institution. Dr. Amboozle's presence at this university sent a clear, no-nonsense message to all: Canberra Polytechnic University was a brand-new school; royalty was at its highest level; however, all that was not enough to persuade Vanetta to acceptthe prestigious tenure-track university professorship offered to her earlier.

It was not enough to entice her to accept the tenured mathematics professor position; she had had enough of Canberra Poly and was poised and ready to move on with her life. Dr. Molluck called Dr. LaMack and thanked him for all his graciousness and generosity; however; he insisted that, due to issues of trust at the school, they had their doubts. Afterwards, Vanetta herself contacted Dr. LaMack and thanked him for all his kindness; she explained to him that she wanted to do a second doctorate in a related field. She told him that Canberra Polytechnic University was a warm and superb institution; but because of the Spoon stain with Dr. Kbergnes and fresh interest in astrophysics; it would be to her advantage to move on to a crisp, fresh environment with new life.

Vanetta told Dr. LaMack that she craved a novel ambiance, free from the viscous stain of the past and that World University in Jerusalem had the best astrophysics program in the world. She wished him all the best and expressed great remorse for the Spoon incident; they both cried on the phone and wished each other great success. And so ended Vanetta's adventurous academic journey in the land down under! The sticky stain that the Spoon incident left dogged that academic institution for years. Dr. Kbergnes had disappeared into the murky foam of obscurity and oblivion, but politics and public life for this most ingenious scholar were far from over! And in the ripe season of things, Dr. Kbergnes was smack back there again.

And within a short time, this ingenious man was running the student body at that university again! And though suspicious people raised concerns about his presence on campus, Dr. Kbergnes' exquisite engineering and manipulation of things quieted the many understandably suspicious and concerned voices. In this quaint world of secrecy and falsehood, these moral stunts and miracles happen virtually every day: The dashing man of gab and swank was right back where he was years earlier; and, of course, he had undergone much change: He was quite a different chap.

His excellent criminological regression models were invaluable to that lovely city; he worked arduously for the Canberra Police Department in reducing crime in that city; and by the time Dr. Kbergnes had left Canberra, he was hailed a civic hero! This very clever mathematician thrilled the city and left its denizens spellbound; he was looked upon with great respect and as a man of intellectual genius and community vision. He'd done much for that police department and was viewed as a wonderful community person; his criminological models had helped the Canberra Police Department to solve some pretty tough crimes and cold cases that did not turn up any shred of leads for years!

CHAPTER 9

THE SPOTLESS COAT OF CHANGE

Oh, what a pity, what a pity; things that could have been so different turned out like that! Suddenly, a professorial career in mathematics was so strangely derailed; but what a terrible place the world would have been had she yielded to him? Yea, had she driven from Spoon Restaurant to Yarralumla that night! What a different place the world would have been? But destiny had different ideas; and wise, resourceful people always seem to wriggle their way out of life's jams; yea, they always seem to find their way in this world, irrespective of the circumstances. And though the fog seems to appear from nowhere and entangle them in a web, they always find a way to extricate themselves from all of life's obscure jams and tight corners.

Such was indeed the case with Vanetta, now Dr. Firne with a Ph.D. in mathematics; and with the cavalier attitude of a true cosmopolite, Vanetta moved on to Jerusalem. Oh, World University of Jerusalem, thou foudroyant star of the Great Sea; what glorious honor has the gleaming star of bloom and beauty conferred upon thee! What great accolades has the noble presence of gentility bestowed upon you! And what a marvelous cynosure that gentility's star has become, smack in thy midst! Though many eyes gazed at her, she adopted a very matter of fact perception of things. From her point of view, finishing her second Ph.D. meant the whole world to her.

In the spirit of an eternal student and a true genius, she shouldered the wheel of things; accordingly, she buckled down to business and began to devour the program. As a brilliant, prototypical mathematician; the astrophysics was baby food for her. She maintained absolute mastery and excellence in all her many courses. Within a year and a half, she was ready for the qualifying doctoral examination; and, in dashing style, she devoured that exam with plenty of time left. Her stunned professors proclaimed her an astrophysical genius, and the word got out! As a result, she began getting offers to teach mathematics and astrophysics all over the world.

Presumably, she must have learned a thing or two from the great Dr. Kbergnes; and indeed, the whole world was watching and taking very careful notes on her. There had not been any major foul ups involving her love life in four years—she had outperformed the global community's sour faces and cynical expectations. The Spoon Restaurant fiasco was circumspectly covered up and nicely tucked away; nobody but the Canberra Police Department and Canberra Poly school officials knew—yea, those were the only people who had concrete information about the incident. These stakeholders and power brokers had the information but concealed it.

Spoon Restaurant management had been briefed about the case's sensitive details; everything was nicely covered up and put safely away from public view. And the spirit of genius flowered again there, at World University in Jerusalem. The world of science gazed and gaped at Vanetta's scholarly research in star physics; many of the brightest scientists alive were stunned by her uncanny knowledge of things: The glory of her genius had astonished scholars at Tel Aviv's distinguished multiversity. Vanetta's doctorate in astrophysics was completed in record time, and oh, the hoopla—the hoopla it generated around the world of science, stunned by her brilliance. It brought her accolades from virtually everywhere! And the phone began ringing.

Vanetta's biological parents, overcome with shock, went into rapturous delirium; they were exceedingly joyful about their daughter's brilliant performance all around. Godparents and well-wishers jammed the university switchboard with telephone calls; her email inbox and fax machine were smothered with congratulatory comments from friends and well-wishers around the world. Oh, what a life, what a life; what a beautiful and glorious life! She completed the doctorate degree in astrophysics in three and a half years: Before the ink dried on the doctoral certificate handed to her, the record passed into the archive of history. Oh, how true was that old adage—limes do not fall far from their tree; as brilliant as her parents, Vanetta was as bright as a star—and she shone!.

A Flaming Star from the Past

Oh, the glory and magnificence of Vanetta Firne, flaming in the world of science; and what a splendid commencement scene it sparked in the City of Jerusalem! By this time, Dr. Kbergnes had advanced quite a bit in his political career; known around the world as an electrifying speaker, he was in great demand. As the story goes, he was asked to speak at a Jerusalem graduation commencement; it so happened that Vanetta was in that very graduation ceremony that year. Oh, the flags, the flags; the florid, flaming, daintily painted flags were everywhere. The One Earth flag, the City of Jerusalem's flag, and the World University flag—see their fulgurous lights; oh, hear their fluttering noise in the whirring whiff of the wind! See the polychromatic flags, flapping like colorful curtains in the lively, velocious wind.

Here and there, a ballot of swans scurried across the sky; rumpling the moment's pomp. See the picturesque parasol they created in the bold, dusty abyss of the air. The phalanx of umbrellas, spread across the sky, was quite a spectacle. And oh, the colorful sounds of jumbo jets that stuffed the air with the fume of noise: The rumbling Jerusalem airport, like a flaring storm, was no small nuisance. See the long, winding stream of police cars and motorcycles; flickering like sparks. Oh, the lights' prismatic, gleaming flashes looked like flaming gardens in the wind. Why were they there at such a tame, innocent graduation ceremony in Jerusalem? They were there to shield and protect a prized global aristocrat from the arrow of harm.

They were there to honor and protect scientific aristocracy's revered princess; they were the quaint private eyes sent there to protect that prized pearl, Dr. Firne; but that was not the explanation that was given for their stately presence there. The crashing blaze of flickering lights circumfused the entire parking area. Oh, the pageantry, the pomp; and the fanfare that flamed about the graduation area! The graduates' cheeks, as bright as a comet, blazed with the golden light of glee; Their smiles, as white as a glistening alpine peak, flamed in the beam of daylight. Oh, the sparkling sparkle of their smile reflected the unsmudged beauty of a tarn's golden flame, beaming in the sun: The graduates were as happy as a lark.

The full array of Jerusalem's police force swarmed about the venue like flies; and plain-clothes police officers, as friendly as a hooker, speckled the large gathering: Their eyes, as sharp as a hawk's, caught a needle's eye in a haystack. Every now and again, someone on the intercom would thank them for their presence; they reassured the gleeful gathering that all was well and that they were in good hands. As the story goes, World University of Jerusalem had a tradition of honor and excellence; and all outstanding graduates were to meet and greet its graduation speakers. Whether they wanted to or not. This particular year's graduation produced three extraordinary scholars: Dr. Lucy Anderson, Ph.D., Economics; Dr. Ashley Pollens, Ph.D., Physics; and Dr. Vannetta R. Firne, Ph.D., Astrophysics, who was the most revered of the three. The star academic graduates cheerfully ambled onto the colorful electric scaffold.

Suddenly, a svelte, dashing gentleman; swish and handsome; scurried onto the stage! Dr. Jonathan Dawn, the university president, kicked off the commencement with humor; "I love graduation ceremonies: I met my third wife at one in Berne, Switzerland; and oh, what a ceremony that was: It has been nineteen years since we've been married, and her twelfth husband, Arnold Zuggzie, is still hunting her down and wants her back."

Dr. Dawn quickly explained that he was just teasing and that he had only been married once; and without any further ado, he introduced the graduation ceremony's keynote speaker; whereupon a trig, natty gentleman scampered up the stage and waved at the gathering, bouncing like a ball. Oh, the uproarious clatter and feverish excitement that his presence aroused. He waved at the exultant, rapturous crowd that received him as if he were a rock star! The crowd, inoculated with ardor and zest, thunderously applauded the speaker. The audience gazed at him as if he were a solar eclipse, electrifying the entire world! He summarily turned around and began shaking hands with the scholars on the stage: Dr. Anderson stepped forth, stared at him behind those dark shades, shook his hands, and quizzically looked away and sat down.

As she sat down, her facial expression told the whole story; she looked as if the gentleman had a few loose bolts somewhere. Dr. Pollens glared at his dark spectacles, shook his hands, and sat calmly down; finally, it was Dr. Firne's turn to shake this commencement speaker's hand. For some reason or other, she was manifestly unsettled and ill-at-ease about the whole thing. Dr. Firne stepped forward, shook his hands, and slumped back into her seat; twitching like a hamster. She twitched and grimaced as if she were having hot flashes! In the mean while; the young, dashing political star addressed the huge gathering with grace and pizazz:

Oh lovely, wonderful people of victory; you have gathered here to celebrate—yes, you have gathered here to celebrate this magnificent achievement of today's winners. This splendid occasion mirrors the accomplishments and victories of today's stars; it foreshadows the greatness and genius of tomorrow's leaders and shapers of history. These graduates are the superb children of genius, vision, greatness, and triumph. Oh, golden children of today's harvest of greatness; so full of life, and light, and vision: You are the architects of tomorrow's skyscrapers that will reach far into the heavens; you are the genetic engineers who will conquer all known human diseases. The explosive, titanic power of genius and creativity churns within your breasts.

Oh, golden children of the earth, look up and gaze into the skies at your tomorrows; gape and stretch into the boundless reaches of the universe and see yourselves there. Throw your heads into the heavens; reach for the stars and read your names on their faces. Reach into your one hundred billion brain cells and turn your world around—remove life's towering mountains that cordon off your way to success and greatness. Speak to those gigantic mountains that block your path and send them into the sea; For you are the masters of your own success and the wind beneath your own wings.

You've been woven from greatness' quaint fabric; you are the masters of your own success. Your hearts are made of steel and your feet of pure iron. You are conquerors! I say to you today: open your eyes and minds: What do you see before you? Behold the world staring at you smack in the face, calling you to destiny and greatness. Yea; see the bold, broad, sprawling world before you; beckoning you to come—it is beckoning you to conquer its challenges and be the winners that you already are. You can sit idly by and let the world and its eerie storms drown and wash you away; or you can arise from the dingy, dusky cave of complacency and realize all your dreams.

Oh, dynamic powerhouses of the earth, your tomorrow has, at long last, come to you today; Your long awaited tomorrow has paid you a visit today: Do not let it slip away. Arise now from the stoical, somnolent bed of false patience and race into the field of war; Race away in that scampering leap of war to snatch your pearls from life's unruly storms: Hasten your steps and rush into that sulfurous heat of war: Subdue all your enemies. Oh, jolly children of conquest, reach far into the heavens and snatch your stars from there; and bring back to earth all of heaven's treasures for the advancement of the human race.

You are the sparkling lights that flare the caliginous jungle of this world; your achievements, like volcanic flames of flashing streams of fire, are priceless gems. You've come to the fierce lion of academic moil; you've faced its wrath; and you've won! Oh, gracious children of greatness; you've won the sublime trophy of hard work; yea, you've faced its frenzied wrath, you've won the war of perseverance, and you've mastered the spirit of patience and have learned to be, and remain, little in your own eyes, and they've taken you far. You've demonstrated that you have what it takes to ride the angry, galloping bull of life.

You have proven yourself and won the howling war on the academic frontlines. You are today's winners and tomorrow's leaders in a world replete with uncertainty; you are the gleaming arrows of success that hobble in the whir of erratic winds: They announce to the world's far-flung shores that you, the victors, are coming. Oh, children of success, the future is a place that is strewn with thorns and challenges; jump to your feet, pluck up the thorns, and toss them into the fire of victory. Oh, children of genius; you are tomorrow's movers and shakers, leaders and winners; Rise to your feet, go forth, conquer, and subdue the whole earth; for it is yours!

Upon his commencement speech's completion, Dr. Kbergnes waved again at the crowd; he waved and wafted kisses at the swooning crowd, inoculated with vivacity and verve. The mammoth Jerusalem graduation assembly roared with swoon, exultance, and glee; many screamed and hollered, "The voice of God and not of a man: God has come to us." And after that stirring, Demosthenic speech; the gossip mills went into overdrive: Many began to speculate about Dr. Kbergnes' political prospects on the world stage, and not a few began to view him as the soon coming ruler of the whole earth.

After electrifying the graduation ceremony, Dr. Kbergnes turned around and looked: There were some fences to be mended; but, by then, all the bricks had been removed. Vanetta, awash in shame; scurried away from that lively, scintillating graduation scene! Her long retinue of godparents, overcome with shock, could not believe their eyes; but unwilling to resurrect an old, troubling story of the past; they took the high ground. Dr. Gutierrez consoled his goddaughter, sobbing vehemently in his arms; and Dr. Firne, busy with a host of other things, opted to just leave the matter alone. And again, the silver-tongued genius walked away unscathed by quaint admirers.

A Gleaming Stream of Suitors

And like luscious, nectarous peaches that bloomed in the splendorous gleam of daylight; Vanetta's trophies and accolades shone like stars in the world's picturesque skies. Her marvelous graduation ceremony filled chatterboxes' mouths with vain gossip; her day of wonder and astonishment had illuminated the world of science. Many of her Jerusalem professors, enamored with her beauty and genius, hounded her; they treasured the fulgid flowers that bloomed from the lovely vase of her soul. Ensorcelled and bedazzled by the awe and brilliance of her starry lights; they hounded her life like fortune's slaves, passionately pursuing her hand of success.

And though all the burly, handsome bachelors were quite well-intentioned; celebrity's friend remained chary and very watchful of her many smiling comrades. Who shall take the beautiful princess into the enchantingly delightful land of romance? Who shall take science's flaming star sightseeing across Jerusalem's pictorial landscape? Who shall hold the royal hand of beauty and take her into romance's land of adventure? Oh, the breath of brilliance that suspired from the majestic tree of science! And wrapped in the incarnadine flame of beauty, a bevy of swains swirled around her. See Jerusalem's erudite, brawny bachelors; like a gleaming motorcade of Aston Martins.

They hailed from all areas of science and paraded in the beautiful princess' golden presence; in the glorious reflection of a galactic flare, they blazed before her like a forest fire. Oh, see how they flared before her bright, pretty eyes like a forest fire in the wind; behold the starry Vanetta, a stirring pond of fire that ignited that raging pyrotechnic blaze. Yea, Vanetta; no longer anybody's little girl; was an exquisite connoisseur of swains. But she was even more eclectic at selecting brawny men with weighty bank accounts: The corrupt Jerusalem urban political machine tossed their golden hats into the ring; many well-established politicians, indicted on rape charges, muddied up the waters.

Their disgraceful mud-slinging machine did not dissuade Vanetta's choice of love. And oh, the phony stories that they invented to sabotage love's careful choice; but the husky, brawny suitor of choice edged out the urban machine's mudslingers. Bodybuilders, fresh from the Mr. Universe Contest, swirled around her like flies; and what a distinction that was, marrying Mr. Universe who himself was a billionaire! Oh, the vanity of man: What a strange casino that her choice of a spouse turned out to be. The world's richest, brightest, and most burly scientists filed before the pretty princess; and like an obscure slot machine, she had to pick one with more money than she had: Scooping up a wheel barrow of gold in such a rich and beautiful goldmine was not easy. But what is a rich gold mine in the eyes of those who own so much of the earth anyway?

In spite of the quaint comedy, clearly evident in the selection process of destiny's swain; the stirring, picturesque showroom of suitors brought back flickers of an earlier period. But alas; Vanetta refused to see her adventurous past as an obscure place of misfortune. Her golden day of true love and romance had arrived; and her garden of love—oh, her beautiful garden of love was blooming with so many colorful, graceful flowers! She remembered the benumbing pain of Anush's betrayal and loathed a repeat of that. And though pursued by the most dazzling embers of amor's wonderful moments, Vanetta's life was never entirely free from the rueful frown of the past.

The rain of broken love's pain did pour from the scarlet faucet of her eyes for some time. And even in the heyday of her romantic hegemony in the holy city of Jerusalem, she had had a few flashbacks of her painful, ungrateful romantic past; and oh, how it hurt! And sometimes, even in the brightest of moments and most propitious of seasons; shoving away love's pain of the past was still like lifting up ten thousand elephants! But eventually, the ugly stain of Anush's betrayal faded from her life forever.

It had wilted entirely from the psychedelic screen of her thoughts and memories: The starry flame of passion for life and love emblazed her cheeks with beauty's light. Moreover, she endeavored to honor her father's instructions for selecting a life partner; she did not quite hit the mark, but came rather close to that bull's eye target. Scientific aristocrats must flat out reject romantic overtures from mongrels; and, according to the scientific aristocratic code of dating, mongrels are people with a lighter wallet than yours!

Their bank accounts have a lower balance than yours. But finally, the lady of dash had come to her own conclusion about this matter. Amidst a galaxy of witty, burly bachelors; Vanetta prayerfully chose a swain! The pretty lady frequented massage parlors and fitness centers in the Holy City; she had a tenured professor position at the gleaming World University in Jerusalem: The experienced university faculty's vetting board had been eyeing her for quite a while. And after she had completed the astrophysics doctoral program in record time; they just could not afford to allow her to fade from their view and be lost forever. Within weeks of graduation, the board began besieging her with phone calls and emails; and, almost in a flash, they scrambled her up like gold dust for a tenured position.

Her worldwide family network applauded from afar; some flew in to catch a glimpse; they wanted to share in the wonderful moment of their world-famous child's success. And, in the Jerusalem World University's signature style of pomp and fanfare; much show and pageantry accompanied the board's high-profile hiring of Dr. Firne. There was a big university parade with orotund speeches and popping champagne corks; and so, the magnificent lady of dash had sealed a deal to work in the desert city.

And, of course, there were always leisure moments for the golden lady of dash to unwind; for whatever reason, she loved the outdoors; especially during the evening's candlelight. Oh, the pretty vespertinal moments of twilight and its quaint medley of sounds—its colorful, mystical beauty that so warmly and gracefully ushered in the night! The lovely lady enjoyed the twilit sky's quiet elegance and would take a leisurely drive; she was always closely watched by a dizzyingly sophisticated network of private eyes. They fanned out across Jerusalem and watched her every move around the clock; and heavily armed bodyguards were never far away from this most special, classy lady.

Vannetta's Eclectic Choice

It was a windy, dusty evening; smothered with the smoke of dust in the air; and there was another burly bodybuilder stepping out of a navy-blue Lamborghini. He smiled at her and took off, revving up the automobile's engine and climbing into great speeds! The dashing show-off went from zero to seventy miles per hour in five seconds. He wheeled the automobile around and pulled up next to Vanetta, saying "want a ride!" She smiled, jumped into her Aston Martin, MSRP and did the same identical thing. The young man said, "Wow, you are a race car driver—a bad American mamma!

Vanetta had just pulled out of Mood Massage Parlor and was on her way back home. This was their initial meeting, but much more happened at the Jerusalem Gardens the very next day, where they officially met and began knowing each other. Things happened very fast, and within weeks, the lady of dash had selected a spouse; and oh; what a quaint, eclectic choice that was! The world gasped at his unveiling. Tall, sleek, and slender; he was that perfect glove for the beautiful Miss Australia: Oh, yes, he was that perfect glove into which Vanetta svelte, gracile, pretty frame fitted; the whole world stared and glared at this pictorial couple's new charm and swank. Oh, see the two glamorous lambs, clad in the scarlet vesture of youth and bloom; see how they gamboled on the green, sprawling meadow of courtship's refreshing world.

And oh, the beauteous role of poetry's painterly language in the museum of new love! Their amorous words, like a showery faucet of beauty, filled the world with pretty flowers; and, as fluttery as flaming butterflies, they went everywhere that lovers frequented. They visited the posh, jaunty bars; they went to the chic, romantic restaurants; they frequented lively, pretty gardens and spent much time at the movies and museums. They were here at the opera, there at the movies, and over there at a blaring concert; and perhaps, things had proceeded too rapidly for the pungent lovebirds in the dusty city.

Oh, what larksome scuffles they began having on the verdurous playground of new love; perhaps, a chaperon, with good referee skills, would have done them a world of good. The picturesque lovers' language waxed from warm and tender to angry and boiling! Oh, their moments, filled with pugnacious sentiments and poisonous comments and outburst—the two lovers' boiling sentiments bubbled over with wrathful, poisonous words that often caused their neighbors to call the police. And how quickly things deteriorated between these two seemingly mismatched lovers! It was as if their world had been wound up like a carelessly assembled Seiko Watch; and, for some quaint reason, time was winding down very rapidly right before their eyes.

The folks seemed to have made the leap of serious commitment without first looking to see if it was a good idea; but, for some reason or other, they thought that they were tailor-made for each other. They decided that they wanted to be together for the rest of their lives: The droll, brash, amusing commitment generated powerful verbal storms between them. Simeon Auckner, an Orthodox Jew, lived by the Book of the Law—the Torah; he had been thoroughly schooled in the Torah and was quite conservative and staid. A little showy at times and beside himself about his handsome, James Bond-like looks; he made harmonizing the seemingly jarring colors of the relationship very difficult. Quite often, they got into overheated arguments about relatively picayune matters.

He charged that Vanetta was a hypocritical Christian bitch who lived a double life; but he added that if she would let him, he would help her to be a more sincere Christian; thus, she would see more clearly on her confused, foggy straight and narrow way. Vanetta was upset because Simeon was too rigid, prissy, priggish, and unrefreshing: She charged that he was way too showy and bossy at times, especially among his friends. She said that he was too prudish, old-fashioned, and lacked the modern urban pizzazz. Vanetta told her friends that Simeon lacked the sassy flavor of modern urbanism; she called him a jack ass and nincompoop out of touch with modern cosmopolitan life.

Simeon shot back, calling her a vile, loose Yankee woman obsessed with erotic adventure; he said that she was consumed with the forbidden and had her boundaries and values Confused. And that confusion created jarring colors that caused them to clash frequently; the loud, ructious quarrels sometimes seemed like boisterous, inner-city brawls; and this one evening, things got so bad that the neighbors looked out their windows. Yea, they opened their windows and yelled, "Stop it or we'll call the police right now!"

At that moment, something happened to Simeon and Vanetta; it was a quaint watershed. It marked a crucial turning point in their relationship: They cried and forgave each other; and in order to keep things cooled off, Vanetta quietly slipped out the country for a reprieve. And oh, what a beautiful picture that she painted about things to her parents in Malibu! The charming Vanetta had to convince her mother that Simeon was right for her—and that was quite a Herculean task that she had to execute in Malibu, but she really didn't mind. She was confident that her relationship with her lover boy Simeon was solid.

Oh, the blazing shawl of falsehood that veils the smoky chamber of the human heart; and after the fire has run its course, the whole house simply vanishes from view. What is so wrong with the plain truth, and why does man toil so hard to distort it? Why is it so hard to line one's life up with that which is right, and truthful, and wholesome? Poor Vanetta—so much in love with an illusion; so out of touch with reality! Unaware that the frail tent of earthly life was erected from the wattles of falsehood; Vanetta set out to convince her mother that

Simeon would make a fine husband. She failed to see that all that glittered was not gold, but rather brass and copper. Yea, brass and cooper, gilt with the glistening glaze of gloss' gleam and glister!

Oh, earthly life; like a gleaming lawn sparkling with dawn's dewy, pretty lights: And when the blazing sun arises and burns off the pearly dew drops on the sod; the plain, grassy tops look like husk beneath the flaming, fiery fruit of daylight: Dawn, the flower of the rising morn, has come and gone! Dawn, dawn, oh, dawn! Its golden icy crystals that cover the naked sod soon vanish and leave the dross behind; oh, the splendorous veneer of dawn is gone, lost in the gleam of the starry morn: Its royal glory that covered the bare grass looked far prettier with its gleaming crown. And so, it is in this world's uncanny mirage—people are gaffed by the veneer of gleam; once the thin coating of glister is removed, what remains is hardly ever worth a dime.

And oh; liars, clad in the dross of falsehood; waste their time in the dense fog of guile. And like the glistening pearly crystals of dawn, life's showrooms are flush with gleam—gleam and glister that only thinly cover the brass that lies just beneath the surface. But Vanetta failed to realize that the world was largely made of copper and brass— yea, copper and brass, glazed with the gloss of worthless beauty and nostalgic wounds. Oh, the fake furniture store of this world, so filled with luster that wilts tomorrow. See the world, its people, and their beaming smiles—smiles imbued with deceit's dross. Who will tell the truth tonight and dine at the king's sumptuous, twilit dinner table- and who will tell it after tonight?

There is no one to dine with the king, for there is no one who will tell the truth tonight; moreover, there is no king in this world of subterfuge who really wants to hear it anyway! And Vanetta, woven from the fabric of falsehood, must lie to her mother tonight. She must tell her parents tall, fanciful stories because she is afraid to lose this one: She is afraid to release this bruised but much coveted pearl that tantalizes her soul. Yes, the pearl is bruised and replete with imperfections; its scars are evident to everyone: But where would she find another one? And besides, which pearl is perfect anyway? Oh, what a vain, empty world of bruised pearls; sheared of the paint of truth and honesty! Why is this blank unbuttoned age so full of bruised pearls, damaged in the spin of things?

Oh, so many pretty birds with broken wings, flying high with borrowed ones! Behold life's many tanagers, flaming with fulgor; lost in the spin of things. Why must religion poison such a luscious crimson fruit of love and gladness? Why must such golden chords of beauty and love be shattered in the storm of discord? Oh, the beautiful flower of love; sullied by the smudge of lovers' vain, fake pride! See the golden chords of love; snapped in the howling tempest of angry, poisonous words—words so cruel and unkind, even hardened felons use them ever so sparingly. Oh, false religion; thou bold, brash fence that parts the tender breasts of lovers; What great and irreparable damage you have done to the lives of so many millions!

Why must false religion's sharp, iron teeth crush the bones of innocent lovers. Oh, religion, when will thou reveal the one true God that rules in the heavens? You've turned the world upside-down and sent so many spinning in a merry-go-round. Why should thy apoplectic drug be used in a world that is blind to the one true God? Oh, how you've soured the angry, splenetic world of man; so filled with bruised pearls. How many gods are there in a single world, replete with such brilliant scientific minds?

Why hasn't the one true God stepped forth once and for all and set the record straight? But yes, he already has: He stepped into the blind, dusky cave of this world of man—he sauntered into the dark night of this world from the golden crib of a virgin's womb, and he demonstrated love's unvarnished beauty and interrupted nature again and again. Yes, he did. And to top it off, he debouched from death's empty tomb for all men to see; but the sightless, unlighted world of man did not behold him: It did not acknowledge him.

Man, a Beast in Fine Clothing

Man has not been able to recognize the Christ Man because of his contact with falsehood—the viscous paste of darkness and untruth over man's eyes has blocked his view of things. The false Prince of this world has veiled the view of man, making him opaque to truth; hence, the gleaming garment of telluric life is but a mere charade—a world of sham; and, accordingly, all that you see in this world is not real—it is all just a mirage; but you would never know that this world's gleaming showroom is but a sham: It's a secret.

And that is the reason that man cannot cease fighting and killing his fellowmen; his assumption that the false world about him is one of truth creates a web of conflicts: This is because terrestrial life is one interminable stream of lies covered with the shawl of sham. And that endless river of falsehood causes conflict, after conflict, after conflict. This is the reason that man cannot stop arguing, fighting, and killing his fellowmen; with all his sublime enlightenment and sophisticated technology, man is still fighting because, at the core, he is a beast with God's image and the devil's nature. Man is a monstrosity; he will build a beautiful mansion and turn around and smash it to pieces with his bare hands—does that make any sense?

Man continues to be a warmonger because he has been blinded to the plain, bare truth; he can see physical objects quite well, but he cannot see and recognize plain truth: What is truth? Truth is well balanced, unbiased, undistorted understanding of facts. Facts emanate from the bowels of nature: There is an incessant stream of facts there. Though man can see physical phenomena about him, he cannot see truth staring at him; and though he may see flickers of truth from time to time, he just cannot accept it. And just like a fish must live in water; man, in his natural state, must live in darkness. But the difference between man and a fish is that man can live in both worlds: He can live in the comfortable world of darkness and in the uncomfortable world of light.

As it turns out, the darkness of man's nature is the very coffin of his own destruction; and when he shuns the light of truth, he has purchased a one-way ticket to his own doom. He senses that life is a mystery, but he does not know what the mystery means for him: Somehow or other, something stops man from embracing pure, plain, unalloyed truth; accordingly, man's vision is merely partial because of his mystical opacity to truth. And that being said, it is very clear that man is not in charge of things in this world: He is merely allowed or beguiled into thinking that he is really in control of things; hence, man is inadvertently and unwittingly cooperating with the forces of destruction: Whose destruction—his own ruin and calamity; but he does not, and cannot know that on his own. The substance of that information is incorporeal, and that is the area which man spurns. The cosmic machine of human existence is a conveyor belt of man's own destruction, but he would never know it because he is not willing to look outside of himself. His insular, provincial worldview incarcerates him in the quaint cage of this world.

Money and youth are wonderful things to have, as long as you stay young and alive; but this is a feat that no one can ever accomplish. So, in the world, man is asked to carry water in a basket. Somehow or other, man only looks at one end of the ledger; he cannot see the other side—he is not allowed to see that other side because of his innate blind vision to his world. And man's blind vision is merely his rank opacity to truth that he ordinarily should see; man is stark blind to truth that he otherwise should be able to recognize on his own. But the real problem and tragedy here are that man is not even cognizant that he is blind; thus, there is no need for him to look around for an optometrist or ophthalmologist.

The problem with man's insular reasoning is that no one stays young and alive forever; somehow or other, he seems to evade that point: He marginalizes that nude, stark truth. And thus, man sails from this world; lost in the swirling smoke of half-truths. It is not that religion has failed to reveal the eternal, monotheistic God of heaven: Rather, it is man's wanton inability to simply assimilate truth clearly visible to him. His blunt refusal to open his own eyes to the glaring truth that stares him every day—his brash willingness to wear damaged goggles impairs his visual view of things; accordingly, man is hamstrung by an incorporeal chain of uncertainty and falsehood in the world.

Because he is not really in charge of things; he is like a fish in the whirling ocean: The fish swims in a challenging environment of uncertainty, with a finite shelf life. Though the water is the fish's own environment and home, it does not belong to the fish: It's there, and will be there for some time; but it is not going to be able to stay there. Though the world belongs to man; he does not own it, and cannot stay here forever; man cannot stay here forever—even though he would very much like to do so. And so, although the garment of telluric life is beautiful, and gleaming, and flaming; it has been woven from the strange fabric of falsehood; thus, it is merely an illusion. And anyone who is really honest with himself would quickly and plainly see that this is true.

Man cannot tell the truth, even when he wants to do so. Why? He is not in charge! He cannot even be truthful to himself, even when he tearfully wants to do so. Man is a slave to lies, and that is all that he does in this world because the world is a lie! Challenge this position if you wish and look at your own life to see if it is one of truth; folks, you would be shocked to see how many lies you've told others— unintentionally. Thus, man is an automatic machine of falsehood; but he would never admit that; he would never admit that he cannot tell the truth; he is too sophisticated for that.

Oh, vain man of caprice and a few days; who has blinded the eyes of thy mind? Who has scarfed thy eyes with darkness' veil that you cannot see the plain truth before you? Tell me, tell me: Who, on earth, has separated genteel, scholarly people from one another? And why can't society's brightest minds simply solve their petty, picayune problems? Why must Simeon and Vanetta glow with such fiery anger in order to solve their problems? They are rich and went to the best schools in the world: They belong to society's astral circles. What's the problem here—two people, too afraid to stare the truth in the eyes and let it sink in; and oh, my, the incandescent heat that built up between the two multiple Ph.D. holders could melt raw iron.

Cooling Down the Heat

But though man cavalierly shoves away the light of truth from his darkened presence; he does recognize its concrete existence, but for some reason or other, cannot apply it. Simeon and Vanetta both recognized the towering complexities they faced; nonetheless, they both laid claim to each other's love, regardless of the consequences: Something had to give between the two distinguished, world-acclaimed scientists. The fire had gotten way too hot for sustainable dialogue—someone had to run; and run someone did: Beneath the shadowy veil of night, Vanetta slipped away. Yea, she slipped out of Simeon's sight; far, far away across the boiling, billowy sea!

Her mind wandered and tossed back and forth and to and fro, all through that anxious flight: Fully cognizant that a steaming argument awaited her at her parents' mansion in Malibu, she twitched and bit her nails for the entirety of her journey from Jerusalem to Malibu. The Godwit jet, the fastest plane in flight, ate up the almost eight-thousand-mile journey: Flying at two thousand, eight hundred miles per hour, the jet got there within three hours; and, in a flash, Vanetta was in the flaming sunshine state of California, putting up a front. Oh, what high fences she had built far from the stable of that wild, angry horse of their love. She went to Malibu to convince her parents that her litigious relationship was so wonderful, but she's a woman, and she is in love. As she stepped into the mansion, it was as if her mother had been agonizing about, and waiting for, her; and this was the way the conversation went:

Mrs. Firne (Vanetta's Mother)**:** Oh, Vanetta, Vanetta, why hast thou let us all down! You were raised in the love, safety, and beauty of a fundamental Christian home; you have been thoroughly schooled in the alphabet of world scientific aristocracy. We are the sacred children of truth who observe the laws of the Bible and nature; these are the only two reliable and holy channels of truth in the world. You have been exquisitely trained in these two impregnable pillars of reality and life; they've carried us through so many of life's storms and brought us safely on the other side. Nature is the mirror of the Holy Writ: The whole Bible is embossed on its tapestry.

Vanetta: Mommy, I really think that you have not looked at the whole picture here: This whole thing has been overblown; you have absolutely no confidence in my choice.

Miss Firne: How do you expect me to trust your judgment when you've cooked the truth? You've enmeshed yourself with a cruel illusion—you've turned to the liars of this world. The Bible is consummately etched on the very motif of nature—you were raised by its laws; for that reason; the liars, the charlatans, and the fraudsters have not been able to cook the truth: They have not been able to find a consistent train of evolutionary links in nature's library.

And, against this backdrop; we've taught you how the Bible says the world works: My daughter, the world works the way the Bible says it does—not how you think it does! You've violated a radical Biblical tenet: Christians ought to be yoked with Christians. You know the roles of the respective sexes and how they are to be played in our world: Why hast thou violated and profaned the sacrosanct, clearly defined principles of Christ and have connected with an unbeliever.?

Vanetta: Jesus is a Jew—isn't he? Then how could my lover boy, Simeon, be the devil? He is the child of righteousness, plucked from the branch of holiness and truth—are you telling me that you are an antisemite and are training me, your daughter, to hate Jews?—is that what you are teaching me to do, Mom?

Mrs. Firne: I'm not training you to hate anybody—I'm just telling you that you cannot marry a none-Christian Jew: It would not work. Oh, he is your lover boy, hah? You have violated all my sacred parenting rules; you've gone to the raging foam of the Bay of Biscay to find a life partner. Oh, Vanetta, why hast thou gone to the turbulent waves of the sea in quest of a spouse? You've pelted your life into the angry, boisterous billows of religious confusion; you've tossed the seraphic virtues of truth into the swirling, churning mouth of the sea.

 Oh, my dear daughter, you've thrown your Christian upbringing into infatuation's miscreant wind. And oh, dear, my little girl; you've so eagerly searched for love and loyalty; but my dear daughter, loyalty is the golden fruit that sprouts from the flower of truth. You and Simeon are too different to be in love with each other. Oh, what a mess! Is this all that I've done to raise you: Is this the daughter whom I've raised? I must be going out of my mind!

Vanetta: But how could this be such a mess when it feels so right, deep in my heart? I feel as if you are not even giving judgment and choice a living chance to prove themselves; you've already made up your mind what you want for me, Mom.

Mrs. Firne: How could I—do you want me to give you a dose of poison and a chance to kill yourself? What a great mess that you've created for yourself—your business is everywhere; the whole global scientific community has been laughing at us: I am ashamed of you! Riot police were called in to handle your relationship with that bright and shining armor. The tenants around his apartment are tired of the raucous noise, day and night! The contention between you two is as stiff as an iron bar, much too difficult to be bent; good heavens; it is so difficult; not even the steel knuckles of Hercules could bend it: Even Samson, in his prime, would not even touch it with a ten-foot pole. Oh, Vanetta, Vanetta; my dear daughter; men are like trains—they pass by every hour: There's never a shortage of men in the world; especially when you are so pretty.

A Mother's Deep Sense of Caring

Vanetta: Yes, Mommy, men are like trains; they pass by every hour—that is quite true; however, my lover boy, Simeon, is neither a train nor a passing automobile: He does not pass by every hour: He is the lover who comes only once in a lifetime; he is neither a bus nor just a mere man: Simeon is the lover of my life, and I am determined to prove all the naysayers wrong—watch me, and you will see what I mean.

Mrs. Firne: Well, you have insulted your mother on several occasions here this evening: I'm ashamed of myself for raising a child who insults me to my face in such a shocking way. I can't believe that you have the nerve to tell me, who raised you, what men are and are not: I've been around much longer than you; I have dealt with all kinds of men—they are trains. And a lady of your pulchritude and caliber is a very busy train station, flooded with noise—yea, it is a busy train station; bristling with the noise of amor's dulcet horn. And though the joy of youth's folly tingles all day in your breasts—though the chirpy voices of passion's song sound like such rich, unforgettable music in your breasts; the ugly stain of an unhappy marriage's pain would smudge your soul for life.

Vanetta: Mom, there is no ugly stain in real love, and I am positive that our love is real; The least that I can do is to be positive and keep negative stimuli and sentiments from my ears; this is what you and Daddy have taught me; it is my best calling card.

Mrs. Firne: How dare you talk to me like that (bang! she slapped her face in a fit of pure rage). Oh, my daughter; allow not the unsightly, inscrutable beast of divorce to hound your soul; tossed in the boiling fury of marital discord, the roof of your love will collapse. Oh, my dear, life will leave you behind; trampled by the angry mule of aborted love: Writhing with a broken heart in the dusky cave of gloom, life will pass you by.

Vanetta: Yea, Mommy, life may pass me by; but love will not: All true love lasts forever. What I have with Simeon is plain and true love: It will never die; for we truly want it and will do everything, in the world, to preserve it.

Mrs. Firne: Oh, Vanetta, Vanetta, flee the unfathomable folly of youth's infatuation; oh, my dear precious baby, my youngest child; for God's sake, listen to wise counsel! Infatuation is full of sorrow, remorse, and distress: Truth's unvarnished love lasts forever. Today's illusion of love is tomorrow's poignant heartbreak and a jarring jar of tears; let that sink beneath the folds of your breast; let it hide in the sinews of your flesh: Little Pumpa, let truth's unanswerable counsel and wisdom settle in the recesses of your soul.

Vanetta: Little Pumpa—who is that? That has been such a long time—oh, so long ago! But Mommy, you have not even heard my side of the story as yet: Yor are taking sides.

Mrs. Firne: Oh, my dear daughter, I've heard just about all that I needed to hear! Loyalty cannot bud from the twig of folly's kiss; it can only sprout from truth's rich soil: Love and war are such bitter and savage enemies; and sometimes, such strange friends.

Vanetta: But Mom, we've already been betrothed to each other: We've made that step. We've solemnly promised to love each other and to stay together for life; that is a promise—a solemn promise! Yes, we are having some problems right now—and there are conflicts. But oh, Mom; we are not as perfect as you and Daddy have been. You two are perfect—your marriage was a wedding planned in heaven: ours is planned on earth.

Mrs. Firne: Are you being fresh with me (bang, she slapped her again and turned away)? I will not have you insult me like that: You do not know the hell I've been through with your father; yes, you have no idea of the hell that I have gone through with your womanizing daddy. Our marriage was made in heaven—what a crass insult that you have thrown in my face—on top of all that you've already done!

Vanetta: Mom, I'm so sorry about that pert comment regarding you and Daddy: All that I've ever seen of you two were happiness and joy in a world fraught with pain. Mom, that was not by accident; my daddy must have been a very good man to you.

Mrs. Firne: Yes, he did have some womanizing issues earlier in our marriage; but he underwent a dramatic moral transformation that changed his life forever. And we both have raised you in the nurture and admonition of the Lord Jesus Christ: Oh, my dear, you have wandered so far away from your magnificent Christian heritage; and now, you are exquisitely preparing yourself for a wedding made in hell: Is that it, Vanetta?

Vanetta: Mom, if Simeon is a Jew—an Orthodox Jew at that—and Jesus is a Jew; how can he be the devil? He has much higher moral principles and values than I.

Mrs. Firne: My daughter, my dear child; go ahead with thy betrothal to that wild man of the desert; go straight ahead in your mess with Simeon, thy love; the nimble man of thy hips. Have all of Simeon, that flaming apple of thine eyes; that blazing star of the East—oh, that blazing star that glisters beneath the pictorial sky of the holy city of Jerusalem. Jerusalem, Jerusalem, oh Jerusalem; that quaint and picturesque city that never dies! Just remember one thing: As a man makes up his bed, so must he lie on it.

Vanetta's Unwavering Love for Simeon

Vanetta: You taught me to be positive and to always approach life in a positive way; but now, you are spewing all these negative sentiments into my ears, my soul, and my heart—how do you expect my love for Simeon to work?

Mrs. Firne: No, I'm not spewing negative sentiments into your ears; I'm speaking wisdom: You are so consumed with his rod of amor, you've been transfixed and spellbound by him. Oh, Simeon, Simeon; that playboy thug who has poisoned the soul of my tender, little shoot; behold Simeon—oh, those rough knuckles that have bruised the tender twig of my womb. See how he has blotched and bruised that glistening pearl that I have polished; oh, that gleaming, beautiful gem that I polished and painted with my own hands! And now, I am so estranged from my dear child, Vanetta, the crimson flower of my womb.

Vanetta: Oh, my mother, my father's golden vault, you are not estranged from me; you just don't understand how a young mind ticks and the love and passion that bubble in her heart. I can't help myself, Mom: I am just in love with my boyfriend Simeon; and he is madly in love with me, too.

Mrs. Firne: My child, you are seeing things from the screen of illusion and vanity. Oh, that I can reach back into the useless archives of the past and pluck that lusty fruit—that priceless, precious child that I used to know, and had grown to love so much! And though the bloomy flowers of my womb have shriveled up and wilted; yea, though they have wilted in the blazing sun of slipped years and faded thoughts; I certainly still believe in miracles and would begin afresh at the drop of a hat!

Vanetta: But think about it for a moment: Isn't it easier to believe for my love's success; isn't it easier to believe that my love for Simeon would last than to start all over again?

Mrs. Firne: And here you go, telling me what choices I must make at this stage of my life. Oh, that I be Sarah, the mother of faith's children; scattered about the earth like wild seeds; and oh, that the eternal God of heaven would look down upon his humble handmaid and grant her one last daughter—one last chance to raise a child to follow his ways and to walk in the way of righteousness.

Vanetta: Oh Mom, Mom; if that is where this engagement to Simeon is going; I do not want it anymore—I value my mother's sanity way beyond the fairy tale of fake love! I will break off my betrothal to Simeon and keep my mother's sanity.

Mrs. Firne: But Vanetta, Vanetta; this has nothing to do with Simeon and you; it has to do with my own disease of uncontrollable selfishness, insecurity, and vanity. You see, my darling love; you are our youngest child: I just hate to see you go—oh, how I hate to see you go and leave us alone: We have everything that we need: Oh, my dear, we have everything that this world has to offer other than our own children.

Vanetta: But Mommy, you and Daddy have us: We have not died; we are still here with you and love you so very much. I don't want you to sound as if your children have abandoned you—that's what you are saying, and it hurts deep down in my soul.

Mrs. Firne: Oh, Vanny, you do not understand; we are here alone, apart from you all; and that makes all the difference in the world— our children are not here with us: I would rather have all my children than all the many billions in those Swiss Accounts.

Vanetta: Do you mean that you love us more than all those billions of dollars, Mom—do we mean all that to you? You are the most wonderful mother in the whole wide world.

Mrs. Firne: All of it, my dear! The truth of the matter is that we will not be here forever. I would rather spend the rest of my time with all my children than be merely watching money; in fact, money is only valuable when it is enjoyed with those who mean the most to you: Other than that, it is nothing more than useless paper locked in a bank vault!

Vanetta: O Mom, you really love us, don't you? You aren't as sick as you think you are. You are a woman who is so full of love; you would rather have your children—you would much rather have your children than all the rubies and the gold in the world, hah Mom?

Mrs. Firne: Amadyn, Arnold, and Sasha; our other children; have all left us—they have all abandoned the empty nest here at our Malibu Palace; we are like hermits. They have all gone out into the world to carve out a life for themselves, away from us; they have been long gone: They hardly come around anymore—oh, we have lost them.

They are busy with their professorships far, far away in the distant reaches of the earth: You are all that we have left, Vanetta; and now, you are engaged to a lost soul!—it's a double loss: We've lost you, and you've lost yourself. Oh, Lord, take me out of this world; I can't handle it anymore. We're all lost now!

Vanetta: But Mom, Simeon is a well-trained Jewish lad and a distinguished scientist: He is also an eminent and skilled scholar of the Torah and an accomplished musician; Simeon is a very conservative young man with excellent morals and values and talents. Oh, Mom, his mouth is full of words that express his thrill and yearning to meet you; he is so vehemently desirous to meet you: Oh, how he yearns for that day when he will finally meet you and Daddy and shake your hands! Mom, he talks about that day all the time. He loves you because he cares for me.

Simeon Accused of Being a Playboy

Mrs. Firne Why would he yearn for the day to meet people who do not want to meet him? I am not disputing the fact that he might be a good Jewish boy; he is just not for you, and I want you to understand that.

Vanetta: Believe me, Mommy, I understand your perception of things; it is just wrong. And I firmly believe that, in time, our God would lead him to our Lord Jesus Christ: Simeon admits that Jesus was a great prophet and a very powerful man of God. He only has doubts about his true identity as humanity's messiah; he believes all the rest. He does not see Jesus as the Old Testament's promised messiah—that is the only issue.

Mrs. Firne: And that, oh, my dear daughter, makes all the difference in the world; that is just another red flag, warning you that your fiancé is a child of the devil: He is not saved because he does not believe that Jesus Christ is the savior of the world.

Vanetta: Oh, Simeon, though so capricious and finical, is far from being a playboy thug; though draconian and showy at times, he is so far from being a bratty child of the devil. Simeon is a fine gentleman, an accomplished pianist, and a brilliant academic star; his academic accomplishments have distinguished him as an outstanding scholar and a sublime man of contemporary society.

Mrs. Firne: Yea, we know that he is a world-class mathematician; we are not ignorant of that; but that is not all that he is—he is a Jew, and Jewish men are taught to marry Jewish women. And where does that leave you? Out in the cold, on the outside looking in! Why would you want to put yourself in such a situation?

Vanetta: He has attended the prestigious Jewish Institute of Theology in Jerusalem; and his sparkling achievements have impressed me greatly; I truly admire him: He is a man of ingenious thought, acuity, and vision with numerous brilliant stars in his future. Simeon is a fine gentleman with splendid dreams and many golden moments ahead of him: He is a man of sterling character, unblemished stature, refreshing thought, and sparkling vision; but there have been some problems—and there are problems in every relationship! His provincial, conservative disposition often jars with my liberal cosmopolitan views.

Mrs. Firne: And oh, what a match that is; and what a marriage that is going to be—your liberal American ethos and his conservative disposition would make quite a match: Oh, the fierce intellectual and spiritual dogfights that you two are going to have. And what a picturesque dance of love and war that you two will be doing for a long time!

Vanetta: But Mommy, everything in this world is subject to change: Isn't that true, Mom? Nothing remains the same—and besides all of this; we have made some agreements; we have agreed to stay in love and respect one another, no matter what. Mommy, we have agreed to disagree respectfully with one another—what a great thought! It is a challenging arrangement, to say the least; but we are committed to making it work and to love each other for the rest of our lives.

Mrs. Firne: Now, Vanetta, do not believe that I do not care about your wonderful choice: I certainly do, but I am thinking in terms of what I know that is best for you; my little baby: You are just infatuated right now; you will overcome it.

Vanetta: But Mom, at what point do I get to figure out what is best for my life and future? When do I get to make that crucial choice of selecting a mate whom I believe is right for me—I feel lock up in a dense fog?

Mrs. Firne: You are way too young to see it in its right light at this point: It is an illusion; but you cannot see that right now, for your eyes have been blinded by the lust of youth. I have your best interest and future at heart, not a few moments of lust in bed with a wild man whom the devil has sent to destroy your life.

Vanetta: We believe in ourselves and the love that is burning in our hearts for each other; in time, things will get better and our relationship will bloom for the whole world to see. Despite all our many problems, we have respected one another's views.

Mrs. Firne: The world is not what you think it is, and things can change in a flash: Young love changes with time, and what used to be so wonderful changes with passing years.

Vanetta Though we disagree on a number of issues, why must issues ruin our love? Feelings and attitudes about issues are like shifting sand in a whirring wind on a scary desert; they change all the time, but our love for each other is genuine and would never change: The world is made out of problems—that is all you find in this fake world of man. The whole world is a lie—you see it around you every day, but it is veiled from your mind: Our love is real and true; it is pure gold that will never rust, wilt, fade, or become mildewed.

Mrs. Firne: And so is the love about which you have been prattling all evening long; it is funny, Vanetta; people often get beguiled and hoodwinked by the fallacy of sexual lust: They get caught up in the moment and the seemingly beautiful feelings, but it never does last; other things get in the way—new lovers appear from the blue and smudge yesterday's thrill, turning it into a fog.

Vanetta: And yes, we do have skirmishes; but who doesn't? The world is not perfect; but despite all our skirmishes, despite our quarrels; what respect that we have for each other! Oh, respect, thou pretty, colorful flag that flaps all day before us; dousing anger's fire: Oh, glorious banner of respect that flutters forever before love's eyes, quenching anger's ire; What a wonderful friend you've been to us, love's hardy children—what a referee you are! Though contention's unpredictable wind blows from the chasm of nowhere; the referees of respect and forgiveness have always been there to break up every fight; and amidst it all, we pledge to fight in peace in a world filled with oxymoron and cynicism. In the sincerity of our hearts, we stand as good a chance of succeeding as anyone else—why shouldn't we go for it?

Mrs. Firne: And a pledge to fight in peace is bekissed with the spears of war and heartache; oh, Vanetta, you are so naïve and out of touch with things, it is pathetic!

CHAPTER 10

AN OBSCURE VISIT AND LONG CONVERSATIONS

And while Vanetta was in Malibu, lobbying for her relationship with Simeon and trying to convince her mother that Simeon was the right man for her; Simeon took some desperate measures to fix things and tie up some loose ends in his relationship with Vanetta. No one would have ever thought that he had taken things so seriously: His friends kept telling him that, if he did not see a relationship therapist; he would lose Vanetta, the most precious gem in his life. They began sneering at him, calling him a weak man who couldn't keep a woman: They bantered, mocked, and jeered at him; and he began getting tired of it. As they continued piling on the heat on him, he could not take it anymore—he caved in. Simeon secretly checked into Azza's Globe Behavioral Science Center in Jerusalem for counseling. On his way in, he ran into a very good friend, Dr. Lackman, from Oxford College in Edinburg, Scotland; and the old buddies began chatting up a storm.

Dr. Lackman: What brings a genius like you into this part of Jerusalem? Your name has been all over the news—you are dating that Firne's Princess from Malibu. I've heard great things about you: Things are certainly looking up for you—way up, actually! Have you come to see a friend? I can show you your way around; come right on in.

Dr. Auckner: Well, Dr. Lackman; things may not be as rosy as you are making them. You've painted a splendorous picture of things, one that is as pretty as the stars of light; but that is the problem with what you are saying: It is merely a beautiful picture; real life is more complicated than that. However, I thank you for lifting up my spirit.

Dr. Lackman: Well, I am so glad to see you. We have not seen each other in ages! What is going on with you, and how goes that beautiful Princess, Vanetta Firne? Oh, what a lucky man you are to have been thrown into that type of circle.

Dr. Auckner: Well, you see, Dr. Lackman; it is kind of difficult to explain. I am in here for some help. Yes, I am trying to find a good psychological therapist.

Dr. Lackman: And what (holding his breath and slapping his hand on his chest)! You are looking for a psychological therapist—have you lost your mind, Dr. Auckner? You are such a brilliant man with four doctorates, and you are looking for a therapist! Unbelievable! That sort of thing ought to be left to the little guys like me.

Dr. Auckner: Dr. Lackman, it is geniuses like me who stumble over little things like these: The ordinary boys have to deal with much more complicated matters in their lives.

Dr. Lackman: What are you trying to say—are you talking to me backwards, Dr Auckner? Little boys stumble over trivial matters as well—life can be quite complicated at times in a world with so many unknowns.

Dr. Auckner: Now, you are talking, Dr. Lackman; do not put me in a place where I do not belong. I struggle with things just like everybody else: I am just an ordinary guy like you. All people in the world struggle with a variety of issues—genius or no genius.

Dr. Lackman's False Perception of Reality

Dr. Lackman: My one doctorate in clinical psychology makes me look like a fool before you! What in the world has gone wrong now? You have everything working for you—have you been listening to the wrong voices? Did a ghost speak to you or something? What is wrong with you, man? I wish I were in your nice situation; you are dating the daughter of the world's most colorful and successful billionaire, and you have a problem? Is there something that I do not know or understand here?

Dr. Auckner: In fact, yes, there is; and if you would just listen, I would explain it to you: You see, Dr. Lackman; I do have a problem—and quite a serious problem as well. All my girlfriends get tired of me and walk away—they say that I am no fun; they tell their friends that I am too staid, old-fashioned, and conservative for them; they say that they need a man with the sassiness of modern urban life and erotic pizzazz: These girls say that I do not have it: I am too religious, modest, and out of touch with things for them. And this sort of thing really hurts and destroys one's self-confidence—I've gone through so many, I just feel ever so useless because my morals are so out of touch.

Dr. Lackman: I see the peril in which you find yourself: You feel as if you are in a jam. But let me tell you something: All people, at one point or another, do find themselves here; jams and tight corners are common in life; human society is filled with jams, and strangely enough, life is a war: You were born in a war, but it does not seem that way because the world is an illusion; the world is a place of make believe where people flaunt and show off things that they do not really own.

Dr. Auckner: It has been especially distracting to my professional life; and now, there is her. All my buddies have been jeering and scoffing at me, saying that I cannot keep a woman; these cynics say that I need to go back to Bible school and study to become a priest. I've had a stream of painful, broken relationships; I am tired of them now—I need your help! Dr. Lackman, if there was one thing that I learned in theological seminary was humility; I have a problem that I am big enough to admit; I cannot love a Ph.D. in mathematics. I need a good woman with whom to share my life; I am hurting really badly right now. I need some help, and I need it immediately because I do not know what I would do—I do not know what I would do if Vanetta walks out of my life right now: I've had it—I'm tired of losing valuable love!

Dr. Lackman: First of all, if Vanetta walks away from you today, just find another lady; you've had them beating down your door to go out with you; they do not see you that way. They have been knocking down your door to be your lovers—haven't they, Dr. Auckner? Some of them have even sent threats to Vanetta, who has hidden that matter from you: You are a real man; do not let a woman be stronger than you. You cannot be weak. And right now, Vanetta is showing more strength than you—and you cannot stand it: She has refused to fall apart amidst the howling storm of your truculent relationship.

Dr. Auckner: That could not be possible—I just spoke to her last night; she's in the city. Where could she have gone—that is not the kind of relationship that we've been building!

Dr. Lackman: Well, I am not trying to shock you; but Vanetta Firne has left the city. I have connections in high places around here; I stay abreast with the latest in popular culture: As per the Internet version of the *Jerusalem Times* this morning, Vanetta is not in Jerusalem; she has gone seeking private counsel about how to make her troubled relationship work. The story is that Dr. Firne is seeking counsel on how to keep the swish man she loves; so, if you think that she is about to leave you, your mind has read the wrong newspaper.

Dr. Auckner: I know the senior editor of the *Jerusalem Times;* I will see if this is really true; the *Jerusalem Times* is a major channel of journalism in Israel.

Dr. Lackman: Well, you appear to have some very good connections as well: Go for it! Your darling girl is madly in love with you and is bent on making the relationship work; you are in a much better place than you think: Things are not what they seem to be.

Dr. Auckner: I am ashamed of myself, and my friends do not make it any easier for me: Do you know anyone around here who can assist me and make this dilemma go away?

Dr. Lackman: I certainly have several friends here who are specialists in this area; they can help you; but perhaps, a real friend is what you need, and he may not be far away. Right now, he may not be far away: Real friends help and build each other up; yea, real friends build up—they do not tear down: I had some similar problems myself. I went through a dry spell in my life when the girls just did not seem to be coming; at first, I thought that something was wrong with me; and then things began to change. And boy, did things change: My wife came to me at that crucial turn of things, and what a source of encouragement that was to me.

Dry Spells' Universal Existence

Dr. Auckner: Well, Dr. Lackman, it seems as if you are the very solution to my problems: You are quite a life doctor yourself; you have a beautiful spin for just about everything.

Dr. Lackman: Life, my friend, is a stream of riddles and puzzles that have to be untangled: All of us experience various kinds of difficulties in life—and that, Simeon, is just life! And that is because what we think life is and how we view it is entirely wrong; our perception and view of life is false. Life is what it is—not what we think it is. The world is such a funny place with so many inscrutable twists. and turns. and quirks: We gaze at the world and believe that we see what our eyes behold; often, we are wrong.

Dr. Auckner: I'm very much encouraged by this wholesome pep talk from a dear friend: I used to think that my eminent degrees were all that I needed to be happy in this world; however, time has taught me that academic degrees are only part of the story; life and all of its complexities are the other part.

Dr. Lackman: We gape at the sprawling world before us through our prism's distorted lens: The world gazes back at us and laughs at the fake, foolish perceptions we form of it. We all look at the world as it appears to us, not realizing that we are looking at a mirage: Things are hardly ever what they seem to be: Everyone in the world is wearing a mask. Why do tellurians wear masks? The world's people wear masks to conceal who they are. Dr. Auckner, they are trying to cover up the very kinds of problems that bother you; they wear the mask of guile to befog the fact that they are not as cool as they appear.

There are very few people who do not wear masks; and oh, how they are spurned—how they are loathed and rejected by this artificial world of charade and subterfuge! Masks are the style of this world; virtually nobody tells the truth, except the few real ones who look beyond the moment's pleasurable enticements: These are the children of God. Masks are driven by the awareness of the real cost of being truthful because this world is the kingdom of darkness and falsehood, but few are aware that that is the case; if they were, fewer people would go to hell when they die.

Dr. Auckner: Now I truly see what you are saying, Dr. Lackman; The world is a bold-faced lie: What we see is merely an absurd pretense that we would never believe—we want it that way; life is the existential process by which we realize that it is neither what we think it is, nor what we want it to be. And that is quite a rude awakening to me: It is as if I am born all over again.

Dr. Lackman: As you can clearly see now, the world is one sprawling, living university; at least, Dr. Auckner; you are honest enough to recognize that something is wrong—you are perceptive enough to recognize that something is wrong with the world about you. The world just shrugs its shoulders and goes right on smiling as if everything is just fine. Human existence in this world is the greatest cover-up there is anywhere in the universe; but you and I would never know that there ever was such a problem in the world of man. There is a war, followed by a peace treaty never to fight wars again: It lasts for a while; and then there's another war and another peace treaty, and another war and another treaty, in an infinite stream of wars!

Dr. Auckner: My, my, it appears as if man is born in the outer court of secret knowledge; but presumably, in view of the complexion of terrene reality; some are privy to that wisdom, and others are not.

Dr. Lackman: I've never thought of it in those dark terms but you may very well be right. Why can't man stop fighting wars and killing his fellowmen? Something is wrong: something is wrong with man that he himself cannot fix, and there is a cover-up—oh yes, there is a cover-up of the truth in this world: They are not telling us the truth.

Dr. Auckner: I've always wondered about the senseless row between science and God: If God does not exist, why should that matter to modern science? Is modern science God? When you think about it and put all the parts together, a disturbing pattern begins to emerge about human society in the world.

Why People Wear Masks

Dr. Lackman: And the pattern that emerges suggests there is a vested interest in the great cover-up. Yes, something is wrong with the human system; they are not telling us what it is—and they are not teaching us what it is at all levels of the educational process. There is concrete effort, at all levels, to canopy the plain, pure, truth. They teach us evolution, Freudian Theory, and about the Frankfurt School of Sociology; but oh, my friend; they do not teach us what is wrong with man and the world—and we need to know that!

Dr. Auckner: If I did not know what you've shared with me, I would have asked you…I would have been asking you silly questions like what they are trying to hide from us: but I've moved into the big leagues now; those questions are painfully redundant; suddenly, the whole scheme of life has been splattered on the quaint billboard of my mind and understanding. I have a clearer understanding of things now.

Dr. Lackman: I know that you are a genius, stumbling over picayune matters like these—yea, tripping over petty matters like these are for the smaller boys like me; not for you; I know that you've spotted the entire machinery of the subterfuge that is running the world. This exquisitely engineered global cover-up has bruised and damaged all of us: The world is a place filled with people who can only see life from the prism of their experience; and it is this flawed, narrow, and provincial point of view that makes people put on masks. They do not understand, and are ashamed of, who they are; so, they disguise as someone else: People, burdened and shackled with the world's sorrows, mask up themselves with pretty smiles to give others the illusion that they are cool.

Dr. Auckner: In this regard, I do not really need to be ashamed of my strange weaknesses anymore; these are badges that flawed, dishonest folks have ascribed to me: They've put them on me. But I do not really have to accept these misguided labels from women who are lost in the fog; these are women who do not know who they are and are trying to find their identity in others; oh, they paint their faces with the mask of gleeful smiles to illude the world around them.

Dr. Lackman: Dr. Auckner, they have the same kinds of problems that show up in your life; but they mask them with colorful, arrestingly delightful smiles and happy, mushy faces. And then they walk away and commit suicide, passing from the scene in utter ignorance: They pass from the phony, plastic scene of this world that they thought they knew so well; but they were deceived by the vulpine power brokers who run the show here on earth.

Dr. Auckner: So, you are telling me that my friends have some of the same problems with which I grapple? Are you saying that all people have the same problems that I've been hiding all these years?

Dr. Lackman: And all people respond the same way; they lie to themselves and to others about their problems. They present themselves to a false world as people who are *cool* and have it all together. Dr. Auckner, the world can be quite cruel at times; it crucified Christ. Quite often, people with big problems work arduously to cover them up with sham and to make themselves look and feel good; thus, they would pick on you. But if you are smart, you would smile and show them the mask that they are wearing; And they would get mad and wonder what a crazy sucker and sick nut you are! Dr. Auckner, if you would still like to see Dr. Clark, I would take you to him now.

Dr. Auckner: Dr. Lackman, you've solved my problem already; oh, what a friend! Not only have you solved my problems; you've shown me a world that I never knew exists—thank you so much for your kind words and wonderful sentiments!

Dr. Auckner's Meeting with Dr. Clark

Dr. Clark; tall and lanky, with thick, bushy eye brows and a thin moustache; greeted Simeon; he was somewhat overwhelmed, but he needed that; he thought that additional help would not hurt at all: He felt that he needed all the counseling that he could get at the facility and that it would help him to better engage with the issues with which he was grappling at that time in his life.

Dr. Clark: Yes, Dr. Auckner; your kind friend, Dr. Lackman has suggested that we talk: This is not a counseling session; it is not psychological therapy either. Let us just talk. I have heard so much about you recently and about that extraordinary relationship; oh, what a lucky man you are! How did this happen? That lady is so special; where did you meet her—she has a thousand bodyguards and a network of private eyes that work around the clock, monitoring her situation!

Dr. Auckner: We met at Mood Massage Parlor's entrance, and it was quite a meeting: The next evening, we met at the Jerusalem Gardens' fountain; perhaps, God was directing our steps. That lady means the whole world to me, but I have been constantly messing things up. Oh, the pain of my childhood: My mother had a difficult—well—a very difficult marriage. And presumably, the dramatic scenes and episodes of that marriage are still bothering me: Sometimes, I have flashbacks of my father yelling and screaming at my mother; and I am yelling and screaming back at my dad, "Oh, please, Dad; please, don't hit her. Don't hit my mamma; oh, please, don't hit my precious, priceless mamma or I'll kill you; I'll shoot you dead—leave my mamma alone."

Dr. Clark: Young man, I can see that you have been hoarding up quite a bit of your past; and those painful, destructive moments are like weapons, attacking you day in and day out. You've become like a zombie and do not know how to deal with these issues.

Dr. Auckner: You see, Dr. Clark; I am a very transparent man—I cannot conceal things: Sometimes, even though I want to hide my childhood baggage from Vanetta, she sees it. Dr. Clark, I need your help; I do not want that to happen in my marriage to the princess: Her father would throw my remains in the garbage bin, and no one would ever see me again. Therefore, I have to be very careful about how I deal with her; she's a princess.

Dr. Clark: Young man, I will say this to you: I deeply admire your profound sense of sincerity; You have chosen to take the high road: Many, in your position, strut about; acting ever so cool. You have a winner's mentality and attitude: I perceive that you two would have a happy marriage and a successful life together.

Dr. Auckner: After you've seen so much in a world that doesn't seem cruel and wanton; what else can you do but endeavor to create an atmosphere and context of truth in your life? I want to be a model husband to my wife Vanetta Roslyn Firne: We love each other dearly! Oh, I love her with all my heart: I do not ever want to lose her—she's so precious to me; she is the darling of my life, and it feels so bad when she is angry with me. It hurts so much, but it seems as if I always go back to those childhood nightmares that irritate our relationship and cause problems between us.

Dr. Clark: Well, Dr. Auckner; I can feel your pain and the urgency of your concerns; oh, the agony that you've endured as a child—you must clear your slate and start over. This prestigious center would give you two months of free psychological therapy for this; that should be all that would be necessary to clear your mind from this distant nightmare. And don't worry: The Firnes would never know anything about these clandestine visits.

Dr. Auckner: Dr. Clark, the past has been quite an offense and stumbling block in my life; somehow or other, I have not been able to cast this mighty burden away; it has defied all my efforts to correct and clean up this mess in my life.

Dr. Clark: I am glad that you have adopted this stance of humility and soberness; many, in your shoes, have opted to simply pretend as if they do not have a massive boulder in their lives—they pretend as if that huge stone before the door of their lives is not there… and oh, my, my! What damage that they have done to other people's lives; they've created an utter mess because of their deceptive behavior!

Dr. Auckner: Yes, I am fully aware of the senseless games that people play in this world; in fact, interestingly enough, if the truth be told; the whole world is just one big dirty game that has been hatched by some very clever and skillful societal engineers.

Dr. Clark: Young man, although you've been greatly damaged in the grillwork of the past; I perceive that you have much hidden and unexplored talent, for you are very perceptive. In order to properly cover things up, you would come to my home as a math tutor; you are one of the best mathematicians in the world, and my son does need some help. We will take care of this baby and no one—absolutely no one—would ever know about any of this. I admire your brilliant, academic spirit; our interaction does hold great mutual benefits, and no one would ever know about any of this.

Dr. Auckner: I will be ever grateful to you for this indelible kindness and stamp on my life; this splendid human courtesy shall never be forgotten or expunged from my mind's archive. Oh, the tender deed of kindness, like the pretty smile on the lips of a blooming rose, must be returned. Kindness is an old friend that never leaves a true heart.

Dr. Clark: there comes a time, at least once in, a person's life, when he needs God: He may not view it that way and may choose to flutter about the place, looking for help. God made all of us, but we rebel against his authority and go wandering over the earth's face; we assume that we can fix all of our problems; but you see, we really cannot deal with all—here and there, a problem crops up where outside help is definitely needed; and not tomorrow: Right now.

Dr. Auckner: Yes, I do agree with you, Dr. Clark: Some things cannot wait on our acumen. There are some things—some matters— that are urgent: This is certainly one of them. Every man deserves the love of his life; and when it comes, nothing should get in the way. This matter is entirely confidential because, if it ever gets out, it can greatly harm you; all of us have brought some of our childhood baggage into the world of adulthood: I am quite happy about your new-found love; you deserve all the joy and beauty that love brings into a life.

Wrapping Things up in Malibu

Eventually, Mrs. Firne began to budge on her firm stance against the Jerusalemite who was dating her daughter; time had brought enough reason to enable her to see the other side of things. However, it so happened that Dr. Clark was a Firne private eye who took care of business for the family in the Jerusalem area; judging from his discussion with Simeon, no one would have ever thought that that was the case. In view of the context of what was transpiring in Jerusalem between Simeon and Dr. Clark, there was active communication between Dr. Firne and his private eye, Dr. Clark. In view of Mrs. Firne's seeming change of heart about Simeon, it appears as if very positive interaction had occurred between the Firnes and Simeon's counsellor in Jerusalem.

Mrs. Firne: Mildren, we've checked out the young man thoroughly: we've found nothing. After all, what is wrong with that which is Jewish anyway—Jesus Christ is a Jew! All the investigations that we have done on this chap have turned up very good results; all one thousand private eyes have brought back very favorable reports on this case. A host of private eyes and exquisitely trained professionals have been working the case, and we are confident that our fresh understanding of things is correct.

Dr. Firne: I've spilled some good cash in the hiring of these private eyes; they are among the best in the world, and I expect nothing less than sterling results from their sophisticated private investigation and experience as information gatherers.

Mrs. Firne: All their findings on this fellow have assured us of an excellent son-in-law. He is a Jewish man above repute—and a tenured professor at a prestigious university there in Jerusalem: This Jewish lad has never been involved with the law; he is a splendid gentleman. My God, how many more reports must we analyze before we fully accept the truth? God has sent this man to our precious last baby to take it from where we leave off; and Mildren, we are pleased— yea, extremely pleased—with what we've found thus far; we shall continue to rake the colds over his head to verify all the original findings.

Dr. Firne: Well, I've been quite impressed with our ongoing inquiry; I'm pleased with the results thus far. My daughter was well trained in Biblical tenets; moreover, I've circumspectly instructed Vanetta ln choosing a spouse from the pool. My dear daughter is fully cognizant that she is not to get involved with mongrels: We, of the scientific aristocratic community, have built tight seals to our world's access;

we cannot afford to allow mongrels to water down the virtues and values that we cherish.

Mrs. Firne: Well, my dear love; our prime concern is that the young man be clean-cut; We would like him to be rich—very rich, but his being clean-cut rises above everything else. We want our son-in-law to be sane and solid.

Dr. Firne: Margolyn, you are my dear wife of more than twenty-five years; isn't that true? I really thought that you understood the fundamentals of our revered scientific aristocracy.

Mrs. Firne: Well, I certainly do—what do you mean by saying this to me, my dear love one? We have our strict code of ethics by which we live: Did I step out of line—I stand corrected!

Dr. Firne: Oh yes, you did: You said that Simeon's being clean-cut trumped everything else. That isn't quite true: After love, the entry route to our tight-knit society is our gold standard; And what is that? Our children cannot marry mongrels or dogs, people with less than they. While being straight-shooting and clean-cut are important to us, money is even more so. It is part of the aristocratic scientific tradition to marry men who are just as wealthy, or even wealthier than you.

Mrs. Firne: Well, you know what I meant—and I did say that he had to be very rich also: I do view being clean-cut as a top priority for marriage to any of my children, but I get it. I get your point: People, with a poverty mindset, have an incurable disease; we don't need it in any of our family members.

Dr. Firne: So, in a sense, we aren't saying anything that is contrary; we're on the same page: It's so important that we be on one accord, and especially when treating our children's lives. Our scientific aristocracy is fundamentally a Christian institution— one of great repute: We are the children of light; and as such, we value the unpolluted principles of the Bible; these rust-proof ideas have been the cornerstones of the financial empire that we've built. We are strong tithers and givers to worthy causes—we do not spill money into the wind; And we do not allow our children to marry paupers, for we firmly believe in endogamy.

Mrs. Firne: All scientific aristocrats are aware of the need to keep our children safe: We are fully cognizant of the need to ensure that our children do not connect with mongrels; but even more important than that; we must ensure that they find upright, godly spouses.

Dr. Firne: All candidates who are qualified to marry our children must meet this criterion: They must have a minimum balance in their account that is higher than our children's; And as of now, our daughter, Vannetta, is worth, in excess of, forty billion dollars! It all started when she was being Christened—she was a mere infant; God made her a billionaire from the very outset.

Mrs. Firne: Well, Mildren, everybody knows that Vanetta was made filthy rich at birth: That is no secret, but we must maintain a smooth equality around our home at all times; we don't want our other children to think that they are inferior to this most gorgeous princess: They are equal—they are all equal.

Dr. Firne: All her monies have been very carefully managed by well-trained professionals: Our exquisitely trained team of lawyers and financial specialists has been at work; they have done a superb job in putting and keeping things exactly where they belong. And oh, the graciousness and generosity of our darling daughter, Vanetta!

Sasha: Vanny has always been so kind and loving to us, her siblings who love her so much: We aren't jealous because we do understand the special circumstances around her wealth; forasmuch as God didn't grace us with such fortune, we're all satisfied with our lot in life—we just have a different role to play.

Dr. Firne: It's so wonderful to hear you say that and be so accepting of your sister's wealth: Her accounts have been carefully stashed into some of Switzerland's finest banks; She was only given access to them if her swain's net worth was a quarter of hers. Due to the curious and unique circumstances in Vanetta becoming a billionaire at birth; we have made some exceptions to the general rule and would accept the above figure; we do not have any qualms about those who do not qualify to marry our children. There are thousands with children who just flatly qualify to be our daughter's bridegroom; thus far, our research has shown that this young man does qualify to marry our child. We have raked the coals over his head and found him to be a reputable character.

Mrs. Firne: Oh Sasha, you've done so well for yourself—Arnold and Amadyn are so proud of you: Your brothers do cartwheels over your success in graduate school; they are so proud of you. And you do not even have to be concerned: Vanetta has made huge grants to the family; oh, that you really knew who you are!

.

Sasha: Mommy, money is merely a tool; wonderful relationships with people mean more. And I am greatly enjoying my chosen line of work as an architect; I bring people so much joy for the homes which my company has built.

Dr. Firne: Have you seen your brother-in-law as yet; you kids are all over the world? He's quite a gentleman and someone whom I know that you all would love.

Sasha: I've heard so many wonderful things about him from my dear braggart sister, Vanetta: She brags about his magnificent build—oh,

I cannot wait to see my dear brother in-law: I can't wait to see, with my own eyes, what my sister has been saying.

Dr. Firne: Well, we are all glad to hear that *Little Pumpa* has come of age: I can't wait either. I've heard so much about him; our private eyes' steller reports have piqued my curiosity; furthermore, he appears to be quite a fine gentleman with a couple issues here and there: We are still working the case, and a final conclusion will be arrived at soon. Our expert private eyes have dug into places where no one has ever gone before; and boy, are they good at what they do! I am very proud of them.

Vanetta: Oh, Daddy, Daddy; tell me: you knew about all this ten months ago? How did you know about this? Who gave you all this information?

Dr. Firne: Oh, my dear daughter, you've just heard what I have said, didn't you? And you know how we, scientific aristocrats, operate busines in this world, don't you?

Vanetta: Yes Daddy—and you know all about him, too? That is incredible—I am stunned! I really thought that I was going to break the news to you about everything that happened; but it seems as if you've already been fully informed about the matter.

Dr. Firne: The gate bell is ringing—who is that at the gate, and what do you want? Oh, how annoying it can be to be interrupted when you are having fun,

A hearty Family Chat

Mr. Stutes: I am Mr. Stutes, Dr. Firne; I will be driving you to the airport this evening. How wonderful it is to be right on the clock; I am a stickler with time.

Dr. Firne: Come on right in and join us. We are chatting up a storm here. Oh, Vanetta, this is Mr. Stutes, the fine gentleman who drove you to the airport—yes, this is the gentleman who took you to the airport seven years ago; since you've been away, Mr. Stutes has married a wonderful lady who is now our maid. And they have been a splendid addition to our family: Oh, how dearly we love them! His wife Margaret is one of the fifteen cooks who work on this residential campus, and his chauffeur business is doing very well; in fact, he is all over the place! We are especially proud and honored to have him and his precious family around us.

Mrs. Firne: Don't worry, my dear child, Vanetta (comforting her); we know everything! We have chosen not to discuss some of the more sensitive matters that have transpired with you: We watched the Australian News very carefully and have been monitoring the rogue; in fact, he is one of our friends: We have the whole story covered from beginning to end, and you have nothing about which to worry. It has all been taken care of for you.

Vanetta's countenance dropped to the ground like a leaf in autumn; she had no idea that her father was fully aware of what happened to her at Spoon Restaurant that evening.

Mrs. Firne: Yes, my dear daughter; we were there, too. Things have been nicely handled, and there is no reason for alarm; You have been covered on all sides, and we believe that you are in good hands. We've never left your alone; we've always been there.

Vanetta: Daddy, you have been tracking all of this: How long have you been tracking us? I thought that this was my business, and that I was managing things to share with you all! I thought that I had it all figured out and that I was going to impress you all.

Dr. Firne: This morning, we have also spoken to Dr. Lackman, who is close to the case; he has inside information about your fiancée and has spoken very highly of him: We are particularly pleased with the rave remarks that he has made about your lover; he said that the gentleman was very considerate and ardent in his desire for you,

Vanetta: I am curious about all these names that I've never heard in my entire life: Who are these people—James Lackman, Ernwin Powel, Stephen Cage…Edward Marl? I am simply stunned by all this fresh information about my life: What else I do not know?

Sasha: Why are you so shocked, Vanetta? You know our daddy already; he does not play: He knew what dress I wore when I went on my first date with my precious lover boy. What makes you think that he would leave you out there all by yourself!

Dr. Firne: Well, Sasha; I was not expecting you to tell all my business; I love my children. The young man Simeon has been taking strict measures to ensure your relationship's success; per Dr. James Lackman, he is going overboard to ensure a happy marriage to you, his wife.

Mrs. Firne: Do you know this gentleman, Dr. Lackman? Have you heard about him before? How did you know about him; he is Simeon's personal assistant!

Vanetta: (With a smile on her cheeks): No Mommy, all this is entirely news to me. His name has never come up before: Is he one of the private eyes whom Daddy hired?

Dr. Firne: Oh, my daughter, he is more than a private eye: He is our right-hand man there. Oh, my dear, relax and be happy: Your dad has been to the Holy City of Jerusalem; in fact, I've been to Canberra and

Jerusalem on numerous occasions, unbeknownst to you. Why do you think that I would leave out there all by yourself?

Mr. Stutes (Licking his fingers): Oh, good heavens, what a delicious meal this is! And what a wonderful boon my wife has been to the world of scientific aristocracy. This food is finger-licking good; he who finds a virtuous wife finds a wonderful life!

Dr. Firne (smiling): And just think about it: Your wife Margaret has been so wonderful: She has headed the culinary department of this residential campus. You know the big functions and bashes that we have around here several times per month—we need a whole culinary staff to handle the food department around here, in order for things to run smoothly; and what a gracious lady she is. What a superb job that she has been doing for us here—she is a marvelous cook! Oh, that girl is such a fine cook—and you found her online: You are guided by angels. What a blessed man you are: He who finds a wife finds a really good thing; Your wife Margaret is a good thing for you and for us—and we tip around here very well, too. She is in good hands here. Oh, Margaret, would you like to work elsewhere? We are not suggesting it, but would you—have you thought about it.

Mrs. Stutes: But no, Dr. Firne; what a funny question that is—no, no, no, thank you; I'm just fine here! I got my big break here, and you people are some of the finest people in the world: I wouldn't work elsewhere for a million dollars!

Vanetta: This meal is so delicious and spicy; oh, this curried mouton is so dainty. And these fresh delicious grapes are all the way from New Zealand—they are great: Oh, the glory of technology; thank God for Godwit jet planes that fly at the speed of light! You think about it, and there it is right before you: The world has become so small.

Mrs. Stutes: Oh, Vanetta, Margolyn and Mildren have never ceased thinking about you: You've been in their hearts and prayers every single minute of the day; be a good girl wherever you are. And remember: Your parents and we will continue to keep you before the Lord, our God. We understand all the challenges that new adults face in today's naughty world; you have to keep close to Jesus in order to avoid falling in all the traps that are scattered in the world out there. You see, Vanetta, the world is a lie and a nasty booby trap, too; only the eyes of Jesus can guide you safely through all the gins out there.

Vanetta: Thank you, Mamma Stutes; thank you for your faithful service to my parents: The Lord, himself, will recompence you for the superb service that have been rendering here to my family: You handle things so well, I'm utterly impressed.

Mrs. Stutes: Oh, that wonderful jet plane that will take you to your destination this evening; I can see the joy on your cheeks; oh, I can feel the enthusiasm that you exude in anticipation to get back to the desert city—all the best to you and your lover!

Vanetta: This new class of jumbo jets is out of this world; they are built on a new speed model. These new mathematical models for assembling airplanes are straight from Star Wars; these powerful jet planes fly at the speed of light and would have caught fire in an earlier age! Oh, how things have changed, and have changed ever so quickly—oh, so much change! The world is changing so rapidly, it is afflicted with the disease of change overload: Stark changes occur just about every day. And by the way, Daddy; you know about all the Jerusalemite's credentials as well, hah?

Dr. Firne: Well, if you are just talking about his four doctorate degrees; those are not what have impressed us—we hobnob with those people every day. You know that, Vanetta: We are not just impressed with educational credentials—we are more consumed with the idea of his qualification to marry our daughter. We are fully aware that this young man is one of the finest mathematicians in Israel, and perhaps, in the world; but his mother's business dealings and accounts—his mother is incredibly wealthy with a number of business ventures in the world.

Mrs. Firne: She built that business from ground up with a paltry two thousand dollars: That woman has developed consortiums and syndicates practically all over the world; Firne Enterprises has even made overtures to work with her media business in Jerusalem.

Dr. Firne: And that young man, Simeon, is filthy rich by world standards; the boy sits high. That young man is sitting on some solid cash—fifteen billion Euros to be exact!

Vanetta (Gloating over all the evening's menu)**:** Oh, Daddy, there is so much food here. Spicy curried mouton, rice and black eye peas— and oh, such exquisitely cooked fish! See these fresh grapes and bananas, Seneca plums, mangoes, and an array of salads.

Dr. Firne: Oh, my dear, precious, little one; you are almost begging the question; that question seems to intimate that you have forgotten who the Firnes of Malibu are: We are that great African-American family—pert and rich—who lives by the sea. Our pantry is stuffed to the brim: Our children attend the finest schools in the world; our table always bristles with the most superb of aliments from all over the world. The papayas, bananas, and pineapples that you are eating were brought from New Zealand and Fiji. You think about it, and we can get it for you within minutes: That is the Firne brand!

Mrs. Firne: We just want our daughters to train men to follow their lead and remain pure; we're the richest folks in Malibu—God made us superrich; people consult with Firne Enterprises on every continent. Our home is one of the most explosive and sumptuously furnished in the entire world. We are among the great peoples of the world, yet we've learned to remain little in our own eyes; and oh, the joy that it brings to all of us to practically live in the world of disguise.

Sasha: But Mommy, do you remember what grandma Angella Firne always used to tell us? Grama Angie always told us not to take pride in deceptive riches: They cannot be owned; so, though we might be the richest people in the world, we must remain lowly and little in our own eyes.

Dr. Firne: We are not bragging here Sasha; everything said here this evening is true: We are the fat cats of the Hills of Malibu; but you know something: My dear daughter: The people of this vicinage would hardly ever know that this is who we really are.

Vanetta: Daddy, we do not have to be hypocrites; everybody knows exactly who we are, and we aren't little in their eyes: They borrow money from our banks and shop at our stores and shopping centers.

Sasha: It's all good; we don't need to feel badly about our being the richest folks in the world. Although the whole world knows that our daddy is a humble man, they also know who we are and respect us greatly for that.

Dr. Firne: When I was a little boy, my mamma always told me to remain little in my own eyes; thus, my dear little ones, I have always remained little in my precious neighbors' eyes. The world is a mysterious place where the perception of little is far greater than much; yea, it far exceeds the vain, pompous perception and understanding of having too much.

Vanetta: Oh, Daddy, is that a whole brand-new Cartesian system of philosophy? but Dad, you really knew that I was coming, hah? You've prepared all my favorites!

Dr. Firne: No, my dear daughter; it is no new philosophical system; it is merely wisdom. The minute you booked the ticket, the airline alerted us that you were coming; the Firne Business Enterprise is one of the largest business corporations in the world, and we have agents working for us on every inhabited continent on the earth. We keep track of everything, and business has never been better in a long time; our neurological operation has expanded worldwide, and is doing very well. The total body of knowledge has been doubling virtually every twelve months, and our line of business, repairing neurological disorders, has been greatly benefited from the knowledge explosion.

Sasha: Daddy, you have really treated our dear mother with great and admirable respect; this has been the essence of our childhood conversation: Daddy truly loves our mommy. We admire you for that: I cannot remember a moment when I saw Mommy with a scowl. You've treated our mom like a queen; on top of that, you've treated us that way as well.

Dr. Firne: You are all my glory: I feel great when my home is honored to the highest degree. Your mother, free from the thralldom of children and home duties, travels with me! And we are like free godwit birds with incredible flying power around the world. Today, we are here; tomorrow, we are in Wellington, New Zealand. And by the way, one Dr. Kbergnes has recently been elected prime minister there.

Sasha: Prime minister of New Zealand, Daddy: Doesn't that name seem to ring a bell? You know that fellow; he has been around. He is prime minister of New Zealand—what a great honor!

Mrs. Stutes: I tell you what: That name has been ringing bells around here for a while; only the great God of Heaven has saved that man's life, for he had overstepped the line. And even good old Mrs. Stutes was ready and willing to throw a rock at this depraved man; but God saved and placed him in our hearts, and we've been praying for him ever since—we have him all covered.

Dr. Firne: And he pole vaulted from tenured professor to Prime Minister of New Zealand: It is rumored that this lightning rod has been positioning himself for chairmanship—it is widely believed that he will be running for the chairmanship of the world. This may be the very man about whom there were some suspicious activities in Canberra several years ago; yes, some very suspicious activities that transpired at Canberra Polytechnic University. But good heavens; he is quite a speaker, and is now Prime Minister of New Zealand. This up-and-coming political star has everyone talking about him; he's the buzz of the day: Is he the new world leader, and would he succeed my son, Amadyn? He's a very polished man.

Vanetta's Knowledgeable Return to Jerusalem

And oh, what a delicious dinner that was! The dinner party had eaten up a storm, and it was now time for Vanetta to fly back to Jerusalem with a lot to think about. Dr. Firne apprised her of his complete knowledge of that west side area of Jerusalem; he told her that all his private eyes were watching things very closely there. And within twenty minutes, her farewell party was ready to take her to the airport: Again, Mr. Stutes; a big, burly gentleman; scooped up a few suitcases and walked out; he was followed by Dr. Firne, Mrs. Firne, and Vanetta: No one seemed worried. The company was quite genial and jovial, smiling and cracking jokes at one another; finally, Mr. Stutes flipped the hatch of the blue Lamborghini sports utility vehicle; and then he fumbled and stumbled, as a bee buzzed around his bristly countenance. He brashly brushed it away and gingerly placed the suitcases into the vehicle's back; the beautiful vehicle sparkled with dazzling brilliance in the evening's gleaming light; It seemed as if it had just been driven off the lot, fresh from the dealer's showroom.

It was a pungent, stunningly delightful automobile; speckled with scarlet and gold. Mr. Stutes opened the back doors for Mrs. Firne and her daughter Vanetta. He gently closed the door and proceeded to open the front door for Dr. Firne, whereupon Mr. Stutes was informed that it was all right and that he had it. The drive to the airport was a smooth, relaxed, and wonderful evening ride; and though traffic was somewhat on the heavier side, things went quite smoothly. Vanetta was conspicuously quiet, and occasionally put her chin in her right palm. What was going through this beautiful lady's mind? She seemed quite agitated; she was worried that her parents had the scoop on just about everything in her life; she was distempered because her private life was an open book before her parents.

The pretty lady wanted to have more control over the privacy of her personal life; she had no idea that the private eyes were that good and were watching things so closely: The golden girl wanted to reveal her private life to her parents at her own discretion; she wanted to have more personal freedom to manager her own life. What she found quite disturbing was that, when she was ready to break the news to them, they had already known everything about it from the very moment it happened; thus, Vanetta was quite puzzled, and flurried, and evinced very little interest in conversation. And though her curious mother tried to strike up a chat with her, she just was not there. Business was doing quite well for the Firne Global Enterprises; cash poured like rain.

Many of the houses that they had bought in the economic downturn paid off handsomely: Dr. Firne, a world-class architect, used his expertise to turn these houses into plain cash; they were repaired, refined, and gaily adorned with marble driveways and gilt gates. Their backyards were exquisitely landscaped and fitted with sprawling swimming pools: The homeowners associations in the various areas were circumspectly studied. If the thorough overhaul indicated that these local government entities were too obtrusive— yea, if the evaluation revealed that a particular area's government was too presumptuous; quite often, Firne Global Enterprises would simply dethrone that area's existing government. It did so either by picking a fight with it in court or buying all the homes in the area: It was truly a case of *you cannot fight with City Hall*—and no one even tried!

Now, once Firne Global Enterprises picked a fight; all existing stakeholders simply left: They knew better than to stick around, trying to fight City Hall: They politely walked away. At times, Firne Global Enterprises negotiated a workable deal with the association; when that happened, all the stakeholders benefited, and the association stayed intact. And so, at the time Vanetta was returning to Jerusalem; the Firnes were doing very well. And Dr. Firne and his wife were scheduled to fly off to Pretoria the very next day; and from Pretoria, they were to do some quick business in Wellington, New Zealand. The Lamborghini sports utility vehicle arrived at the airport and pulled into the parking lot. Within minutes, Vanetta had cheered up and was back to her normal self again; She thanked Mr. Stutes for his kind and courteous service, and wished him all the best—yea, she told him that she was very happy to meet his wonderful and gaily painted wife; and that she wished them, at least, a thousand years of nuptial bliss and playful moments!

Vanetta ecstatically kissed her mother and father, bobbing around them like a little girl. "Oh Daddy, Daddy; when are you going to come to the holy city of Jerusalem?" Her parents smiled and kissed their once "Little Pumpa" as she joyously walked away; and as she walked through the terminal, she waved heartily at the jarred farewell party. They waved and wafted kisses through the air at each other as she was swallowed in the fog of the moving mass of people;

and then, finally, Vanetta disappeared into the smoke of the crowd beneath nightfall's veil. Suddenly, she vanished in the thick mist of the moving travelers that faded in the dusk.

The airplane on which she was travelling taxied out onto the runway, took off, and leaped into the air like a rocket; and with the flashing beauty of a meteorite, the lovely aircraft zipped her away into the night. What were her thoughts on that airplane, going back to Jerusalem? What was simmering in her mind on that lovely aircraft: About what did she muse? How was she going to still the tempest which was roaring there in Jerusalem? Did she communicate with Simeon while she was away from the city of the desert? Evidently, her relationship with him was about to enter into a very critical and trying phase, with many twists and turns; she must have sensed the change coming and decided to remove herself from the locus of smoke and fire. Was her visit to Malibu a success?

She had already received some pretty distressing and poignant phone calls from Simeon's ex-lover, Avanah, who was bent on repossessing her lover, Simeon; and their very distressing nature may have also certainly played a role in her taking off from the Holy City. Insisting on a sabbatical, away from the thorny Jerusalem scene, was a sage move in order to cool off and calm her mind and thoughts. Interestingly enough, Simeon, himself, had to run away from things in the desert city and avail himself to a much-needed cooling-off period. This massive weight is the kind of pressure that relationships often bring to people who are trying to get their lives together. Because people come in pairs, somehow or other; being single does not feel normal; especially in view of the tremendous importance placed on having a love relationship with the opposite sex.

For a variety of reasons, people want romantic relationships—and most people only want one at a time: While sex often plays an important role in that longing, most people want to be loved by the opposite sex; and when that side of things becomes cloudy, most people wax very unhappy and depressed, Thus, in the light of these facts, it is very understandable why Vanetta was so uptight about her relationship with Simeon and fled the city, in view of getting some much-needed rest and refuge from the storm in which she was caught. It seems as if her entire life had been thrown into upheavals: Can she handle what she perceives is coming?

CHAPTER 11

ANOTHER CRACK AT THINGS

Dr. Lackman's phone had rung at least twenty times during Vanetta's absence: He was busy, coordinating a dense network of private eyes who worked for him; and by then, Simeon had already seen Dr. Clark for more than three sessions. It was revealed in the therapeutic sessions that he had much pent-up anger in him; all that fury from his mother's divorce had been bottled up in his soul. Dr. Clark told him that he was a walking time bomb that had to be diffused; he was instructed to get it all out in his quarrels with Vanetta, one day at a time. Simeon assured Dr. Clark that he had been cured of his psychological traumas of the past, but he agreed to quietly spew any residue of old rage left in him in his quarrels with her. And, as a fine gentleman, he also promised that he would tell his fiancée about it; but upon Vanetta's return, they seemed to have gotten back into the same old rut; only that this time, their quarrels were less visceral, calmer, and more subdued.

And though Simeon had quite a bit that he had to offload from his mind, his circumspect avoidance of coarse brashness seemed to sooth Vanetta's heart. And like a man on a mission; Simeon began to throw all that stuff off his chest; it was the kind of weight that no man, in his right mind, should be carrying. He had been weighed down with that old, stale baggage from the past; and oh, what a release it was for him to finally cast it all away! What glorious relief he felt when he finally jettisoned all that unwieldy baggage of the past. Old, distant nights of visceral screams and anguish; his mother's head, being banged against the wall, frightened him: He would scream to the top of his voice, "Daddy, stop hurting Mommy; you are hurting me, Daddy, when you hurt my mommy like that, *stoppppp, stopppp* hurting her!"

Sikh Auckner: If you don't shut up, boy; I'll fling your little "F"ing tail through that window. This is my house; I pay all the bills around here: Shut up now and go to your room! Your "so and so" mother is a *da gone* harlot; she is not what she used to be! Let me handle all the affairs in my own house; you are a child—just be one!

Simeon: (Running into another bedroom, screaming, "I beg your pardon, Daddy"!) Oh God of heaven, come down quickly and help me and my mommy; don't let Daddy hurt us anymore: Don't let me buy a gun and shoot my daddy: I want to do it; help me not to do it!

Oh, my! What an abusive house of hell in which that young man was living—could he make it through childhood in those dire circumstances? Not only was he being abused, and clobbered, and battered by his drug-abusing father; he saw his mother being beaten and trashed, day after day, after day—and it began to get to him. It began to affect him psychologically; he started to lose his mental stability and balance, and wanted to do away with his father. Although he cried out to God for help, he constantly pondered doing away with his father—he hated him; every blow that Sikh gave his mother, he felt it and took her physical and verbal abuse very personal. This young man was literally boiling over with rage and wanted to fix his father up; he did not even understand the extent to which his son had hated him and thought of consulting a clerk at a local gun shop.

However, this was the environment in which Simeon grew up; he had witnessed way too much abuse for a young man; thus, when he reached the age of young adulthood, all that rage was still there, boiling up in him; and woe be unto the women whom he dated.

Unfortunately, Vanetta was one of those women; and what a hell into which she walked! He claimed that he loved Vanetta; yet he picked all kinds of fights with her, just in order to survive: His childhood abuse bothered him like a serious case of drug addiction, but he loved Vanetta and did not want to lose her. He did not want to make it seem as if Avana's words were true; he trembled at the thought that he was not a real man and could not do anything with a woman. Simeon dreaded being called a eunuch or asexual—it scared the daylights out of him; however, he realized that he was not as highly sexed as his peers, who had already had several children. For this reason, he insisted on entering into this tournament of forgiveness with his dear love, Vanetta. Having made it through the crucible of childhood, Simeon wanted to go on and reap adulthood's benefits.

A Tournament of Forgiveness

See the pristine, white, satin gloves of courtship; so often stained with lies' blotches: Those ugly blotches of falsehood, so hard to see at first; and then, they are everywhere. And though youth's beaming glory and vestal beauty were so conspicuously present; the flaming paint of beauty was rarely ever noticed in the castle of their presence. Alas, love had become so much work; at times, the toil seemed unbearable; eyes that once saw beauty's flame waxed dimmer and dimmer by the moment. Oh, the subterfuge of beauty, that guileful paint that deceives man's shallow heart! After it had been arduously sought for so long, why should lovers simply ignore it now? And when the pretty lovers are bruised pearls in a sprawling, whirling, vitreous world; how gingerly and circumspectly should they handle the glassy pearl of one another! And this was the course that these two wonderful people had decided to follow.

This colorful, quarrelsome couple had finally struck a feasible deal with each other: They decided that, in order to grow deeper in love, they had to work harder at it and that they would participate in what they called a "Tournament of Forgiveness". However, a tournament of forgiveness requires superhuman might to make it work; and like skilled managers of a brash, new franchise; they recorded everything. They kept squeaky clean accounts of all their feisty rows and angry quarrels; their relationship's quaint accounting system was carefully balanced at nightfall. Oh, the splendid glister of a new day's morn never glinted on yesterday's sour frown: The old quarrels of the day were always ironed out just around nightfall; and sometimes, there were many acrid aches over the day's rowdy storms.

Each day was as new as the one before—it's slate as clean as a whistle! And though, at times, the contentions were stronger than the iron bars bent by Samson, every effort was made to turn an imminent war into an opportunity to be courteous; but in a world where so many disparate things were merely thrown together; wars broke out like angry storms, crashing from the mystical chasm of the blue. Simeon's soul was scarred by Sikh Auckner's physical abuse of his mother; the graphic sounds of her loud screams howled in the archives of his thoughts.

He had to overcome this powerful childhood trauma in order to function effectively as a spouse; he had to clear himself of all this mess in order to behave as a normal adult. He had witnessed the horrible verbal and physical abuse of his mother by his dad: Those childhood memories had poisoned his soul with hate for the system of the world. He knew that something was wrong with the world, but he could not put his finger on it; he saw the world as a place with sick people who seemed perfectly normal. In his view, the world was a strange mental asylum with people who behaved normal; and the charade of earthly life puzzled him for most of his childhood and young adulthood.

He loved his father and mother dearly—they both seemed like normal people; but, according to him, they were anything but normal—and it puzzled and bothered him: "How could this be?" he reasoned and wondered. And it bothered him for a long time. And he could not see why his father, Sikh Auckner, would abuse his very beautiful mom. In time, the mask of the Aston Martin stunt driver was slowly removed from his face; and gradually, Simeon began to unload all that old rage that had built up in him. And again and again, he brought unsettling charges against his adorable fiancée: He charged that she had been beguiled and hoodwinked by twisted, sloppy theology; he told her that her splashy contemporary Christian ideology had soiled her soul.

Simeon's Long and Strange Tirade

The world is filled with cynicism: A big, fat laugh seems to hang over everything; how things got this way is anybody's guess—it is the tenth wonder of the world. As it turns out, more often than not; we are not living in the world that we've come to know: The world before our eyes is quite different from the one that we think we know so well. Simeon; a dashing, comely gentleman; had had a very negative run-in with the past: He had witnessed his father's brutal, barbarous abuse of his mother and was crushed by it; he thought about killing his dad on several occasions and had even visited a few gun shops to get the tools to do the job. One night, around 11:30 PM, his father, Sikh Auckner, came home in a drunken rage; and, as was his custom; he picked a fight with Simeon's mother, Marlene Auckner, saying nasty things to her and calling her whoring bitch. And, of course, all this was utterly inappropriate and untrue.

Egging her to answer him back; Sikh rushed into her, slammed her head against the wall, and threatened to throw her and Simeon out the window; it was a watershed moment, and violent spirits entered Simeon: He wanted revenge. In fact, he vowed to disassemble and thrash his abusive father at his earliest convenience. Because of that incident, Simeon could not consummate any intimate relationship; his violent thoughts, old bruises, and acheful wounds hindered his intimate life. His movie-star appeal, flashy walk, and the pizzazzy air about him meant nothing. Simeon was hurting—and was hurting really badly; but again and again, he had to save face. And when he fell in love with the princess, he had to clean up his act; and he knew it—and he did! Simeon had resolved to release all that rage and pain by feigning fights with Vanetta. After an earlier connection at Mood Massage Parlor on the previous day, they met at the Jerusalem Botanical Gardens and followed things up with some very interesting dates; including membership in car clubs and auto speedways.

It was in these environments where Simeon got to show off his driving skills—and he certainly did. The early part of their courtship was rather unconventional; Simeon got to show off his stuff, racing his Aston Martin in large race-car arenas. Though his lover was impressed with his driving prowess, his being a show off did not escape her notice; but the love was there from the very beginning. The moment that he glimpsed her, there was an instant connection: Vanetta was very impressed with him; and he constantly upped his driving talent a notch, showing off his skills as a race car driver.

For some reason or other, Simeon enjoyed sightseeing and wheeled Vanetta all around Jerusalem; however, as time went by, and the newness of their love wore off, the rubber began to meet the road. Vanetta and Simeon began having issues that waxed progressively intense; this is an episode of their quarrels on one of their sightseeing tours. Simeon was still hurting from his childhood woes and sought to take it out on Vanetta and her hedonic, libidinous American ways to see if it would ease the pain.

Simeon: Oh, Vanetta, the one and only woman whom I love; I'm not angry with you: I'm furious with those scoundrel ministers in America, who have dishonored God's sovereignty. Secular contemporary Christian theology in the United States is drowning the world: Yea, it is drowning the whole world in the seething, roaring sea of *detabooization*. And before you ask me what that is, I'll tell you what it is. *Detabooization,* my dear, is the process by which corrupt societies remove all the sacred taboos from their presence. Yea, it is the process by which base societies; sheared of morals; systematically cast away all of nature's sacred taboos, as has been done in America.

Vanetta: Yea, oh, strange man whom I do not understand: I know what you are trying to say: As society's vision of fun, mainly sexual, expands; great change occurs. People become generally less tolerant of taboos, and the society undergoes dramatic decline. This is the trigger of societal decay, and it has darkened every major civilization's door in the past.

Simeon: And this jarring pattern is clearly observable in all major societies of the past; hence the reason we see such a graphic replay of Rome's decline in American society today. All Western societies today are on life support; they've utterly divested themselves of morality and are among some of the most dangerous places on earth. America delivers as many as three shooting sprees a day: This is the very essence of an insane society—how long can your society continue shooting up its own people in this barbarous and utterly disgusting manner: has America lost its mind—what happened to those people over there! Sometimes, I wonder how safe I am with you; oh, my, my dear love; sometimes, I wonder if you would shoot me, too.!

Trying to Make Sense out of It All

Vanetta: Now, let me tell you something, Simeon; and you listen to me well. The history of man's existence on the earth has been one of curiosity and intrigue; the earth has bristled with rising and falling powers, exhibiting growth and decline. Man cannot help it; it's not Americans' fault: The world is a place of design, and each civilization has been appointed a certain amount of time for its existence; once that time expires, that society is stone dead—it just cannot go on anymore. Even the world has been put on history's clock: This current spiritual darkness is on clock and can only go on for six thousand years; and, as far as I know, that time has already expired. This explains why all this nonsense is going on in America; thus, it is not just America that is running out of time; it is the whole world. Because of what happened in the Garden of Eden, mankind and the devil had been awarded six thousand years to play house on this earth.

Why six thousand years? Six is the number of man: God created the world in six days and rested on the seventh day: That was utterly symbolic; accordingly, because of man's grand treason in the Garden of Eden, at the dawn of human civilization, he has been awarded six thousand years to do his thing on the earth: Once that time expires, man has to vacate the earth and go to his place of eternal torment in the endless lake of fire. You might ask, "Why are you so harsh—why such harsh words for mankind? Well, I'm just explaining to you what's ahead—have you noticed how strange the world has gotten recently? The world has gotten strange because man's time on it is up; he can no longer do his thing here in this world, and what is his thing? It is fighting, game playing, cheating, robbing one another, having sex with other people's husbands and wives, bombing, and killing one another.

Those are the things that man does to his fellowman because he is fundamentally evil and lost in the fog of sin and doom: People in the world don't want to hear this—they want to hear how wonderful, and creative, and innovative man and the world are because they are humanists; they believe in the inherent goodness of man, but that is a lie: man is inherently evil because his spiritual father is the devil, and he is doomed without Jesus. If that were true, the United State would have been getting better and better as it wanders further and further away from God, but that is not what is happening in the United States today: Every major poll taken in the United States, since the year 2000, has hands down indicated that American society is in a moral meltdown and may career into another civil war if things swing too far away from the center.

And all this is against the backdrop that American society is one of the most humanistic, secularistic, and liberal societies in the world right now—and what an exorbitant price it is paying for that distinction. American society in a mess, and the mess is caused by its liberal stance against the God that made it great. The godless, liberal media; the humanistic academic machine; and the broad amoral sociocultural environment are the principal driving forces behind this burgeoning growth of lawlessness in America today. And again, this is not what your average Joe wants to hear: He wants you to tell him how wonderful his society is.

The truth is that this world is not wonderful; it is a heartbreak hotel in which people play games with, and tell lies upon, one another. This is why the Bible says that human society is condemned: This explains why one atmospheric river after another swoops down on California and washes dozens of homes away; and you look at it and say to yourself, "Oh, my God; my, my, my; all that person's livelihood has been washed away—what is that family going to do now: All they have left are the clothes on their backs?" And this scenario is repeated again, and again, and again; in a seemingly interminable cycle of gloom and doom. America is being smashed to pieces because of its rebellion against God and his word. America's greatness came from God, and he is demonstrating that to America and Americans.

Why is nature so unforgiving and cruel to man? And oh, my; when it is not an atmospheric river; it is some crazy wild fire burning down your home: When it is not that, it is some disgusting shooting spree gone mad; and when it is not that, it as an earthquake that has left unspeakable horror in its wake. Why is mankind subject to so much trouble? According to the Bible, the world is condemned for rejecting Jesus and trying to enjoy God's world without God; and it is so easy to dismiss this sentiment as mere organized religion. Thus, that is what mankind does: Dismiss the truth as some senseless rant; hoping that the world is not condemned, as the Bible says it is; and go on trying to enjoy God's world without God. Does it work? *Look at the mess the world is in right now!* And God is a gentleman; he does not argue with mankind—he merely gives him time to change his mind and to repent and turn back to him.

Do not be deceived by humanistic psychologists and other behavioral scientists that tell you that human beings are basically good; if that were true, they have had plenty of time to prove it—and have they done so? No, they have not! The history of human society has been one of war and bloodshed. Do you notice that the days are getting darker and more and more sinister than ever? It is because man is showing his true colors. He has been given six days to do these things that he does so well; the seventh day is God's, and that day is upon us. Thus, Jesus will return and repossess the earth from mankind and the devil. His return will inaugurate a new age of supreme peace, tranquility, and prosperity during the Millennial Reign of Christ; and again, this is dismissed by the secularists and humanists as mere senseless rhetoric of organized religion.

It is viewed as mere foam that floats from the mouths of silly people who have nothing better to do than to fool themselves about some Galilean, named Jesus Christ, who made a fool of himself in Jerusalem, two thousand years ago. There is nothing to it than mere silliness. But that is far from the truth that I am trying to get across to you, Simeon: I want you to know and understand the concrete reality of these truths, having to do with our relating, one with another. Thus, I have a moral responsibility to make sure that we understand our respective roles as lovers; in this regard, I must continue to expound this matter to you, the man of my heart, so that we can be on the same page and respond to each other as two polished, educated human beings. Oh, my dear Simeon; this is not a joke, as many secularists and atheists suggest; mocking, and scoffing, and laughing at this most solemn matter. Jesus will come back to the earth and repossess it from the devil and mankind. How will he do that?

Jesus Christ is God himself; but when he came to the earth, he laid his divinity aside to defeat the devil, as a man, in order to free mankind from the bondage that he created in the Garden of Eden by disobeying God. Jesus had to enter the fight with the devil as a man; he could not do it as God because that would not have been fair—it would have been no contest. Thus, having done all that heavy lifting; Jesus will rule the earth, with an iron fist, for one thousand years; and there will be great peace and prosperity all over the world—peace and prosperity like never before. And then, in the wake of all of this overwhelming change; the denouement, or the end of all things, will occur. One might ask—and quite justifiably so—" Why doesn't God just end things right now, cold turkey: Why mess around with all this this, and that, and the other?"

There are many things about which the Bible is silent; however, when you clear your head and do some logical thinking, the answer seems to appear to you. Apparently, God has to clean up the earth first before reconstituting and making it brand new, as part of new heavens and new earth. Don't you notice how chaotic and confused the world has suddenly become—am I the only one noticing that the world is not what it used to be? It is because man and the devil no longer have any legal authority to function in this world; this explains why national governments are no longer working effectively and why there is such a massive movement of people over the earth right now. Governments are failing left and right, all over the world—the world is ending.

Hundreds of millions of people are crossing national boundaries illegally, in quest of survival: What those people don't know is that they were born rich, talented, and educated in order to be a blessing to their respective societies. Well, if that were true, why are they leaving their respective countries to illegally invade other people's countries? And the answer is very simple, the modern university system has indoctrinated the world with the heresy that God does not exist and that the universe created itself. Well, that teaching has now come to fruition; and nothing is working in the world anymore—and people are going hungry like crazy!

That evolutionary point of view is killing human society, one society at a time; and now, societies are becoming rogue and fading away fast; transmogrifying the earth into a whirling wasteland. Look around: What do you see? The clouds are falling; and the world is ending—fast! And if you don't think so, sit tight and hang on to your front row seat; the show is just about to get started. The world is falling down: Oh, my! What a pity. To save face, the nations of the world will switch to world government, as if that would do them any good; and Jesus, himself, will come back and wreck and crush the devil's world government. Sit tight; the world is ending right before your eyes, and I can certainly handle my nutty fiancé's moodiness and quarrelsome behavior. You are just confused, Simeon; it's not just America: It is the whole world—can't you see that?

Simeon: Oh, you seem quite at home with the Bible—don't you; Oh! Dear, but America should know better than to disrespect nature in such a shabby manner: Liberal American Christianity has not only darkened the skies over the United States; today, it has turned the whole world into a howling moral cave of gloom, and doom, and ruin. Also, it has literally brought the world at the mercy of the evil minions from Tartarus—oh, at the mercy of the Bohemian Groves' evil gatherings and their distinguished guests; so many politicians gather there, it's not funny! Yes, such arrant falsehood has brought the world at the mercy of the denizens of hell itself. I think America and its politicians truly need prayer—don't you: I really think so.

Vanetta: And yes, we see the startling replay of the *Rome Scenario* in the West all over again: I agree with you there, Simeon; but why do you have to attack my country and its political leaders so fiercely, calling them devil worshippers—don't you think that is wrong? Something is bothering you, Simeon; and you are trying to take it out on me: You are too afraid to say what it is. You are petrified! You are angry about something, and you are trying to pick a fight with me because of it—what is at the bottom of all this senseless wrangling and bickering over irrelevant stuff—what did my country do to you?

Simeon: Vanetta, you are not my psychologist: I am angry with American Christianity: That is what has messed up America; I am not angry with America—she's our dear friend. Oh, the senseless moral destruction that this damned hypocrite has wrought in the world! Liberal American theology has blurred the line between right and wrong, good and evil: It has removed God's power from the Church and left his children with no defense—it has thrown them into a dark world with no armor to fight the titanic war against evil. In the process, it has ruined the entire world's moral fabric and put all of us on edge.

Vanetta: Why do you inculpate the Church; American society has been ever muddy: Are you saying that it is the Church that made America a muddy place—that is so absurd!

Simeon's Clobbering of American Christianity

Oh, my! What a terrible thrashing that was; this young man is as angry as a wasp—and he is not angry with America; he has made himself very clear about who his pet peeve is. It is the spiritual whore of phony Christianity in America with whom he is angry. He has expressed his hatred and animosity for hypocrites in the most searing and passionate of ways. Simeon believes that hypocrisy in the Christian Church in America has been the cause of America's downfall because many an American went to Christian Churches in America and were devoured whole by so-called Christians who make Jesus look like a sleazy used car salesman or some untrustworthy con artists. And so, he continued his visceral rant against the American Christian Church.

Simeon: Oh, Vanetta, forgive the pain that I feel every day; you help me to go on from one day to the next, but I cannot believe you said that. I cannot believe you said that America is not the only muddy place in the world: whatever mud is in America, the dark American Church is the cause of it; it is the main cause of all the woes in America today. it was once clean, and then, it became vile: Oh, what a mess it has created for the human race; what moral lawlessness it has fostered! Such maddeningly disturbing darkness, which has overwhelmed and consumed the entire world, has turned everything upside-down; the mayhem and moral lawlessness in America bud from the tree of false theology. Oh, that tenebrous cloud of heresy has yielded so much moral anarchy and woe in America; its streets are as dark and eerie as daybreak, and people walk in the shadow of trepidation. Shooting sprees are as plentiful as air, and human sanity is as scarce as gold.

Vanetta: But Simeon, you must remember that America is no longer a Christian nation: More than fifty million people in America identify themselves as devilists and occultists; when you really get down to the plain truth, you would be shocked at what you'd find. Now, tell me how the Christian Church is responsible for so many people serving the devil; they've resolved not to serve the one and true God—how is that the Church's fault, hah? What you are saying does not make any sense.

Simeon: And now, my dear, you couldn't have asked a better question: I'll tell you how. Hypocrisy in the Christian Church has bred an atmosphere of heresy and falsehood in America; this darkness and rife hypocrisy have sapped the Church of its spiritual power to get the job done. Blood-thirsty hounds roam the streets in murderous gangs with no respect for law and order: They spray innocent bystanders with powerful pellets of sorrow, death, and doom. They wander about the darkened streets in their savage rampage of societal ruin; they disport weapons, normally used for ground combat, before horrified onlookers. They've turned the society into a heap of confused people.

Vanetta: To some degree, I can see your drift and logic here; the Church is not inculpable: At the same time, you must remember that *church* means different things to different folks; most Americans today view the whole idea of *church* as a joke, and are they wrong here? Some people are sincere and take their Christianity very seriously; others don't. Things have deteriorated—and will continue to do so as the age winds down.

Simeon: Well, the people could not see the Church as a joke unless they actually saw its hypocrisy in living color; where did they pick that up? They got it from the Church itself—they picked it up there because the Church is supposed to be the example of right and wrong in society. And oh, Vanetta, you know that if the Church is a joke, the rest of the society is plainly false. Trepidation's flame blazes in the streets like wild fire, flaring in the whir of the wind; fearless goons flaunt powerful guns before the goggled eyes of civilians, bristling with fear. See their grotesque, unwieldy ammunition; ordinarily used to hunt wild beasts: The goons drive colorful classic sports cars that gallop like a horse in the screaming streets. Boom boxes; as loud as an atomic bomb; blare in the brawling, sprawling thoroughfares; they blast off like high-powered cannons in a war zone, strewn with fallen warriors. Oh, how pathetic and sad: When will things turn around? They are as much turned around as they are ever going to get.

Vanetta: But regardless of the Church's sins, why must you so fiercely attack my nation? You talk like a fool whom I don't ever want to see again; what a way to show your love to me! Why don't you pray for America—why must you so fiercely attack my country of birth—what has America done to you? And then you say that you love, and don't want to lose, me.

Simeon: Why are you attacking me—what did I do to you? I am blowing off steam way down in my soul; if I do not try to pull up the weeds in America's spiritual garden, I will explode like a bomb. Vanetta, this is the type of in-your-face lawlessness that one finds on America's streets: The polish of courtesy and good taste has become mildewed; good manners are gone forever; the strident, doomful roar of moral decay is everywhere you turn on America's amoral streets.

Vanetta: I do not want to marry you anymore; you are tearing me to shreds; I really mean it: I'll catch the next plane to California, and you will never see my face in Israel again. I really thought that you had some sense: Why do you break down the one you say you love—why do you tear me down like that?

Simeon: Love must have strong muscles to endure difficult things to understand and digest; if you know that something is not right, why don't you fix it and reassemble all the pieces? What you see is not what is happening in my world.

Vanetta: Am I a bone specialist or some medical doctor; I cannot do any of that kind of work. And the way you are acting, you will break me in pieces—what, on earth, is wrong with you? You've never even tried, one day, to kiss me; you are like a man without any masculinity—I don't even know what kind of man you are.

Simeon: I can't believe you said that; I'm angry with myself: all the atrocities transpiring in America are what is wrong with me. Oh, the picturesque, surreal chariots of moral chaos on the jarring streets of Columbia! Innocent street bystanders, gripped by the iron teeth of fear, shudder at every noise: Sporadic packs of barbarous psychopaths gambol like lambs in the howling, boiling streets; gunfire's eerie blasts rip from no where's quaint chasm as folks dodge and coup in the rain.

Simeon Clobbers American Society

It was a day of wrangling and trying to put things in their proper context; but the argument continued, even after they had shoved, and pushed, and wrestled, and tussled with each other all day. Obviously, this is no way to neither find nor have love; the very concept does not dovetail with this kind of scuffling and wrangling. However, the same thing is true about spousal abuse, and the terrible effects that it has on people to whom it is delivered and those who witness it firsthand every day. Spousal abuse is societal perversion, and it affects people in sundry ways; because of its terrible blows on Simeon's mother, it had virtually turned him into a fool who has to show love by being mean and unlovely—and that was so unnerving and confusing to his girl, Vanetta. She detested every moment of it, but she had no idea that he had been instructed by his psychotherapist, Dr. Clark, to do just what he had been doing in order not to fall apart.

Although Simeon knew that his behavior was not normal and that he was suffering from a severe affective complex, he never ceased to connect with his lover, Vanetta, and to endeavor to improve his relationship with her. In this regard, he kept on the move, driving around the Holy City; thus, on this particular afternoon, they had decided to visit the Jerusalem Gardens where they'd met initially. At first, they sat around the large, tranquil pond and exchanged flowers and amorous words; somehow or other, though, he behaved like a rank asexual and did not attempt to show any raw affection. Nonetheless, Vanetta was very happy with what she got in that venue and even complimented him for his improvement in showing, giving, and receiving love. For one thing, the venue was intensely romantic; flowers were everywhere and were flush with bloom and beauty. Thus, it was an ideal venue for love and romance; and Simeon did evince some measure of improvement, but then, he retrograded back into that America bashing again.

Vanetta: Oh, Simeon, like an austere prosecuting attorney; you have attacked us: You've attacked our wonderful land of the free; you've wounded our country. You've filled my soul with all those poisonous thoughts that you've cherished for years, and you've viciously attacked me today—again: Just when it seemed as if you were getting some sense, you slip right back into that negative trend and pattern again, but I refuse to give up on you. And, of course, I would be lying if I say that your words do not hurt: They are like a massive falling mallet— yea, your sour sentiments are like an unwieldy mallet, dropped from a thousand miles! And you've asked me repeatedly, "what has liberalism done for America?" What has violence done for Israel? When will Jerusalem's streets be safe? When will its citizens begin to see Jesus as their promised Messiah—just when? They've allowed us, Gentiles, to see what they've refused to see.

Simeon: What have corrupt democracy and the emblazonment of lies done for America? Moral lawlessness rules supreme beneath the dark cloud of American society: The air; like a swirling, pictorial chasm; is replete with the streets' howling shrieks; subterfuge and witchcraft, like invisible Lilliputians, darken every city. And like an uncanny flock of fluttering birds, speckled with gorgeous colors; the weird and the unfamiliar seemingly appear from just about everywhere— pedophiles, psychopaths, jailbirds, and weirdoes appear from the temple of the blue and create all kinds of problems for people who live in America.

Vanetta: And what else do you have to say about us? These people are found in every society. They are the essence of the good-evil dichotomy in the world.

Simeon: But we aren't as colorful a glass case of liars and psychopaths as in your society. Plain-clothes witches and undercover convicts disguise as good guys and ordinary people! Come on, Vanetta; how did the great land of America get this way? What has happened to such a great and wonderful land of opportunity and freedom, now a land in which millions of children go to sleep hungry every night? Where did all that varnish and polish of good manners and moral virtues go? Liberalism's *detabooization* of American society has eclipsed the light of morality: Liberal theology and moral relativism have destroyed our great society; They've transmuted America into a tenebrous cave of angry, unhappy, confused people.

Vinetta: I do not know why I am still standing here, but I must see the end of all this: Something is wrong, and I do not know what it is; but I am willing to see it to the end.

Simeon: America is hurting; Columbia is lost, and the Church is not helping the situation either; America's churchgoers agree with the liberals that the Bible is too strict. The strange dance of greed and guile keeps everyone working overtime: Venal political gamesmanship and dirty, under- the-table deals spin many into criminals: These nasty, shabby, unmoral tricks move crooked politicians in and out of crime; oh, the corrupt political process flings people in and out of crime— and time. Where did America's sublime morals go—they've simply faded into the golden sunset. Who taught church people in America to be hypocrites and to mock the Holy Bible? Did the Angel Gabriel bring that message to America, too—what happened, Vanetta—three shooting sprees a day? Are you really serious—is this real, Vanetta? Am I dreaming this?

Vanetta: But Simeon, tell me: what do you get from this; flinging a volley of insults at me? Your politicians are as crooked and venal as ours; politicians are crooked and oblique—period. They commit egregious crimes—they rape their secretaries and tell them to just relax and hold on; they will enjoy it. And when I fire back at you, you say that that is unchristian, and vengeful, and pert; why are you trying to make all the rules in this relationship and treat me like trash? However, I must forgive you in order to win this tournament; all the points are piling up on my side.

Simeon: I'm not so much angry with America as I am with her phony churches—and what does one do when he has a gripe? He must vent his rage, lest he explodes like a bomb; every man needs an outlet that allows him to uncork his mad world of pain, and strain, and posttraumatic stress within; he does need some sorry scapegoat on which to unleash all his strain and stress. But you are not my scapegoat here: I wish you were just a soft pillow or a good friend; oh, but you are so visceral and untame; you take so many things so personal, it really hurts and bothers me greatly.

Vanetta: Well, you are acting so weirdly; I do not know if you are the right guy; you have done nothing but confuse me: I do not understand your weird behavior. I hang on for the sake of love because there must be something at the bottom of all this; I am winning the tournament.

The Collapse of Morality in America

Simeon: When I lash out at America's deadly sins, I'm treating the witchcraft in the church; I am addressing the hypocrisy in the church and the blackness in the school system. That City of Angeles' schools—oh, see the folks in long, black hats and pointed boots; they *shit and piss* over people's innocent children, turning them into hardy young criminals. Oh, America, America; your crummy schools turn zealous teachers into lost child molesters: You've lost respect for the God of heaven and for nature's grandeur and sublime beauty. You worship the dark and promote its values of selfishness and corruption. You are the mercenary children of vanity and greed, and you make people's children twice the children of hell as you yourself are. Shame on you, schools of Angels.

Vanetta: I cannot disagree with you on some of these issues; things are very strange now: The wrong people are running the show, and societal institutions are run by some pretty strange folks, with absolutely no morals. Nonetheless, blasting the system with these lurid comments is not the right approach either; moreover, if something is wrong with your world; all problems can be solved with love and understanding—not with hate, and animosity, and confusion.

Simeon: Vanetta, my love; none of these sober comments were aimed at tearing you down; I agonize and animadvert against all this moral insanity that has flowed from the Church. If the Church can't serve as the right role model of what is right and wrong for, and in, society; then what else, in the world, can? In this regard, marginalizing the Church's moral transgressions is a very egregious blunder; if the American Church is flush with witches and wizards, then America is a lost cause—and this is pretty much the case nowadays.

Vanetta: Our world has gone to the dogs, but that does not mean that we must cease praying; we must continue in prayer, engaging the universe's Supreme God for answers to today's woes and tomorrow's strategies and solutions.

Simeon: Everything is so politically correct in America now, nothing is right or wrong anymore, and the Germans did not commit any atrocity against any Jews: Shame on you, America; your dabbling in witchcraft's parlor hasn't escaped God's notice. You'll pay for it, and are already paying for it in nature's incessant stalking of your shores;

the witch doctors who run the show have sabotaged your political and public education systems. These are the people who are running your country and schools today and driving them into one ditch after another.

Vanetta: But Simeon, I thought that you were born in Jaffa and migrated to Jerusalem; you've fooled me and filled my ears with a blizzard of lies: You had to be born in America. How could you know all these intricate details about American life—you know so much! You seem to have the inside scoop on a lot of things that baffle, jar, and worry me so much. How do you know all of this—who taught you all of this about America's schools and their problems?

Simeon: What have I said that worries you so much? I have gotten all my facts on the Internet. Your country bristles with nuns of the night who serve in noble places and work for the dark; they kiss children's cheeks, feed them intimacy's broth, and rip their tender parts asunder. Now, tell me Vanetta; is all of this stuff news to you: It blares on the daily evening news. What is new here: Nothing! These are everyday Los Angeles news telecasts' sound bites: Why look as if you've just seen a ghost or unidentified flying object: Come on, Vanetta. This is the real world; it is much stranger than the wildest fiction that you have ever read.

Vanetta: And yes, those things may have happened in my noble and wonderful society; and not a few public-school districts are merely covens, infested with the wrong people. We are not perfect, you know: Bad these things happen everywhere—and you know that, Simeon! What do you say of your government officials who violate their secretaries—isn't that rape, and is that right?

-

Simeon: That sort of corruption does not occur in Israel: our politicians are gentlemen; first of all, I am not talking to you: I am talking about phony American Christianity. Oh, Vanetta, you say that

I am not a Christian; yet you loathe my basic Christian values: I am not a Christian in the liberal sense of that watered down American perception of Christianity: I am a Christian in the true context of the holy word of God and its moral principles. Oh, how sad—America's brash, titanic *detabooization* machine is bringing the world to an end! If the crucified Jesus returns to America today, most Christians there will wonder who is that and what is going on. And Jesus too will wonder what, on earth, is going on in the Christian Church in America. Christian ministers and pastors have betrayed Christ again by teaching false doctrine and refusing to teach the Bible; they refuse to teach the world's fast-approaching destruction, eternal hell, weeping, wailing, and gnashing of teeth. No one delivers these sermons anymore; thus, people no longer fear God.

The Effects of Christianity's Decline on American Society

One might ask, "Has the Christian Church's decline had any genuine effects on American society—is this just the senseless rant of a very confused young man who has experienced much abuse during his childhood?" Well, only the facts can answer this question; certainly, Simeon has had a very rough childhood, but are his seemingly extreme sentiments far out of facts' and reasons' reach. Naturally, the Christian message is the most noble, altruistic, and distorted message in the world; at the same time, the world is the unhappiest place in the universe because it is the only known place with life in the universe, and the only place where everybody dies. But what does that have to do with Christianity's noble and sublime role as the ultimate solution to human problems? Flashing an empty tomb and a resurrected Jesus, it would seem as if society should heed what Christianity has to say; on the other hand, defining who is a real Christian and how to become one is extremely difficult because that standard varies very widely from one sect to another; but the standard, presented in the Bible, does not change—it is the same standard, presented in the Bible, does not change—it is the same standard.

However, what does not vary is the soothing, comforting peace that comes from the Bible's inspiration and its clear understanding of what is necessary to be a Christian—you must be born again because you were born in sin, due to Adam's treason in the Garden of Eden. Christianity has something that none of the other religions have: Peace, and love, and a chance to begin all over again by being born again; this has nothing to do with other people. You must either accept it or reject; it is a personal decision that every person has to make; however, forasmuch as Christianity is a supreme relationship with God, Christians' behavior carries a lot of weight.

And unfairly enough, people judge Christ by the actions of his so-called followers: The devil runs the world, but nobody judges him by the action of regular people in the world; it would seem as if it should be as broad as it is wide, but it is not; the cards are stacked against Jesus because the world is run by the devil. Thus, Jesus gets a bad and unfair rap in this world; and while many who claim to be Christians turn out to be hypocrites, all Christians aren't hypocrites; and many take their Christianity very seriously. And so, here we see this couple, pushing envelope against one another and demanding answers from each other. Moreover, as it turns out, Simeon may not have been as off the wall as one may have initially thought after all; his sentiments were quite well-founded, and Vanetta may not have been as silly as she first seemed.

Vanetta: I can't argue with you about all the silliness transpiring in American churches today: Our society has backslidden from God, but our relationship is not a church growth program; it is an intimate, man-woman relationship. At least, that is what I want, and I've had it—I've had it with you, Simeon; you've confused me enough.

Simeon: Oh, my sweet darling, Vanetta, you are supposed to be patient and longsuffering; should you speak like that to me? Oh, my dear love; the God of Abraham, of Isaac, and of Jacob has sent me to you—he has sent me to love and cherish you as a gleaming pearl to be adored by the world; and you, my dear, are that glistening gem prepared for the jeweler's glass case. But oh, Vanetta, my love; Abraham's God has also summoned me to tell you the truth; and that is what you do not want to hear: I love you with an everlasting love. Oh, Vanetta, my sweet darling girl; I love you with the love of truth, trust, and loyalty.

Vanetta: But Simeon, love is kind, and soft, and tender, and beautiful: It is not tart and nasty; it is not as unkind, and sour, and tasteless as the poisonous words that you've been pouring into my ears. How much more can I take, Simeon—how further can we go with this?

Simeon: I've been trying to set the record straight, but you are very upset about this, and that, and the other: You are violently disturbed by the truth; though you are allergic to the truth, I still love you. I cannot ever stop loving you; oh, my darling, my darling: You mean the world to me; but I must tell you the unvarnished truth about the nonsense called American Christianity. Christians, there, view God as an American: God has no nationality; however, Christians in America give people the impression that God is like them. As a result, when they mess up; people blame God, assuming that God is like them that mess up. Accordingly, Christians, like those, wind up becoming enemies of God more than anything else: They block people from entering into the Kingdom of God by virtue of their corrupt, sinful lifestyle and hypocritical behavior.

.

Vanetta: Why do you think I want to hear all of that: Is that all you can do to criticize me? Don't you think that I want more from my knightly hero? Are you my harshest critic or lover?—I don't understand you, Simeon; you seem to confuse me more than anything else.

Simeon: No, Vanetta, I am your most wonderful friend and chivalrous lover: Why do you see me as a critic because I tell you the truth? Oh, my dear sweet love, the Jesus of the Bible and his wonderful teachings are pure: They are as different from American Christendom as night and day; yes, it is true. The line of morality in the American Church is so blurred, it is as if it is not even there; And that is the reason that it seems as if morals no longer exist in American society today.

Vanetta: Well, it was nice to hear you say those beautiful words; they soothed my heart: They mollified the bruises in my soul, and you must remember that morality is fading—interest in, and attention to, morality is fading worldwide; not just in the United States. The guy Jerry who came up to me this morning had just met me: He said that he wanted to take me to his home and make me feel good: I was so angry, I asked him if he thought that I was whore; He told me that it did not matter; life today is fast and quick—there is no time for flowers and poetry. I was shocked at his effrontery. That is the reason that I put up with all the nonsense that you throw at me: I want more than just being made to feel good from coition's excitement: I love— and want, you, Simeon.

Simeon: And how sad that is, but morals are fading the fastest in the fairy land of Columbia. White-collar technocrats, in glass offices, have no more morals than Tartarus' unangelic beings. What a sorry plight and dark cave into which the world has plunged; what a dark chasm it has become! And who would rescue the human race from the umbrous, somber dungeon of false Christianity? Oh, the acheronian prison of false American Christianity: What a cruel, abject parody— so fraught with senseless scams and empty gimmicks; Oh, so close to the beastly gremlins of hell; so far from the real God of heaven! See the earth, a howling chasm of doom; so tied to phony American Christianity, and so lost in the dark wilderness of sin.

Venetta: Oh Simeon, my dear; would you simply revert to those beautiful earlier lines? We cannot fix this old, evil world on our own: Can we just stop trying and focus on fixing our love life? You've used words that touched my heartstrings: Say what you've just said there again—say it again; it rubbed me the right way. Come on boy; you are making a lot of sense now—say it again! Tell me how sweet and pretty I am again.

Simeon: We'll never be able to fix our love life without positively contributing to the world around us. False, barren Christianity has polluted America and darkened the minds of its people; in turn, polluted Americanism and false religions have poisoned the soul of the whole earth—false religion, phony science, and religious terrorists; lying on the universe's God; have poisoned the world. America is corrupt because Christianity's pure elements are sullied with gimmicks' alloy: Yea, they are vitiated with the poisonous alloys of false science, guile, gimmickry, hypocrisy, and fraud; accordingly, a churning chasm of meaninglessness has opened up and devoured the West. But we must also remember that there are many good Christians in America; they are the very reason that America still exists; without them and their prayers, America would have been washed away a long time ago. Do you know how many nations are trying to destroy America, but they can't? Why? It is the steadfastness and prayers of the millions of Christians who are, forever, praying for America—and they live right there in America.

The actions of evil, corrupt hypocrites make it seem as if Christianity is a bad thing; God cannot stop half-stepping Christians from being who they are, and he cannot stop corrupt human beings from starting churches that he did not initiate. For example, God did not initiate the false religion of modern science: Modern science came out of God; atheists stole the idea of science from Christians and godly men like Charles; Boyle, the father of chemistry; Descartes, that brilliant French mathematician; Newton, the father of mathematics and physics; and Francis Bacon, the father of modern science and the scientific method. These Godly men are the true inventors of modern science—not the sour atheists who are around today, proclaiming to be the initiators of the concept of modern science. In this regard, modern science is a Christian phenomenon—not an atheistic invention; but that is the way the world works: Lies are told to promote evil, and people are tricked into believing that right is wrong, and wrong is right.

The world is a lie, and the watered-down version of modern science today is no exception to that rule of falsehood in the world. The fact is that modern science is a religion—a false religion, raised up by the devil to oppose God. Check modern science out and see what it is doing; modern science is solely oriented around opposing God and the Bible with its liberal program—who do you think is behind that—God? You must be crazy! Modern science is crafted by dashing secret societies to solely discredit God and the Bible—and oh, what a magnificent job that it has been doing in doing just that!

The wild and crazy world that you see today is the unmistakable creation of modern science's pagan ideas. This explains why society is so sick and why love doesn't stand a fighting chance in this rapidly changing, crazy world: it explains why couples are divided along moral lines and why homes break up. And Vanetta, my dear, it explains why you resist the truth that I present to you; but I'm not going to give up on our love because I'm not a quitter—I am a Spartan.

Accosted by Aggressive Hookers

Well, this seemingly odd couple had made considerable progress and had gotten along pretty well during the past three or so days; they had gone to the Jerusalem Botanical Gardens and had made quite a few friends there. Their friends were quite impressed with their fancy cars, flashy clothes, and other fineries or adornments as they took turns to chauffeur each other to the gardens and around the city of Jerusalem. On this particular day, Simeon drove them in his orchid

Aston Martin; actually, they took turns, driving each other around the city: This day, Simeon did the driving; and the next day, Vannetta drove her Bugatti Chiron. These were extremely wealthy folks who knew how to handle themselves in public, and their friends were not poor either. On this beautiful afternoon, they went to the movies to see a movie and mingle a bit with their aristocratic friends; and then, they went sightseeing again.

As they drove around the city, they made occasional stops at places of interest. Vanetta had had an interest in this particular beauty shop for quite some time; so, as they swung into its parking lot and got out to enter the beauty shop; four young women approached them and inquired whether or not Vanetta was Simeon's sister and if they had any need of a maid. Well, this is the Holy Land; what it appeared to be couldn't be true; at least, so the couple thought. However, that was not the case: Where there is smoke, there is usually fire—and indeed, there was. This was raw fire: These were young Jewish hookers, trying to make a connection with a *John*. After winking slyly several times at Simeon, they daubed business cards into his hands, that read "Hot kitty at your disposal; available right now or later on tonight. Please connect with us as soon as possible."

Having had the business cards plastered onto his hand and noticing the girls' wink, Simeon winked at Vanetta; motioning to her that they needed to get back into the car and get away from that hot zone as fast as they could. This is rather worrying because Jerusalem is the Holy City of David, and these harrowing and unnerving things should not be occurring in this city; however, history hardly matters when sinners and evil secularists are running the show. The Jerusalem of the Bible is not the Jerusalem of today: Today's Jerusalem is a hedonistic, secularistic urban culture where, just about, anything goes; it is occupied by secularists and heathen Gentiles, fueled by an array of false religions, including modern science.

It is also under the influence of a watered-down form of Christianity; thus, the ideological context of today's Jerusalem explains its active urban prostitution culture, with young girls running around and telling men that, if they are horny, they can furnish them with some *red-hot ass* not far from that location. You might be offended by this kind of rhetoric about contemporary Jerusalem, seeing that it is called the Holy City—and, of course, it must be clarified that the secular government in Israel has passed laws; outlawing prostitution; but it might as well have never tried to curb the moral travesty.

As you already know the score; most laws today don't amount to a hill of beans. This kind of stuff is even thriving in Muslim societies, and it is a massive boulder for many Muslim government officials; unfortunately, we are living in the age of sin and darkness; thus, most people don't take such laws like those seriously because, sometimes, the very government officials who passed the laws, are in the brothel that same night, fishing for some new sex from someone who is young enough to be his daughter. Accordingly, this Jerusalem is quite an illusion; it is not the Jerusalem of old: It is rather regrettable that many of these girls enter the prostitution trade as early as twelve and thirteen years old, and most of them were either raped or sexually molested, earlier in their lives by their relatives. It is a rather unfortunate and sad situation, and many of the girls work the prostitute business just to survive—oh, what a pity.

CHAPTER 12

MORALITY'S COLLAPSE AND PUBLIC EDUCATION IN AMERICA

Well, what an experience that Simeon and Vanetta had out of the clear blue; they looked around, and it was there, enveloped in a gaggle of prostitutes: Women begging them to be brothers and sisters, but they were not; they were lovers. The same thing happened at several other boutiques and malls that they'd visited, spooking Simeon. Vanetta was shocked and lost; she could not believe her eyes, and three of the girls were no older than fourteen years old. Prostitution is illegal in Israel, but many young women get lured into it from a very early age, even as early as thirteen years of age. After that incident, the sightseeing couple then went to several other malls and bought a few items; including hats and dashing beanies, in preparation for their circus date later on that week. But even while they were at the mall, Vanetta met one of her friends from Malibu who told her that pastor Nathan Johnson had committed suicide; and she was crying.

This suicide pattern has become a mainstay in many contemporary Christian churches today, in the United States; presumably, as more and more ministers pull away from the Bible, in favor of pop psychology, telling lies on God; suicide has become increasingly popular, even among some of the most noteworthy pastors. Evidently, after all pop psychology and fake revivals fail, these pastors become depressed and throw in the towel on their ministry. Thus, a high level of failure exists among so-called contemporary Christian churches in America; In 2019 alone, nearly five thousand protestants churches closed their doors, while only three thousand new Protestant churches were started in the United States of America; the numbers tell the whole story of the massive damage that hedonism and secularism have done to the Christian Church in the United States of America, and this is because psychology and fake revivals just don't cut it.

People are looking for truth and meaning—not gimmicks and fake revivals; and, of course, the suicide rate has gone off the chart around the world, with more than one million people taking the plunge every year—and that number is climbing! While Simeon had been doing his very best over the past few days and keeping the senseless argument and controversy at bay, the news of Pastor Nathan's suicide drew him back into that captious mood again; and the argument continued all over again. They began sparring over cultural issues all over again: It started out by addressing the need to fix their love life and to leave the world and its problems alone; and then, it spiraled into the whole mess of drug abuse and public education in the United States.

They began wrangling over the breathtaking collapse of morality and public education in the United States; they jostled each other over the dramatic breakdown of morality in public schools and teachers making babies for the young lads in their classrooms—and, in some instances, for children as young as thirteen years old! These moral catastrophes never used to occur when people had more respect for the Bible and there was more honor accorded to moral laws: What happened—what changed? Well, as the couple wrangled about fixing their love life, that argument dragged a number of other things into the ring—and oh, what a slush that it created! What an endless array of problems it created.

Vanetta: By fixing our love life, we will be much more able to contribute positively to society: The problems that you see in

American society today were not created by us—were they? They were created by religious people who've disappointed and deceived many Americans; these are the very ones who no longer consider Christianity a valid religion, but many of these were the very people who flocked Billy Graham's altar calls, not too long ago! Those are some of the very ones who've deceived many younger Americans in churches years ago; they've all left church now.

Many of them have violated and perverted themselves; they've given up on the Christian message of love and forgiveness and have embraced the lies of sex perversion out there today. They are out there, promoting all kinds of false behaviors. Many of these people were once Christians; they've given up on that message now—they are no longer Christians; they are now perverts. But the problem is that the whole society has swung that way and is being smashed to pieces by the evil that it now serves. So many problems are cropping up, lawlessness is everywhere; and things are utterly out of control because the only people who seem to be in charge are the anarchists.

Simeon: You cannot enjoy this world by focusing on yourself and your problems; you can't. However, you'll do much better by living the vicarious life that Christ asks of every Christian, and the tainting of Christ's light has created a jarring cave of moral and spiritual darkness in America. Too many people are too centered on themselves; and so, the society doesn't work anymore.

Venetta: Vicars play a critical role in the world in strengthening the conscience of men; their selfless sacrifice, on the behalf of others, changes and sublimes the rugged hearts of men, turning them from stone into human flesh. Look at the exemplary work that Mother Theresa has done.; her vicarious labor in India has saved millions of people's lives and made her name a household name.

Simeon: I know you say that you are not a vicar; you are just an ordinary lady; but we must remember that we ought to live the ideals that inspire and mold our lives; we must not allow ourselves to lapse into the depths of debauchery that has befallen America. With the absence of the pure light of Christ, Americanism has become a quaint eclipse; and wherever it has gone, it has polluted and corrupted traditional societies, around the world, on a massive scale. And it is in this despicable moral landfill where most of the world's people live today.

Every day, one hears about some new revival breaking out somewhere in America; yet the whole society has continued to degenerate spiritually, morally, and otherwise: The only plausible conclusion to this strange conundrum is that the revivals are faked and false. But what a strange world in which we live—how does one fake a revival: I think that all these phony people need to stop playing with God— what they are doing is deadly serious. Can't somebody tell them to stop doing what they are doing and putting all of us at risk? After all, God is not a teddy bear; and you've had the nerve to talk about Mother Theresa's noble and magnanimous contribution to world society; you should be ashamed of yourself to cite such a revered vicar, who abandoned her life for the sake of others.

Vanetta: And you must remember that Christianity is essentially transcendental in nature; it takes time to soak into your bones: While its principles are true, they appear to be false. And Christianity appears to be false for the very reason that Christians do not live pure lives; accordingly, it seems as if God is calling people to be Christians and to live Christian lives that they cannot live; many say that the Christian route is not broad enough: what they are saying is that Christianity does not allow them to meet their needs, such as their need for sex: What they are doing is that they are trying to bring God down to their level, but doing that brings God under the rulership of the devil—and that will never happen in this world.

These people want a God that they can control—there is no such animal in the universe: At the same time, however; Christians, themselves, are not living holy, upright, godly lives. Thus, we have a paradox on our hand; and God seems to be the rogue in this very unfair life program. Hence, you cannot be too hard on Americans who have to live side by side church-going hypocrites. The ultimate fact here is this: America would never have been this messed up if Christians were true to the call; their hypocritical behavior soured most genuinely searching Americans' hearts against God and church. The problem here is that, if Christians would live like Christians, it would encourage others—it would inspire others to live and follow the Christian life, but the example itself is lacking; and that is from what most Americans have turned.

They've seen far too much hypocrisy in American churches to be Christians—why would they want to be as messed up as most Christians; however, the paradox is interesting. Many who've rejected Christianity are not here with us today—they've committed suicide and have gone to hell. The irony here is that rejecting Christianity on the basis of how other Christians live is a snare because it condemns Jesus himself, and no one has the right to do that; Jesus is way beyond repute. The take away here is this: You follow Jesus—not phony Christians because Jesus is not like phony Christians. Jesus does not need to prove himself to anyone; he has already left his record here.

Simeon: While Christianity symbolizes the purest truth in the world, its bar is the issue; many Christians feel that the bar is set far too high; it is so high, it is way beyond their reach. They think that they can never jump high enough to reach it, and that is so because Christianity is a supernatural experience; they are trying to experience it in their natural strength—and that would never work; thus, the dilemma of impure Christianity and fake revivals remain: If Christians feel that they cannot live the life that God himself has called them to live, why should non-Christians attempt to live it? And indeed, the point is very well taken. As a result, America has gone to hell in a hand basket.

What most people don't understand is that there are only two kingdoms in this world: Christianity and all other kingdoms; people are born in those other kingdoms that are all presided over by the devil. The issue that people must clear up in their minds is that the world is not what it appears to be: Look at the illusion that sex creates in this world. People run after sex but frown upon family life and kill the babies that sex produces: This kind of mentality alone should alert you of the fact that the world is not what it appears to be; the world is not a place of fun and games—it certainly is not a place of happy, joyous, free sex. Rather, the world is an illusion; and it is not God who has set the bar too high: It is the devil who has tricked man about the availability of free sex—there is no such animal in the world.

Ultimately therefore, what appears to be a bar that is set too high is there for your protection from the devil's illusions about sex and fun in this world. If you do it God's way; not only will you enjoy the sex; you will have a father for your baby and will not have to suffer for the rest of your life, agonizing over having killed your own baby and having all kinds of night sweats and nightmares over that abortion. This is how the world lies to people, and they swallow the lies hook, liner, sinker, the fisherman, and his boots. The ultimate fact here is that you cannot enjoy God's world without God; that is why evolutionists are telling people that God does not exist: Listen to me; it is a lie.

 You might ask, "Why is it that people do not see these deceptions?" They see them, but they downplay them and run after the world. How do people run after the world? They run after fun, and sex, and other things that jack them up later on; and after they get jacked and messed up by the world, they run from it by committing suicide. The world is an illusion; you better not let it illude you, for it will carry you to hell where it is going.

Vanetta: And yes, Christianity is a tall order because it is not any ordinary, natural life; it is a transcendental, supernatural existence in a natural body—the Bible teaches that, when a person becomes a Christian, he or she is born again; and God, himself, comes and lives inside his or her body. However, this is not language that ordinary people understand; and so, they run from God and the Bible and run to the world, that smashes them up in pieces; and they are sad and dreary. Thus, it is very little understood, and those who initiate fake revivals are fooling themselves and playing with God and the devil; and as surely as the sun hangs from the string of nothing in the sky, those who fake revivals will pay for their foolishness and utter absurdity.

The Importance of Faith in Christianity

Hence, what God is asking man to do is to step out on a limb and and truly trust him Here is the issue: God would never ask anyone to do anything that he knows he can't do. Christianity is a transcendental lifestyle, lived by faith; not in your own power, but in God's. Christianity is Jesus Christ, himself, living his life through you, a natural person—and God won't have it any other way: That is the way he has designed the system to work! Thus, the error is not God's: It is Christians' unwillingness to trust in a God that they can't see, and there is where faith comes in. You have to believe that God is real and start acting that way in order for real Christianity to come alive in you; it is when you do that when God begins to manifest himself to you and to show you that he is real.

This is why secular professors don't believe in God; they are not functioning in an environment where God does manifest himself;

thus, as far as they are concerned, he does not exist—not in their world. He does not exist where they fish; thus, what they are saying makes sense to them; especially in view of their allegiance to the other side.

When Christians act the same way as these college professors, they get the same results; and so, they become discouraged and walk away from Christianity, choosing to believe the vanity of psychology. The reality is that, when the chips are down, psychology will not be able to help you; it is merely a demonic illusion—and this is true. How many people do you know that psychology is really helping? Folks, it is all an illusion, and this is pretty much the conclusion to which this couple came; the more they talked to one another, the closer they got to each other. and the more they saw how compatible they were.

Vanetta: The truth of the matter is that serving God requires faith and self-sacrifice; but it also requires abandoning the world that you see and its deceptive, sophistic reasoning. The secret here is that the world that you see is a lie, but you must inculcate that fact: You must understand that the world in which you live is a lie; thus, you must leave it alone and move in the environment in which God operates, which is the one the Bible recommends. Have you ever wondered why there is so much pain in the world? Most people do not see the world as a lie, and this is the fundamental fact that you must first imbibe into your soul if you are really going to be successful in this world.

The first fact that you must know is that the world is a lie and a pretty dangerous place, too; that is why friends change so drastically and become such bitter enemies; and sometimes, you have to ask yourself, "Are those the same two people who used to be such friends—what happened?"

You can't enjoy God's world without God, and you can hardly enjoy friends without his presence. To connect with God, you have to get into his environment: God's environment is the Bible; faith, through your words; and conscience. You have to connect in God's environment; he will neither operate in yours nor in scientists'. The Bible; your words; and, to some extent, the human conscience are the programs by which man connects solidly with God; you will not find him in your reasoning—he is not there, and this is why people's minds play games on them.

To connect with God, you must exercise faith that he is there and would respond to you. If you say, "God, save my soul" and really mean business with him, you will see how dramatically your life will change. Why? It is because you asked him to change your life and save your soul, and so, he did just that. This is a simple test of God's existence, for he deals with you through his word by your own words; this is why words are so important. God created the world with words, and he is waiting on you to cry out to him for salvation through your own words; and when you do, he will respond and deal with you as if you can see him.

Simeon: What man does not understand is that the world is a lie, but he doesn't know that: The world is dark and controlled by the devil, and man is directly under demonic control; this is the reason that serving God is so difficult, even though it is the right thing to do. Isn't it interesting that God is asking you to do the right thing, but you prefer to do the wrong thing? Have you ever wondered why you are subconsciously drawn to doing that which is wrong?—the thing that you naturally do is wrong and doesn't require much effort because your words are directly controlled by demon spirits, unbeknownst to you? That is why your life continues to be messed up; your life is directly channeled and controlled by your words, whether you think so or not; and those words are controlled by the devil, utterly beyond your knowledge. Check out your words and what you've been saying; you'd be shocked at what you've been saying all your life.

Vanetta: But how do you get people to admit that something is truly wrong with them? No one wants to get that deep; people just prefer to see the world as some mysterious place—that it is, but that is not all it is.

Simeon: And with that I agree: A mysterious place it is, but it is much more than that: It is a spiritual decision: The world is a place of deciding spiritual destiny, where you make up your mind about reality. And you do not even have to believe that; you can act as if there is no decision to be made here. The truth of the matter is that you were born under the dominion of spiritual darkness: You are programmed to tell lies and do evil, but you would rather not admit that that is true; no one can live for the Supreme God and operate per the tenets of this false, evil world.

Vanetta: This is the very reason that we need to concentrate our effort of fixing our lives: The world is a supernatural place where spiritual forces call all the shots in folks' lives—people who don't know God. We must decide whether we are just going to follow the false, evil track of this world; or whether we are going to reprogram our lives according to the bold principles of Christianity outlined in the Bible. It is very obvious that Christianity is a clear reprogramming of life that is very different from the program here in this world; people clearly see the difference, but they ignore and downplay it.

Patching Things up

Oh, my! It seemed as if they had gotten back on the right track again; their words were quite congruent. Suddenly, they seemed to be on one accord, speaking the same things. Well, what had happened to this seemingly mismatched couple? As was stated earlier, these were not poor folks; and they had the whole world at their fingertips. However, Simeon's childhood abuse was not quite the whole story; he had intimacy issues and had been degraded by other women who said that he was not a real man and that he shied away from intimacy. And you know that such behavior would irritate any real woman—and it did. Simeon was fully cognizant of his erotic troubles and had sought help in that regard: He detested being called "a no-man"; and so, he wrestled with himself in order to balance his many intimacy issues.

However, there was one particular issue which he never mentioned; and perhaps, if his previous girlfriend, Avanah Heim, had settled her score with him, she might not have been able to take the load—and Simeon knew that. Sometimes, people think that they want certain things until they get them; and Simeon had discussed his problems with his mother, who had made certain suggestions to him; but he told her that things would all settle down, pan out, and he would be just fine. She had suggested to him to connect with clean, seasoned prostitutes who are skillful sexpots; however, he insisted on nature running its course and things panning out down the road. I guess you can see that this young man had a number of issues that needed to be fixed like yesterday.

Well, after all, these are some of the problems that people who work with God have to solve. All people have problems—all kinds of problems, and they often struggle with them: Simeon was no different--he had an oversized penis which could have been a challenge to most women—and it was certainly not that for which Vanetta was hoping. It is amazing how people go about and create realities that are entirely false. Vanetta was most certainly not anticipating her fiancé with a ten-inch penis, but that was what awaited her—and she had not even a clue about that.

Simeon: And oh, my dear; that is good talk: Now, you are talking, my love; and that is what I've been trying to say all afternoon: This is the reason that we must thrash out the issues and problems stalking the United States. What a curious, inscrutable, and eyebrow-raising place Columbia has become; oh, my, my! Though church revivals break out like wildfires, nothing seems to change in folks' hearts: The society still bristles with charlatans, crooks, witches, weirdoes, thieves, and scam artists. You might ask me if there are thieves in your Columbian society and animadvert about how insulting I am: Who do you think scam artists are—they are thieves, stealing people's identity and hard-earned money. Televangelist after televangelist continues to disgrace themselves and their congregations, and many have several wives—have you heard of those! I once saw a televangelist, draped between his two young and pretty wives: I almost fell out; I didn't know that the moral decay had gotten that deep and advanced.

Vanetta: This is the reason that we must focus our attention on fixing our love life first: Those people need prayer; but if our love life is in a mess, we cannot even pray for them—they and we are in the same boat. We must fix our lives first before trying to fix others'. Doesn't that make a lot of sense? I think that it does—don't you?

Simeon: Again, Christianity is transcendental; Christians are called to live vicarious, altruistic lives. Oh, the deadly toll that American society's moral wreckage has taken on life in America, and this would not have been so bad if America was not so busy in so many other countries' business. The burgeoning growth of witchcraft and sorcery has turned off the light of truth in America; America's backslidden Christian Church is lost in the fog of societal disgrace and ruin; oh, the church, that obese slob; trampled by the hooves of anarchy; shuns confronting evil and following the right path; as a result, virtually everything has gone wrong.

Vanetta: Simeon, tell me something: What has gotten into your head, all of a sudden? We have much patching up to do, but you keep prattling about false American Christianity: Why is that so important to you? Why are you so obsessed with the problems dogging Christianity in America?

Simeon: Oh, my dear love, with the softest and prettiest lips in the world; we cannot stop here: We cannot cease loving and being concerned about others, even while we build our love. Lost in the maddening noise of a vicious moral storm, the church is unable to respond; it's shrill, empty, feeble cry; devoid of God's power; is mocked by evil's brawling army. Its virtually meaningless presence has become irrelevant in a society that has gone crazy: Who will wake up America's Christian Church, lost in the fog of fraud and materialism? Not even the brawling, noisy hoodlums on the streets and on the Internet would try. The savage tempest of moral declension is raging in the dark streets of Columbia and making millions tremble for fear.

Vanetta: But you know, Simeon; you are so strange; you know the tunes that I love: You understand how to play them on the jukebox of your thoughts, sentiments, and words; but for reasons not fully understood, you've chosen to starve my heart for those tunes and to only play them once in a blue, blue moon. Oh, my dear, I look forward to some very wonderful intimate moments with you, my dear. I am just a woman who yearns for my love's wonderful kiss; it is just right and normal to desire that for which you are starved, and no valid reason is given.

Getting Around Town

Simeon: Oh, my dear darling love, the moral tempest is raging in the land of Columbia: Everyone's so sound asleep in his comfortable cubicle; he cannot hear the noise—oh, he cannot hear the angry, doomful noise of the groaning, fiendish storm about him. Lost in the moiling epicurean mist of a good time, his ears have been corked; his spiritual antennas have been snapped like matchsticks in the storm's groanful roar. The epicureans were drunk, lying on the gorgeous carpet; having sex in an orgy-like manner. They could not care less what was transpiring outside.

They could not hear the confused noises of the Philistines' horses' hooves, galloping nearby; the world's powerful billionaires could not hear the drumbeat of the haters, just a stone's throw away. Oh, the horsemen of America's ruin are coming—the Philistines and Achaeans are coming! They came before and did much damage; they woke the Columbians up, but they went back to sleep again— the phony Christian Church in America sent them back to sleep again. See the false Christian Church of America, gallivanting on the meadow of guile and believing that others would not recognize its shallowness and deception.

Vanetta: And Simeon, to top it off, you have the nerve to splash poetry in those golden sentiments; and when you do that, you cause my heart to crave your love and that poetry even more; and then, you take it all back. What a strange and funny lover you are; you must have some very special love in store for me, but I'll just wait my turn because I doubt that you are a man of such virtue; you bring so many doubts to my mind.

Simeon: Behold those stout, gamboling lambs on the green, poisonous meadow of earthly life; see how they gallivant like wild horses on the tawny grass of the wilted pastures. They've wandered so far away from the fore, they are almost unrecognizable; so many prosperous Christians—their waistlines are as wide as a sports utility vehicle! Well, that is the only prosperity that they know and want— food; they do not want to grow spiritually and get closer to God.

Vanetta: You have dragged me into this long, drawn-out discourse about human destiny: There are so many other things about which I would prefer to be talking at this moment, but for the reason that I am discussing these matters with you; I truly do not mind at all, for I know that, sooner or later; all this senseless stuff would drain off, and the real you will appear—the real romantic Simeon will show up.

Simeon: Groping in the whirling, cosmic fog of misleading, mendacious prosperity teaching; they've wandered so far from the truth: Many wondered about these strange, weary people; they wondered if these unblessed, obscure carnal Christians ever knew the man, Jesus Christ. The backslidden American Church has darkened the conscience of the entire society and have sent Americans down the wrong path. Many who longed for romantic marriages wound up with things that they could not handle and which they had no idea were there: They are like women who run after sex; and when they get it, they run from it. Why do some women assume that all men are the same, carrying the same rods of iron? Well, I guess; that is just a woman thing.

Vanetta: Yes, my love; a backslidden church is bad news for any society whatsoever; despite that fact, yet there is hope: Prayer makes all the difference in the world of man. And as for iron rods whirled around, passion can handle anything thrown at it.

Simeon: My sweet darling, oh, how you've warmed my heart by merely sharing my thoughts; it fills my bosom with so much joy to hear you utter a thought that means so much to me. America's fallen Church has sold its spiritual interests to the inscrutable Bilderbergers: It has left them to virtually run the show; and oh, what a quaint, dramatic show they've put on. Oh, the vociferous roar of spiritual darkness and moral decay in American society today! What a pity that I have to deal with so many issues that my dearest love hardly ever seem to understand; I'm a man wearing so many hats.

Vanetta: Has it occurred to you, Simeon, that America is not the only place undergoing moral decay? Human beings are the devil; they are always up to some kind of mischief; do you know why their minds are under the influence of demons. Why are you pouncing so much on America? I think that you are unfair and are not giving our country a fair judgment, but I understand what you are saying—I understand your ire with the Church.

Simeon: But how can you say that? You are not supposed to utter such dark, deep truths: Human beings are not supposed to know that they were born wrong and need to get right; you are supposed to sugar coat the truth for them, pampering them with deceitful comments and preparing them to go to hell. That is the program that is designed for the world; it is a program of deceit and falsehood, leaving people with the wrong impression about the world and how it really works. Men, arrayed in shaggy hair dos and mysterious cell phones, came from afar; their phones whistled like trees in the wind, and oh, my. No one was expecting what happened next, but I'll personally help you pray for America; it has wandered too far away from God, and he has given it up; he has simply moved out of America's way, allowing it to do its own thing. And what is that? America 's three and four shooting sprees per day have jerked the slack out of her.

Vanetta: What utter folly—what foolishness! Jesus came to bring light to a dark world; thus, isn't it our commission to talk to the world and explain these dark truths to people? Well, that is our job to pray for America, no matter what is happening. America is in the wilderness right now; she has wandered far away from God and needs all the prayer in the world right now.

Simeon: But you may not be able to tell Americans that; they have a different understanding of things: They see Christians as jokers— the American Church has backslidden right before their eyes. Its clamorous clanging has deafened the ears of the battered, beleaguered soldiers of truth. Moral darkness' bellowing roar has drowned out all the voices of reason and soberness; their maddening horns' brash, loud decibels daily disturb the restless, untamed peace.

Vanetta: My heart goes out to the untamed children of moral decay in our society; may their restless spirits reach out to the timeless and vicarious Jesus who died for them.

Simeon: And may the surge of utter mayhem and lawlessness be staunched in Columbia: The growth of sociopaths, serial killers, and weirdoes has created a virtually new society; they are the product of the corrupt, venal school system. This obscure, eerie showcase of moral decay has earned Columbia a new distinction: The strange, new ochlocratic gathering in the West, where morals don't matter anymore. America's picturesque, jarring showroom of societal decay has left many breathless—it is hard to see where Columbia is today, and the moral slide just continues on and on. Such behavior is clearly not sustainable—what do you say?

Suddenly, there was a switch to longer sightseeing destinations; and instead of just spinning around in Jerusalem, this pert couple opted for more distant destinations and wheeled their rented jeep to the Dead Sea. As they went, they continued discoursing on the matter of the moral collapse in the United States; they had talked enough about phony American Christianity's fake revivals and the intense lawlessness that has broken out in Columbia.

They just hoped not to run into anymore molls and courtesans around the Dead Sea; however, they seemed to have switched from Simeon's personal erotic problems to the outbreak of societal breakdown in Columbia. As they pulled into the Dead Sea's parking area, the entire desert area around the quaint pond was spangled with Dead Sea fans: Some were showering under a pipe close by; some were walking around in exotic swimwear, taking a strange sunbath; some were making connections for later on. Others were sitting smack in the sea itself; reading books, riding on the waves, or just chatting up a storm with a friend or lover nearby. It was a rather pictoric scene to behold.

As the couple pulled into the desert pond's parking lot; they stopped, parked, and continued talking and soaking up the beauty of the obscure environment. It was a rather picturesque scene and pictoric scenery indeed, with so many people strewn on the shore of this very curious desert pond; this dashing couple just continued talking—and they behaved as if they were quite at home. The environment's mood did not seem to change their perception of what was important to them; they'd already defined that—each other; and so, that was their entire focus. However, that did not say that the environment didn't matter to them; obviously, they were there to enjoy the flaming scenery and were somewhat swallowed up in it initially. Notwithstanding, they quickly reconnected with was really important: Patching up their love lives and reconnecting with fixing their various issues.

Vanetta: Oh, my! What a difference an environment makes; this pungent seaside made quite an impression: Wouldn't you say, Sim? So, what are you doing—are you celebrating evil's utter triumph over the West? Where is your compassion for the fallen human race that has chosen the broad, wrong road to hell? Are you celebrating the Western World's downfall or emphasizing the Church's call to prayer and repentance?

Simeon: I'm neither celebrating America's moral collapse nor the West's downfall: I'm merely highlighting the sheer moral drop that these societies have sustained: Yes, Vanetta; your society has fallen from a great height; sociologists ought to discuss that. Oh, Columbia's messy, polluted public policy has made her the tenth wonder of the world. See America, the land of the free and the Godless, lost in the uncanny parlor of witchcraft: Oh, behold America, the land of liberty; dancing in the venomous smoke of amorality! Pull her muddled children from the howling sandstorm of moral insanity and sorcery; oh, God, stretch forth thy hands and pluck them from the angry jaws of pauperdom. Reach down to her with mercy and fill the stomachs of the many children who go to sleep at night hungry, right there in America—and that number has ballooned into millions in recent years!

Vanetta: Oh, how I pray for the souls of confused lovers who've been lost in the fog. The world is filled with addled, broken-hearted people who are stuck and lost in their yesterdays. Even though their parents inflict heavy blows on each other, they don't have to take it out on their lovers; and they can certainly fill their lovers in with these secrets—the secrets that they've kept from everyone else and be a source of refuse, comfort, and understanding.

Columbia's Careless Ride to Hell

Well, could they have just sat there and talked to one another for two hours or so? The ambiance was piquantly arresting, and they seemed to have been enjoying this seemingly endless discourse about morality. They'd been on that topic for several days now; but now they seemed to have exhausted it. In that regard, they switched the conversation; and it assumed a more serious tone, involving the growing threat to public life in America. Somehow or other, though, Vanetta seemed to agree with Simeon's attitude about the problems weighing down public life and the American Public School System, but she was somewhat bemused by Simeon's obsession with American culture and his thorough knowledge about the American Public School System. She wanted to know how he came by all that knowledge; he seemed like a rank authority on the problems facing American public schools and the society as a whole.

Simeon: God of heaven, reach forth your hand and extract America's children from ruin's mouth: Oh, America, many of the day's brightest thinkers now express grave concern about thy strayed path, even the fieriest of thy cheerleaders now question thy hold on world dominion. You've lost your grip on world supremacy's rudder and on just about everything else; thy children of bloom, mesmerized by drugs and promiscuity, now grope in the dark—yea, they flounder in the tenebrous hall of suicide and confusion; lost in the cave of moral relativism. Who will reach out and give Columbia a helping hand back to safety's shores?—just who will do it!

Vanetta: And do you think that you can stop hard-core pagans from taking their own lives? As I said earlier, each person must decide whether or not he wants Christianity's truth: Christianity is the ultimate truth in the world of man, which is a flagrant mosaic of lies; but the world doesn't see itself that way—and that is the problem. Because that route of lies is broad and easy to follow, with no major inconvenience to my fellow Columbians and inhabitants of earth; billions go along for the ride; and oh, what a ride it turns out to be for so many people—what a ride to hell that it turns out to be for so many people in Columbia and in the rest of the world! I hear you, Simeon's; you begin to make sense now. Evil is fine for those who revel in its short-term benefits; but do not deceive yourself: Those long-term consequences are certainly coming, and you will discover them all in hell after that long ride on the broad, messy road of this world.

Simeon: The seductress of drug addiction has sucked Columbia's children into its vacuum of doom; and working with the guileful enchantress of suicide, it has washed millions away, many of whom once reveled in hell's short-term benefits. Ultimately, the piper soon came around and had to be paid; and for many people, the payment was their souls: They had sold that to the bad shepherd and were doomed for the rest of eternity.

Vanetta: And yes, millions—and even billions—are washed away on life's false road; they follow the easy, broad, and enticing way of this world with its impunity-driven tort. We are told that life ends at the end of this life; this world is all there is to it: Live it up and have fun; when you are dead, you are done.

Simeon: The world is a sick place of sorrow and woe; the multifarious issues multiply by the day: Morgues, overflowing with corpses, greatly complicate the toil of staff workers; and jails, jammed with criminals, regurgitate them back into the dark chasm of society's streets. And there they continue their slaughterous campaign on the innocent and unsuspecting: Cash-strapped cities, bedeviled by financial shortfalls, throw reason out the window. Benumbed by the mushrooming growth of crime and a declining tax base, America's once dynamic urban political machine has virtually ground to a halt.

Life, as they have always known it, has disappeared in the swirling fog of fiscal troubles: large urban centers, sucked into the chasm of societal decay, shut down vital institutions; releasing millions of insane people on the streets. Oh, the streets, awash with shanty towns, turn aristocratic city areas into shabby slums—and they are everywhere you look. Can't you see, Vanetta, America is dying, floundering in the dark; the strain of sorrow is everywhere in America. Who will rush to her aid?

Vanetta: Make no mistake about it: The wages of lies and ruinous behavior do add up; people pay an exorbitant price for following the broad and easy way of this world. The evening news, flooded with sorrow, makes even the devil himself want to cry! Society has made its decision; it has built its house on the sand of lies and deceit, and oh, what a bumper crop it is reaping.

Simeon: Whole cities, as wide as the sea, are gobbled up by urban blight; these sprawling cities file bankruptcy and are virtually turned into trash. Waste, mismanagement, corruption, and weeds; growing in their city halls; poison whole cities! Critically needed mental asylums are summarily closed, tossing everyone into the streets; sprawling penitentiaries, flush with business, pelt hardened criminals back into society. They shoot at police officers at the drop of a hat: Police go down every day, falling like leaves from autumn's naked trees. Half-naked girls, attired in the colorful garb of hookers and harlots, roam the streets; yea, they wander about the streets around the clock, throwing themselves into every man's arms. They fling their bulging bosoms in the sickening glare of everyone's glowing eyes. Lawless middle school girls, more brash and brazen than hookers on the streets, shower classrooms with verbal sewage more nauseating than Bombay's slum dwellings.

Vanetta: Simeon, the world operates on the agricultural principle; no one shall escape: Those who are now busy, sowing wild oats, will reap a bountiful harvest down the road; somewhere in the future, a bumper crop of ruin and trouble patiently awaits them. But oh, how pathetic: People are wired to lie, to do wrong, and then to be destroyed later on! Is that the essence of human society, but that is not what they tell you; they sugarcoat it with all kinds of lies and wangle you into believe all those serpentine falsehoods.

America's Public Education Travesty

Simeon: My dear, sweet bunch of summer fruits; what a thought that you've brought forth! School children, who are taught to disrespect both teachers and parents, sow wild oats; vile, profane words; louder than the noise of a cannon, rip like slugs from students' mouths. They sound like roaring, hungry lions deep in the bowels of night's dark, uncanny jungle; girls, shamelessly garbed, fling their legs on classroom desks before male teachers. Stunned and horrified at the sight, these bruised angels wonder what, on earth, is going on!

Downcast, burnt-out teachers stand there; puzzled and bewildered; lost in confusion. Oh, teachers; trapped in the fog of moral chaos; feel helpless, lost, and demoralized. Groping in these vile factories' dark smoke of moral decay, they feel so alone and lost—oh, these moral slums that turn teachers into aborted babies, lost in the cave of evil. Many innocent teachers; lured by hookers in middle school; are enticed, trapped, and sent off to prison for twenty years!

Vanetta: Somewhere, somehow, children are taught to disrespect parents and teachers: Schools conspicuously omit moral training, and teachers who emphasize it are spanked; they must choose between violating the appropriate code of conduct and keeping their jobs because administrators don't want to shake things up. The rarest thing that you would find in public schools today is a morality-driven teacher and school policy: Why is that so? That is so because public schools in America are not set up for children to obey authority and get an education. Any honest teacher who is not tied into the system of lies, deceit, and fraud would agree.

Simeon: But oh, my lover girl, I never thought that you would say that—oh, how honest you are! Schools, turned into moral slums, manufacture a vile company of criminals and jailbirds; see the wriggling fetuses of helpless teachers, brashly snatched from the moral slums of public schools and sent to jail forever! See how these crass public schools mold and corrupt these passionate, innocent angels. Oh, teachers, the very juice of their lives is wrung out in the moiling mills of these factories of moral decay. And ever so often; these very molders of young, lost minds fall through the cracks: Floundering in the whirling fog of a broken school system, many well-meaning teachers fall prey to folly. Yea, many teachers become victims of the lecherous motions of vice around them; Teachers, the golden fingers of social nurturing, ever so often, lose the moral war and are shipped off to prison for twenty years and more. By the time they are released, their lives are over; and all their juice has been sapped in the prison system.

Vanetta: But why should teachers lose the moral war in a totally amoral environment? If the psychological ethos of their world is conducive to teaching well-disciplined children, shouldn't they perform spectacularly; seeing that they started out with so much passion? Where did all that passion for education go? It was stolen from them in the vile factories of ruin. Somewhere along the way, they lose that passion for educating young people and developed a passion for sex with lusty, bloomy girls, hornier than they.

Simeon: Oh no, no, Vanetta; you cannot say that—that is politically incorrect, you know! Draped in zeal and innocence, these teachers become soiled by the stain of false public education; enticed by the guileful enchantress of lust, these well-intentioned professionals give in. Oh, these revered people of honor yield to the enticing, deceitful bait of lust and vice; and what irredeemable ruin that false public education brings upon honor's servants! They lose their way in the dark, dreary halls of public education; so, filled with vice, so flush with opportunities to get into trouble with young girls. Oh, public education in America, so filled with vanity; so lost in the cosmic fog of folly. What a guileful and deceptive machine it has become.

Vanetta: Why must teachers, our strong angels, be gaffed by such seductive bait of lust? Why must they fall prey to the picayune music of a few overheated moments of venery? The truth of the matter is that many of the girls are not children; they are thoroughly schooled in adult life and understand adult men's hot zones; and, as you know, boys would be boys, and men would not be challenged by little children; especially by little girls. So, unfortunately, many innocent teachers are booby trapped and shipped off to prison:

All too often, male teachers are not the only ones yielding to this uncanny bait. More often than not, female teachers; spurred on by the same chaos-driven, morally slimy environment; are among the many *Great Whites* who are caught in this drag net; many of whom make babies for their students. This is how loose the public-school system has become, and to put some icing on the cake; even administrators sometimes bite the bait, are caught in the net, and are sent to prison for an extended period of time. This gives you an idea of how corrupt society and the public school system have waxed.

Simeon: Oh, these strong angels lose their way in the dark halls of sin and moral debauchery. Reason and soberness; like frisky little children, clapping their hands on a hill far, far away; forever try to reach the dark ones in corrupt public schools: They scream and bellow. Oh, see the little children: Their tender, tiny hands have been clapping for decades now. Who would listen to them—no one; the voices of reason and moral decency have wilted; and now, the guns and insane shooting sprees have entered the picture and muddied things up even more. Yea, reason and moral decency have faded from the picture: Their pungent voices of reason and soberness have been drowned out in the loud, crushing din of human hebetude; they are the merciful attorneys of public schools' fallen heroes—those ruined children of honor. Thus, in this cruel, frenzied war of moral travesty and human vanity; so many losers are born, and so many live behind darkened prison cells.

Vanetta: As I've stated earlier, the world is a lie; its context is mendacious and sophistic: Formerly passionate teachers who turn into child molesters simply learn the truth about life: They learn the hard way that this whole world is an illusion, instituted by the devil himself. By then, though, it's way too late for them: They heard it before; but it sounded like a fairy tale to them, so they paid it no mind. I tell you what: It is no longer a fairy tale; is it? Behind those darkened iron bars of prison life, there are no skeptics. Man has a choice: He can choose the Bible and create a glorious society; or he can choose his own selfish desires and become a slave to them, winding up in prison for the rest of his life. This, unfortunately, is the choice that many teachers make and wind up reaping lengthy prison terms for going along with the world's devilish way of doing things.

Simeon: And why should there be any skeptics behind the dark, cruel bars of prison cells? Amidst the fog, the vanity, the sophistry, and mendacity of this world; so many losers are born: They are the little children on a hill far, far away; who are, forever, sounding the alarm of impending ruin of guns blowing their horns in the hallway. The are the once zealous teachers who've tripped, fumbled, stumbled, and fallen in vice-driven hallways; they are the students who are trained to become whores, hookers, weirdoes, witches, and jailbirds! These long-forgotten groups are the real losers in public schools' moral frenzy's vicious war—and you know that I'm just speaking the truth and telling you like it is, but this is not what you want to hear.

Vanetta: And where are the children of honor: Who've taught them to be losers? Their intentions were so noble; and they were so filled with zeal, passion, and fire—where did all that go! Oh, Simeon, Simeon; why did they fall through the cracks? Tell me more; tell me more! These are human beings and valuable lives, thrown away like trash: Is this that to which human civilization has come—is this what our great society is promoting in the world today? Well, I must say that I am shocked and lost in the fog of this truth!

The False World's Teachers' Sorry Plight

Simeon: Who are the children of honor—those who have sex with minors? No, not at all! Honor's real children are the once gentle human beings who've been soiled by the putrid system of public schools in America; public education is a factory of corruption that its workers learn to relish over time: They just didn't become fans and consumers of oversexed children just like that; it was a slow process after the truth about public education soaked into their bones. Once it touches your world, it changes you forever! Honor's children are teachers who've been gaffed by the cruel traitors who run public schools; these heartless mercenaries, sheared of morals, are the bubbly children of the devil himself; they are the ones who do all the dirty work.

Vanetta: No teacher—society's very angel—ever got into public education to go to prison; no teacher ever intended to disgrace himself and his family's name by molesting minors. Every teacher, seduced by the bait of lust and venery's few steamy moments, was sucked in—gradually: He or she was dragged into that kind of zone in environments where that kind of stuff goes on: A teacher's steaming escapade with a student reflects a culture of naughtiness and debauchery. Day after day, it is tossed at your feet on a gold and silver platter; the girl begs the teacher to meet her at some cozy place where no one, *in the know*, will be around. The cozy location is far out of regulars' reach, and the corrupted angel feels utterly safe: The female teacher invites her favorite male student over to her pad for the weekend, under the guise of school-related work. In both cases, the environment seems relatively safe until someone drops the ball; someone gets careless and overconfident, or someone becomes pregnant. And, in these strange days, the female teacher is the one who is increasingly becoming pregnant by her underage male student.

Simeon Oh, my dear love; we've hardly agreed all evening; but I have to agree with you here: We must pray for the many teachers who slip down this dark pit—they've been devoured; yea, these well-meaning human beings slip through the cracks, down into this dark, dangerous pit and vanish forever! Oh, my sweet darling dear; they are the bruised pearls, corrupted in society's umbrous moral slums: They spend virtually the rest of their lives behind the obscure, shadowy veil of prison life. With their intrinsic vulnerability ignored by the shabby, unthankful wolf of society; their only sympathizers are the cynical, hard-core criminals; carrying on in the adjacent cells.

Oh, the harsh, wanton lash of society's whip of ingratitude on lost, forgotten teachers' backs! Many of these imprisoned female teachers, stashed away in caliginous prison cells for a good while, are raped and impregnated again by unscrupulous prison guards who are supposed to be their custodians. This, however, hardly ever makes the news because prisoners are supposed to be mistreated—after all, they are prisoners, aren't they? More than a thousand pregnancies occur in the prison system every year; and many of these are the work of prison guards, preying on helpless female inmates: Many of these females are lost teachers, trapped in the fog of a captured environment and tempted beyond their control.

Vanetta: Oh, Simeon, Simeon, stop it; you almost make me want to cry my heart out; society mistreats teachers, every day, by paying them a salary that forces many to live on the streets. How shameful, and abominable, and inhumane human society is! It disrespects the most important people in its midst by disregarding their need to survive in the world and shoving them into prison at its earliest convenience. I'm telling you; many teachers were raped by their students: Things went too far with the student; and by the time the teacher looked around, it was too late to stop the moral trainwreck— the damage had already been done.

The student caught the teacher off guard, in one of her weaker moments, and pushed the envelope: Losing face and not knowing how to stop the complicated situation, things rapidly spun out of control; and before the teacher knew it, she had already bitten the dust. The student, thoroughly experienced in matters of adult life, had already ignited all the female teacher's intimate zones; causing her to fall flat on her face. Having been overstimulated and not in touch with reason and herself, those erotic juices gushed like water from a broken pipe; and sometimes, that is all it takes to create a total mess.

When the teacher woke up the next day, her kitty was filled with the student's love: She was utterly lost in the wrong lane; and before she knew it, she was in all kinds of trouble that she had never imagined. Oh, Simeon, you make me want to cry when I realize how vulnerable and unprotected female teachers are: Their innocent kitty is so unprotected from the strong winds and virile sperms of aggressive male students, who take advantage of the moral mess in the dark, confused school system in America.

Simeon: And cry, you should; this is the world in which we live and the people we see on the streets every day. Oh, the whip of injustice, splashed across the bruised backs of these humble public servants— behold ingratitude's indelible scars, branded upon the backs of these fallen angels. Yea, teachers who've toiled long, hard hours in the horrid trenches of moral chaos are summarily dismissed and thrown away, into dark prison cells like trash! Yes, they are teachers, children of honor who should have exercised better judgment; but they are disrespected and lampooned by their students, day after day, and are taunted by the bait of steam and fire.

Simeon's Studious Research

Vanetta: Simeon, tell me: How do you know all of this? Who told you all this stuff? Who gave you all this information about my society and its moral problems? You seem to know more about my society and its problems than I do, and I am angry about it! Who told you all of this?

Simeon: That is because you belong to the bourgeoisie class; you are an aristocrat—aristocrats hardly ever notice the pain and anguish that the rest of society feels every day; and besides, this is the dynamic, titanic Age of the Information Revolution in the world that refuses to prosecute plain criminals. The mess in your society is everywhere—brain science is not needed to find it. And again, I'm not vilifying and vituperating you, my darling dear, the most beautiful woman in the world: I am blasting the crass, callous, abject system of false Christianity and the evil that it has encouraged in this world.

Vanetta: I understand your feelings about hypocrisy and its negative effects on mankind; but I'm not responsible for people's misrepresentation of the pure teachings of Christ. I know that there are people who intentionally distort the Bible for their own gain; they present Christianity as a *get rich quick* gimmick, extorting millions of dollars from misguided church people: Quite frankly, that kind of Christianity is illegal and regrettable. There are people out there who are quite unscrupulous and merely take people's money away from them; but there are others out there as well. These are honest men and women who execute their ministry to their parishioners with integrity; these are true men and women of God, like Dr. Price, who are called to the ministry and present the Bible in its entirety and proper context. Unfortunately, these are far and a few about whom you hardly hear.

Simeon: But for every Dr. Price, so many others misrepresent the Bible and its holy agenda. We are thankful for the few Dr. Prices in this world and the great good that they are doing; moreover, this gentleman, from Los Angeles, has had an impeccable record.

Vanetta: Wherever you go, Simeon, there will always be those who misrepresent the truth; but many will choose not to lie and give people false hope, and that is comforting indeed. Some people were produced from the good side of the fruit that Eve ate in the Garden of Eden; others came from the other side of things and choose to mirror that side.

Simeon: Whatever moral decay there may be in this world, phony American Christianity has done it; and the damage is virtually irreparable; I'm deeply frustrated with those who play games—I'm livid with people who play games, flashing the veil of secrecy to hide the darkness and the mysterious world to which they belong: Oh, the caliginous veil of secrecy that hides shadowy covens, splattered across America. Evil serpents, clad in human flesh and as pretty as a star, work in the secret world of darkness: Their grin, as charming as an angel's smile, takes Jesus himself to detect their guile and identity; these dangerous human beings, quaint demon spirits themselves, are the essence of fraud.

Oh, these serpentine school districts in America, rank secret societies, play games with people's children; oh, my, the hell that has been carved out for them is beyond words—it cannot be described. What a world that awaits them after this short vacation on earth is over! They're black, bloated owls and fat rats that hold positions handed to them from the black curtain of the middle of the night. Oh. good heavens, Vanetta; I wish I can tell you more, but I must close it here now. My dear, my dear; there is so much more to say; it can only be whispered into your ears.

And above all, you need to know about fourteen-year-old girls, right here in Israel, who are forced into prostitution; these things do not know any national borders; they are ubiquitous and know no skin color either. Many of these girls were raped by their fathers, brothers, and uncles as young as three years old: As time passed, they've come to know nothing else but wrong living; and with badly wounded and bruised-up intimate parts, they eventually evolve and graduate into becoming prostitutes; many hardly make it out of prostitution alive!

Vanetta: But oh, my dear, why all *this*, and that, and the other that has absolutely nothing to do with us—is it that you do not know how to talk to, and what to do with, a woman—is it that you do not know how to make a woman feel like a real woman? These are not the things that I want to hear: I want you to tell me how much you love me and teach me how to have a good time with the man of my dreams. Tell me Simeon: Don't you know how to talk to a woman—I know you do because all these women here in Jerusalem are after you.

Simeon: There is more to life and love than sex: Oh, my, it does so much damage to people's lives: We live in a world society that worships sex and kills the babies that it produces; and when they are done, the nightmares that the abortions cause drive many women out of their minds—and thousands commit suicide! They are constantly crying and are a mess: You have no idea of the many women whom I've met and had, and the many times when they moved me to tears about the abortions that they've had and the horrible experiences that they've had with it. Oh, the many abortions that they've had and the jarring nightmares that they have every night, waking up in a pool of cold sweat: They've soured my heart about love, sex, and relationships. Moreover, I told you about my childhood abuse and my father's physical and verbal abuse of my mother: I'm still struggling with all of that. I spoke to Dr. Akiva Kaplan, Chief Counsellor at the Jerusalem Christian Center, and he recommended that we attend a relationship repair workshop that is going to be held at the church there in two weeks.

Vanetta, we are both broken people whose lives need to be repaired; you told me about the devastating break up that you endured with Anush, so this is not just me: We both need psychotherapeutic repair; and I talk like this to find a coping mechanism to relieve the posttraumatic stress that I've endured, growing up in that hellish Jerusalem home with my father and mother, and watching him ball up his fist and throw it into my mother's face—I went through all of that in that home. Vanetta, I'm still hurting from the pain that I endured, witnessing all that physical abuse that my father delivered to my mother; and I want you to be there for me and try to understand what I am going through because you are going through it, too.

Vanetta: Well, at least, this brings some closure to this most tenebrous mystery of your penchant to address other matters that have nothing to do with our love life; I'm glad that you've shared this matter with me again, and I will endeavor to be more understanding of the crisis through which you've been going. Love making has very little value in the brunt of this kind of storm. I just wanted to know and to ascertain that you, indeed, know how to talk to a woman and to make her feel like a rock star, my dear Simeon.

Simeon: It is not just me going through this crisis; it is us, and you need to see it in its proper context. The world is filled with broken people, and this explains why most of the marriages today fail: Billions of people, out there, are struggling with untreated or unprocessed emotional and mental wounds that have hamstrung their lives; devastating their self-esteem and sense of direction in life. Vanetta, we've talked about this; I've shared with you my vulnerabilities, and to hear you humiliate me like this is just rank painful—"You want to know if I know how to talk to a woman and to make her feel like a rock star": That is so humiliating!

We've agreed to leave the falling knife of sex until we are married: I do not want your father 's hitmen coming after me if you accidentally get pregnant without a ring on your finger. Those were some very crushing words: You know how many women have had abortions for me in this city—what do you mean by saying, "You were wondering if I knew how to talk to a woman and make her feel like a real woman?" The last thing that I want now is to hear you tell me that your period did not come for this or that month; that would mess up everything.

CHAPTER 13

MEASURED EFFORTS TO FIX BROKEN PEOPLE

Most people can see why the poor generally suffer from a variety of mental and emotional problems; they often do not have enough money to address the full range of their needs, and nothing causes emotional and mental problems and worries like money troubles. However, they are not the only ones who endure painful emotional stress and disturbance. Poor people often see rich folks as happy and having it all together; and they just wish that they can be like them: Rich people, on the other hand, know that there is more to life than mere money: The two groups of people often live in entirely different worlds and see things from a completely different point of view. However, this was not the sentiment that Simeon and Vanetta shared; they had endured intensely painful emotional scars that had affected their lives and ability to give and receive love like emotionally healthy and well-adjusted adults.

Against this backdrop, Simeon and Vanetta agreed to procure professional help in order to fix their confused, broken lives; although they were billionaires, they were very confused and unhappy people. Vanetta wanted to take the relationship to the next level and begin enjoying sex with her partner, but Simeon had been soured about sex, after meeting dozens of women who had been through the sex rush and trap and had been slammed by sexually transmitted diseases, abortions, abortion deaths, and its jarringly cruel and harsh nightmares. Simeon had had an earful of broken women's painful moments of disgust and sorrow over sexual experiences that went wrong—sex that produced pregnancies, and pregnancies that either drove women smack out of their minds or to commit suicide!

The Jerusalem Relationship Repair Workshop

Ultimately, Simeon had had it with the massive overrating that has been attributed to sex and the tremendous damage that it has wrought to, and in, society; in addition, Simeon knew that Vanetta's father was a fool who would shoot first and ask questions later if any man messed with his daughter and impregnated her, outside the context of marriage. For this reason, Simeon held his orgasm and resolved to work on himself and process the very raw and wounding abuse that he had endured as a child, growing up in Jerusalem. In that regard, he persuaded Vanetta to attend that Jerusalem relationship repair workshop and then to consult formally with the Dr. Cohen Consulting Group in Arnoma, Southern Jerusalem, about their relationship troubles. Obviously, a relationship workshop of this nature would normally be, and reflect, the disposition of a more conventional relationship repair workshop; the people, presenting the workshop, would assume a more secular approach to, and understanding of, the whole issue of a relationship of this ilk. However, the opposite was true of this relationship repair workshop.

The people, presenting the workshop, were more religious and tended to approach the whole topic of long-term, serious, intimate relationships from a theological and religious point of view: This was because the relationship repair workshop was presented by church people with secular educational credentials. At the same time, though, modern behavioral science—and science in general—have been greatly overrated; in terms of what they can deliver in these types of settings. Broadly speaking, in a workshop of this ilk, science and its liberal spin doctors are what is expected to be presented as law; in view of the understanding that God does not exist.

The world has been gravely brainwashed by the societal engineering that science is right, and God does not exist—and that is all too bad. In most cases, what modern behavioral science has to offer the world's broken people is a rank waste of time; and if you don't believe me, just look around and listen to the news. People have been pumped up with more liberal psychology than ever; at the same time, the world has waxed crazier and crazier than ever, a flagrant testimony to the fact that modern behavioral science is a waste of people's time and money; yet it is vigorously being promoted as the solution to people's problems while the world becomes wilder, sicker, and crazier than ever before. I wonder who is fooling who here.

Psychological counselling and drugs do not solve people's problems; they just sedate them and cool them down for a little while before their demons flare up again. Dosing up people with a whole lot of drugs merely sedates them and quiets down their demonic flaring, but it does not cure their problems. In many cases, the psychologist who is delivering the consultation has been divorced several times; and his life, itself, is riddled with serious problems that nobody can solve—is anybody home: is anyone hearing this? The Bible has been burlesqued and thrown out as being old fashion and uncontemporary, yet its solution of Jesus and his love for mankind is still straightening out people's lives today; as it has always done by separating them from the devil and their sinful ways, the very essence of the problems that they are having.

Sin is the cause of human problems; popular psychology utterly dismisses the whole idea of sin and presents itself as the solution to man's problems. All this is merely stated as *a buyer beware of the* fraud of psychological counselling, being presented as the societal panacea of human woes. While psychological counselling can do some good in relaxing people, presenting it as the sole solution to man's problems is a dangerous crutch and a curious snare. People's problems are caused by the devil, and only God can fix that: Only God can fix people's problems; all the other fixes are mere illusions—and you can take this to the bank!

For whatever all this was worth, Simeon and Vanetta attended the Jerusalem Relationship Repair Workshop and were pleasantly greeted by some of the finest behaviorists in the field; overall, the workshop was quite well-attended—the church auditorium, that seats about five thousand, was jammed; in fact, several people had to be turned away, as there was no overflow building on the church campus. Simeon and Vanetta were not cognizant that the world was that messed up and that that many people were hurting. The workshop was executed by Dr. Akiva Kaplan, Theologian and Counsellor at the Jerusalem Christian Center; Dr. Arleen Amsel, Marriage and Family therapist; and Dr. Emily Fertral, Self-Esteem Therapist.

The topics addressed were very raw and profound: Overall, the speakers accentuated the central notion that human problems are caused by sin through the agency some physical, mental, or emotional wound in the past; and, or present; that has not been, or is being, properly processed and healed. Thus, it continues to cause mental and emotional problems up to this point in the person's life. This was the backdrop against which the workshop was presented; in this regard, the presenters did not focus so much on relationships and their repair per se: Rather, they treated the cause of relationship problems: A wound of some kind in the past or recently. The first workshop was presented by Dr. Kaplan; he addressed the issue and problem of *Bad Connections from Past Trauma*; and as was stated earlier, he is a theologian and tended to focus on some of the more unconventional aspects of relationship trauma—and with reason. He briskly walked to the podium, smiled, and addressed the audience.

Dr. Akiva Kaplan: Good afternoon, ladies and gentlemen; what a dazzling summer afternoon this is, and how blessed we are to have been so warmly graced by your crowded presence; I am so pleased and touched by your warm presence here this afternoon, and I firmly believe in what we can deliver to you. All people in the world are seeking something, and what better search could there be than to find and maintain warm, healthy, and happy relationships with others. Well, we live in a very crowded and lonely world; and what a miserable oxymoron that is; nonetheless, it is so true. What we are going to do this afternoon is to set out to demonstrate to you that your problems are caused by wounds, of one kind or another, in the past, or by something that has happened recently. Thus, there is no mystery to human misery: If something happens now; in one minute from now, it has already slipped into the past.

What typically happens is that these painful incidents transpire and, sometimes, they are so painful, that they split the personality into two because the person cannot handle the level of conflict that the wound causes, as one person; it is too much for him to manage as one individual. Thus, his personality splits off in order to enable him to handle the pain from the wound created. In other situations, some behaviorists maintain that the painful experience gets frozen into the persons mind and emotions; causing him to consider the painful emotion as being himself, thus associating himself with the pain.

The wound causes the person to identify himself with the pain, thus pasting him to that moment and rendering him unable to separate himself from the painful, disgusting emotion. In other words, the horrible event and the emotions associated with it become the person and that becomes a bad connection with the past, a jarring fog that has to be cleansed and removed in order to clear up the person's life; and sometimes, with split personalities, the task is a Herculean one that can last for a very long time. The world, out there, is much more delicate and complicated than most people realize, for the simple reason that the real world is not what most people think it is: The world is a spiritual place—it is not as physical as it looks, and this is what confuses and deceives most people.

Dr. Kaplan: Awareness of Key Facts

What am I saying here to you? For example, in reference to what was just said, old childhood trauma; frozen into the person's subconscious mind for decades, can hold that person in that defective past moment past for years. The problem gets lodged in the person's subconscious mind, causing him to get, and remain, stuck in that nasty moment and leaving him wounded for decades. He is perfectly unable to separate himself from the wounded moment, which becomes his life. The young man identifies himself with the moment when his father picked him up like a sack of salt and was about to throw him through the window, when the police rushed in at that moment, scrambled his father up, and took him to jail that very night.

In another situation, a twelve-year-old girl may have experienced a similar situation with the same emotional effect. Her drunken father may have come in around 11:00 pm and ruthlessly raped her; plunging his ten-inch phallus into her womb, impregnating her, and forcing her to bring forth a baby into the world at that tender age. In that regard, in order to escape the searching arm of the law; her father told her to tag the baby on the boy, Asher, down the street. Because of the nasty event with her father, she was forced into adult life and to bringing a baby into the world at that tender age. At the same time, she was also forced to lie about the baby's father: She could not get away from her father until she was of age and got away from that home environment.

In both situations, the two bad experiences tore a wound in those two children's mind and ripped up the fabric of their emotional system, thus predisposing them to having the wrong attitude to the world. Accordingly, they became muddy, angry, sour, vengeful, and unforgiving human beings. People's behavior is conditioned by their past and present experience, their heredity, and their awareness of these influences on their lives; and even more importantly, that influence over their lives is amplified if they are not aware of it, or are aware of it but not aware that it is spiritual in nature. This helps us to see how dangerous the evolutionary point of view is: People's problems are spiritual, but evolution tells us that spirits do not exist.

Their unawareness of these facts renders them unvigilant to these booby traps and more vulnerable to falling prey to them. Thus, awareness of these key facts is critical to treating and cleansing yourself of these old childhood traumatic situations. In this regard, all relationships should revolve around understanding the other person's past and present circumstances—good and bad experiences because those experiences are the principal factors that influence their current behavior and attitude towards life and the world, one way or another. However, this oversimplified humanistic understanding of reality omits the broader spiritual machine or aspect of life that humanists, secularists, and modernists claim does not exist.

Negative experiences are caused by demons that shape people's lives in a negative way, and they don't care whether you think or believe that they exist or not. These dark spiritual forces are the principal engine driving human life in the world, liberal scholars cogently argue that these things do not exist; thus, human society is a lie—it has a hole in it and cannot be fixed as such. This explains why wars and divorce continue, despite all the progress that human society has made in the past. What is so paradoxical here is that these dark spirits are the very beings that are motivating liberal scholars to disown God's presence and spirits' existence.

The question that one might ask here is this: "Where did these spirits come from, or better yet; what is the origin of these bad spirits? But this is not how modern scientists think; this is not modern man's epistemology. What is epistemology? It is the study of where knowledge originates; and as far as I know, the modern theory of knowledge is evolution, the idea that there is no God: That leaves out a world of information that is absolutely necessary in order to understand life and the world. Do you see the problem? Evolution is the prison house of human society; life cannot be understood with it.

Dark Spirits' Origin and Work in the World

These are the original fallen angels that were cast out of heaven and have developed a great spiritual empire in the world; they rule over the darkness of man without God; this explains why the world today is so adamantly opposed to anything that is Christian because the current world has been crystallized by godless, atheistic modern science, based on evolution; thus, the corrupt world that you see today is the production of modern science, a totally godless, pagan institution that is utterly opposed to Christianity and God and open to anything that is pagan and dark. This explains why women are killing their babies and having sex with dogs.

Thus, two civilizations exist in the world; and all the religions that you see, except Christianity, belong to that same dark civilization. They are made to look and sound different from each other in order deceive the world: It is called *the mosaic of falsehood*. These were the same spirits that controlled the ancient, pagan world and that had erected all those huge stone temples and henges around the world without the aid of modern commercial cranes. These are found in South-West England, in Salisbury and Avebury; in Propriano, Corsica, France; in Sardinia, Italy; in Egypt; and in a host of other places around the world. Wherever you find them, they conjure up images of darkness and mystery—a mystical presence with no explanation and one which no one can understand. However, after the resurrection of Jesus, a diametrically opposite power; this ancient, pagan influence waned somewhat but has made a spectacular comeback during the

Enlightenment Age, when those dark spirits deceived the whole world again.

As you look at the world today, you can definitely tell that something is wrong with it; what is wrong with the world is that those dark spirits have made an ingenious comeback and have turned the world upside down: They've convinced modern science and other dark systems that Christianity is a joke; and because darkness is associated with falsehood and death, the world has become a death trap; and people are dying in all kinds of strange ways: Strange things are happening that make no sense, and people are committing suicide left and right; the world is rapidly rushing to its end. Why? The devil has deceived mankind again, and homosexuality and gay marriage is spreading like wild fire: You don't need rocket science to figure out what that means—mankind is phasing his own self out.

Man has opened up himself and his society to the devil; and those dark spirits have conquered the world of man and have made a mess of the world itself. These are the same spirits that cause emotional and mental problems among people, causing women to have sex with dogs and boys to have sex with their mothers—the whole world has been turned upside-down. These da gone nasty spirits represent the domain of darkness; these were the same spirits that cause destruction of the world's great civilizations of the past. Now, that the world has bluntly rejected Jesus; the whole world has become dark again and has opened up to the devil again like never before.

Notice that they can only function in a *DeJesusized* world. However, that is not the whole story; what we are looking at is the end of this dark age of human and the devil's control of the world—the world that you used to know is ending, and all the wickedness that you see in the world today will be burnt up and done away with forever! This explains why the world is so dark and sick; thus, psychology's shallow understanding of things is but a vain bluff. Just a cursory glance at the world today tells you that something is wrong with it—and what is that? Man has opened up to darkness again: The whole world is run by secularists, humanists, modernists, and naturalists—and they all adopt a purely humanistic understanding of the world, without the presence of spirits; and when you pull the blind away from all this madness, you would find that the essence of the world is spiritual.

 The world is essentially a spiritual place—God and the devil; anything else is false. While liberal psychology is correct in identifying the cause of human problems—a wound of some kind or the other in the past—it does not, and cannot, identify the real source of the wound. It is demonic in nature and hides behind man's inability to see these superhuman forces. The girl turned into a whore because her father savagely raped her when she was just twelve years old; ripping up the fabric of her emotional system, and thus giving her a false sense of reality: Her father gave her an appetite for the wrong kind of sex, thus turning her into a whore in the tenderer years of her life.

Dr. Kaplan: Psychology's Fraud and Shallow Answers

Why is psychology fraud? It pretends to solve human problems, a job that should be left to God; but it can't: It can only deliver answers that any good friend or keen observer can: To pretend to be able to solve human problems, when, indeed, it can't, send the wrong message to society about its very essence; especially one that excludes God from the picture. Psychology recognizes that dog sex is wrong and extreme but cannot tell the origin of the extreme energy that causes women to have sex with dogs; thus, the idea that human problems originate from some wound, delivered in the past, is only partially correct—and this is true whether it is child abuse, incestuous rape, or a sour and deep-seated rejection.

They all have the same source: Demon spirits working behind the scene. Ultimately, the original wound occurred in the Garden of Eden; but the Pope says that is a fairy tale: Do you see why human beings cannot get along and why human problems cannot be solved. Thus, ultimately, all your problems' solutions lie in the spiritual world where God and the devil operate; and disowning their presence is simply spinning your wheels. That is what evolution and modern science have done to the human race. These are concrete realities that exist in the world of man; they just exist at a level that cannot be seen with the naked eye. Saying that God doesn't exist is like saying the wind does not blow: You can't see the wind, but you see in which direction it is blowing, and you can feel it on your person; and if you get in the way, you will learn the hard way.

Here is the problem with psychology and most of the behavioral sciences: They waste people's time, take their money, and often leave worse than they were before. The truth of the matter is that psychologists are not God; human problems are very deep-seated and often involve aspects that are way beyond the psychologist's grasp. Moreover, as society becomes more and more derailed by the rogue liberal agenda; psychologists are going find it increasingly difficult to treat their clients, as they wax progressively demon-possessed. In view of the fact that society is largely demon possessed right now, practicing behavioral science; such as counselling, psychology, psychobiology, and psychiatry will become a rather risky undertaking indeed—and some of that is already happening now.

The darling world that used to exist has vanished, and the world that exists out there now is plainly no joke; you better know what you are doing, tampering with severely mentally and emotionally disturbed people—and you better be careful with the people with whom you become intimate. The idea of calling seriously demon-possessed people's behavior delusional possession and paranormal behavior is again only doing lip service to the problem and the truth. It is high time that behavioral scientists recognize that these behaviors are dangerous and rest the case of dealing with these risky human beings who are severely emotionally disturbed.

Thus, to wrap things up; the best relationship repair that can be delivered to well-meaning people; seeking help; is to locate the wound, process it properly, face the experience again in a new light, separate yourself from that experience, remain vigilant for that and similar ones in the future, and deal with the demons at the site. It is rather noteworthy that, unless the demonic element is treated, the problem remains. If you think that you are ugly, there are scores of things that you can do to improve your appearance; and remember, all people eventually lose their physical appeal over time. However, if a demon is telling you that you are ugly; no positive affirmation can fix that; the demon of rejection has to be cast out and the site (your mind) cleansed before the healing is complete. Beauty is merely an illusion—a passing cloud. Thus, you may want to view that rejection that you got as a child in a new light; knowing that all people are eventually going to lose their beauty and sexual appeal over time—it goes without saying.

If you are whorish and tend to want to cheat on your spouse, that is a moral wound that can sell you rather cheaply and diminish your self-esteem. Thus, you may need spiritual counselling and even exorcism to cast out that whorish, lustful spirit in your body and to remove from around you that licentious attitude to the world. Moreover, being a whore also predisposes you to being rejected by people: Nobody wants anybody who has been intimate with everybody. The wound of lust and whorishness may be connected to your heredity, and the solution is the same: seeing sex in a different light and recognizing that sleeping around with so many people puts your life in danger and robs you of the virtue of enjoying the person that you were meant to be.

Though it may seem as if I were verry rough, uncouth and unkind to certain groups of people; I want you to know that I'm only here to deliver answers—pragmatic, life-changing answers; and I said what I felt would help those who are genuinely seeking help. I was rudely awakened when I realize that everybody does not want help, and many people just like things the way they are; they don't want to change—and that's okay; it is their lives; but those who truly want to change have gotten enough meat on which to chew for a good while. Good evening, ladies and gentlemen.

What a very profound and honest workshop presentation that was; Dr. Kaplan truly addressed the powerful forces that shape relationships and cause them to go amok; most people, not aware that the world is a booby trap, are not vigilant and circumspect enough; they do not look for the invisible traps and landmines that are scattered all over the place. Many go around, looking for sex and treat reality as if it is a sex shop; they ignore the fact that sex is a family affair that produces serious responsibilities: It produces sexually transmitted diseases, many of which are deadly; it produces pregnancies, many of which contain several children.

When the pregnancy becomes obvious, it forces people into dangerous behaviors; many women die on abortion tables, and the abortions themselves generate nasty spells of darkness, depression spells, night sweats, and suicide encounters. Dr. Kaplan did his best to show his audience how to repair existing relationships and to create healthy, well-balanced ones. As he strolled away from the podium, Dr. Arleen Amsel, a marriage and family specialist, cheerfully walked up to the podium; she addressed the problem of *Fear of Intimacy and Success in Relationships.*

Dr. Arleen Amsel: Fear of Intimacy

Well, good Afternoon; I see so many smiling faces that reflect the perception and attitude of people who have been thoroughly nourished by Dr. Kaplan, a profound scholar of theology and modern counselling theory—his doctorate in counselling, from one of Jerusalem's most prestigious universities, was well earned! Would you all stand and give Dr. Kaplan a rousing applause; he has truly delivered a breathtaking presentation to all of us here this afternoon and has opened my eyes to many things that I had never seen before. We treat human behavioral problems as if they are an end in, and of, themselves: We know that these mental and emotional disturbances are caused by wounding events that unfolded in the past—we know that, but those events do not occur in a disconnected world or vacuum; it is abnormal for a father to rape his twelve-year-old daughter; but what makes people do these things—what pulls people across the line of truth and good judgement, causing them to do crazy things like these?

That part is hidden from us because the agents, responsible for those behaviors, hide behind the scene or stage of the visible world, and this is why we have and this is why we have no business saying that there is no God. All of us, behavioral scientists, are looking at the same things: We are just looking at them from a different point of view. Something is wrong with man—what is it? We only know in part because we are only allowed to view part of the broader problem. Why are people afraid of intimacy and success in intimate relationships? Intimate relationships seem so natural, and real, and desirable—why would someone be afraid of something as wonderful as that? being snuggled and caressed by a member of the opposite sex feels so real; the people feel as if they belong to each other—how does it get so perverted and strange, and how does it get to the point where people become afraid of each other?

It is obvious that fear is real and is caused by some concrete entity within one or both of the parties: How does a man become afraid of kissing his charming wife? It is obvious that people relate to higher powers with a fearsome demeanor; and when you come into their presence, you can tell that something is wrong with them that they themselves don't know what it is and cannot relate effectively with their own selves. All my colleagues are atheists and think that I am crazy to embrace the foolishness of Christianity, but I was raised in a home where Bible reading and prayer were daily family activities; and Christianity had been riveted into my bones. Though evolution had been hammered almost daily into my system while I was working on my doctorate, it failed to take root; and all the while that was going on, I knew that modern science is false and belongs to the other side.

I simply never bought the trash that they were tossing at me: It is cool to believe that God does not exist at the university with a bright future ahead of you; however, no one stays young, pretty, and beautiful all the days of her life. Sooner or later, youth's luster and shine begin to fade away; and you begin to lose the self that you knew and to gradually become folded up trash, ready to be taken to the human landfill of meaninglessness—ouch, that hurts! Despite the fact that we know that this is true, it is not what we want to hear nor believe; thus, we wind up deceiving our own selves about truth.

Dr. Amsel: The Consequences of the Wound

In dovetailing and conforming to Dr. Kaplan's wound theory, fear of intimacy is caused by a wound, of some kind or other that transpired in the past. I am a marriage and family therapist and tend to approach this kind of issue or problem in a deeply Socratic way; the particular prism from which marriage and family therapists approach fear of intimacy is through digging into the person's past, in particular, his childhood. On the other hand, a teacher who got pregnant for her student but did not get caught can also develop a deep fear of relationships because she underwent a great shock, on realizing that she was pregnant for the little boy over whom she had been given custody. Just being pregnant is a shocker, in and of, itself, much less finding out that you are pregnant for your student.

Generally, when such a lusty shock occurs, it creates a gaping wound in that teacher's spirit; and the relationship often comes to an abrupt end. Sometimes, the teacher gets caught and is sent off to jail, accentuating and magnifying the shock. This explains why, not too infrequently, when many of these female teachers go to prison, they they often fall prey to the prison system itself, becoming pregnant again for the prison guards. This is because of the gaping wound that that first pregnancy for their student produced. Along with that wound is a massive shock that threw her system out of compliance.

These two negative consequences, arising from having sex with their students, have blown their sockets. Overcoming that condition would take a long period of deshaming therapy and forgiving themselves and the students with whom they've belittled themselves. Can that teacher-student relationship ever be restored? It most definitely can but will be extremely difficult: That teacher crossed a forbidden boundary and created a false behavioral dynamic with her student, and that false dynamic has been etched into her subconscious mind.

Facing the Fear of Intimacy

Because this kind of wound is related to very extreme behavior, demon spirits are often involved in these abnormal, extreme types of relationships. All abnormal relationships have demonic ramifications: Why? Because the behavior is abnormal, something has to be done to impart some special quality to this relationship in order to keep it going; thus, it produces intensely strong orgasms in order to tie the two people together and to bring them back into the same situation again, and again, and again. It is somewhat akin to an interaction marriage: While you may view black people as inferior, when you find a black lover whom you truly love and admire, no one better call her inferior in your presence. The bond that is formed in these interracial marriages is generally stronger than that in normal relationships. This is why these kinds of relationships are so difficult to break; thus, they produce wounds that are not that easily healed; thus, the hate that you'd have for family members who dislike your black lover can be very strong.

Even if the teacher did not see the student for years; when she eventually sees him again; that perverted bond is still there. However, by then, the age difference hardly matters anymore. These relationships are so intense that, quite often, the parties involved don't even try to tackle the problem because of the fear and insecurity that was generated in the initial encounter, especially after the teacher discovered that she was pregnant. However, regardless of how much fear and insecurity that have been generated, the problem has to be solved by facing it with a different mindset. Instead of viewing Miss Adams as your teacher, you must now view her as just another woman with whom you had a fling earlier in your life or just a few weeks ago. Because the incident breeds so much fear and insecurity, as a coping mechanism; you must do some role playing with a trusted friend to face down that fear and insecurity that the relationship has generated. This would help you to treat the wound and clear yourself of its painful agony.

What you don't want is to get stuck in the teacher-student relationship episode and make that become a part of your life; you must separate yourself from that event and moment. Because you cost your teacher her job and career, you may carry around much guilt. Thus, you would have to forgive yourself for impregnating your teacher; you would have to see her as just another woman with whom you've had an affair that ended in pregnancy; and you would have to see the pregnancy as not being your fault. Rather, you must see it as your teacher's because she encouraged you into the illegal act.Because of the guilt factor, even though you may try to make the relationship with your teacher work, that guilt may not be that easy to overcome because, every time you make a step forward, you make two backward. This keeps you stuck in that rut and afraid of relationships. You become afraid of relationships because of the wound and shock from that which was so wonderful between you and your teacher.

Obviously, professional counselling, therapy, and prayer may be necessary to help you overcome this hugely difficult event that has overpowered your life; it may have also changed your perception of relationships and sex forever! Because this is a very traumatic event for both student and female teacher, it must be carefully treated, cleansed, and healed before either of these two human beings can get involved into anymore sexual relationships. However, this is not the way the world works: More often than not, without working on themselves and repairing the breach; these selfish people go right on into new relationships, infecting others with their germs.

This explains why society is so dysfunctional and perverted: People are too sex-driven and irrational; they are emotionally and mentally ill but go around as if all is well. In the process, they infect society with the germ of their emotional and mental madness; and society—and the world, as a whole—become more corrupt and confused with mentally sick folks. This highly defective program creates marriages that don't work and babies that turn society upside-down; as a result, this is the world that we see out there today, riddled with sick and very selfish people. Evidently, the audience was very impressed and touched by her sentiments. As Dr. Amsel finished her presentation, the packed church auditorium erupted in a rapturous applause that went on for about three minutes; she then ambled her back to her seat in the audience, at the front of the auditorium.

As she walked back to her seat, Dr. Emily Fertral went to the podium and waited for the clamorous din to quiet down; all this time, Simeon and Vanetta sat there relatively quietly and just soaked up all the information that had been delivered to the audience. They were quite shocked to realize that most of the problems discussed were similar to theirs—and even worse, and it comforted them to realize that their situation was not that bad after all; most of the attendees there, that evening, had serious moral, mental, and spiritual wounds that were much more severe than theirs. However, eventually, all the noise did quiet down; and Dr. Fertral was able to address the audience, as she warmly and cheerfully greeted the massive weekday gathering; which was somewhat of an anomaly, for the people had come out in droves.

Dr. Fertral: Self-Hate and Negative Self-Esteem

Oh, how gracious and thankful you are; what an ebullient applause that was! Well, Dr. Amsel certainly deserved that marvelous exhibition of your appreciation; and what she had to say was so life-changing and poignant. These workshops that are held here in Jerusalem are landmark events, and there is absolutely no reason that Jerusalemites should go around with broken hearts and lives when there is so much assistance available to them, in that regard. We are armed with an immense volume of vital and invaluable information, and we are eager to deliver it to all those who are sick and tired of living mediocre lives. My discussion, this evening, is the topic of *Self-Hate and Negative Self-Esteem*.

If you've been vigilant and have been taking good notes or taping the contents, you should have noticed that all the topics discussed here tonight are tightly connected and have been addressed from somewhat different angles; this is because they've been treated from the lens of different disciplines. Different academic disciplines look at the same issues and problems from a different point of view, in view to getting what the other discipline missed in its observation and circumspect analysis of the problem. Thus, I will discuss the topic of "Self-Hate and Negative Self-Esteem" with you from a psychotherapeutic point of view, which looks at the broad array of forces, factors, situations, and circumstances in the person's life and sees which ones impinge on the current matter at issue and how its use can help to solve the problems being studied in those people's lives.

Dr. Fertral: Doomful Societal Currents

Although the notion of self-esteem is not new; the idea of using self-esteem and the elements that impinge on it to improve overall mood and heal people's emotions is quite new. We've all agreed that human problems are caused by negative incidents that caused hurt in the past; for example, to a large degree, diseases—especially degenerative diseases are caused by poor dietary habits; poisonous ideas, and intensely negative feelings of hate, disgust, revenge, and unforgiveness towards other people. Most of the degenerative diseases are directly caused by these intensely poisonous feelings and ideas. No one harbors these feelings in him without a reason; they are directed at others; and quite frequently, they are directed at the person himself—and this poisonous attitude towards himself causes self-hate and low self-esteem.

If you do not love yourself, you are going to hate yourself and others; and when you do, you will have low self-esteem. No one with such feelings and attitude towards himself can ever love anyone else; and these are the people that you meet on the street every day; they are getting married, having children, and divorcing their spouses. They load up the streets and society with their destructive children, with no fathers. This is the perfect recipe for a doomed society that is already placed on the clock. This pattern reflects the doomful societal currents that will wash society into the yawning landfill of obsolescence and destruction.

In addition to these crazy trends, the problem of fatherlessness is exacerbated by war, due to the action of someone or some group of group of persons in the past. World War I was caused by a single bullet from a gun: World War II was the result of unfinished business from World War I. War removes millions from society in a flash; forcing more and more women to find intimacy in their own gender, pitching society out of whack, and crystallizing the currents of doom. In addition to wars and poisonous ideas and emotions, people eventually get tired of living defeated, meaningless lives; and they commit suicide.

As society waxes progressively complicated, social scientists have noticed a sharp rise in the incidence of suicide; exceeding more than a million people per year in recent years. In addition, the level of food allergies has shown a meteoric rise; but what are food allergies? They are nothing but a negative reaction to man's poisoning of the environment. The air, the ocean, and the soil have all been poisoned. Many of the diseases that are around today are a reaction to the toxins that are released, both in the food chain and from our bodies. They emanate from our bodies and from the destructive wars that men fight.

When we look at suicide, it is directly caused by the poisonous emotions of loss, rejection, anguish, revenge, sense of devastation, unresolved conflict, open or hidden emotional wounds, and old unbearable pain. Though these problems are fixable on a personal level, they are unfixable and irredeemable on a broader secular level; these problems can only be transferred from one person to another. For example, a diseased can be cured, but man cannot remove it from the human cosmos; he can only clear it away from an individual—he cannot eliminate it from the world of man. Where is psychology's solution—where are the secularists, and the humanists, and the modernists: Where are they? Their pride and swollen vanity are also part of the doomful societal currents that stalk human society today. Interestingly enough, these very people are some of the leaders in the meaningless suicide race in the world today.

I guess more and more people are beginning to see that the world is not as wonderful as they've been once led to believe. Thus. they are choosing suicide in droves: Nobody has ever told them that they were born rich, talented, educated successful because they were born in the outer court of secret knowledge. Another batch of doomful societal currents are the dishonest ones who cheat on their lovers. Cheating cannot be fixed on a human level because it is a lie; it is the product with which human society is built—lies. Human society is a lie; thus, people cheat and tell lies: Cheating is the purest form of a lie. When people lie, they are merely being human; thus, whatever is human cannot completely fix world problems, and this includes evolution and its companion of atheism.

The solution has to come from a divine source that is not involved in the games that people play in this world. People cheat because they are liars and enjoy cheating—and they enjoy cheating because it is corrupt and evil just like they are; thus, only that which is corrupt is good for human enjoyment. People cheat because they enjoy the lie of having sex with someone else's spouse—and many swap spouses, merely to have some new and exciting sex. The idea of having sex with someone else's spouse is the very essence of a lie and the undisguised betrayal of human society to evil; it just doesn't get any darker and plainer than that—but yet it does.

Dr. Fertral: The Betrayal of Human Society

When people crave adulterous sex, their action betrays the very essence of being human and what it is like; it is saying that to be human is to be a lie. Thus, whatever is human is intrinsically false: Whatever is Christian is purely true because it is not mixed with the dregs of the world. Whatever is mixed with the world is of the world and, therefore, false; this explains the enmity between Christianity and the world. The two diametrically opposite systems exist on the same sphere; accordingly, there are only two civilizations that exist on the earth: Real Christianity and all other systems in the world. Christianity emanates from the virgin birth of Jesus; the world originates from the forbidden fruit that Adam ate in the Garden of Eden six thousand years ago, resulting in the corrupt civilization that we see on the earth today. That civilization can only be repaired by the resurrected power of Jesus; that is why human problems cannot be solved by mere human beings, like liberal psychologists.

Look at this world: Does it seem like a place that is being repaired? While a person can free himself from cheating through the execution of a massive array of efforts; such as therapy, exorcism, and prayer; the human race cannot be free from cheating on its own because the bad shepherd is the spiritual father of the corrupt Adamic race that came from the Garden of Eden. Have you ever wondered why modern scientists are so insistent on the idea that God does not exist? The secret society of modern science knows that, if it accepts the presence of God in the universe, it will also have to accept the Garden of Eden scenario; and that would help people to see the connection between what happened in the Garden of Eden and why society is so sick and pathetic today.

Adam betrayed human society in the Garden of Eden bychoosing evil over good: People today are doing the same thing when they choose swinging or spouse swapping over family life. They are, in essence, betraying the nature of who they really are: Liars, thieves, crooks, cheaters, mobocrats, and on and on it goes.. The whole world has been adumbrated by this false devilish power because the people pattern their lives after the world's model of lies and deceptions. Because most Christians are mixed up with the world's falsehood and are so loose and false themselves, they disguise in the darkness because they realize how unpopular it is to be real. Not realizing that Jesus recaptured the whole world from Satan on the Cross of Calvary, two thousand years ago, Many Christians still play cat and mouse with God and the devil, thus jeopardizing their spiritual destiny. What people who choose the world's way of doing business do not understand is that,

The paradox is this: this world is false and ephemeral; the world after this one is the real deal and eternal, but it doesn't seem that way—and that is the catch. God who made man out of dust is able to reconstitute and resurrect him from the dust itself; however, contemporary man doesn't see things that way—he doesn't look that far and is not that deep. People choose the corrupt path because it seems more real than the true path, it is easier, more attractive, and more rational—it makes sense because it is all that you've ever known. You've never seen God; thus, he does not make any sense. So, the world's way seems like the right way; but it is dead wrong on many counts, even by merely taking a closer look.

From this logical perspective, the world's way seems like the right way to go; even though that is the very path that causes all the wounds and emotional problems in the world. People choose the corrupt path of cheating on their spouses, but what does it do? Cheating kills marriage stone dead, and a mother who elects to have sex with her son kills that mother-son relationship too; once she lies with her son, that mother-son relationship can never be resurrected again—it's lost forever.   In conclusion, in the spirit of this repairing relationship workshop; relationships can only be genuinely repaired if the parties involved understand that only emotionally, mentally, and spiritually whole and healthy people can have successful, healthy relationships.

Therefore, you must understand the cost of healthy relationships and be willing to do whatever it takes to make them happen in your life. sex is an illusion; it is a falling knife that cuts on both sides. If your life is dysfunctional, due to past unprocessed wounds, stuck in your subconscious mind; you need to process those old emotional hurts and wounds and clean up your mind and emotions before getting into new relationships with anyone. If you are already in a caring relationship and have chemistry for that person, you should search your heart for weaknesses that may make you vulnerable to cheating and refrain from all those Achilles' Heel situations that can mess up the relationship that you already have: A bird in the hand is worth two in the bush. Don't fool yourself; if you are a whore, you should not be in a sexual relationship with anyone: You should get the help that you need before giving yourself to anyone.

Don't fool yourself: Having a bunch of sex partners doesn't mean that you are happy; it just means that you are a whore on death row and that your moment may come at any time; for someone in your sex pool already has a deadly sexually transmitted disease or that lethal injection that will end your earthly life, and it is just a matter of time before it gets to you. Whoredom, therefore, is a lethal injection sex line on a time clock, spinning towards you; and it will be just a matter of time. Clean up your whorish behavior before getting into a solid relationship in which you can be honest with yourself and with the other person; lest you go on, creating fresh wounds and emotional and mental disturbances in your own life and in the lives of others. If you are currently in a marriage and are not getting enough sex, you should let the other person know how you feel: This matter should be fully addressed between you and your marriage partner or romantic lover.

It had been candidly discussed long before this relationship had crystallized; but just in case it wasn't, you should address this matter bluntly, sincerely, and sensitively with that current partner. You should not go messing around with this other person, crossing forbidden moral boundaries with him and causing more confusion in your life. You would be just setting yourself up for another failure in the future—the kind that you've had in the past. You must recognize that sex is neither love nor a good relationship. Great relationships begin with truth, honesty, and work: Nothing good happens on its own—and many who didn't think so are dead today. Every day, at least, three women, in the United States, die at the hands of their romantic partners. Good relationships are worth fighting for; they would bring you a smoother, happier, and healthier life; thus, remove those gaping wounds that have been messing up your personality and driving away all those potentially great lovers from you.

CHAPTER 14

THE QUESTION-AND-ANSWER SECTION

Well, the Jerusalem Relationship Repair Workshop had come and ended; and so much valuable information had been shared that the attendees did not want to leave: They wanted to wring out every drop of juice that they could from it. Thus, they requested a question-and-answer section; it was still early in the evening, and the experts who executed the program did not have any more engagements for the rest of that Friday evening; thus, they agreed to a brief question-and-answer section. Three chairs and two tables were brought to the stage, thus allowing them to sit at the tables and face the audience; and things kicked into an entirely different gear. The audience directed its questions to specific members of the discussion panel, and the whole atmosphere changed. Dr. Kaplan tersely addressed the audience, thanking them for attending and supporting the workshop so wonderfully well.

Dr. Kaplan: I am intensely delighted at the moral support that you, Jerusalemites, have given our unwilting effort to help our beautiful city of Jerusalem to be a better, safer, and more wholesome place for all of us. When you are free from moral, emotional, and mental wounds; our city will be a much safer place in which to live. Our doors are always open to people who want to clean up their lives of hate and of the many mental and emotional disturbances that confuse so many people today. We are very happy that you've enjoyed our presentation; and with that, I now introduce you to the question-and-answer session; you may begin with your questions.

Maya Naftali: Dr. Amsel, this is for you: I was a high school teacher in the Jerusalem Unified School District and have lost my way; I lost my career because I drifted into a sexual relationship with a seventeen-year-old high school student and became pregnant for him. When I realized that I was pregnant, I resigned the position on the pretext of having lost interest in teaching; I got a job in another setting, but due to guilt, I aborted the baby and ended the relationship with the young man. However, he keeps coming back; hounding and telling me that he cannot live without me, and I seem not able to live without him either. Thus, I keep taking him back: What do you think I should do. While I love him, it seems as if my whole life has been defined and wrecked by this egregious mistake. What do you think that I should do, Dr. Amsel?

Dr. Amsel: Based on what you are saying, it seems as if you met this young man a virgin and broke him into physical intimacy with you; and from what you are saying, it appears as if he is addicted to you—a bond has been formed there. At the same time, *the Grapevine Press* is very busy; and careless handling of this matter can land you behind bars for ages. Thus, this requires a very tenuous balancing act: If you get any closer to him, the school may connect the dots and implicate you in a wash of criminal charges, wrecking any future marriage to this young man.

It seems to me that, if you are serious about having any future with him; moving to another city may be a safer route to take. At the same time, though, the fact that your sister aborted the baby and the young man did not broadcast the matter around the city, it seems relatively safe to marry him because there is no way the school system can know why your sister resigned from her teaching job. At the same time, too, school systems are notorious for sweeping these things under the rug and keeping quiet about them, letting sleeping dogs lie. While moving to another city may be a safer route for your sister, Ada, going ahead with the young man may not be such a bad idea; in view of the context of this matter. Do you understand what I am saying to you here?

Maya: You've told me much more than I thought I needed to know, and you've given me some very solid and sapient information. I will discuss the matter with my sister and hear what she says. Oh, Dr. Amsel, I think that it would be rather politic and expedient that we have a private consultation with you in your office; these matters often require more formal drilling and research, and I understand exactly what you are saying to me—the double language and all.

Dr. Amsel: Call the church's secretary on Monday for details about my office hours in Talbiya, and we will talk some more, privately about this matter.

Dr. Gidon Pasternak: Dr. Fertral, this is for you: Although this transpired a long time ago, when I was a little girl; I sometimes feel as if I still need professional therapy, and I occasionally suffer from guilt and shame. I was educated right here in Jerusalem, have a doctorate in computer engineering, and work for an artificial intelligence company here in Israel. I seem to have it all put together, but something rather traumatic happened to me when I was just twelve years old: My father, Jonas (the name is veiled to protect his identity), came home drunk, around 11:00 pm, one night; walked into my bedroom; and raped me. My mother and he were separated; she had had issues with drugs, and my father was given custody of me. Three years had passed, and we had developed a relatively decent and normal father-daughter relationship but for that night. I don't know what had happened—I was still a little girl and had not even thought about sex with anyone, much less with my father: I was a tween!

For some reason or other, though, my father chose that night to enter my bedroom, plunge his tongue into my mouth, suck my emerging nipples, plunge his ten-inch phallus into my womb, and crush my girlhood. It was as if I were having a baby when he plunged himself into my innocent body. I felt him way up by my navel, and it felt as if I were going to die: my father was merciless as he drilled himself into my body. I screamed and bellowed, but no one was close by to help me. And needless to say that my bed was a mess; the sheet had been messed up, and I felt like a dog: He burned the sheet the next day. I did not know how I was going to face the future; when I asked him why he did that to me, he told me that he wanted to teach me about how the world really works. And from that night, my father has had sex with me, every night, for the next fifteen years until I mustered up enough courage to run away from him.

I had just begun to see my periods when this dastardly incident occurred, and he taught me how to avoid pregnancy. Well, needless to say that I grew up very fast, and even my neighbors, a block away, noticed that I began looking like a woman at fourteen years of age. I loved my father but never saw this coming; and being trapped in the cage of that environment, I felt lost and wheedled into being his wife for that long. He told me that no man could love and sex me like he could; though I strayed and engaged in sex with other men, I just could not escape my father, and sex with other men did not feel the same—and this is the issue—I am trapped in this moral cave and can't seem to get out.

Though I've drifted away from him, from time to time, and even refuse to tell him where I was; either he would always find me; or I would go back, looking for him. Because he got to me when I was so young, it seems as if the bond there is indissoluble; and this is the issue with which I struggle now. I told my neighbors that my father has a lover in Tel Aviv, and we go by to see her ever so often.

Nonetheless, deep down in my heart, I cry out for normalcy; and my father seems to be the only thing that is normal to me—nothing else seems right, and no one seems able to make that kind of love to me that my father does. We just seem like the right pair of gloves for each other: Nothing else seems to work; but I struggle with this huge cognitive dissonance every day of my life, and it seems as if I've been robbed of a normal life. I keep leaving him and going back for the more of what I cannot seem to find anywhere else. Any words for me, Dr. Fertral?

Dr. Fertral: It is a pity that your father did not allow you to develop some more; based on what you've recounted here tonight, your father is the first man that you've ever known. Though he'd ripped and thoroughly ransacked your body, reaching deep into the inner parts of your world; sooner than later, you got used to him: Your body got adjusted to his unwieldy sexual tools and began to crave him. What you are dealing with is that insatiable craving for the only man whom you love and who has loved and sexed you to your liking. There are two things which I would like to point out here about incest: First, there isn't anything abnormal, physically, about opposite-sex incest; what close relatives have to do is to avoid noticing each other's nakedness, especially if they live alone. Regardless of the family ties, when opposite-sex physical nakedness is exposed to each other, it can trigger the flow of those intimate juices which set up new patterns of thought that utterly ignore family ties.

As a result, fresh currents of sexual interest develop; and the race is on to put the two things together—and they usually do. Quite often, it is hardly ever mutual initially because it is wrong; in fact, more often than not, it is despicable to the other party. However, as the sexual thoughts begin to goad the other person; his target begins to catch on, especially if he displays his nakedness carelessly. After a while, that which seemed so icky and sour begins to feel much more appealing; and then, it is just a matter of time before the two relatives begin having sex routinely. And this is what was said earlier; sex is an illusion—a falling knife! Relatives are often wheeled into it, and then it spits in their face.

Secondly, because he is your father and physical intimacy has already begun; there is a mysterious mechanism that is built into wrong, inappropriate relationships in order to keep them going. Thus, this mechanism is called *the first-time factor;* this is what drives the drug addict to keep going back to repeat that initial hit: the same thing happens with incest. That first incestuous orgasm is stronger than any other normal, non-family member sex; and that is what keeps it going. What is so interesting here, though, is that, that same *first-time factor* is what ties the incestuous couple together; paradoxically, however, that is the same factor that causes them to become careless with the sex and to cause pregnancy to happen in their intensely secretive sexual association.

And that same pregnancy is what often puts a different spin on the value of the sex, shattering the relationship. Once the woman gets pregnant, the cat is out of the bag; and the disgraceful story is out in the open. Most wise incestuous couples move away to a new environment that is not aware of the incest; however, in your case, Dr. Pasternak, there is just you and your father: I would assume that your mother is largely out of the picture, and your personal life is none of anybody else's business. You did not ask your father to rape you that night, and you did not tell him not to have told you that he was sorry either.

You were born in a captured environment that exploited your spiritual ignorance; and to free yourself from that world would be extremely difficult; in fact, you cannot do it. You would have to, most certainly, get away completely from that environment; and even so, your body will crave him until he or you are no more. From what I am hearing you saying is that you truly love your father and desire him as your ideal sex partner; thus, what started out as a terrible wound has turned into a huge celebration because, whenever you get horny, you declare that you run and find your father; thus, he is your husband, and that fact has been sealed into your brain and bones. I would suggest that both of you move to another location and figure out if you can make children for your father; not all incestuous children come out deformed; some come out perfectly fine.

I wish the world was perfect and everything was done according to the Bible; but it is not that way—and I'm not promoting an antibiblical approach to life either; I just know that the other approach to your situation would be much more hellish and confusing. You've stated that you've had sex with several other men, but it is not the same because you did not enjoy the experience with those men—and it will never be the same unless you call out to Jesus to take your father out your bones and give you sexual feelings for another man whom he picks for you, in which case you would have to change your entire life program and go with Jesus all the way, which will be the better solution for the both of you in the long run.

What you are saying is that you are madly in love with your father; it is a case of forbidden love gone mad, where neither reason nor logic is workable for you nor your father. I've given you one of two choices: Continue going with the flow, especially since you've been doing that for so long; changing partners would be a major disruption of your life. In the course of doing that, seek Jesus for his guidance because he already knows your circumstances and that you did not choose that lifestyle for yourself; your father chose it and broke you in to sex with him, and now, you've fallen in love with him. The other alternative is to embrace the route of walking away from your father, abandoning this world, and utterly revamping your life; starting completely over. This approach would cost you everything but may be the best approach for you in the long run!

Mashla Abeles: This question is for Dr. Kaplan: I went through a terrible break up, and that wound has been very painful; but even since that break up, I've made some terrible choices that have made things even worse for myself. I hate myself: I keep making all these terrible choices; I don't know what I am going to do next. After my last boyfriend left me and walked away, I got a Doberman pincher and trained him to be my companion; but my friends laugh at me and call me a *dog lover*, and it hurts deep down and destroys my self-esteem: Their jeering makes me feel like trash. I tried suicide a couple times, but I could not go through with it; I just wish that spouses were sold at retail outlets where you can go and buy one for life. Men are crazy and change so much; they are here with you today and gone tomorrow.

I feel so lost and confused; it is as if my whole life is one big fog that has no meaning. I've thought about euthanizing my dear lover Skivvy; but I cannot bring myself to doing that either, and I feel very guilty, sleeping with a dog: I feel as if there is no place for me in this world, and my dog keeps my company and loves me better than any man; he never says *no,* and he's always there. Oh, what a wonderful friend and lover he is to me, but I know that having sex with a dog is wrong; it seems as if this whole world is false and wrong—what is right in this world! Oh, what is right that brings the right result every time?

Dr. Kaplan: Well, it seems as if you've turned your mouth over to the devil because all your words are negative: Do you know that all that you are today is the sum total of all that you have been saying. God designed the world in such a way that you become whatever you say; similarly, you become whatever you eat. Your food is your medicine; these are not my words; they are the words of the Father of Medicine, the great Hippocrates of ancient Greece. He said that your food is your medicine, and he is still saying that today: In a similar vein, God who created the world with words is saying something quite similar to Hippocrates: Your words are your life, and you create the life that you desire, merely with the chisel of your words. The first thing that you need to stop doing is talking down on yourself and wrecking your life with your words.

Unfortunately, the humanistic, secularistic world in which you live trains people to see the world as a godless, disorderly machine that just appeared out of the clear blue and would, one day, disappear sometime in the future just as it appeared. Human society has been hoodwinked and wheedled by false religion and modern science— and what is the result?—a world filled with people like you, Masha Abeles, and all that you've just said is a lie; but you don't know better, and that is why we hold these workshops to enlighten wonderful people like you, Masha. As part of a Christian institution and church, I can only tell you what the Bible says about engaging in sexual intimacy with animals—and I guess that you already know what it says: Don't you?

Masha: It says that sex with animals is an abomination to God; but I don't believe in God—and that, I guess is my problem. I grew up in a strict Jewish home where the Bible was honored and revered, but I rebelled against it and heeded the words of my chemistry professor: "God does not exist, and only weak-minded, silly people believe in God." I guess he was wrong because I would not have been having sex with a dog if I had listened to my parents and the Bible. Oh, I feel so lost and misled by society's dignified and highly respected people who ought to have told me the truth, but they told me a lie and sent my life into the black pit of despair; and that professor, Dr. Doron Becker, shot up his family and killed himself—my God, my God; what did I do to myself and family's name.

I've disgraced myself and family! God, if you are out there; help me out of this black and destructive pit in which I've find myself. A dog is an animal—a beast, and I've broken the biblical ordinance; but it is so hard to untie myself from this zoophilic net into which I've tied myself. God, if you are out there; reach down and lift me out of this dark, acheronian pit—get me out of this dense, dark jungle: I feel as if I'm in a heap of trash!

Dr. Amsel: Miss Abeles, I applaud your courage and honesty about fixing your situation: I am aware of secular Israel's drift away from conventional Biblical theology: Israeli society today is a humanistic, secularized machine that only pays God lip service; don't you see that curse has been working Israel over—it can't even pick a leader; it is having an election every six months.

Dr. Kaplan: Well, the Bible doesn't lie—it cannot lie; it says that the wicked shall be turned into hell and all the nations that forget God; has Israel forgotten God, with all of its moral debaucheries today? You be the judge of that matter. The Bible is plain on this issue: Intimacy with a beast or an animal is an abomination unto God: Today, sex with animals has become a fad in a loose, pagan world; it is not uncommon for women, having sex with dogs, to hold animal sex orgies: Are sex orgies a weekend fad today—a virtual amusement park. The number of women having sex with dogs has mushroomed: It has waxed into quite a fad here in Israel, in the European Union, in the United States, and around the world.

Women, having sex with animals, have become relatively popular here in Israel and especially in European Union countries; like Germany, Denmark, and the Netherlands—and all over the world for that matter. Bestiality has become common in the United States and in several South American countries. Many argue that love has no limit nor boundary—and I quite agree; however, man, engaging in sexual intimacy with animals, is the essence of human depravity and a world gone mad. God specifically created an orderly system of sexual intimacy in the world.

Sheep must have sex with sheep; goats must have sex with goats, and man must have sex with the opposite sex of his kind. Because I stepped across my mother's bedroom door and beheld her sexy body does not entitle me to seeing her as a potential sex partner because she is my mother, and I should have greater respect for her than that. I should show greater reverence and honor for my mother than to see her as being sexy and a potential meal of sex—God help us; we've lost our way in this world!

Moreover, the Bible specifically warns against sex with animals and incestuous sex—and especially with one's mother; that is an abomination to God, and that is what is wrong with human society today—people have no reverence nor fear of God anymore; thus, they think that they can do anything that they want—all the taboos have been shredded and jettisoned. We live in a world and society today that has been completely consume with, and taken over by, spiritual darkness and hellish spirits; all the demon gods of the ancient pagan world have come back again and thus, the whole world has been gobbled up by darkness and disease.

The world has become a very frightening place indeed; There are reasons why God opposes man, engaging in sexual intercourse with animals. While a dog may have a longer penis than the average man and you may enjoy its constant humping against your hip bone; that dog may also have, and transmit, fatal diseases to you, its sex partner; and from you to the rest of the human race. Thus, for this and a host of other reasons, sex with animals is a bad idea; and you shouldn't need brain science to figure that out. The very idea of having sex with a dog is a mark of mental illness; it indicates that you are not mentally stable.

A teacher has sex with his opposite-sex student, and they put him away in prison for thirty years; a woman has sex with a dog, and they slap her on the hand and say, "Don't do that anymore; that is naughty." Where is the moral outcry—there isn't any: Oh, God, help us! Though a dog may smell and desire to lick you as a woman, putting you in the mood for sex; it is wrong to engage in sexual intercourse with that dog—and you shouldn't let him lick you either. Of what most people are not aware is that, whatever you treat with tenderness and endearment eventually becomes a sex object and a snare to you, pulling you in the wrong direction sexually. Thus, if you cozy up too closely with a dog; you will eventually begin seeing that dog as a love object because of your wrong association with it, due to the demon spirits goading you to have sex with it. Have you ever wondered why there is so much gun violence in the world?

Sex is God's way of bringing human beings into the world; it is the very factory of human beings and is very sacred to God; the Bible says that sex is the only sin with which you sin with your whole body; thus, wrong sex is innately destructive. Many people can't understand why there are so many shooting sprees today; all this careless sex with animals is a strange form of devil worship, giving him full access to the human cosmos. Nowadays, every time you look around, there are tears in the news: The world was not meant to be lived in the manner in which it is being lived today—and the lugubrious news and incidents seem to be getting worse every day; people have gone stark crazy: They are having sex with dogs and think that they can get away with it!

If you let the dog kiss and lick your cheeks, you will probably allow it to lick your lips, and then your tongue. If you are a woman, allowing a bull dog to lick your lips; it will begin to stir your sexual juices; and especially if you are single and live alone. If that is the case, you have more access to that dog and to stirring him up and teaching him about your sexual parts. In this regard, it will just be a matter of time before you begin training that dog to have sex with you, opening up yourself to all kinds of strange surprises. Thus, as a responsible community leader, my best advice to you is to have your dog, Skivvy, euthanized, and to have some medical checkups in order to cleanse your body from the pollution of that dog's sperms that are now in your blood stream.

When you eventually have sex with a man, some of those dog elements will enter that man's blood stream, especially if it is shortly after the encounter with the dog: Would you be willing to tell the man that you are a zoophile who routinely have sex with your dog—and do you plan to have sex with dogs for the rest of your life. While it is not going to be easy for you, kicking this pastime with your dog and best friend; you must do it for your own sanity, get a Bible, begin reading the gospel according to St. John, and pray to God to deliver you from this difficult situation. At the same time, our church, the Jerusalem Christian Center, has a prayer line, the Jerusalem Cristian Center's Prayer Line: It operates around the clock; and you can connect with us for further assistance in your journey out of that black hole in which you've fallen and find yourself. We have done our part; the rest is on you.

A few more questions were asked, and Simeon and Vanetta were called to say a few words and to express their gratitude for the workshop. Everyone was very happy to see them there and wondered why they were there. Even though the Jerusalem community knew that they'd had some relationship problems, they did not expect to see them there because, in their view; such wealthy, successful people don't have serious relationship problems—or do they? However, for whatever it was worth, they were there and came forward to say how wonderful the workshop was and how greatly it had helped them.

They talked to the audience for about five minutes, signed a few autographs, and then made it to their Bugatti Chiron. The workshop ended with a bang, and the attendees left there nourished up and encouraged to heal their wounds, to solve their problems, and to fix their lives. Most people who attended the workshop had no idea that their lives were that messed up and complicated: it was after listening to the speakers that they realized they had that many problems: Most of the attendees had no idea that they had that many problems. The audience realized that life comes with its problems, and even the most exalted of society's astral circle experience some of the same problems that everyone else faces in the world.

Preparing for Their Fast-Approaching Big Day

Well, the Jerusalem Relationship Repair Workshop had come to an end and had given its attendees much handy and useful insight about how to succeed in intimate, long-term relationships; however, that, in and of itself, was not enough to fix these people's lives; they had to take other concrete steps to fix their complicated lives and learn how to get along with the people in their lives; accordingly, Simeon and Vanetta decided to waste no time to get started fixing their lives and resolving the issues which have dogged them in the past. Dr. Clark's consultation with Simeon had done a considerable amount of good for him; and as a result, their relationship had improved quite a bit. However, their Big Day was fast approaching; and they wanted to be fully prepared for it; for they had looked forward to it for quite some time.

Occasionally, Vanetta would call her parents in Malibu, California, and talk things over with them in order to get their take on things; however, overall, they had overcome most of the issues that had discomforted and dogged them in the past; and so, they were well on their way to their upcoming marriage there in Ajaccio. Thus, the very next day after the Jerusalem Relationship Repair Workshop, they visited the Dr. Cohen Counselling Group in Arnoma, an upscale suburb in Southern Jerusalem. This is a suburban Jerusalem vicinage that is occupied predominantly by wealthy Jerusalemites. Understanding the overpowering role of the ancient sex deities of Ishtar and Bacchus in society today, Simeon and Vanetta did not want to take any chances; they had already seen how predominant adultery had become and the degree to which marriage had been reduced to virtual trash: They wanted to give their upcoming marriage the best possible chance of success, especially in the light of the starkness of their relationship: Simeon is an Orthodox Jew, and Vanetta is an African American woman with red-hot blood running in her veins.

Even after the landmark counseling with Dr. Clark , and the Jerusalem relationship repair workshop, Simeon still had not completely overcome his childhood issues. He had made sizable strides in that regard, but he still had some ways to go. He often took his frustration out on Vanetta, even though he was much less frustrated after those two major events mentioned above. This was the backdrop that propelled them to scheduling a counselling session with the Dr. Haya Cohen Counselling Group in Southern Jerusalem. Interestingly enough, the initial reference to Dr. Kaplan and the Jerusalem workshop came from Dr. Cohen; she urged them to attend that workshop first before their counselling session with her, and they both agreed to attend the Jerusalem workshop. They saw the virtue in attending something like that and realized that it would help them to be a happier and more successful married couple.

When they eventually went for the counselling session with her, all systems were go; they had been properly prepared for the consultation and knew what their issues were and how to approach the counselling session. When the two dignitaries arrived at her office, Dr. Cohen honored and handled them with much care and circumspection. She told them that the counselling session would cost them US $5000.00, but it was not going to follow a straight counselling session pattern; she had to chat with them a little first before treating those sensitive areas of intimacy; such matters, she said, required great circumspection. She told them how wonderful it was seeing them and how happy she was that they'd chosen and honored her office with heir distinguished presence, and they expressed much delight at hearing her gracious words.

Shortly after the routine chit chat and welcome, Dr. Cohen engaged Vanetta and Simeon in some relaxful unwinding, entertaining them with delicious, coffee and nonalcoholic wine; she told them that she wanted to address them as a professional friend and create a warm, relaxing, and friendly environment within which to unwind in order to discuss the issues that bothered them. She told the couple that formal counselling sessions often intimidate clients, derailing the counseling itself; and because she did not feel that she had helped those people, she would reschedule another appointment at her own cost.

She told them that she wants to get into the bones of her clients and get them to see her, not as a professional counsellor but, rather, as a well-educated friend. She explained to them that that kind of approach creates a warmer and more relaxing atmosphere in which to talk to her clients as people she'd known for years, thus allowing them to warm up and open up to her. In that regard, she told them that counselling did not begin until the discussion got to the issues and they began treating them. With that in mind, they chitchatted for about twenty-five minutes before they really got down to business.

Dr. Cohen told them that she had counselled Vanetta's father during his bout with midlife crisis and had helped him to regain equanimity and to come back to the self that he used to know. She told them that her father had slipped into midlife crisis because, as he grew older and drew closer to his own mortality; he waxed increasingly afraid of himself, his family, and life itself. Over time, he gradually slipped away from himself as he became increasingly depressed, lost, and afraid of life. When Vanetta heard that; she perked up, hugged and kissed Simeon, and her mood changed in a distinctly positive way.

She and her fiancé became totally relaxed and ready for the consultation with Dr. Cohen: it was not like they were not relaxed before—they just loosened up some more, and she saw and recognized the mood change; and that was her cue to get things started with the formal counselling session. Now, Vanetta's dad had never told her nor any of her siblings about that part of his ordeal with his midlife struggles; however, Dr. Cohen had spoken to him the night before, and he gave her the green light to discuss the matter with his daughter if that would loosen her up because she had detected some earlier tension coming from her.

The Formal Counselling Session with the Couple

Although the Firnes had consulted with their pastor, Dr. Chappelson, of their Malibu Church where Vanetta had been Christened, someone from that aristocratic neighborhood had put them on to Dr. Cohen in Southern Jerusalem; and they acted on the tip that they got. Now, Jerusalem is a very small city; it is just three-quarter of a square mile, but a lot is squeezed into that little space; and the Cohen Counselling Group, the world's finest behavioral science group, is located right there. When Dr. Cohen mentioned the world cities that her father had built and where he had obtained his doctorate in neurology, Vanetta perked up and became even more absorbed in what she was saying. It was at that point that she eased into the counselling discussion with the couple.

She began by talking to them about relationships and how they work: She told them that, for the past half of an hour, she had just been building a relationship and establishing trust and contextual perspective with them. She then asked them if they trusted her, and they said that they most definitely did and could freely discuss any subject that she brought up in the counselling session: They said that they felt quite relaxed and cheered in her presence. This was the essence of her counselling session with them:

Dr. Cohen: Do you trust me, and would you be my friends: Most relationship problems are oriented around failure to establish a firm sense of trust; and Simeon, you must embrace the trauma that you encountered during your childhood years with the spirit of forgiveness. You must face the hatred that you had cultivated for your father because of the things that he did to you and your mother. You must revisit those painful experiences with a brand-new mindset because they are the very things that have been ruining your life and causing fights between you and Vanetta, the woman whom you love so much. Simeon, you must hate the hatred that you've directed at your father all these years and begin to see him in the light of love and forgiveness, in order to get through this crisis.

See it this way, Simeon: If you continue to hate your father as you've done over the years, you will become an even more hateful person and will have even more fights with Vanetta; blaming her for your unhappy experiences in life. This is the way you have to live in a world manipulated by the devil; there is a literal devil in the world: He works behind the scene to set people at one another and to make them hate one another. The best way to deal with this kind of world is to wear a forgiving mind and treat people as if they are not your problem but merely instruments used to complicate your life. Most of the time, when people come at you; they themselves are not even aware why they don't like you, even though they recognize that you are a very nice person. It is the evil enemy of man that puts him against himself, his family, ahis neighbors, and his friends; causing things to go wrong for him. Simeon, if you continue hating your father, Sikh, it will ruin your relationship with your darling girl, Vanetta. In the Bible, Jesus says that those who subscribe to truth will get more; and those who reject it and have not will lose even that which they have now.

If you keep on hating your father, you will become more hateful and lose even that which you have now. What I am saying here to you is that your problem is not that of an abusive childhood? No, it is your unforgiving attitude towards your father that is feeding that poison of hate that can turn into a stream of degenerative diseases. Is your father abusive now? If he is, get away from him but maintain a forgiving attitude towards him; in other words, what I'm saying to you is this: Forgive him but don't let his shabby and crazy life poison yours. This was the reason that I insisted on getting into such a relaxful and cheerful state with you two because I knew that, if you have someone whom you did not trust, telling you these hard and crazy things, you might get mad and walk away.

The crux of the problem that you are having is forgiving your abusive father because he caused you much hurt while you were growing up as a child, and that has been feeding the toxin of hate in your body. Let go the grudge against your father, and all the other issues will fade away, over time, because it is that poisonous hatred for him that has been getting you so angry and irritable with yourself and your darling girl, Vanetta. Once you understand this and act on it, all the problems that you are having now will eventually fade away.

It is like a hurricane over warm ocean water: As long as it stays over that warm oceanic water body, it continues to be strengthened; however, once it crosses land and that water vapor is cut off, the hurricane simply fades away. The same thing is true about hate and unforgiveness: Once you release the hate and unforgiveness, most of the problems fade away. But notice that it doesn't seem that way; it seems as if hating your father is what you need to do because he physically abused you, and you seem to have a right to hate—even kill, him. However, that is not the way the world works. Hating people produces poisons, and poisons make you sick and sad—the exact thing that you do not want in your life.

And what is my solution to the rest of the problems of posttraumatic stress disorder, fearsome nightmares with nasty expletives, self-hate, fear of the future, inability to give and receive love, romantic isolation, and negative attitude towards life? All those problems are there because of your deep-seated hate for, and anger about, your childhood abuser: You hate him because he abused you and your mother, and you even went to a gun shop to purchase a gun to kill your father because of the bad things that he'd done to you and your mother.

You not only have to forgive your father for abusing you and your mother; you also have to forgive yourself for the murderous thoughts that you harbored against your father. Whenever you sense those thoughts coming on, start hating them as if your life and marriage depend on it and begin showering love upon Vanetta. Lift her up with your big, strapping arms and tell her how much you love her. Do you love her, Simeon? Well then, tell her what, and how, you feel; pour it into her ears—I'm sure she wouldn't mind at all: Would you mind if your fiancé showers you with amorous, romantic words, Vanetta?

Vanetta: Oh, most certainly not, Dr. Cohen; this has been the focus of most of our fights: He has not been romantic and amatory enough to me—I most certainly would not mind!

Simeon: I wish it was so easy as you make it, Dr. Cohen; it was since I attended that Jerusalem Relationship Repair Workshop that I realized how much trouble in which I was. It was then that I realized that those strong, incandescent emotions of anger and rage—those visceral sentiments of violence were demonic, and I realized that they came into my life during those weak moments when my life was littered with holes and weak moments. When Vanetta and I went to the Galilee Revival Hour Church exorcism one evening, I was shocked at what came out of us: Because of her bouts with untruthful lovers in the past; she, too, had weak moments: it was those spirits that were rubbing against one another and causing all those problems in our lives.

Dr. Cohen: I'll tell you what: This is a milestone that we've reached in such a short period of time; even though that exorcism occurred somewhere else in the world, I was not expecting you to share that this early in the counselling session. When you go home later on today, tell your mother that you are a new man with a fresh outlook in life: You no longer hate your father, and she must adopt the same stance towards him, too.

Vanetta: And Dr. Cohen, what is my role in all of this—how do I fit into this puzzle; it has been difficult for me, too; I've walked away from this man on several occasions, but it has never lasted. I love Simeon with all my heart and with the love of compassion, and I guess that that is the only love that matters after all; everything else collapses under the pressure of human weakness.

Dr. Cohen: And how glad I am that you ask that; I do this quite often and let the pieces fit where they may—and they often do. You must love Simeon: Show him that you care and not expect anything back. Don't let rejection hold you back; Remember: you are fighting for the very life of your relationship and for your man. Spiritual powers have been trying to tear up your relationship; thus, you must put up a titanic fight and hold out—you are almost there. Do it as a downpayment on the relationship that you want with him.

Some things are worth fighting for, and you must fight as if you are fighting a lion because you are; the world is filled with hateful people who want your lover and would do anything to divest you of him. Don't pressure him to give you love; let it happen on its own—and it eventually will: he's learning to give and receive love on the other side of all that hate; he'll learn to shower you with so much love, you won't know what to do with it. As he heals, he will begin to respond to your warmth, and kindness, and love with all that love that has been bottled up in him all these years and were corked by his poisonous hatred for his father.

Simeon: And what kind of relationship must I maintain with my father—how do I handle such a complicated relationship with him now; but despite the fact that it may be hard, I will go to see him and hate those feelings that I used to have for him.

Dr. Cohen: Barring your father is still physically, mentally, and emotionally abusive; you must visit him as often as you can, bearing kind words and gifts. Remember: You are not doing all this for him—you are doing it for the life that you want in the future. You are doing it for you, Vanetta, and your family. When you hate people, the hate does not touch the people; but it poisons your blood stream, creating all kinds of health problems for you. You must remember that people do not hate because they are naturally hateful; they hate because they are being moved upon by a literal devil whom their university professor told them does not exist.

Oh, my! What great counselling that was! As the essence of the counselling came to an end, Dr. Cohen slowly eased away from her counselling role and reverted back into small talk again; and as the counselling session was officially completed, they had a word of prayer because Simeon requested it. As Simeon led the word of prayer, there was a sense of wholeness and completeness; the engaged couple felt a sense of joy, wholeness, and strength that they never had before. They recognized that genuine counselling is not just mental; it is a spiritual experience of trust and hope for a new tomorrow; it encapsulated the notion of willingness to apply the counsellor's recommendations and a sense of viewing her as a spiritual parent whom they can trust and would return to see again, even if it is just to say that we did what you recommended, and look at us now:

We are well and have come back to merely say, "Well done and thank you." Thus, in many ways; they viewed the counselling session as a form of parenting and viewed their counsellor, Dr. Cohen, as a friend and quasi family member to whom they can turn for sound advice about important matters in their lives and someone whom they would recommend to others who are serious about cleaning up their lives. They saw her as someone who is trustworthy and who can be recommended to others who are looking for good counsel about the various issues that they face. In many ways, life is work; and many people fail at it because it is not easy; and success is not automatic, even if you have oodles of money. In many ways, this was a very successful counselling session; and great trust was forged: the billionaires sensed Dr. Cohen's sincerity and were impressed with what she told them; thus, they requested prayer at the end in order to consolidate the edge that they felt that the counselling session had imparted to their lives and relationship.

Well, does Dr. Cohen have a word of prayer with all her clients? Absolutely not! She is a Christian but counsels people in view of their worldview and understanding of life; however, she always recommends connecting with God, that higher and supreme power and factor in human lives, as part of her overall solution package for the couple or person; and in view of her parenting style, her clients mostly do not mind a word of prayer from her because they trust her. Accordingly, while she tailors each counselling session according to the context of the person's situation, she always reminds people about the transience of the human experience and their need to connect with the universe's Supreme Being.

And sometimes, because of the innately difficult nature of some of the counselling sessions where she, herself, is overwhelmed by the context of the counselling itself, what else can she do but to talk frankly to the client about man's need for God. In cases where the client's spouse or child dashed herself before an oncoming train in the Paris Subway, or a spouse who has been suddenly snatched away from her by suicide; she has no choice but to invoke the presence of God into the counselling situation.

The counsellor has to deal with a range of life circumstances and has to be very strong herself, exhibiting great internal fortitude and understanding of life's whimsical behavior in people's various situations. Not too infrequently, a bomb goes off at a Jerusalem market, and someone's prized family member was nearby; and suddenly, he needs the support of a genuine counsellor to help the family process such a situation. Often, the need for prayer is so overwhelming, it just goes without saying. Who does the heavy

1) How long have you known each other, and are you having sex outside of marriage now?

2) How do you feel about that: What kind of sexual regimen do you have now?

3) Have you had any sexually transmitted diseases within the past five or so years?

4) Have you attended any relationship repair workshops recently?

5) What is your mission in this relationship—what do you want, and have you talked about it with each other? Is this the result of some sleazy computer hook up or a true effort at love?

6) Have you had any hook-up sexual relationships within the past five years and are you a sex maniac? How do you feel about *swinging* or spouse swapping for sexual variety and fun?

7) Do you sense as if you are on the same page and are going in the same direction?

8) Are you looking for a caring, serious, long-term relationship; or you both are just looking for some short-term, exciting sex with each other—what do you expect from this marriage?

9) Is this a sexual relationship, and are you both satisfied with the amount of sex delivered now? Do you consider cheating as a viable way to spice things up in the bedroom?

10) What do both of you want from each other that you are not getting now—more sex; and in your opinion, how much sex is too much sex in a marriage?

11) Would you ever cheat on your spouse if he or she is sick and cannot perform sexually? Would you consider cheating under any circumstance whatsoever?

12) Vanetta, how comfortable are you initiating love-making with your romantic lover, Simeon? How do you feel about an open marital relationship?

13) Do you enjoy sex: How much sex is too much for you per day and per week, Vanetta?

14) What is your ideal or preferred penis size: Small, medium-sized, large, or jumbo?

15) Are you having sex now, if not, why not? How important is sex to you both?

16) What time of day do you prefer having sex: Morning, evening, or wee hours of the night?

17) What sexual positions do you particularly prefer? Have you ever committed an abortion; and if so, how many abortions have you committed?

18) Do you think that the commission of abortion scars a woman's perception of sex?

19) In view of the stark sociocultural differences between you two, have you discussed any religious conflicts that you are having now?

lifting in these overwhelmingly difficult situations? Thus, in many counseling situations, counselling, in and of itself, is not enough. Anybody can be tough and sexy when the lifting is not too heavy; most marital counselling treats the rigor of an extramarital affair, and even those are strange nightmares that require some heavier than normal lifting.

The Simeon-Vanetta couple had thoroughly enjoyed the heartfelt counselling with Dr. Cohen and formed a bond with her virtually for life; they sensed her sincerity and love and felt that she was someone with whom they'd want to discuss their personal life issues. Not only had they enjoyed the counselling session with Dr. Cohen, she also recommended that they see a psychotherapist in the unit. This counsellor, Dr. Adair Johnson, executed an entirely different style from that of Dr. Cohen and was more matter of fact, but the betrothed couple did not mind at all; they were merely there to improve the quality of their lives and the chances of their upcoming marriage's success.

The Dr. Adair Johnson Counselling Session

Because of the therapeutic nature of this counselling session, it was more scripted and systematic; and Dr. Ruben Adair Johnson adopted a more straightforward approach, ignoring many of niceties that were had in the Dr. Cohen consultation earlier, and to say that he'd roughed up the billionaires was an understatement. Although the lovers noticed the stark difference in the counseling's nature, texture, and arrangement; they did not mind at all because they were both college professors with multiple doctorate degrees. There was a brief period of chit chat; but it was rather summary and matter of fact: They got down to business really quickly, subjecting the lovers to some tough questions that often smacked embarrassment—and again, they did not mind. This was a session of psychotherapy and, therefore, involved pert and stark questions that had to be answered to the point; but it was all a part of growing up and dealing with life's many unusual faces. The following reflects the questions that they were asked:

The Actual Marriage Therapy Session

Well, as you can clearly see; this was quite a different experience from what they they'd had with Dr. Cohen. Although the couple did not mind the rough treatment that Dr. Adair seemed to have handed them; the secretary, Talia Cantal, tipped the group's marketing specialist, Dr. Admon Berenson about Dr. Adair's rough, brusque style in dealing with the superrich couple. He was told to tone down the brusquerie and to apologiz to the billionaires for the abruptness with which he had treated them.

When Dr. Adair realized who this highly decorated couple was, his tone changed dramatically; and he adopted a softer and much more polite stance in dealing with Vanetta and Simeon. He told them that he was new in town and had no idea of who they were and that he was very sorry about what seemed like his very rough, incult, and inconsiderate tone in dealing with them. He also told them that he had worked out an arrangement for them to see Dr. Tamar Abeles, a young and beautiful sexologist whose training better dovetailed with their special circumstances.

Dr. Adair: I am extremely sorry about how I was perceived when I saw you earlier this morning; I am a matter-of-fact scientist who is mainly after results, but I do recognize that I can be gruff and rough at times in executing my services and that my manner needs to be smoothened and polished some more. In that regard, I do recognize that I am not the right person to treat the sensitive and delicate aspects of your sexual situation; in that regard, Dr. Abeles would be a better fit to treat the sensitive situations with which you both grapple.

Dr. Simeon Auckner: Well, I did not see that at all and have been through quite a lot with women who've tried to disgrace my life, spreading lies about my sexuality and saying that I can't do anything—I can't get it up. I've been so humiliated.

Dr. Adair: Well, is that rue—is that correct? You know; women are like that and would do and say anything when they can't get their way. I'm sorry that you've been through that, Dr. Auckner, but I want to go back into your childhood and see what I find there. Tell me about what happened during your childhood that has affected you so dramatically and predisposes you to being so angry and vengeful all the time.

Dr. Auckner: I was raised in an orthodox Jewish home, but my mother was not too keen about religion, and my father was a junky; he often drank heavily, came home late at night, and would beat us up; he would ball up his fist and throw it at us, often injuring my mother; and when I got in the way, trying to shield my mom, I often got clobbered by this insane man whom I called *dad*. However, that was then; this is now: Since that time, I've grown to love my father and to forgive him of all the terrible things that he has done to my mother. Forgiving and forgetting about all that has happened in my childhood: I simply refuse to allow my past to hold my future captive. My fiancée, Vanetta here, has been of immense moral support and has helped me through some pretty dark moments; but it's all gone now. I understand what my role is: It is to choose to forgive my father for abusing my mother during those dark moments—and to do so every single moment of every day of my life.

Dr. Adair: So, are you saying that the nightmare is finally over and that you no longer experience bouts of anger and frustration?

Dr. Auckner: I now understand what being free from one's past is: These are moments when a wound occurred in a person's life, and he identifies with that wound, treating it as if it is him, himself; but my understanding of things has changed now; the abusive moments that I endured as a child, growing up with my mom and dad, are not me. I've separated myself from those fleeting moments when those wounds transpired in my life. Thus, my attitude towards my father has changed radically; and I can forgive—and have forgiven—him for all of that now. Some of the incidents are difficult to treat and remember, but focusing on these negative elements just prolongs the mental torment that I endured years ago; rather, I've chosen to focus on the brighter side of my life now and to look back at those negative childhood experiences with a smile.

Dr. Adair: I notice that you've given more attention to the abuse that your mother suffered than that which you, yourself, have suffered in the past: Is that a testimony of your love for your mother?

Dr. Auckner: Yes, it is a reflection of my love for my mom; she is quite precious to me because, without the strength and inner fortitude that that she evinced during those dark moments in that hellish jungle that I used to call home, I would not have been able to make it through that dark night. I love my mother on one level and love my fiancée on another; these are the two most important women in my life, and they are of coordinate value and importance to me. These two women have allowed me to bear all the pain, and shame, and disgrace of spousal abuse, and anger, and fear, and all the frustration of living in a world like that. Now, all that childhood trauma was stuffed and lost in the fog of my subconscious mind.

Dr. Adair: so, tell me how you managed to escape that dark jungle of child abuse during your childhood—what did you do?

Dr. Auckner: I went back to those moments and undid the wounds of the past by reexperiencing and viewing them from an adult perspective: Those moments are not me anymore; they are themselves because the wounds that they caused have been healed. I've mended the splits and gashes that they caused by treating those polluted areas in my soul, thus initiating a healthy flow of mental and emotional energy in my personality, causing the wound to heal over time. The healing has come about by my own conscious effort to cleanse the polluted areas of my personality and to treat them as non-events—things that never happened. Dr. Adair, I realized that the processing of these kinds of wounds involves reaching back into the past, opening up myself to them again, and viewing them from an adult point of view. This is the process of re-experiencing those nasty events that happened some time ago in the past, that have been ruining my present and future; reliving those experiences in an adult way and putting a new spin on them.

This allows me to separate myself from those nasty incidents; reperceive them; put an adult spin on them by forgiving the culprit at work, if need be; and reclaiming my life—and I've done all of that. Dr. Adair, though it may still hurt, by experiencing those dark moments again; their bite is already defanged; causing some of the pain to drain away from the wound and allowing it to be healed over time. I learned that emotions are transient; they need to be experienced as such and not to get lost in the fog of my subconscious world.

Dr. Adair: Well, Dr. Auckner, you talk to me like a highly skilled social psychologist; and I can see that you truly understand the dynamics of the healing process from mental and emotional wounds that all of us have sustained when we were children and have continued to experience as we trudge our way through life's journey. Sometimes, it was as simple as craving one's mother's love and wanting a hug or kiss from her, and she was unavailable at the time, or she did not respond to the child's request; and in that moment of innocence and pain, a wound was created that damaged the child's personality system.

At other times, it might have just been talking down to the child and telling him that he would never amount to anything; and though the child did not fully understand what you were saying, in his own state of innocence; he understood that you were wrecking his life with your destructive words. As a result, he cried out from his heart, creating that emotional wound that has turned him into a criminal—the very person whom you told him that he would become: You told him that he would not amount to anything, and you were right. Being his caretaker and father, you have authority to speak into your child's life, and you spoke destructive words that went ahead of him and destroyed his life.

Dr. Vanetta Firne: Dr. Adair, all these secrets are printed in the Bible: God created the universe with words, and he expects us to live by our words; speaking those things which we desire to happen. However, because we were born in the outer court of secret knowledge; we are not cognizant of these truths; thus, we destroy our lives every day with our own words: Words built the universe, and words destroy the world of man. The devil used words to trick Eve into eating the forbidden fruit, and he is doing the same thing today to mankind.

If you listen to what people around you are saying, you would be absolutely shocked at the level of destruction that people bring into their own lives—and they do it because they were born in spiritual darkness; thus, they live and are destroyed at the unwisdom of their own words. For example, a woman, craving another woman's husband says things like these; "I'll die to have a man like that; I'll throw my quam at him in a minute and invite him over to my house, even without a thought!" Have you ever heard those lines before? Those and many others like them are the cranes that crush people's lives and dash them into life's landfill well before it was their time: Why? People reject the Bible, and for that reason, the world, itself, is already condemned; thus, when you see the destruction that an F5 Tornado does to a community, know that such things happen because human society has rejected the Bible and has chosen the unwisdom of this world.

Dr. Adair: Well, Doctors Firne and Auckner, you've taught me a thing or two today; and my life would never be the same again; I was sent here to counsel you, but you've wound up counselling me and teaching some very dark truth which I will never forget; and with that, I would like to bring this therapeutic session to an end. Again, I apologize for sounding a bit rough around the edges at the beginning; and I am inviting myself to your upcoming wedding in Corsica, within a year or so.

Dr. Auckner: We will send you a formal invitation to our big day, there in the Sargesse area of Ajaccio, in Corsica: Dr. Adair, we are professional scientists and did not take offence at your matter-of-fact approach to counselling us; in fact, we truly admire how you do things. We've been scheduled for some therapy with Dr. Abeles just before our wedding; we greatly appreciate all that help that we've gotten from the Cohen Behavioral Consulting and Counselling Group here in Arnoma; our lives have been greatly nourished and enriched by this facility's superb services.

We came here with much uncertainty; but we came, putting a positive spin on our various issues. Nonetheless, we followed your lead in this very relaxing environment that you've created for us. The behavioral science professionals at this facility have made us very comfortable in our own skin; we feel that you are a very talented behaviorist and have shown us how to go about solving our conflicts and issues that are so common to all relationships. The world has become so visceral and volatile today, just about nothing is certain; however, your awesome counselling skills have created the opposite effect of a world that anyone can trust—and that is so wonderful.

In the course of learning to deal with life's many hard knacks, we have inculcated the importance of humility and viewing ourselves little in our own eyes. In addition to learning how to use words wisely, we've learned the ways of humility and disguise so that we do not make our identity immediately too obvious to anyone with whom we come into contact because we do not want to be viewed as some advertising agency of who we are; instead, we would rather be discovered than to tell people who we already are; it is people's responsibility to find out who we are and not our responsibility to tell them. There is just much wisdom and beauty in being discovered.

CHAPTER 15

TROUBLING COMMUNITY ISSUES

A few months had elapsed since the engaged couple had attended the Jerusalem Relationship Repair workshop, and they had reported to the Firnes how well they were doing. Actually, it seemed as if the Jerusalem Relationship Repair Workshop had done the trick for them; for, from that time afterwards, they both experienced a considerable amount of mental and emotional healing. One has to give them much credit for the level of humility that they'd evinced, being thoroughly educated people, with several doctorate degrees; holding tenure-track professor positions at Jerusalem's most prestigious universities; and being highly respected world figures, with billions of dollars.

Simeon, himself, had four doctorates (systematic theology, physics, quantum algebra, and epistemology); and his fiancée, Dr. Vannetta Firne, had two doctorates, one in astrophysics and the other in quantum algebra. As you can see, these were not ordinary people; but they behaved that way, and you could not tell that these were such sophisticated human being, just by looking at them—and not only that, these were also billionaires. Dr. V. Firne was one of the richest persons in the world, and she just went about as an ordinary individual: The fact that they did not make a big deal about who they are, Dr. Adair could not tell until he was bluntly scolded about how brusque and gruff he was with them initially.

When he found out how wealthy these people were, he was shocked! At any rate, they walked away from that counselling group, liberated human beings and reported the counselling results to Vanetta's parents, who were ecstatic to hear how well they were doing. The Firnes were very delighted at the news of their counselling results, as their relationship had come upon some hard times in the past, due to Simeon's childhood abuse. However, after the Jerusalem Repair Workshop and the consultations at the Cohen Counselling Group, all their challenges seemed to have dried up; and they were well on their way.

However, the world is filled with problems of all kinds; and money does not exempt you from life's trials and tribulations. As they delivered the triumphant report to Vanetta's mother, Margolyn Firne, a decorated and distinguished Westwood University professor; was so happy to hear that things had turned around. She had been very skeptical about the relationship because she thought that there was too much raucous music in it, Simeon was an Orthodox Jew; and Vanetta was an African American young lady. Thus, looking at things with the natural eyes, she did not quite like what she saw; but Vanetta convinced her that their relationship was as solid as a rock, even though they fought like hell and worked out some kind of deal through what they called *a tournament of forgiveness*, and they came through!

Anyway, after not seeing her parents for about nine months; she called them and gave them a progress report of sorts: It was then that she discovered that her mother was dealing with some mysterious connections: She kept running into the same people over, and over, and over again. Sometime back, she had had a young lady in one of her classes; her name was Sophia Brent, and she kept running into her; again, and again, and again and did not know why. It was really funny and interesting.

Thus, she was bemused by the mysterious meetings. Now, this was after she had taken that class with Dr. M. Firne. As it turned out, Sophia was a virgin and was under pressure by her peers at her school to have sex. They told her that sex was in, and virtue was out of style. All her university friends gave her the impression that sex is everything; and if you are not having sex, something must be wrong with you. However, Sophia took the taunting and all that pressure in strides and did not let it bother her: That was until she began sensing a mysterious connection with a feller named Aubrey Holmes.

Though she was a virgin, suddenly, she began experiencing strong sexual drives for Aubrey; she began to feel like a sex maniacal virgin and as if she was going out of her mind. She began having this mysterious connection with Aubrey and was haunted by visions and dreams of being thoroughly sexed by Aubrey, and she did not know why; but the taunting, mysterious connections had turned her life upside-down, making her feel like a dirty person. Suddenly, it seemed like wherever Sophia went, she ran into Aubrey; and each time she saw him, the sexual drives waxed stronger, wilder, and crazier.

Somehow or other, though, she was shy, even though she felt all these butterflies and raw sexual feelings for Aubrey, she was still a virgin but was ready to lose her virginity with him; and it seemed as if the sightings kept increasing by the day. She went to the park, and he was there: She saw him at the library, at the museum, at the grocery store, at the movies, at the cafeteria—and even at the gas station. Sophia began having sexy dreams and orgasms with Aubrey in her sleep; these dreams reflected all the trappings of real sex with Aubrey although she was a virgin: Hardened nipples, intense blood flow to the genitals, and swollen vaginal lips and clitoris frightened Sophia. She couldn't handle the rawness of the experiences she was having.

One day, she went to Bloom's Flower Shop in Westwood; and when she met him there and wet her under clothes, she knew that it was time to do something about preserving her sanity; she felt lost in a fog, disgraced by her own thoughts and could not make it happen for her. But then, she thought, "What if it happened and she got pregnant?" She would have destroyed her academic life and either have to deal with the guilt of an abortion or bring a bastard child into the world without a father, thus confusing her life even more! Eventually, the meetings waxed more and more surreal and out of control: Her intimate feelings began interfering with her studies, and she became even more lost. Sophia was working on a master's degree in organizational psychology.

Now, she had taken a class in social dynamics and policy from Dr. M. Firne; and she was the star of the show. Thus, she had formed a solid connection with her professor, merely by virtue of her brilliance in the class that she had taken with her: Dr. Firne had even advised her to do a doctorate degree in social dynamics and policy; but then, she began having these strange problems and craving for sex with Aubrey. It was as if her life had been toppled, and she had lost her way. Oh, poor feller: He had not even the slightest clue that all this was going on about him. Often, Sophia's eyes would automatically glance at Aubrey's crotch, and she would rush to the restroom, clean up herself, and weep; and as funny and vulgar as this may sound, Vanetta had a friend who almost lost her mind, dealing with this same bizarre problem.

She convinced herself that she was a whore, and almost became a prostitute; indeed, the world is filled with strange people and even stranger problems. This is no joke: Many women are unable to control their sex drive and purposely refuse serious, long-term relationships with good men. We have our own perception of reality, based on face value; but in most cases, reality is quite something else. Some women were born with that slut spirit and are driven like crazy by it—they must have sex several times a day in order to feel sexually satiated, and woe be onto you if you wind up with one of those hoochie mammas I tell you; you will find yourself in a serious ant's nest. Well, after the disturbing meetings began affecting Sophie's academic life, she went and spoke to Dr. Firne, asking her if she could share a few personal issues with her about a problem that she was having at the time.

Dr. Firne told her that she most certainly would like to talk to her about the thorn of being a woman; somehow or other, she sensed what Sophia's problems were and scheduled an appointment to see her on the following day. It so happened that Sophia did not have any classes on that day, so they scheduled the appointment for the next day, at 1:00 pm. Sophia had to drive to school and took off work for that day, but she did not mind; she needed some wise psychological counselling, and Dr. Firne was a quite sapient psychologist. So, she drove over to the celebrated Westwood university, parked, rushed over to Dr. Firne's office, and knocked at the door; Dr. Firne quickly opened the door and graciously greeted and welcomed her into her office. Sensing that Sophia was somewhat nervous, she kept a smile on her face to calm her down.

Sophia's Consultation with Dr. Firne

Actually, several students were at the door when she arrived; wanting to talk to the highly decorated and beloved professor; but she warmly patted them on the back, hugged them, and told them to come back and see on her the following day: Those whose papers were due and had arrived after the counselling session had begun with Sophia simply slipped them into the chute, waved at Professor Firne, and walked away. From what transpired in those few brief minutes, it was very obvious that Dr. Firne is a very popular and beloved professor and that Sophia was occupying some highly treasured space. At any rate, the crowd around the professor soon dissipated and vanished; and Dr. Firne was ready for the chat with her former student.

Dr. Firne: Oh, my dear Sophia, how are you: I thought about you all yesterday and wondered what was wrong—you are such a brilliant young lady; but don't worry, I think that I've already figured out what the problem is. I think that I know what is wrong with your situation, and you don't have to say a whole lot to me either. I'm here to comfort you and to defang the issue that you are having. You see, my dear, this is a woman thing; and we, women, know how to make it seem as if we have it all together, and we really do not.

Sophia perked up and relaxed; she was shocked when she heard that her highly decorated professor might have experienced the same embarrassing situation through which she was going; thus, the cloud that was there vanished from her cheeks. The cloud was there because Sophia did not know how to explain her complicated and embarrassing situation to her professor. Now, she realized that she had a free pass and did not have to dig her hands and feet into the muck and mire into which she found herself. And so, she perked up and smiled; and doctor Firne smiled, too.

Dr. Firne: My dear Sophia, it is a confusing world in which we live; we are told an endless blizzard of lies and made to feel dirty without being properly educated on clumsy matters: My parents told me that I arrived on jet plane; and when I asked them where the plane came from, she told me to shut up and to never talk to her in that tone of voice again, so I got my education from the wrong sources. You are stressing erotically over some new man you met—isn't that correct?

Sophia: How did you know, Dr. Firne, about the shame and pain through which I'd been undergoing? I just felt dirty as those whorish thoughts kept flooding my soul, and I am a virgin—I don't understand: Is this normal? It's difficult being a woman: Men are expected to flaunt their horniness in society; but when women do that, they are called whores.

Dr. Firne: I was a virgin, too. Our society has gotten virginity wrong: Jesus says that if a man looks at a woman to lust after her, he has already taken her to bed. I went through the same thing through which you are going now when I met my husband—and I stressed erotically over him for months because he is a real gentleman and did not want to do the wrong thing and violate me before we were married—and he didn't; but Sophia, I wanted him to. I wanted him to violate me, and we've been married for more than twenty-eight years now. Marriage is what sex is all about—it is a monopoly on love and sex. Most women have trouble controlling their sexual drives; thus, I'm here to tell you that your problem is a quite familiar one; my best friend, Donna Hasslebeck, had it even more terribly than I, but you have to control it and not let it control you and turn into a whore. So, what is happening to you now?

Sophia: I am twenty-two years old—I'm not a child anymore; but I'm still a virgin. However, as you've suggested, I'm not really a virgin because my mind has been flooded with sexual thoughts, sentiments, and scenarios; so, I've already experienced sex in my thoughts, feelings, and dreams—and those dreams are no joke. However, it had gotten to the point where I've been craving being sexed by this young man, Aubrey, into whom I keep running virtually everywhere I go; and the powerful sexual urges begin disturbing my academic life. For more than two years now, I'd told my colleagues and school friends that I had never been sexed; and they kept treating me as if my mom needs to come and pick me up for the weekend because I am still a little girl. I did not let their jeering and taunting bother me for the past two years; however, since I met this young man, Aubrey, it is like I'm obsessed with him; I cannot seem to get him out of my mind; and the thoughts cause me to do disturbing things that depress my self-esteem and mood.

Sometimes, when I see him, I want to jump on him and carry him to my house, but I know that I would not be able to live with myself after that—and I know. I've often wondered why being a woman has to be so hard. when it's not your period it's crazy sexual drive from nowhere; and when it is not that, it's making babies, stretching your womb out of shape and creating stretch marks on your legs and wrinkles in your face. When it is not that, it is some man who sees you as a sex toy and wants to rape you at his earliest convenience. Dr. Firne, why is the world so hard and complicated: Why is life so difficult? I urgently need some answers! I wish good men were sold at the retail outlet down the street, where I could go and purchase one; and we could go home and have some good, responsible sex, knowing that he is my man and is going to be there tomorrow, too.

Dr. Firne: Unfortunately, Sophia, this is the way the world is; life is tough, especially when you make wrong choices. Opening up yourself to Aubrey is a terrible mistake going somewhere to happen, and I'll tell you why: You are in so much heat right now, you will, most likely, open up yourself to him without proper protection. And even so, you need to research this area of birth control for some time before participating it in sex The last thing that you want to happen to you right now is to open up yourself to Aubrey and get pregnant for him, mashing up your whole life.

I've experienced these crazy, crushing sexual drives, too, but I stayed the course and waited; and eventually, the storm passed; and I came out unscathed. Listen to this: Society and our bodies have overrated sex; and, for the most part, sex is more trouble and problems than anything else. What are the Problems? Sex is an illusion; it is not what you think it is; For one thing, sex is not the unfiltered, unvarnished, recreational entertainment that it appears to be—it appears to be that, but it is not: Sex was designed for marriage and family life; and when you take it out of that context, you destroy both the value of sex and yourself.

Have ever wondered why people walk away from each other, despite having access to all that sex? One thing that is certain about sex is this: As long as you keep having sex, you will get pregnant, regardless of what measures you take; when pregnancy occurs, it often changes the whole dynamic. Suddenly, the urge gets lost in a fog of issues that complicate that original sex drive that was there; thus, sex is a mocker, and thoughtless, horny women are its suckers. The man has sex with you, and the sex is over: The fun is over; he finishes what he was doing with you, pulls up his briefs, puts on his pants, and walks away. As far as he is concerned; the transaction is over—the sex is done; but you see, it is not finished for you yet; you would have to wait until your periods come again and give you clearance that the transaction is indeed over.

You don't generally see it that way, but that is the way it is. If your periods do not come, that has created a whole different ballgame that you are going to have to figure out how to deal with this new thorn in your life. Pregnancy comes with all of its surprises—even in the best of circumstances; however, if you are living with your husband in a loving marriage, the spin on pregnancy is entirely different. When the man is not there, the pregnancy casts you in an entirely different light: For one thing, it delivers a bastard child into your hands, which makes holding on to a man in your situation much harder now because of the child; men are not looking for women with children— they consider them baggage because men view women as sexual objects: Not as parents of children that are not theirs. And the more children you have, the harder it becomes to hold a man in your life; unfortunately, human society is a lie; and these are the things about which most people, particularly women, find out later on down the road.

This is not to say that some men do not stick around with women with children, but those are far and a few. For this and many other reasons, as a woman; you should refrain from getting pregnant as much as you possibly can—even during the first five years of marriage because there is a high failure rate of marriages; and divorced women, with children, fall in the same bag as women with the baggage of children. However, the trouble for women does not end there; what if you choose to have abortions when pregnancy occurs—what would your plight be? Good question: Some of the unhappiest women in the world are those who've had abortions. Call it whatever you want; abortion is cold-blooded murder; and as society gets darker and darker, people's conscience becomes seared as with a hot iron; and nothing is wrong anymore.

Don't fool yourself, though; whatever you sow, you are going to reap—and you don't decide what is right or wrong: Nature does. A sizable number of women die on abortion tables, but that is stuffed under the rug and down the drain Human society is false, and people pretend to have power that they don't have; they behave as if they have all this power to decide what is right and wrong for them. With all the dirty and wrong sex and cheating going on in the world today, the world has been rumpled up and turned upside-down because the Bible says that the wages of sin is death, thus, the world has been turned into a morgue.

Have you ever wondered why, all of a sudden, people are shooting each other down as if they are wild animals? The ship of society has been overturned. The Good Book says in Psalm 9:17, The wicked shall be turned into hell, and all the nations that forge God. Which nations have forgotten God?—those nations in which shooting sprees are happening three and four times a day. Those nations used to be godly; nations like Italy, Spain, France, the United Kingdom, and the United States were once Christian nations: Not anymore.

The people have made up their own minds about what's right and wrong; in the process, they've forgotten God; and God has turned them over to violent, sanguinary shooting sprees, where ordinary people are afraid to leave their homes or to watch the news: Why? They've tossed out the moral rules and redefined right and wrong. And my, my; what an exorbitant price they are paying now for forgetting God—oh, my! But I'm not done with abortion. Now, you can always redefine the rules of morality: What you cannot redefine is whether you are going to make it through on that abortion table this time or the next time around; and sad to say, millions die on abortion tables every year, especially in developing countries: Evil doesn't care how it gets you; it may eat you last, but it will eat you anyway. Bear that in mind.

Most women who choose the abortion route do it out of practical necessity and due to the fall of morality in the West and around the world: Most women who choose abortion do so because the man did not stick around: He pulled up his brief, put on his pants, walked away, and the woman never saw him again. When she called and told him that she was pregnant, that was the last that she heard of him; and rather than confront the juggernaut of a fatherless pregnancy; she opted for an abortion—and who can blame her!

You see, both the recreational sex and the murderous abortion are sins in God's eyes; but society doesn't seem to care because it has redefined right and wrong; and in the process of doing that, it has forgotten God. So, what does God do? He sends messengers, asking man to repent and change his mind and warning him of the risks of not following through. In the course of time, God gives man a certain amount of time to repent; and when he doesn't, God unleashes his clean-up crew on mankind—and what is that? Shooting sprees; cyclonic bombs; atmospheric rivers; squall lines; destructive cold fronts; dried-up rivers and lakes; whole mountains giving way, covering up homes; F5 tornados; category 9 earthquakes; six-hundred-millibar hurricanes; and devastating climate change.

Suddenly, everything that used to go right starts going wrong because man is trying to enjoy God's world without God, and that would never happen. God is a holy God who presides over the universe; that is run by physical laws—so are the affairs of men; they, too, are run by moral laws; When those laws are persistently broken, God dispatches his clean-up crew, which man never understands; and he dies like a fool. Killing a baby in the womb is murder, but people who've forgotten God don't think so. For this reason, a variety of curses drop like a bomb on them.

Thus, some of the unhappiest women in the world are abortion mothers who weep all day long, and run good men away from them in unhappy marriages: They live in a world with a room into which no one else is invited; they go into that room every day and weep for hours.

That is the price that they pay for redefining the morals that God placed in the world; and unfortunately, for many, the abortion nightmare does not end there; they endure an endless river of sleepless nights, getting up in a pool of cold sweat and screaming to the top of their voice. Many fall apart with nervous breakdowns; and sometimes, this personal collapse continues for years. Again, unfortunately, for far too many abortion mothers; suicide awaits them at the end of the road: Was it worth redefining God's moral rules that he placed in this world? Merely saying that God does not exist doesn't change a thing; it just turns you into a fool and fodder for the world's many instruments of destruction.

Don't go about pretending to have power and authority that you don't have, following clearly wrong voices; therefore, deciding to have an abortion does not mean that it is going to be a safe abortion or that it is not going to end in suicide. Sophia, take my advice; grab control of yourself and squeeze back those powerful sexual drives: Do not let them dump you in the gutters like they have done to so many of the world's billions who are not with us today because they made wrong choices that crucified them on the cross of abortion troubles. You live in a false world in which sex is greatly overrated and does massive damage to far too many lives.

Do you notice when the peer pressure for sex comes, you never see images of those whom it has already slaughtered; all you can feel is the sexual pressure in your crotch, but remember: It never ends there. Sophia, I've reawakened your awareness and understanding of the mendacious world in which you live; actually, what I have endeavored to do is to kill the sex drives with which you are currently grappling. While there may be something there for you, opening up yourself to this young man's powerful and healthy sperms is the wrong route for you now. Go back home and cool off: Take a cold shower; let all that steam drain away and forget about Aubrey: he represents nothing but trouble for you now.

Stop thinking about him; and those strong sexual feelings and raw, colorful, steaming dreams about intimacy with him will fade away; especially in the light of this new understanding of the world and its crazy appetite for self-destructive sex. One last thing that I would like to ask you, if you don't mind: Cutback on interacting with those sex-obsessed friends that you have on this campus; Sophia, you are in trouble right now; you cannot fool around with your life and future; avoid people who belong to the dirty sex club and who seem to think that something is wrong with you if you are not having sex by hooking up with anyone who is available—any one-night stand with a penis. Stay away from those people; they are rapidly rushing into their own landfill. I don't want you to see yourself as someone who is sick. because you have craving for someone whom you love; at the same time, I don't want you going out there, exposing your nudity to this man whom you do not know and who can destroy your life.

Don't be ashamed of your virgin status; at the same time, don't run out there and open up yourself to some man whom you do not know, get pregnant, and have to struggle with the decision of what to do with a pregnancy, the status of whose father is in doubt. Remember: Most men would sex you up if you allow them—and you would even enjoy the experience; but, keep in mind that those men do not love you; they love sex: Once they get what they want, pump you up with their semen, and impregnate you; you will see how much they really love you. Keep me posted with your progress, in this regard, and come back to see me again in about two months.

Overcoming Sophia's Personal Problems

Dr. Firne was a great counsellor and steered her through the caliginous jungle of the virginity shame by destigmatizing the whole notion of being an adult virgin and defying that hypersexual culture that controls young people's mind today. She steered Sophia out of the madness that is destroying young people's lives today. The world out there is obsessed with the destructive kind of sex that murder innocent infants in the womb and call it abortion; oh, how terrible it is to slap some kind of fancy name on the plain murder of innocent babies in the womb, the very place where they are supposed to be. They belong there; there is their home—their play pen; and because people have made these sour choices, they reap what they sow, and nature socks it to them smack in their sleep: A hurricane appears from the blue and smashes their homes to pieces, even while they are asleep, an F5 Tornado appears from the blue, awakes them, and shreds their community.

You look around, and utter destruction has gobbled up the whole community, you saw what happened in Florida, in Buffalo, in the

Mid-West, in California; doom is everywhere God sends his clean-up crew. You look at that and say, "Oh, isn't that terrible—they've lost everything!" But no one would ever consider that, may be, that is pay back for all the babies who have been slaughtered in their mothers' womb—and do you notice that some of these things happen in the night when people are sound asleep. Nobody gets away with anything in this world, even though they seem to get away with it for a while. And so, Sophia Brent debouched from that sex spell. She realized that she did not need to have sex just so that she could no longer be a virgin; she should desire to have sex because the person is right for her—not merely so that she could enter the rat race to lose her virginity by a certain age.

Dr. Firne demonstrated to Sophia that sexual experience and love are two entirely different things and should not be confused by horny, one-night stand hookups. These are the things about which Dr. Firne reminded Sophia, with regards to the fire that was burning in her. So, in looking at Sophia's personal problems in their proper perspective, they did not arise merely from being a woman; they arose mainly from the environment in which she found herself: She'd connected with some very unambitious people who did not want anything more than a college degree and hard-driving sex with anyone with a hard enough penis for sex. This poisonous environment polluted Sophia's mind and perception of reality; and over time, it had taken its toll on her, consuming her life like a wildfire.

The bedazzlingly powerful sexaholic environment in which Sophia found herself adumbrated her understanding of reality, handing self-destructive sex absolute control of her life. By virtue of being trapped in that sexaholic school atmosphere, Sophia developed resistance fatigue to self-destructive recreational sex; and it began pouring out of her like water from a broken fire hydrant; she was ready to succumb to its awesome power that she had given it over the past two years, when all she heard was, "Have sex to be normal!" Over time of listening to this mantra drummed into her spirit every day; she, herself, became obsessed with sex. The idea that this message, itself, was false had gotten lost in her subconscious mind; her resistance to the mendacious message simply crashed, and she capitulated to it: It was a kind of sexaholic socialization that she underwent.

Over time, she realized that she was involved in some kind of cabal that glorified sex; thus, when she began having thoughts and feelings to actually go and assault Aubrey and rape him, kissing him without his permission in public; she knew that she had bitten the dust and was beginning to lose it. These problems gradually waxed worse over time and began to distract her studies. She would go to the movies and meet Aubrey there, and she would literally wet her undergarment and could not tell what was wrong with her. Well, by the time things got to this stage, you know that she was in stark trouble. Thus, in retrospect of all these sudden developments in her life, Dr. Firne understood the mysterious connections that she was having in her own life, having to do with her own daughter Vanetta and her boyfriend's mother.

Dr. Firne was running into Simeon's mother just about everywhere she went. She also ran into Simeon at the *Le Jardiin de Luxenbourg* in Paris and shook his hand; she and her husband, Dr. Firne, were spending their weekend in Paris and were just walking around the garden when Vanetta's mother ran into this warm and gentle feller to whom she took a liking; Thus, all the connections were intertwined; and, in that regard, the whole circle of events made sense. Dr. Firne turned out to be a splendid counsellor for Sophia; helping her to steer her life out of that crisis. Sophia pulled herself together and away from that tangled jungle of sexual obsession. Over time, she totally overcame the mess and was eventually able to connect with Aubrey after she earned her Master's degree in organizational psychology.

Sophia's Ongoing Interaction with Dr. Firne

Over time, having cut off her interaction with virtually all of the sexaholics who'd been goading her to enter the rat race to lose her virginity; Sophia worked closely with Dr. Firne; she came right out of it. She utterly exploded the idea of the sex rush by pointing out the many contradictions around sex today, demonstrating that nothing is wrong with being a virgin. Today, people are tacitly told that virginity is a sociocultural value up to some vaguely agreed-upon age range, somewhere around fourteen to seventeen; but that same age range is some also vaguely defined boundary between which people are supposed to be having sex. Thus, young people get contradictory signals from society about sex, highly valuing virginity on the one hand and degrading it on the other; holding that sex should begin somewhere between and after this age range.

The world views and values sex as recreational entertainment that produces the trash of human reproduction which must be thrown away. In addition to the so-called trash of pregnancy, sex often delivers poisonous sexually transmitted diseases. This was how Dr. Firne led Sophia out of the morass of self-destructive sex: She pointed out the contradictions surrounding sex and showed her why, based on the Bible, her values were the only thing that mattered after all. She showed Sophia that, although sex has serious liabilities and consequences, they are often ignored in the frenzied sex rush. Because of the contradictions surrounding sex, it has become very self-destructive and poisonous; and women are forced to bear the brunt of the burden that pregnancy delivers because the world is a chauvinistic place that protects men who misbehave and mistreat women.

Dr. Firne told Sophia that the world is false and is riddled with invisible booby traps that most people don't see; she told her that, people are designed to live according to the dictates of the Bible but are socialized to ignore it; when they do that, the whole world turns into a booby trap. For example, sex was meant for marriage, but when that is foregone, sex becomes a dangerous weapon; causing poverty, disease, societal deterioration, and death among the human race. In this regard, Dr. Firne showed Sophia that the sex she was craving was itself a dangerous illusion that would eat up her life like food; it was not the fun and excitement for which she was looking; rather, it was a dangerous booby trap that was about to trash her life and academic studies.

However, in order to do that, it had to give her some temporary fun in exchange for the treasure of her future success. Dr. Firne told her that what she was looking at was an endless stream of abortions and sleepless nights; or A string of rejections from men who would come, use her body, and walk away because of the many babies with which she would end up. Thus, she convincingly demonstrated to Sophia that sex is not that recreational after all. Furthermore, she pointed out to her that no one can do sex all day; couples eventually wear out their bodies with sex. She told Sophia that, if she really wanted a relationship that majored in sex, she should do a partial or complete sterilization, thus giving her complete control over her sexuality; and she could always adopt children later on in life. However, it is hardly ever that simple. Things are hardly ever as simple as those promoting them; the complexity is often revealed in the plan's execution.

The Aubrey-Sophia Connection

The man with whom she finds herself, later on in life, may want to have his own children and would eventually leave her for a woman who can have children. Dr. Firne told Sophia that it is a world in which you are damned if you do and damned if you don't. because the world is false; in many cases, people find themselves in situations where they are forced to choose between the lesser of two clear evils, like the world in which we live now. Dr. Firne counselled and carefully nursed Sophia out of that dark jungle in which she had found herself—and how did it happen? She was just going to university and met some people there, whom she befriended, who happened to belong to the hook-up culture; as a result, she almost lost her way!

Dr. Firne patiently nurtured Sophie out of that umbrous wilderness of lust: In the process of the ongoing counselling, Dr. Firne recommended a life-giving church in the Los Angeles area to her. In time, she connected with Aubrey, sometime around a year and a half later on, at the Fountain of Living Waters Church; and oh, my; what a meeting that was!

As it turned out, something was really there for her; as is obvious in the Following conversation that occurred in the church's lower bookstore, on the east side of the beautiful church campus. This church is located in the center of the city, just outside of downtown, on the Vermont Corridor. Sophia went to that church that day and decided to visit the bookstore when the service was over. As she was in the bookstore, looking at some books on spiritual warfare; Aubrey walked in and looked around as if he were in a forest. When he spotted Sophie, he pretended as if he was interested in that prayer and spiritual warfare area where she was; so, he moved in that direction, and this was what happened.

Aubrey Holmes (Smiling): Do I know you; I've seen you somewhere before: What is your name. I don't know why you are ignoring me; you used to go to that university on the westside—didn't you?—I know you; I've seen you over there before.

Sophia Brent: Have you come back again? I was so glad when you vanished—are you back again? I know that you know me, and I know you, too. This meeting is one of those mysterious connections that I used to have when I seemed to have met you every day; I, myself, wondered about meeting the same man over, and over, and over again—it was really weird.

Aubrey's Steaming Proposal to Sophia

Aubrey: What is this—some kind of riddle? When I went to that school in Westwood, I used to run into you almost every day; and I even thought that you might have been my wife because I was not married, and I kept running into you. I made several steps to come to you, but something kept holding me back. I went to the park; you were there: I went to the museum; you were there: I went to the movies, and you were there, too; and now, after a reasonable hiatus, I come here to this church, and you are here—what is this, some race on my trail? Are you following me or something, or are you my wife? Is this a sign from God that you are my wife, as sexy and pretty as you are?

Sophia: Well, that has answered your own question: if you find me sexy and pretty, don't you think other guys find me that way, too. Why do you want to marry a pretty girl like me? What makes you think that I'd want to stay with you when all these buffed men are on my trail, too?

Aubrey: By the way, what is your name; though I'd met you a thousand times before, we've never talked to each other, and I never got to share with you what I was going through each time I met you. By the way, can we step outside and chat some more around the fountain?

Sophia: Because I'm serious in my relationship with the Lord, I don't generally find myself alone with guys: All men are the same; they want the same thing—especially guys like you who just want to take a Christian lady to all the wrong place, even before you get to know her.

Aubrey: Oh, dear lady, I have something to tell you; but I cannot tell you here because the bookstore is about to close. Go out to the fountain, and II will come and meet you there.

Sophia: Good bye; I'll see you around: I have much lined up for the afternoon; but perhaps, next Sunday will be a better time to talk to you. I'll see you around,

Aubrey walked out behind her; he motioned her to the fountain and told her that he would make it up to her because he believed that God wanted to put them together, and he did not want to get in the way. He told her that something was interfering with the dynamics of their relationship.

Sophia: But how could that be—I don't have those same feelings for you. I remember when we used to meet quite regularly; and I was bemused about who you are, but I never desired to be close to you. I just saw you there and kept running into you: I don't know who you are; it was just like seeing another person—and besides, I'm not the same person that I was then.

Aubrey: What do you mean; are you telling me something that I don't already know? I have something for you, and I don't want to give it to anyone else but you.

Sophia: Oh, is that right-what might that be, Mr. Mystery man? You are like a brick wall; You are so inscrutable; I do not want any man to give me their penis filled with pregnancy germs; I know how it works and what men say—and it is all an illusion. I've heard all of that before, and my mind has been turned off entirely from men who see women as sex objects. I know what men want and I know what I want—and what we want are different: What kind of work do you do?

Aubrey: My name is Aubrey; I am a middle schoolteacher and have been coming to this church for the past nine months. But you've not told me your name; what is your name, and what kind of work do you do—are you still going to that school over there in Westwood?

Sophia: My name is Sopha; I work as an organizational psychologist for a marketing firm in Westwood and do not plan on having children any time soon. I need to get to know myself some more and the man whom I am going to marry before I can take Long-term, intimate relationships seriously. The world is too false and vain to take people at their word.

Aubrey: But Sophia… and by the way, that is a pretty name; I love that name: You have no idea the hell I've gone through just to get you out my mind; night after night, I kept dreaming you in flaming colors. I kept dreaming you and me having hard-core sex, and the dreams were particularly disturbing on those days when I saw you; it seemed as if you would force me into your bedroom where you lived in Culver City over there: I can describe your body in living colors for you; and then, all of a sudden, when I stopped seeing you; it felt as if I were going crazy because you had become like my wife. When I saw you this afternoon, looking at those books, it was as if God had answered my prayer; and I imagined seeing that birth mark on your right leg and on your breast. I had intimate details of your body because I had living intercourse with you—I am not lying.

Sophia: Well, I don't see how that can be possible—I did not know you and cannot see how you could have had those dreams about me when I have never been with a man; I am a late virgin, twenty-two years old; but regardless of what you have dreamt about me, it just goes to show what your dirty focus was when you saw me. Men often see women as sex toys and food to be consumed, and that attitude casts women as sex objects and not as human beings. I want to be viewed as a Christian woman—not as some dirty old man's sex toy;

nonetheless, I am glad that you poured your heart out and told me what you were thinking about me; your colorful description of my body sent thrills all through my spine and made me feel like a dog—a slut.

Aubrey: So, what you are saying is that my description of your breasts is off; at least, that was what I saw; and since that time, I've been craving your nude, sexy body: I want to have it under my control to enjoy it and the contours with which it is so wonderfully designed.

Sophia's Deep Knowledge and Jarring Admission

Sophia: Isn't that a shame; that is all that you can remember about me; however, just in case something happens between us way down the road, there are some things that you need to know: After those haunting meetings with you need to know. After those haunting meetings with you, all those times, two years ago; I sought sought psychological counselling to determine what was wrong with me; and now I realize that it was your hypnotic spells that were placing me in your path and interfering with my life.

Aubrey: What do you mean by saying that meeting you was interfering with your life—were you having the same dreams, too?

Sophia: No, my mind is not dirty as yours; it is not driven by nasty dreams; I just wanted to see if I were losing my mind because I know that some men work with curious art and science and can cause women to do some peculiar things, such as placing them on their track and controlling their minds. I want you to know that I would never give any man my love who hasn't experienced, at least, a year and a half of celibacy with me to truly get to know me: My psychologist told me that all men want from women is sex; and once they get enough of that from them, they are gone; especially if they manage to impregnate them Many dumb broads, thinking that men's interest in them is all about love and fun, find out the hard way. I had a great chat with my psychologist, Dr. Firne: She. Herself. is an organizational psychologist, with two doctorates under belt.

She told me that many women are just silly; they confuse men's desire to conquer and control women, through sex, for exciting recreational sex and fun. She told me that human society is false, but the human beings, themselves, don't know that because they were born in the outer court of secret knowledge, where they are not allowed to know the ruth. Dr. Firne told me that there is a truth gap in human society; for example, when a man sees a sexy woman and goes after her, he often means what he tells her: he is sincere at that point. What he does not know is that he was born in the outer court of secret knowledge that does not allow him to know who he really is. That is why most women go after the handsome guys: they fantasize about having slap-your-mamma-crazy recreational sex with them.

What these women don't know is that, once these guys get enough of them—once they get enough sex from them; their minds will change. But they neither know that, at the time they are telling these women how much they love them, nor are they aware that they cannot tell the truth and are programmed, from birth, to lie their way all through life. Why? The world is a lie. The world is a lie! A few months down the road, they see other sexy girls; and they begin to change. Out of the clear blue, their attitude begins to turn sour towards those earlier women. As the sourness progresses, those men begin to argue and fight with their earlier lovers in favor of fresh, new meat. And as things progress and become worse and worse, the relationships with their earlier lovers disintegrate and fade away. In a similar vein, what happened to all the love that he told her

What happened to all that love that he told you that he had for you; It was all a lie, but it was a technical lie because that man is not even aware that he cannot tell the truth; and if he sees his mother in her panties or in the nude often enough. Some of those very guys would also gravitate to wanting to have sex with their own mothers. It is not uncommon to hear of young men; fourteen and fifteen years old, whose mom had them very young; talk about how sexy their mother is and how wonderful it is having sex with them. Do you mean to tell me that young boys have sex with their own mothers?—all the time! And what is so pathetic here is that most of these relationships end with these young men moving on to greener pasture, leaving their mother and several children behind. Why do people do these things?—and I can go further with this, illustrating to you why men do not know that they are liars and are mainly interested in the sexual aspect of their relationship with women. Many women are petrified about the aging process because they know that, sooner or later, their lover—husband or live-in partner— is going to dump them they for a younger woman.

Every day, hundreds of thousands of people get dumped by life partners whom they once told how much they loved them: Why? Human society is false; and people were born in darkness, but they are not aware of that fact. Thus, they are bound to make the same mistakes again, and again, and again; and, as it turns, human society is a not only a lie—it is also a mistake. This explains why so many marriages and friendships collapse. In this regard, most relationships are mere phases in people's lives, and there is the dumping phase: This is why millions of women get dumped every day, and most of the dumping is done by men because women are designed and programmed by God to crave men's love.

Even polluted women who crave other women get dumped; many of them end up in intensive care, having sustained a barbaric bludgeoning by their lesbian partner: you have no idea how many same-sex couples die from domestic violence abuse: Why? People get tired of each other because they reject Jesus and are searching for fulfillment elsewhere, in mere vanities, trying to enjoy God's world without God. Have you ever wondered why millions of couples wind up becoming sexless—what happened to all that thrill that was there at the beginning? Where did it go? Now, tell me, Aubrey; Do you still love, and want to screw me; or has your mind changed about me now?—and I'm not done. I have more for you Aubrey.

Aubrey: I've never heard anything like this in my life before; everything that you said is new to me, and I do not know what to do with it. You are scarry, and no one can enjoy sex in fear.

Sophia: And that is my very point, my dear brother—my dear, because I went through the same thing that you experienced, and I, too, was craving you; Though I was a virgin—and still am—I had those same dirty dreams of you ejaculating in my kitty, and I was afraid. I thought I was losing my mind, so I went to see psychologist, Dr. Firne, and she gave me the whole low down on human society and the devious and anfractuous ways in which it works. Had I not gone to see her, I would have become a whore and very well may have been stuck with your bastard: I quite likely might have lost my mind. That was the reason that I said, "I am a different woman now": I know how to protect myself from men's fertile sperms, the ultimate conquest of women. Dr. Firne gave me the inside story about life and how it really works, and now, I have it in my hands and in my bones: No one can ever take it away from me.

This is the reason that I underwent the partial sterilization process, tying my tubes and blocking any man's sperms from getting to my eggs to destroy my life. I know that I'm a woman and must protect myself as much as I possibly can: It is not that I'm an easy target, and I 'll not participate in any kind of sex outside of marriage, and that is no guaranty that one's husband would stay with her after pumping her up with his fertile semen. This is not to say that I can't control my feelings, but a stitch in time saves nine. You see, Aubrey, sex is not what people think it is: For one thing, sex is not mere recreational entertainment; that is just the downpayment on all the troubles and problems that sex brings into people's lives.

You see, my friend; God already knew that, if he had created a different mechanism for manufacturing human beings into the world, human society would have long been extinct because taking care of babies and raising children is a Herculean task; and virtually no one would have wanted to do that without some kind of inspiration because it would have been too unnatural to say, "Babies, be"; and they appeared just like that. God knew that there had to be more to bringing children into the world.

For that reason, he gave man pleasure in sex as a bonding mechanism and an inspiration for him to have sex and produce babies, but what has man done with it? He has rejected God's plan and insisted on sex being merely for entertainment; in turn, God has cursed promiscuity with diseases and death; the destruction comes from four different sources: Either you are going to get it from sexually transmitted diseases that would most likely kill you; you are going to get it on the abortion table; it is going to happen after the abortion through a worried, confused life; ending in suicide; or you are going to get it through rejection from men. And, as I've explained earlier, unwise sex predisposes woman to being rejected by men through a revolving door of unplanned pregnancies that either produces a nasty cycle of abortions or a houseful of fatherless children.

The abortion cycle cheapens the woman's value; depresses her mind and mood; drives good men away from her because she is so depressed and sad all the time. It robs her of valuable night sleep because of the nightmares and night sweat that drown her in her bed at night; causing maddening depression and suicide that often follow that lugubrious and pathetic state into which many abortion mothers find themselves. None of this would happen if the men, responsible for these pregnancies, would stick around and support their women

and children. they often don't because they know that the world is
false, and they can get away with it. They often cut and run because
the world is run by chauvinistic, misogynistic men who protect
and defend one another. Thus, most of these women have no other
pragmatic choice than to abort their babies because they reckon that
they cannot afford to raise them with dignity, on their own; thus,
the abortion murder falls both on irresponsible men and dumb, silly
women.

Now, what happens if the cycle of pregnancies produces babies
whose mothers opt not to murder them in the abortion shredder?
What happens if the mothers decide to keep their babies? How does
the cycle of rejection work in this case? Well, it almost always starts
out with one baby—the first one; and, for all practical purposes, the
woman is still fresh-looking and viewed as valuable and sexy. Men
with hot penises still see her as a good meal of sex, and the fact that
many women make the same mistake that they made with the first
man allows them to get pregnant again. Each time they get pregnant,
their value diminishes because each succeeding guy sees them as
being less and less valuable because the extent and weight of her
baggage get greater and greater with the passage of time and foolish
sex; and, as a result, fewer and fewer men want to stay with those
women.

Thus, they begin to attract older and older men; in some cases, this
can go on for up to twelve children; especially in underdeveloped
societies where people depend on their children to serve as added
hands to work on the land. At the end of the day, in this dark world
of good and evil, women are given baskets to carry water; and men
often get away scot-free because the chauvinistic age is ruled by
men, and women are left holding the bag. In this regard, society is
way out of balance; and justice is not served. But this is the way
the world, run by the devil, is—it is false; and if you fix it in this
generation; a generation or two away from this one, it goes right back

to what it was and even worse than it was before—do you get it now, Aubrey: Do you still want to have sex with me without us having spent quality time to get to know each other? Oh, Aubrey, you don't even know, or have asked, me if I'm one of those women who have sex with dogs: Shame on you, Aubrey!

Sophia Delivers the Rest of Her Message

And that is not even all, Aubrey: Many women have young children without a father in the home; these children often grow up undisciplined, and much disrespect occurs in the home, especially among boys. This, by no means, indicates that this is what happens in every situation. But in a large number of cases, the loose mother begins to see her oldest son, growing up and becoming man; and not having a regular man in her life, she begins to see him as the man of the house. Unfortunately, this attitude often leads to the wrong perception of her son; and in many cases, he begins having sex with his mother; impregnating her, further confusing her life even more, and branding the family with generational poverty.

 This same scenario unfolds in situations when married women have children too early in the marriage, and it fails. More often than not, the boy children grow up without their dad; and the oldest son becomes the man of the house, in the context of an intimate relationship with his mother. Often, incest is almost never an issue at the beginning of things; in fact, such a sentiment is entirely ruled out by the mother and her young, innocent children. However, virtually everybody knows that children do not remain innocent; and a lot happens behind closed doors; especially when adult males and females are involved. While this is not the standard and does not happen all the time, all too frequently; these mother-son sexual relationships do develop; and sometimes go on for a long time, even after the son gets married.

These types of relationships develop in cases where women are single or divorced; moreover, they even develop in cases where there is a man and a loose woman in the house. And it gets even worse, my dear, Aubrey, who wants to enjoy my quam, even before he has gotten to know who I am: All too often, the world is a very lonely place; and sometimes, neither a man nor kids are around: The woman lives alone—and this is increasingly becoming the case now. In the light of the loneliness in the world, many women have gotten way down low and dirty; instead of subjecting themselves to a partial sterilization tie off, an increasing number of women are choosing dogs for their partners. They cite the fact that the sex is crazy, the dog is a virtual sex toy, and the woman can never get pregnant.

Many view it as the emergent trend of transhumanism, combining technology and science with human reproduction to produce various types of the human species and societies; and surprisingly enough, women, engaging dogs sexually, have become quite popular. Part of the problem is the mushy love for animals in North America, and many people have gone way too far with dogs; it's kind of interesting that people abort their babies but go overboard, loving and taking care of dogs and cats. And in a world where shame and disgrace have been abolished, many women have sex with their dog lovers in orgy-like situations, without a shred of shame because it is a world of anything goes: Nothing is shameful and disgraceful anymore.

So, where are we, Aubrey? Do you still want to sex me up without even trying to figure out who I am, and whether I slept with a dog last night. I want to galvanize you into seeing the world differently, not so much because the world has changed—and it has, but because it has always been this way; and because of what men have done to women, many women have been motivated to take action and create a world that they deem right for them. Unfortunately, for far too many, that world has become a world of dog sex—and some women even wish that they could make babies for their dog lovers because they never tell them no and are always there at their disposal. Unhappily, many of these brave new souls are allergic to their dog lovers' semen; and as a result, quite a few have drifted over to the other side—they die while having sex with their dog lover.

Aubrey: I know that you have said all that to discourage me, and I understand that the world has changed; but none of that has dissuaded me from seeing you as my wife: I do not see you as a sex toy: I see you as my wife, as has been indicated by all these mysterious connections. When I was having all these sex dreams of liberally being with you, I knew that it was a foretaste of what was to come, so when will my year and a half of celibacy begin? I was raised in a single-parent home, and none of that mess that you've described there happened in our home. I was raised to respect my mother, my peers, and adults. However, though none of that occurred at my house, I know of homes where it was rumored that those things were happening; and I suppose that, if some women can masturbate, they can—and will—probably have sex with their sons if, they would go along with it: Sex makes a fool out of people every single day because it seems real but is not.

And I get your point; you were not merely trying to be vulgar and nasty; you just wanted to demonstrate to me the reality and degree of human society's complexity and the level of depravity to which it has sunken. All those things are happening, yet people go about their lives as if these things have never happened because they no longer have any respect for truth and God. I would be highly upset if I learn that my girlfriend or wife has been sleeping with her dog. Personally, I feel that, if you agree to have sex with your dog, you should also be prepared to divulge that information to any potential or prospective human lover: No one should have to learn that after the fact; especially in view of the idea that many women drink dog semen, which is an extreme act. In view of that, I feel that, at least, any potential lover needs to know that, going into that new relationship with that woman.

Sophia: It was very difficult for me to tell you what was happening to me during those dark times when we kept bumping into each other; I felt like a whore, even though I was—and still am—a virgin. I never knew that virgins could have those kinds of feelings, seeing that they've never had sex. For that reason, I tied off and would not have children in any marriage for, at least first five years because, as a woman, I know that I'm so vulnerable to the male sperm and its destructive power. Men destroy women with their sperms and sell them to society for next to nothing. The more children a woman has, the harder she has to fight to keep the man who has impregnated her with all those children; it is a strange paradox—and the very opposite of what God had intended initially, when he made men and women. Sex was created for marriage and family—and for nothing else in this world.

When people go about it in their own way, it becomes satanic and distorted; causing all kinds of problems in human society: Why? Sex was created for marriage, and marriage for sex; in fact, when you get right down to it, sex is marriage because it is the only human behavior that thoroughly mixes the erotic juices, blending up the opposite-sex couple and making them one. Moreover, the offspring from sex produces features of both the man and the woman; amplifying the fact that these two had sex that produced this offspring, and thus ratifying the event and putting their stamp on it.

Aubrey: But why do you sound so much like an attorney; this is just a light chat around a church fountain; we haven't even gotten to know each other as yet, and you've begun talking about marriage and children: When do I begin my year and a half celibacy regimen; I sense that I would need to finish that first before the relationship formally begins, and I will follow your lead because of the enlightening things that you've taught me here today. I never saw the world in that light before; you've truly enlightened me here today; I can't wait to join your crusade against the wrong way in which the world works.: Other people need to know and see this for themselves.

Over the next two years, Aubrey matured in his Christian life, as he recognized the destructive power of sex; he caught Sophia's drift and vision to empower women in society, and he never hounded her for sex one day—he saw the destruction that a careless, irresponsible penis does to young women's lives and to society, as a whole. Aubrey saw how society has been deceived by the devil and how people destroy one another's lives without realizing that that is what they are doing; men destroy women with their penises because their sperms wreck and destroy their value and future, creating houses of incest, depression, poverty, and suicide. After Sophia and Aubrey were married, Sophia took up writing and became a societal powerhouse, changing women's lives. But the story does not end here, Sophia's friend, Christina learned the hard way; because of the false nature of the world, suckers are born every day, and reality dating television bristles with them. Thousands get used and dashed away like trash by penis-whirling bachelors.

Christina's Very Unfortunate Plight

Many women have come upon hard times, finding the right opposite-sex lover; and in the light of the drought of good male lovers today, quite a number of women have opted to search and ransack the available dating services on the circuit today. And where are they, and how do they work? Well, there are quite a few that may be worth a woman's time; but many simply aren't. In this regard, there is a considerable range of dating services; showing people looking for love. Unfortunately, to a large degree, these are people who are looking for sex and not necessarily love, for many of them wind up getting screwed and lost along the way, as happened to Christina.

There are those abominable adulterous websites, catering to those who are tired having sex with their spouses and want something new—and this is one of the reasons that the world has become so complicated and splattered with domestic violence. Wrong sex is one of the causes of violence in the world, but the world is not that enlightened to see that. However, extramarital websites have been rapidly growing and the number of women slaughtered by their romantic partners every day. Ashley Madison alone boasts an active membership of fifty million, and the total membership of adulterous websites draws closer to a quarter of a billion married folks. This is what has become of marriage and civilization in the West.

In this regard, married women, contemplating an affair, may want to give heed to this warning: All men may not take this moral beating rolling over. If you are married and are contemplating an adulterous affair, fold our legs and stay with your husband or ask him for a friendly divorce because adultery often brings out the beast in some men; and yours may be one of them: Don't risk your life, taking dangerous adulterous chances. Yes, you may get away with it for a while; but eventually, somebody is going to tip somebody; and you'd pay for it in a way you never dreamed. Hang in there with your marriage, seek counselling, and turn to God to repair your life. Remember: Every sixteen hours, a woman dies in the United States at the hands of her romantic lover; spare yourself the trouble and be a good girl—all right!

In addition to the extramarital sites, there is a range of hookup dating arrangements; from Christian sites to those showcases exhibiting hookups, dressed in the nude and ready for the sexual act. Possibly, at the top of the list are the virtual reality television dating programs; thus, you can see that there is quite an assortment of dating arrangements on the circuit today. However, reality television dating has become very popular; wheeling singles all over the planet and splattering all kinds of occult activities in their audiences' faces in the process. Some of the shows pull no bones about what they are doing—and it is low down and dirty. Well, obviously, there is much legal paperwork and moral beating involved in these sleazy reality television dating shows; some of the acts are quite questionable; but presumably, the clients who participate in these shows are duly warned about the pain of rejection and the risk of pregnancy and contracting sexually transmitted diseases. In other words, these television dating shows take no accountability for what happens on the show: Contestant, you are on your own.

Whatever happens is your responsibility; but in looking at these shows more closely; even with the best of intentions, the number of men these women are asked to kiss tells the whole story. No woman who kisses that many men in such a short period of time can make any virtuous wife anyway. The number of men that these women are asked to kiss gives these sleazy television programs away, for any woman who kisses that many men, in such a short period of time, is a whore anyway. And in most cases, these betrothals and marriages don't work: They are based on the notion that every woman is a slut, and marriage is a phase in the broader game of falsehood in this world.

Despite these glaring drawbacks and warnings though, many women flock these reality television dating shows; it so happened one of Sophia's bosom pals, Christina Johnson, went on one of these reality television shows, called the Golden Bride and had made stunning and remarkable progress; she went all the way to the last two contestants for the dashing bachelor's love. It was her, Christina Johnson, and Adela Haynes. The pert, spanking bachelor; Earl Johnson; had made sure that he had sexed Christina up really well, the one whom he knew he was not going to choose; even though he had assured her that she was going to be his wife. In this regard, Christina was fairly confident and certain that she was going to be Earl Duncan's pick for the upcoming engagement.

However, Earl had promised both women the engagement ring and assured them that they were going home with him that night; and they were all excited about being engaged to him. But you see, this is the way the world works and tells, and gets away with, lies. Obviously, these horny bachelors can only choose one woman and can greatly simplify the process by making it easier on the candidates whom he already knows that he is not going to pick. The bachelor just does not; suddenly, out of the clear blue, at the last minute; make up his mind about his choice; or the one whom he definitely favors for the spot of being his fiancée; he already knows who she is. Thus, he can simplify the other girl's life by letting her go the night before the selection is transacted; but is that what they normally do?

By not telling the other woman that it's not going to be her just amplifies the magnitude of the rejection that he is handing her, the woman whom he eventually does not pick gets a bad rap: Even though he does not pick her, he already decided to have sex with her ahead of time, on the eve of the selection day. This was exactly what happened in this terrible situation. On the selection day, Earl shared these shocking sentiments with Christina, the one whom he screwed and rejected, "I love you, Christina; you are such a wonderful girl, and I really enjoyed being with you. However, Christina, I'm going to pick Adella because I love her more than you. This is even after he has squirted semen into the other woman's womb the night before! How, on earth, can that be fair to that woman whom he already knew he was going to reject; even after he'd been treating Christina like his wife and having sex with her, regardless of what he'd promised all the girls.

The fact that he broke his promise and had sex with Christina intimates that she ought to have been the one whom he should have selected to be his wife. If he had already decided that he was going to pick Adella way ahead of time, then he should have had sex with her instead of with Christina. Having sex with Christina, when he already knew that he was not going to select her, was beyond wrong. And for the sake of policy, he should have selected the woman in whose womb he had played virtually all of the previous night; subjecting her to the likelihood of becoming pregnant with his child. Well, as it turned out; in an all-night, rough-and-tumble, fiery sexual escapade in Mexico City, the night before the selection day; Earl and Christina had a mess of sex. Their steaming sexual romp lasted practically all night—and it was quite a carousing in that hotel that night. However, it was romp that came with a nasty frown—and tears in Christina's eyes.

A Nasty Sour Turn

Obviously, Christina is not a fool; she would not have acquiesced to sex at such a crucial point in the game if she was not reasonably assured of clinching that engagement ring on the following day. As a gentleman, knowing that he had already settled in his mind to choose Adella, Earl could have easily told Christina that she was not the one and let her go home that evening; obviating the crushing rejection on the following evening. Evidently, it still would have hurt—the rejection still would have stung with the pain and venom of a poignant sense of loss. However, knowing that he was going to choose Adella ahead of time and opting to have sex with Christina on the eve of the selection is flagitiously wrong.

On that evening, when he picked Adella; he smiled and told her that he knew that she was going to be his wife from the very moment when he saw her: This, my friends, is how the world lies and gets away with it. But that is not all of the story—there is more. It so happened that the sexual escapade in Mexico City occurred during Christiana's ovulation period of her cycle; and oops: A terrible accident occurred, and Christina's egg was cooked without a kettle. When Earl turned her down the next day of the selection, a tornado cloud, from nowhere, dropped on her face because she had sensed that she might have been pregnant during their sexual romp in Mexico City the night before. However, this was one of those cryptic pregnancies where the regular cycle continued; and the inspector—the pregnancy—did not show up for months. When it finally did, on the fifth month; it was way too late for the safe abortion of four babies. It was alleged that, due to Earl's sheer size, the condom broke and messed everything up; however, the escapade was so wild and crazy, it would have been a miracle if it did not snap; notwithstanding, none of that mattered now.

Earl and Christina went on for another four hours of roasting, hot sex. In the context of the whole situation, though, the rejection was harsh and unusually cruel; nonetheless, it was nothing, compared to the awareness that she was, now, indeed, pregnant with quadruplets! Christina's cryptic pregnancy escaped her notice; and by the time she found out that she was pregnant, she was already five months into it. Her parents, frantically exasperated over the matter, sued the reality television program; but by then, Christina was too devastated to hold up; thus, she jumped the exit: She just could not believe that such a disaster had befallen her out of such an innocent bid for the selection to be married. Christiana wanted a man of her own—and she went for it and lost her very life—oh. what a lugubrious turn it was for her!

She really loved Earl and wanted the selection; thus, she went after it with all her might and lost everything—even her life. Looking at the situation, Christina just could not see any way of rehabilitating her life. In the light of the edgy circumstances in the matter, her doctor, Dr. Leon Allsworth, cautioned her against any abortion attempt, at all, at that stage in the game. Though her parents sued and prevailed in the case, their daughter, Christina, was gone; and the windfall of US $7 million did not benefit her and her four babies on the other side, at all. The judge ruled that, despite the fact that reasonably measures were taken to circumvent this kind of outcome; in the context of the events leading up to the final selection, Earl Duncan deceived Miss

Johnson; and an injunction was signed to block any further appeal of the matter.

That precedent-setting case made it illegal for any kind of sex to occur in these edgy, dicey, sleazy reality television dating competitions; and from that show onward, these sleazy reality television dating shows' rating dropped like a stone in the middle of the sea. Though many women still continued flocking them, they'd lost the edge that they once had; but you might wonder, why are so many women flocking all these various dating outfits; especially sites that offer easy adulterous affairs? Is it that the normal process of social interaction doesn't work anymore; or that changes that have occurred in world society since the Great Recession have greatly cheapened the value of women, driving billions into prostitution.?

Quite naturally, because it is difficult to correctly ascertain the exact number of women working in prostitution, ant numbers floated on the Internet would, most likely, be grossly inexact and false; this is especially true, in view of the fact that some of today's most sophisticated women now work as plain-clothes, undercover prostitutes or whores. The problem is particularly acute, as moral standards have plunged all over the world. Nowhere is this moral decay mechanism more obvious than in the cities of Paris and Jerusalem; and it is such a shocking travesty to see how Jerusalem, the Holy City, has been utterly swallowed up by prostitution. The unnerving number of women—and in most cases, little girls—working online as prostitutes, in Jerusalem, is, at best, disturbing.

And with regards to these little girls who enter the prostitution dance: How old are they? Many enter the ructious carnival as young as thirteen and fourteen years old—and sad to say, many of these children never get out of this dark smoke alive. It is like you look around, and virtually everything has been polluted and poisoned. The number of little girls, working as prostitutes in Jerusalem, should generate a worldwide outcry for polluting the holiest city in the world—where is the outcry? Where is the Pope and his influence? They are conspicuously absent, and everybody seems to be involved in the pert, masqueraded dance of prostitution and dirty sex.

The Jerusalem School of Divine Value

The Jerusalem Christian Center was pastored by Dr. Akiva Kaplan: His mother was a prostitute before she came to faith in Christ and understood that the world as a lie: The Bible says that there is a way that seemeth right unto a man, but the ends thereof are the ways of death; in other words, the world is an illusion, and things are not what they seem to be. Dr. Kaplan's mother, Dena Kaplan, followed the charming and whirling drives of youth and sex and wound up in the cave of prostitution: Her husband, Idan Kaplan, met her in a women's virtue class; had compassion on her; fell in love with her; married her; and had Dr. Kaplan and his sister, Maya Kaplan-Sift.

Thus, in view of his background, Dr. Kaplan has always had a soft spot in his heart for prostitutes because he knew that his mother was once a whore, and God had lifted her out of that miry clay and turned her into a woman of God. He had changed her to such a degree that she could not even remember that she once was a prostitute; God had stripped her of the memory and experience of prostitution and turned her into the wife of a minister of the gospel. When Dr. Kaplan assumed the role of Pastor of the Jerusalem Christian Center, that compassion, deep in his soul, welled up in him: He was profoundly compassionate towards prostitutes, and he created the Jerusalem School of Divine Value—and what is that?

It encapsulates the idea that all people come from God and have divine potentials; however, because of Adam's treason in the Garden of Eden, they are planted in a world of sin, falsehood, and evil and are told a blizzard of lies: People are socialized to believe that God does not exist; in fact, that is the first message that you get in college: Your college pulls no bones in delivering this lie to you and cramming it down your throat. You are not even allowed to voice your own opinion, and your professor will fail you if you insist on voicing the opinion that God exists because modern science is not about science; it is a dangerous secret society that is programmed to hate God and engineered to create a totally Godless society where belief in God is viewed as treason and a form of mental illness.

It is out of this godless moral trash heap from which the whoredom, that produces prostitution, springs. Prostitution is a product of pornography, which is the handiwork of modern science. Pornography started in social science classrooms where professors taught human sexuality, displaying hard-core pornography through videos and DVDs; and gradually, it went from there to plain pornography in the classroom. Today, in many human sexuality classrooms. the sex taught is raw, hard-core pornography; where students have sex in the classroom as part of the class requirement. DVDs are hardly ever used anymore to demonstrate the sexual mechanism and process; Thus, you see that modern science is a naughty little feller and is responsible for the dire and hopeless state of the world today; modern science has created a world that is unsustainable.

Well, what does all of that have to do with Mrs. Kaplan's prostitution?—everything! Women are the toys of prostitution; they are the principal objects sought to display raw, hard-core pornography, and nothing stimulates you sexually like some out-of-this-world pornography. In fact, millions of lives and marriages have been wrecked by pornography; and the marriages, families, whores, and incestuous relationships that it has spawned came in its wake. Came in its wake. Nothing destroys homes, marriages, and parental relationships like pornography does, and nothing creates and ignites the fire of prostitution or whoredom like pornography; it salutes you today at your every turn and destroys your life. I said all that to say that Mrs. Kaplan was sabotaged and turned onto prostitution by the raw, undisguised brand of pornography that is on the circuit today. Nonetheless, Dr. Kaplan's father fell in love with her, married her, and had him and his sister.

In time, he became the Pastor of the Jerusalem Christian Center; and in view of the rampant prostitution swallowing up the city of Jerusalem today, he remembered from whence he came and started the Jerusalem School of Divine Value that strives to redirect women to their god-ordained purpose. The school endeavors to clean up prostitutes' lives and to develop marketable skills that would enable them to live decent and enriching lives. Each class contained ten girls, and Dr. Drafna's class was particularly interesting; he calls it the Drafna Training Gymnasium; he claims that his class trains these girls' minds to only think living, productive ideas. He insists that a person's life is the clearest reflection of his mind's thoughts and ideas and that, whatever he allows to come into, and to dominate, his mind soon reflects the condition of his life. This episode is a jarring capture of Dr. Drafna's classroom.

Dr. Drafna: Oh, my beautiful children and unforgettable friends, welcome to our life studio and mental gymnasium; we are going to talk about your new, productive ideas today. Your homework assignment was to generate, at least, one idea that can turn you into a millionaire within a clearly defined period. And by the way, Dr. Gefen Chanin is our distinguished visitor today; she is the President of the Anoma Community College, right here in Jerusalem. She has heard heard some pretty swell things about our school and has come by to see what we do here at the Jerusalem School of Divine Value. First of all, our school is based on the principle of God's ubiquitous existence in the universe, now called the multiverse by some astrophysical scientists.

The idea that God does not exist is an embarrassment to science and to normal people who think for themselves; thus, we get off on the right foot, honoring and glorifying God with our lives and work. To them, life had no meaning, other than to sell their bodies for ninety shekels just to survive. When they come to us, they are manifestly in bad shape morally, spiritually, physically, mentally, emotionally, and psychologically. Notwithstanding, we take them; teach them the Bible; tell them who they are; and get them running on all cylinders again. We tell them who they are—not who society and the devil say they are—and, quite often, within weeks; the change is unmistakable. And we've had some fantastic results from, and with, these girls—they are dynamite. Today, we are going to address yesterday's homework assignment. Starting with you, Hanit Eskin, what is your brilliant idea that you think can turn you into a millionaire within the next five to seven years? You must share with us the idea and the mechanism that you would use to bring it to fruition.

Hanit Eskin: Good morning, Doctors Drafna and Chanin; and all hail my awesome classmates: You are the bomb, and I love you all with all my heart, and soul, and person. As you know, I love to tell stories; and because I already know that people like to laugh, I love telling funning stories. Our fabulous life coach, Dr. Drafna, has taught us that life is lived in moments of time; and those moments belong to our purpose for being alive, so I produce new stories every day. These are both short and long stories, and I never get tired of writing these wonderful stories. I've already written fifty-one books in just five short years, and I'm about to graduate from the Jerusalem Academy of Storytelling. Nineteen of my books are best sellers; and I would not tell you how much I earn per year on those books.

In addition, the speaking engagements are beginning to come in from all over the world; I cry when I see people viewing me, an ex-prostitute who had zero self-esteem, as their role model; but I know from whence I came. I came here as a confused prostitute; a desperate young woman with my body ripped up by all kinds of men, just to survive: I am shocked when I see people viewing me as a rock star. But you know, the world has it all wrong: Rock stars promote and celebrate this world's slimy message of lying and cheating; thus, I don't want to be viewed as any rock star; I want to be viewed as a messenger of truth that tells the world that God is real and is a living and gracious heavenly father. God is awesome, but the world is a lie: It is a whirling carriage, rushing headlong into the black pit of doom. The world is rushing into its own destruction.

Dr. Drafna: Dr. Chanin, that is just one of our girls, and she has made me as proud as a peacock: This is what we do here in this neck of the woods. We are off on the right foot, but the world has been running on the wrong foot for millenniums, with broken ankles and hips out of joint; and oh, my, look at the unqualified disaster that the world has turned out to be! You don't have to wonder who is right in a world in which scientists claim that truth is no longer valid in executing scientific analysis and where more than half a dozen shooting sprees and eight high-speed police chases occur every single day. The matter is a simple one: Where Christianity predominates, these evils of this world are blocked by the power of God; and where evil predominates, the peace of mind and the peace, quiet, and secure life that people want are blocked by the devil, the world's spiritual ruler and father of man.

You will either have one or the other, but you cannot have both. When man pushes away God, evil consumes his world; and when he opens up to God again, normalcy returns. Today, you look around, and the whole is ruled, trampled, and mauled by chaos and doom; and even secular commentators are saying that the world is I want to be viewed as a messenger of truth that tells the world that God is real and is a living and gracious heavenly father. We now live in a world that is riddled with prostitution, and pornography, and crime. Violence, crime, doom and ruin are ubiquitous. Dr. Chanin, the world is trampled and mauled by the anarchy of moral decay and lawlessness: One doesn't need to ask who is right anymore; it is obvious that something has gone terribly wrong with our world. Now we see who had been running the world all the time.

Things are way out of control; Jerusalem has been transmogrified into a moral trash heap, and the symptoms and vestiges of moral decay are everywhere. Jerusalem has been virtually turned into a whorehouse, in which prostitutes flit around like butterflies; selling their bodies and disgracing the human race—and to whom do they sell the sex? Well, you would be shocked to know who many of their clients are! Our ex-prostitutes have provided us with shocking and concrete information about who extract sex from prostitutes in Jerusalem and give lip service to abolishing it; naturally, it is difficult to abolish prostitution because men rule the world and love the sex that women provide them for a few dollars. Prostitution allows men to have sex with women without the responsibilities that go along with having sex, making children, and creating a family; as a result of those terrible mistakes that our chauvinistic politicians make every day, I get to do what I do so well: Reprogram and reorient these girls back to their God-given purpose of being mothers and making significant contribution to society.

CHAPTER 16

THE JERUSALEM CHRISTIAN CENTER'S PRAYER LINE

Jerusalem is hailed as the holiest city in the world and home to three major world religions: Christianity, Judaism, and Islam; and with such a record of reverence and holiness, one would think that this city is the most peaceful and reverential place in the world. Unfortunately, it is not: it is one of the most turmoil-ridden cities in the world. Ripped and torn apart by shattered dreams, frenzied polarities, broken people, sociocultural problems, and foggy circumstances; Jerusalem is easily the most curious city in the world. Locked in a titanic, internecine struggle for religious and sociocultural supremacy, this mysterious city is engaged in an interminable conflict between Jews and Arabs, both Children of Abraham. According to the Bible, God had promised Abraham a son after he was well advanced in age.

His wife, Sarah, had lost hope after she had been, presumably, unable to make children. For that reason, she egged her husband to go into their maid and raise up a son to them; and he begrudgingly went, did what he had to do, and impregnated Hagar. She, being young and fresh, brought forth a son unto Abraham named Ishmael. Years later on, God made good on his promise to Abraham and Sarah; and she brought forth a son, whom she called Isaac. From that point onward, there has been an interminable and internecine rivalry between those two sons of Abraham: Isaac and Ishmael, and that is what has been playing out in the Middle East since 1948—and will go on until the end of this age of darkness.

Against this backdrop, there have been disagreement and discord over a range of religious and ideological issues; causing different types of community conflicts in the region. For one thing, Israel is an Abrahamic covenant that God made between himself and Abraham: He made the covenant with Abraham and for its blessings to fall upon Isaac's linage—and this is the essence of the massive and unending conflict that has been going on there in that country, and in Jerusalem, in particular. However, though Israel is in covenant with God, it has bluntly refused to follow the dictates of the Old Testament; and the Jewish Authorities have flatly rejected Jesus as the son of God and his messiah to the world. As a result of Israel's blunt rejection of God and embracement of secularism and humanism, Israel has been in constant turmoil and has had to fight in his sleep in order to survive; thus, it does not subscribe to biblical and Christian morality, and that is the essence of all of its troubles.

The following reflects some of the moral problems with which modern Israelis now grapples—stark poverty, political corruption, rife incest, rampant prostitution, skyrocketing crime, extensive drug addiction, and widespread violence are some of the strapping issues with which Israelis now grapple. Many young girls are molested by their family members—fathers, stepfathers, brothers, and uncles. For many of these girls, the molestation begins as early as three, four, and five years old; from here, most of these girls who've been molested go on to become prostitutes—a kind of graduation of sorts. Many become prostitutes as early as twelve, thirteen and fourteen years old.

In working in the prostitution industry in Israel, thousands of these girls suffer great violence, and many die before ever being able to extract themselves from this massive, hellish darkness and thralldom: Oh, what a pity! According to one news outlet in Jerusalem, 26,000 men purchase sex every night In Israel, a tiny country that is just 8,630 square miles. Recently, the government has been trying to wrestle the behemothic problem of prostitution to the ground and bring it under control. In this regard, a new law has been enacted in Israel that fines users of prostitution services US $614,00 (20000 Israeli shekels) on their first offense, and something like $1,228.00 on their second violation of the new June 30, 2021 law.

However, this is merely a rubber stamping of the age-old prostitution problem in Israel; the real problem is that the police do not enforce the law: They already know that this law is doomed to fail because other similar ones have suffered the same fate in the past; and business, as usual, has continued as it has always done in the past. The prostitution in Israel is a whopping $1.3-billion-dollar industry per year. For this and other reasons, Jerusalem has become a very muddy city, ruddled with moral decay. But the Jerusalem Christian Center's Prayer Line has arisen as a solid bulwark against the moral darkness raging in the city. It operates around the clock and responds to thousands of prayer requests per day. It was against this backdrop that these beleaguered people had called the prayer line for prayer on this particular evening; and their prayer requests reflected a range of tangled and complicated issues.

The very nature of the prayer requests underscores the level of spiritual darkness in the city itself and the disturbing condition of the world. The prayer counsellor that evening was a charming young lady, a former Muslim named Aliana Bronke; and it was a rather dramatic stream of prayer requests indeed. Initially, Aliana, herself, was a recovering disillusioned atheist who'd wandered into the Muslim Faith; but after several years of that and the spiritual hunger persisting deep down in her soul, she gave the born-again experience a chance; and she found Jesus to be quite a helpful friend.
Aliana was raised in the Jerusalem area and had attended a prestigious university in the city; she had a relatively good job, but the spiritual

poverty and emptiness were there—and when her boyfriend, Fevil Altman, dumped her for the girl, Bat Bruik, across the street; that was a watershed moment in her life. Aliana walked into his apartment and caught him, smack in the act, making out with Bat—and she was crushed! The crushing incident made her realize that the world is false and untrustworthy; people are not who they say they are: Aliana recognized that the world is a lie and cannot be depended on. Awash in tears, she called the Jerusalem Christian Center's Prayer Line for prayer from a broken heart, and she wound up giving her life to Jesus and being born again that very evening.

That was truly a turning point in her life: From that day, she began attending the church, the Jerusalem Christian Center; and over time, she, herself, became a prayer counsellor. On this particular evening, Aliana was at the switchboard, manning the phone; she was working the 3:00 to 11:00 evening shift on the prayer line, and this gentleman called for prayer as soon as she got in and got settled down. The gentleman who called in was her ex-boyfriend, Fevil Altman, who was on death row; he'd recently discovered that he had an aggressive and incurable strain of gonorrhea that was resistant to the most potent form of antibiotic on the circuit.

He hadn't seen the doctor for some time. and he was shocked at the level to which the disease had progressed, and Dr. Heram Azel literally gave him up. Dr. Azel compassionately patted him on the shoulder and told him that his journey in this world was about to end; make his peace with Allah, Jesus, God or something, quick! His friend, Elon Castel, had told him about the prayer line and about how many people had had miracles from its prayer warriors' prayers, so he decided to call in. It so happened that he called when his ex-girlfriend, Aliana, was handling things.

Aliana Bronk: Ring, ring, ring: Good afternoon, my name is Aliana Bronk; how may I help you this afternoon? Jesus is the answer to all human problems; he has brought me from a mighty longggg way! What is the issue… how may I help you?

The young man wept and sobbed on the phone; he did not know how to handle this sudden and strange tangled-up situation and did not want to deal with the moral and spiritual crisis, so he hung up the phone and called right back, thinking that a different person would answer the phone. Aliana recognized the phone number, for she had kept it in her purse and had been praying for her cheating ex-lover for almost two years now. Though he'd dumped her and hurt her feelings, she still wanted him to have what Jesus had given to her.

Aliana Bronk: This is Aliana Bronk, how may I help you? You've just called; I recognize the phone number, and you should not play with God like this—he's not a toy. Do not be afraid of the sorrows that have come upon you; God is able to deliver you, for he delivered me from a cheating lover nearly two years ago, and he can certainly deliver you: The question is not whether Jesus can fix your problem; rather, it is whether you believe he can.

Fevil Altman: I am Fevil Altman; I believe we know each other: The doctor has given me up. He said that I just have a few days to live; my body has been ravaged with a fast-moving strain of gonorrhea. A friend of mine told me that people are getting all kinds of miracles from this prayer line, and you are my first miracle: I looked everywhere for you and could not find you, but I found you today; and I'm so happy to meet you for one last time.

Aliana: No, Fevil; that is a personal opinion: You've found the answer to life—you've found Jesus, and he will take care of you; however, before I pray, you need to understand your spiritual condition and clear it up with Jesus, the hungry detergent of human mess and sin. All people were born in sin; all things in the world are composed of matter, and the smallest unit of matter is the atom; in a similar vein, all people were born in spiritual darkness because of what Adam did in the Garden of Eden. It sounds funny because the ruler of this world makes it sound that way: When I was in my mess and sin; I called out to Jesus, and he was there for me. Fevil, people are messed up in this world because of sin, and the devil tells them that there is no such thing as sin and that God either does not exist, or he is trying to take away your fun. I guess, Fevil, you were having fun when you caught gonorrhea—weren't you? But you weren't having fun; you were living in sin, and the wages of sin is death and destruction—and that is what has visited you, my friend. But if you are willing to clean up your life and turn it over to Jesus, he will fix whatever is wrong with you and straighten out all the loose ends in your life—he did it for me, and he will do it for you.

Fevil: Well, how can I argue with you; it's like arguing with my doctor: Do you mean to tell me that that Garden of Eden stuff is not a fairy tale that some strange, weird people made up as a crutch on which to lean in this world—do you mean that there was a literal Garden of Eden?

Aliana: Let me ask you this: Was there a literal Jesus who died on the Cross of Calvary for the sins of mankind—where do you think he came from, and where do you think you are going now? Why do you need to accept Jesus as part of the healing process? The devil is both the spiritual leader and father of the human race and the world because of what Adam did in the Garden of Eden: He allowed the bad shepherd to trick and deceive him with a lie; and from since that lie in the Garden of Eden, the whole world has been tricked by, and has been a lie ever since: That is why people cheat on their spouses, girlfriends, and boyfriends; lies confuse the world and turn it into a fog. What is the essence of that lie? It is trying to live without Jesus and to enjoy God's world without God—no one can do that: This world can only be enjoyed in God's presence.

This, Fevil, is what your life has become: A fog; it is not your life alone that has become a fog; the rest of the world out there is nothing but a fog. Lies, my friend, turn the world into a fog; causing all kinds of collisions and people to meet each other who never should have ever met each other. I cannot pray for you in your present state because you were born wrong: People do wrong, not because they are bad people—they were just born with the wrong nature—and what is that? They were born with the devil's nature. I was born with that same nature; and when I saw that I was about to destroy my life, I howled and called out to Jesus on this same prayer line that I currently man. You don't have to call out to Jesus; you can go on living the way you've been living, using up whatever life you have left in you—It's your choice. Jesus cannot heal you in your sin because it was sin that caused the gonorrhea that is killing you now—wouldn't you agree? It is sin that causes people to cheat on their lovers.

Fevil: Why would I argue with you and God; I've sinned and done many wrong things to people and would do anything to make amends for my wrongdoing. Pray for me, Aliana; go ahead.

Aliana: Fevil, repeat this prayer after me as you call upon God for help; it is sad that many people wait until it is this late to call upon God for the help that they'd always needed. Say after me: Oh, God of heaven; I've sinned against you and against my body: I'm not even worthy to talk to you; have mercy upon me and forgive me of all my sins and cheating on my many girlfriends. I repent of my sins; wash them away from me; wash me in the blood of Jesus and make me a new person. Break any curses that may be upon me and give me a brand-new life; I surrender my life to you, oh, God. Show me where my wealth, success, talents, and greatness lie. Make me the star that I've always been but was led astray in the fog and darkness of this world; Show me why I am here, and what I am to do to accomplish it: If I've spilled most of that time, grant me more time so that I can fulfill my purpose in this world, in the name of Jesus, Amen.

Within one day all the wall eating, while peeing, vanished; the painful swallowing faded away; and when Fevil went back to see his doctor, Dr. Azel, he was shocked and asked him if there was a resurrection from the dead—after extensive tests, he gave Fevil a clean bill of health. What is so significant here is that this young man did not ask for healing: He just ask to be forgiven of his sins and to go to heaven after it was all over; as he recognized that his time on earth had ended. Fevil had faith for salvation but none for healing, but Jesus went ahead and healed him anyway, and he began attending the Jerusalem Christian Center, the church to which Vannetta and Simeon had been going while they prepared for their bid day. However, Fevil was not the last prayer request for the evening—it was just the first one. Fevil tried to reconnect with his ex-girlfriend, Aliana; but she told him that she was quite contented living for Jesus and being celibate.

God's Grace as a Father's Love

Aliana: Ring, ring, ring; My name is Aliana Bront; how may I help you this afternoon? There is no cross from which Jesus cannot deliver you?

Harel Beckman: My name is Harel Beckman; I need prayer just to make it through this night: Two storms have blown into my life at the same time. I am a businessman here in Jerusalem, and a rather lucrative deal has fallen through for me; and I've been swindled out of a considerable amount of money. I am not in the best of mood now; I've already contacted the hit man to fix things for me, but I feel restless and convicted in my soul—I need prayer. I'm about to do something foolish; I want to go out into the Sea of Galilee in my motor boat and dash myself into the sea, forgetting everything for which I've worked so hard. Would you please pray for me?

Aliana: First, Mr. Beckman, calm down; the world will not end tomorrow: I understand your pain and frustration, and life is riddled with storms. You are not the only one facing a storm today. I know that this brings very little comfort to you, but you must calm down before we pray. So, calm down, Mr. Beckman, God will fix it for your; just calm down!

Mr. Beckman: Really, he will! You are such a wonderful lady who cares so much about everyday people: I used to go to a church here in Jerusalem; it was so corrupt that I stopped going because I began getting confused in the darkness and wrongdoing. However, someone had been telling me about this prayer line and church for almost a year now; and when this situation struck me like a bolt lightning, I just could not wait any longer. I guess God has been on my track.

Aliana: Well, Mr. Beckman, it is so good see and know that you've calmed down; tell me the matter that is worrying you again so that I get a better vista of the problem.

Mr. Beckman: I am an agribusiness farmer here in Israel and had been contracted to furnish fruits and vegetables for this grocery chain here in Jerusalem; and suddenly, two of the grocery chains cancelled the deal; in addition, my son and chief accountant, Ariel Beckman, stole two hundred thousand shekels from my business account and has run off to Hobart, Tasmania, with his girlfriend: I am devastated—I don't know what to do but to seek prayer!

Aliana: Well, I have good news for you, Mr. Beckman; the Holy Spirit has just told me there that you are a wandering son who has walked away from the church, and he has allowed these conflicts in your life to get you back on the right track. Go back to your church and pray for your pastor; I've fixed the problem; by the time you get home, you would discover that the issues have been resolved and that the deal has been doubled. You'd also discover that the hitman you were about to hire has become a Christian and will be attending your church.

On his way back home, Mr. Beckman's cell phone rang; it was the manager of the second largest grocery chain in Israel, offering him the opportunity to provide fruits and vegetables for four times the number of stores who had cancelled the earlier deal with him. When he realized that he didn't even need those two store managers' business anymore, he did cartwheels and was very happy. The next day, his daughter who is working for an engineering firm in Paris, France, called him to let him know that she'd sent him a check to help strengthen his business. When he inquired how much it was, it was 400,000.00 Euros, an amount double that which his son had stolen from him.

The next day, he flew to Paris to thank his daughter for helping her father's business in a time of crisis. This particular daughter, Margo, was the one that he had spoilt silly when she was a child, and his son, Ariel, had worn a grudge against him all these years, trying to destroy his father's business. As a thank you note, Mr. Beckman wrote the Jerusalem Christian Center a sizable check, for his business had quadrupled during that year of his initial loss; and despite his son's ireful and vengeful actions, he went looking for him and found him at a famous pub in Hobart, Tasmania. He told him that he loved him but that he had lost his inheritance. His girlfriend was very sad when she heard that, and she walked away from him: he never saw her again, and he was heart-broken! At any rate, as the evening wore on, the calls waxed more and more bizarre; it seemed as if the darker folks kept their prayer requests for last.

The Thorn of Prostitution in Israel

Aliana: Ring, ring rink: Good evening; my name is Aliana Bront: Praise the Lord; what is your name and prayer request? Whatever it is, God has your number and knows you by name; there are approximately one hundred trillion cells in your body, and God knows them all by name. What's bothering you tonight, if I may ask?

Adva Abramov: Yes, I'm not going to beat around the bushes with my issues: I'm fourteen years old; I'm a prostitute and was raped by my father I am pregnant again and don't know what to do: When I was nine years old, I was impregnated by my father twice and aborted both babies. Since then, I am currently a part of a teen prostitution ring here in Jerusalem. I am pregnant again and don't know what to do: My pimp has broken by hand twice: He told me that, if I try to get away from him, he would kill me; and I am really scared. Someone gave me this prayer line's phone number and told me that it is a miracle alley: I must call it; God would fix my problem, and so I did.

Aliana: Have you ever called us before? We have facilities at the church here that address the needs of people like you. Naturally, you are involved in this messy lifestyle because of economic distress; and you fit the typical model of young Jewish girls who've been molested by family members when they were, characteristically, very young. So, don't feel bad about your situation; it's not your fault; I, myself, was in a very messy situation in the past; and God delivered me from it and from myself, who was a disaster going somewhere to happen! This is the way the world is without Jesus; the world is a dark spiritual jungle that is enclosed in a fog, filled with drunk and crazy people who can't see where they are going because of their drunken state and mental illness.

Adva: Well, I almost never do any of my business on the street; I work online and set up all my appointments online: It was when I was looking for clients online that I saw the ad for this church's prayer line on the Internet, and I took down the phone number. It was my friend who drew my attention to the number online and suggested that I call it for prayer out of my situation. And boy, am I glad I did: You are so warm, and kind, and sweet; I wish you can be my sister. I will do anything to get out of prostitution and find a real job and life; I am tired of being kicked around by heartless clients who, although they want sex, they want to to beat me up too. And sometimes, they don't even pay the ninety shekels that I charge. Some nights, you can't sleep for the pain from the self-destructive sex that you had with them on that night or on the night before.

Aliana: Yes, Adva, that is why we are here; and you would not understand it now, but you will later on. The world is a war field, and two opposing forces are fighting—good and evil. The battle started a long time ago in the Garden of Eden. Man believed the devil's lie, and that lie is reigning in the human soul and cosmos up to this day. Most people who get trapped in prostitution love sex and don't mind being paid for it until the piper shows up at their door with a death sentence, and a strange death sentence because you can only do it for so long before you pick up a deadly sexually transmitted disease that drives you away from the world. I'm going to lead you into a prayer, and I want you to go and see Tova Efron tomorrow at 9:30 am: Tell her that Aliana, the prayer counselor, sent you to see her; and she would connect you to the Jerusalem Christian Center's Ministry for Women in Distress. Now, I'm going to lead you into a payer that is going to begin the change process in your life.

Adva: Oh, gracious God in heaven, I was misled and molested by my own father, whom I loved so much; but he misled me in life and and led me down the wrong path. As a result, I killed two of my babies, his own children that he planted into my womb. I killed those babies because I could not afford to take care of them, and he did not care either. Those actions were sinful and wrong in your sight. Come into my heart; wash me clean and clear me of these sins. I repent and am exceedingly sorry for having done these abominable things. Oh,

Lord God, cleanse my soul and wash me whiter than snow: Change my heart and life and turn me into another person who is just like Jesus. I am sick and tired of being a prostitute; I am weary of living wrong and having my body ransacked and dug up by dangerous, uncaring men. Oh, Lord God, I reach out to you for a brand-new life and am willing to follow your way for me. I am a gem that has been mistreated and bruised up by wrong living, but I surrender all to you in exchange for the life that you'd always wanted me to have, and to enjoy in your glorious presence, Amen.

The Spiny Thorn of Incest

Aliana: Good evening, my name is Aliana Bront; welcome to the glorious kingdom of God, the place with all the answers to your problems: How may I help you? What can Jesus do for you this evening. He has the key on every lock in this world.

Shift Pasternak: I've been listening all evening to this prayer program: I'm an academic and atheist, but I admit that there are problems in my life that I don't understand nor seem able to solve on my own. I am not as ordinary and poverty-stricken as the other people who've called in earlier: We are not poor; my father is very rich, and that is why this is all the more shocking. The general consensus of opinion is that rich people have it all together. The name that I've given is an alias in order to protect my family's identity. Early in my life, my father and mother divorced, and I opted to live with my father because my mother was on drugs and could hardly take care of herself; thus, naturally, living with my father seemed to be the better of the two choices—and things went well for a while.

My father seemed to embody all he attributes of a good and loving father until I was twelve years old: I'd just begun exhibiting the features and signs of puberty: seeing my period and showing breasts on my chest. Because I did not understand what was happening to me,

I sought all these intimate answers about my body from my father; at first, he told me to talk to my female teacher, Miss Adrish. However, somewhere around eleven, he began showing more interest in me and answering all my questions; I'd just begun learning about sex from my classmates, and I did not consult Miss Adrish anymore: I'd begun to sense what these intimate matters meant, even though I'd only had a modicum of sexual knowledge.

When I became twelve years old, my father began showing more fatherly love to me; I had never thought that he would see me as a sex object, but that was exactly what happened. Well, they say that gas and fire don't mix well; and perhaps, men and women don't either without sex, even if they are of the same blood. One evening, when I was twelve years old, my father walked into my bedroom and raped me. He pushed his tongue into my mouth and did some other disgusting things that reprogrammed my mind and body and bonded him to me for the next sixteen years! I've run away from him on several occasions, trying to reprogram myself to a more normal life; but it has been of no use. I keep going back to him for more of the same sexual abuse because that is all that I've ever known, and I've grown accustomed to him; but it is a kind of cognitive dissonance.

I want to be around him because he is my father, but I feel trapped in his booby trap of incest abuse. Sometimes, I ask myself if I'm my father's wife, and if I want to be; so, I'm somewhat between and betwixt in this troublesome, vexatious conundrum; and it is tormenting: It is like being in a prison in your own body. and it is tormenting: it is like being in a prisoner in your own body. My father has trained and oriented me into having great sex with him, and now it's hard to let him go; even though I agonize over the shame of being my father's girlfriend. I am not a needy, uneducated person either; I have a Master's degree in computer engineering. I've changed my voice print so that my friends would not detect who I am, even though it is highly unlikely that they would be listening to a station like this: They are all modernists, humanist, and secularists—they are all atheists!

Aliana: Well, I've listened very carefully to what you had to say; and, as you already know that sex with your father is an abomination to God; but it is not against the law here in Israel if both parties are adults: We get thousands of calls like these every day from girls whose fathers, uncles, and brothers have raped them as young as three years old; when your father got to you, you were a virtual adult—you had already begun seeing your period; for most of the girls who've contacted this prayer line, they were mere infants. Most of them have turned out to be prostitutes, like the young lady to whom I've just ministered. Your situation is vastly different from theirs; and because it is not against the law, I cannot tell you to leave your father because you are an atheist.

However, you do have conscience problems being in an incestuous relationship with your dad; and because it is an abomination in the sight of God, your conscience worries are God telling you that you are destroying your life with an illicit relationship with your father. Whichever way you go, it will be difficult for you, for you have already bonded with your father sexually. And for all practical purposes, you are already his girlfriend or wife, whichever way you choose to see it. Your body has already become accustomed to a sexual relationship with him, but God can set you free from that; however, you would have to be willing to let it go.

You cannot play with God; if we pray against this booby trap into which your life has fallen, you would have to mean business with God. What do you think you should do—should you wait and give it some more time and thought, or should you just let it go, cold turkey? I'll tell you one thing: You'd never make up your mind to stop this as long as you are in it—you can't: Not as long as your body will continue to torment you for more sex with your father; sex binds people together, creating a kind of oneness. This is the nature of a mess, and this is exactly what sin does: it confuses your life! You see, being as atheist cannot help you out of this suicidally driven paradox and messy situation in which you find yourself. You are not happy, but you would always like it as long as you are in it.

Shift: Aliana, I want you to pray for, and with, me so that I can get out of this messy lifestyle: I hate myself. Having sex with my father is wrong, but I capitulated to the principle of first; allowing myself to become addicted to his germs. I don't want to be an atheist anymore because all atheism amounts to is the pampering of one's selfish vices, and it is easy to be an atheist so that you can live the immoral life that you want to live; but when that immoral lifestyle entraps and entangles you and turns you into a fool, atheism is not so *cool* after all.

I don't want to do anything about which I'm not proud; and I don't want to go out there and lie either, telling people that I'm proud to be my father's girlfriend or wife—because I'm not! I'm ashamed of the acts in which I've engaged with my father; and he is not a good father either; he's a dirty old man who has taken advantage of his daughter's innocence. One fashion mogul was ashamed to be whatever he was, and he took his own life when the conscience noise got turned up in the dance hall of his mind; and he could not handle it, so he left the dance hall of life behind, with all its trappings of glory.

Aliana: Repeat this prayer after me; we shall give you some assistance that we believe would help you along the way. Repeat this prayer after me: Oh, Lord God; forgive me for saying that I'm an atheist; both atheism and incest are sins against your glorious presence and kingdom of this great multiverse. Wash away all my sins and all thoughts of incest from me; wash me clean with the hungry detergent of your presence and word, and take away all thoughts of sex with my father from me. Break all curses that were spoken over, and put on, me unbeknownst to me. Cleanse and wash me, and make me stand up to my father and tell him that what he has been doing to me is wrong, and I will not participate in it with him anymore: I'm free from the bondage of incest in Jesus name. My body is now free from those crazy urges to have sex with my own father. I reject those nasty desires and thoughts and repent of the sin of incest that had overtaken my body. I am free indeed; Jesus has set me free. I was once consumed by that lustful, incestuous spirit; but I am no longer bound by incest and lust. I am free indeed.

The Ridiculous Crisis of Sex with Dogs

Oh, my! Just when you thought that you'd heard and seen it all; there was more, but it was the kind of more that no one had expected to hear on a prayer line. We've heard of mothers calling and crying about losing their sons; they'd had a romantic relationship with their sons, and they left them for younger girlfriends. Even though these types of prayer requests were somewhat along the fringes and border lined the outrageous, they still had a modicum of rationale to them; at least, a young man, having sex with his mother, is still having sex with a grown woman. Even though it is plainly inappropriate and morally distasteful to the social palate, it is still somewhat tolerable because some women have children very young. Some start their sexual lives as early as eight and nine years old, as is clearly exhibited in Israel and in some European Union countries.

Unfortunately, the world is moving so fast and is so chaotic now that, even before you can catch up with one dramatic change or turn; there is another equally, or even more dramatic one that just blows your socket. This was the case with the incestuous father and daughter relationship mentioned earlier—and now, there was the case of the dog lover. In each of these cases, the person is clearly crossing a forbidden boundary and shows no remorse nor guilt. Let us see what happened in the case of Masha Abeles when she called the prayer line. This was the same young lady who had expressed, at the Jerusalem Christian Center's Relationship Repair Workshop, her affection for a Doberman pincher with which she was living and with whom she slept. She had been advised to stop having sex with the dog and to have it euthanized: What did she do? Well, let us see what steps she took.

Aliana: Ring, ring, ring; Good evening, Aliana Bront speaking; welcome to the Kingdom of God: How may I help you this evening? Whatever your problem may be, there is no issue that Jesus cannot resolve, fix, and solve; but I reckon that this is a heavy one—what is it?

Masha Abeles: I was simply tired going through rejection after rejection; when my last boyfriend walked away from me, I just did not see it coming. We were seemingly doing so well, when he just walked away, and I never saw him again; When I called and asked him what had happened, he told me that he had had enough of me and needed to move on to his next catch. He also told me that things were getting a little bit too loose and that he thought that all women knew what to do to themselves in order to keep things tight and exciting; when I asked him what he meant—if he could speak in plainer Hebrew to me, he hung up the phone and walked away. When I discuss the matter with my friend, Vered Geller, she asked me how long we'd been together; when I told her that we'd been together for two months, she told me that I was lucky: Her last relationship lasted five days. Vered told me that that is part of the woman curse; men leave their wives for younger women with tighter body parts all the time—I was not even his wife: What did I expect!

Aliana: So, what are you saying: What do you want me to do about that—bring him back to you? You should be singing your happy praises that you've gotten rid of another good-for-nothing man. If there is anything that I can do for you is to pray for you that you connect with Jesus and get born again so that the Holy Spirit can divert those kinds of men away from you in the future.

Masha: I don't want that either; that is not what I want. After I was so brokenhearted, I felt as if I were through with men; so, I went and bought a Doberman pincher and settled down with him. He has been such a wonderful companion: He was always there, and he never told me no. However, there was only one problem; I made a mistake and told my friend, Amy Zuffe, about how well my partner and I were getting along; and there was where my problems began: she was so jealous, she began calling me *dog lover*; and it hurt to the bone.

A few months ago, I went to a relationship repair workshop at the Jerusalem Christian Center; and the counselors there told me that I was crazy and that I needed to euthanize the dog and get my life together. However, I know several young ladies who haven't had a boyfriend in years, and they brag about how happy they are with their dog boyfriend. Now, I've tried that, and there is a bother—Why? Why can't people just live the life that they want to live? Why do I have to give up the love of my life because of people? Although it is against the law; thousands of women, in our society, regularly have intercourse with their dog lover in the privacy of their homes; isn't exciting sex just exciting—why does it have to be wrong? Why can't people just accept others for what they value?

Aliana: so, Miss Abeles, is that the reason that you've called this prayer line tonight, and do you expect me, a prayer warrior and servant of the most high God, to encourage you to continue having sex with a dog?—is that why you called this prayer line this evening? That is wrong on every count, regardless of who else is doing it: Sex with a dog is against the law, and it is also an abomination unto God. Miss Abeles, how do you have sex with a dog—does that make any sense at all? Doesn't that tell you that something is wrong with that?—It's a dog, not a human being!

Miss Abeles: I discovered intimacy with my Doberman pincher by merely showering him with my love, and he has responded to me in ways that I was not expecting. This happened over a period of months; initially, I was afraid and ashamed of the thought; but it was there. and one day, it just happened; I was shocked at the level of excitement that I enjoyed with him. However, after I told my friend how much excitement I was having with my dog boyfriend, Skivvy, she got jealous and started calling me dog lover. As a result, I began to feel ashamed of what I was doing—it felt wrong, and the experts at the Jerusalem Christian Center advised me to euthanize the dog and turn my life over to Jesus. Some of my friends who are dog lovers and have dog orgies advised me not to euthanize the dog because I may get into trouble with animal rights activists. Hence the reason that I've called for prayer; I want some more clarity, as to how to move forward; separating myself from my dog boyfriend, Skivvy.

Aliana: Do you want me to pray for your salvation so that Jesus can lead you out of all this fog and confusion; I was once just as confused, as you are now, in another situation; I called out to Jesus, and he delivered me from myself and my destructive selfish desires. May I pray for your salvation? All right, repeat after me:

Oh, great God of the universe, I now reach out to you and repent of the darkness that I've allowed into my life: Wash and cleanse me from all my sins and nasty behavior; take away all this perverted love for Skivvy, my original lover, and give me normal human desires again. Lead me to my purpose in this world and help me to shine like a star in executing my purpose. Come into my life and make me a new person, in the name of Jesus.

Masha finally realized her error of lowering her humanity and self to mate with a dog; she also became aware of the fact that, in making her way back to love with men, she would have to convey to her prospective lovers this dark secret of having mated with a dog; and that may not be easy to do. What she realized is that some things may not be as attractive as they looked when you first saw at them in the heat of the temptation—and having sex with a dog is certainly one of them; for once you make that decision, you've crossed a critical line. And some men may no longer see you as a potential lover nor want to have sex with you in the future—you also now carry the stigma of being a dog lover. At the same time she was dealing with all these mentally tormenting issues, many of the other dog lovers had been rounded by police: One of the girls died in a dog orgy party: she was allergic to dog semen. Somehow or other, the information got out to the city's animal activists; and they stirred the Jerusalem Law Enforcement Department to raid the girl-dog love ring, and dozens of arrests were made.

Shocking Community Storms

Well, Masha Abeles, the girl who fell in love with the Doberman pincher, had been advised by the counsellors at the Jerusalem Relationship Repair Workshop to release the dog to to be euthanized. She was told to refrain from any further romantic involvement with dogs—and she agreed. Realizing that she could not handle this very dramatic and overpowering situation on her own, she called the Jerusalem Christian Center's Prayer Line for prayer and counselling. Aliana Brank; the prayer counsellor, in no uncertain terms; recommended that she refrain from any further sexual intercourse with Skivvy, her dog lover, and that she euthanize the dog. She opted to do that and asked Jesus to come into her life and clean it up; she decided to do just that and felt that she had done the right thing, but her troubles were far from over. In fact, they had just begun.

Even before she had called the church's prayer line, she had been undergoing great depression; knowing that she had to give up her dog lover, the only one who had been loving and kind to her in years. Thus, she had been undergoing considerable depression. Masha had called the already busy Jerusalem 988 suicide and crisis hotline: When she called, she was connected to a mental health professional, Dr. Drafna Bronk; he told her that he was a specialist that dealt with prostitution and that he would recommend that she call the church's prayer line. Well, after a few days of calling the prayer line and talking with various prayer counsellors, she agreed to euthanize the dog—and she begrudgingly did. However, that action triggered a shitload of troubles for her and ignited a powerful firestorm for which she was not nearly prepared; it literally turned her life into hell.

It so happened that Jerusalem has some very strict, nitpicking rules about dogs; Jews love animals and respect animal rights, in part, due to the Jewish ethical obligation to treat animals with kindness: This obligation is unique among Abrahamic religions. At the time when Masha called the prayer line, several people who worked for animal shelters and with animal rights organizations overheard the comments made during the prayer request and her comments about euthanizing the dog. The incident set off a lurid and visceral firestorm of protests from animal rights organizations, and a mob of dog-loving animal rights' activists surrounded the church; claiming that it was doing business with people sexually abusing animals and calling for the church to be shut down.

These frenzied groups sued the church, demanding that it be closed down; but the church prevailed. The Jerusalem judge, Dena Cerf, ruled that the Church is God's holy institution on the earth and should not be blighted, tampered with, and sullied by the stain of secularism and humanism, currently tearing Israeli society to shreds. The judge continued, stating that the Doberman pincher belonged to the girl; if she chose to euthanize it; the crime was committed by her—not by the church. And furthermore, the church has legal and spiritual right to pray for, and to advise, people who call the prayer line for prayer, in line with the law. It certainly has the right to pray for people who engage its prayer line for spiritual counselling and prayer.

Israeli Society in Shock and Chaos

The angry judge roared and bellowed that the church did not break any law and ordered that the mobsters be put away for two weeks; after she cooled off, she advised the plaintiffs to see what could be done regarding the girl euthanizing the dog. The animal rights activists did not seem to mind the church's inculpability. Even after the first group of mobsters were given steep jailtime for surrounding the church and disturbing the peace, several other noisy groups surrounded the church again. They demanded that it be closed down for allowing the atrocity of young girls, sexually abusing dogs and forcing them to have sex with them several times per day.

They called for the church to be padlocked and for an injunction be imposed against any further activities. Nevertheless, the church sued this other batch of zealots, called Pets in your Arms. In the meantime, a liberal judge, Nelly Folk, invoked the injunction against the Christian church and padlocked its door; initiating an incandescent and turmoilous outcry against her.And in a flaming display of a humanistic, secularistic society at war with itself; the conservative Jerusalem mayor arbitrarily revoked the court-ordered injunction, calling it an act of judiciary insanity.

As the dust settled and the din boiled down, the court backed down and acquiesced to the mayor's revocation of the church injunction and for the injunction against Judge Folk, being able to serve as a Jerusalem judge for ninety days, be stayed.In actuality, this judge's license was revoked amidst a hail of death threat. As a result, the judge fled to a resort in the Dead Sea area, thus, allowing the turmoil to boil down After the church was exculpated from any wrongdoing, it sued the animal rights organization, Pets in your Arms for interference with its spiritual and community activities—and it prevailed big time. Because of the cloud that the liberal judge had created in the city, the moratorium placed on her ability to function as judge; for making dumb, hebetic decisions; literally revoked her license to serve in the Israeli judiciary—and there was much talk to do just that. In view of the church's victory over Pets in your Arms, that animal rights organization was ordered to pay $1.7 million to the church for violating a sacred institution, disturbing the peace, and defacing and damaging private property.

Having lost their battle against the Church, the various animal rights' groups sued Masha Abeles for murdering the Doberman pincher in all her silliness; but again, the conservative Jerusalem Court exculpated Masha from any wrongdoing for euthanizing her Doberman pincher. In spite of a whirling spate of legal rulings against them, the animal rights' groups refused to back down and give up the fight. Being connected to some higher-ups in the legal system of the government, they lobbied for a law to criminalize people who have sex with animals. This was directed mainly at women who lived with a dog, or had several dogs and were suspected of being too close to comfort with them. These placed hundreds of women's living arrangements in stark jeopardy.

The animal rights activists also lobbied to prosecute anyone suspected of sexually abusing a dog or any other animal, and to give landlords the legal right to exercise more leverage in dealing with women living alone with dogs. This ignited another firestorm against animal rights' activists who wanted to prosecute women, living alone with a dog, or with several dogs, and are suspected of having sex with them. They also went to the neighborhood in which Masha lived, surrounded her flat with noisy screams, and began taunting her; calling her a slut and dog lover. Some had rocks in their hands and began threatening to trash her home: These rabble rousers, too, of the baser sort, were rounded up by the police and given steep prison terms for disturbing the peace and making frightening threats. Many of them were put away for years!

The pesky matter has never been brought to closure; and in a liberal society, like Israel, it is difficult to clamp down on such extremes. Marginal behavior; like having sex with animals, freedom of choice, and boundaryless love; is the day's mantra. People just want to be left alone to live their own lives however they choose. And in a world where nothing is wrong with anything anymore, people are expected to look the other way at clear violation of the law; even if they see a woman having sex with a dog. Even if they behold a woman making out with a dog, in the greatest show on earth; in a shady, shadowy world like this one; they still ought to understand that it is none of their business. In the light of the litigious atmosphere in Jerusalem, most people tend to mind their own business and do whatever they have to do. Even the police look the other way at prostitutes transacting business with their Johns, an act that is clearly against the law. If they honor prostitutes like that, you don't have to wonder what they would do; on spotting a woman having sex with a dog, reputedly the greatest show on Earth!

Vanetta and Simeon Back in the Spotlight

Well, several months had elapsed since Vanetta and Simeon had had that chat with their psychotherapist, Dr. Adair, in his office; he had recommended that they engage in a softer discourse with sexologist Dr. Thama Abeles before their wedding. However, they'd made so much progress and were so immersed in their personal healing that they opted to defer the heavier lifting of the sexological aspects of their relationship; as they'd reputedly claimed that, for religious reasons, they'd not been having sex. Well, that was commendable indeed—wasn't it? However, this colorful and exquisitely decorated couple was about to jump over the broomstick and to experience all the honor that one's big day accords him.

Accordingly, they were advised by Dr. Adair to do some light lifting on the matter of sex with their sexologist, Dr. Abeles. As you might recall, these are the superrich folks who had to be handled like vitreous gems: You might wonder, "Why would people, in their right minds, want to spend all that money just to talk about sex—isn't that a non-issue? Don't people just have sex and enjoy it: Isn't sex something that people just enjoy and do whenever the urge comes to them? Why all this fuss about sex—if they are having an issue with it, couldn't they just discuss that with a friend—can't they?"

And they, most certainly, can do that with a friend; notwithstanding, they are billionaires—they aren't ordinary people like you and me, and there were some legitimate issues indeed that needed to be thrashed out. Moreover, sex is more complicated that most people want to admit: Many people suffer from devastating sexual dysfunction and, for one reason or another, don't enjoy sex. Simeon carried quite a weight in his crotch, and he was afraid that he might hurt his baby doll, Vanetta; however, she did not seem to mine, even though he'd discussed the matter with her. So, you can see that there were valid reasons for this sexological discourse; and after they were there for a few minutes, in walked Dr. Thama Abeles into the counselling room: What happened as she warmly embraced the couple and bade them to sit down?

Dr. Abeles: Oh, good morning, Simeon and Vanetta, how are you? it's so wonderful to see you both again, since I last saw Simeon in Auckland a year ago—and you two hadn't even known each other as yet. So, how did this happen: Can you tell me how you two met and what has unfolded snice. You look so happy and filled with joy.

Simeon: Well, certainly; we met at the Jerusalem Gardens, and from the moment I saw her, I had butterflies and knew that she was my wife. Several other girls were vying for the position, but they were too sex-driven for me—I wanted more than just beauty and great sex; I wanted a solid, well-rounded woman. I wanted more than just sex—and I got it!

Dr. Abeles: Well, what do you mean by saying that you wanted more than just beauty and great sex—what exactly does that mean? I used to think that no one could top that, but I'm wrong!

Simeon: I think that we, in the West, make a great mistake of overrating sex and its entertainment value; there is no question that clean, powerful sex is a great source of entertainment to any relationship. But my ga lee, sex has become the relationship itself, to the point where, if you don't deliver it every day, these women go and scandalize your name; saying that you are not a real man and can't do anything. They went about Jerusalem, scandalizing my name and saying that I can't do anything—I can't get it up. It is rather disgraceful and sad that long-term, caring relationships have come to this: it is sick and sad indeed, isn't it? There is more to love and relationships than mere sex; we, in the West, need to wake up and smell the coffee; our civilization is dying from moral decay, and folks need to wake up before it is too late.

Dr. Abeles: And Vanetta, how do you feel about all this, seeing that you have preserved that aspect for the upcoming marriage; what does that mean to you?

Vanetta: Absolutely nothing, and although sex isn't, indeed, everything in a relationship, it is a large chunk and sets the tone of the whole relationship itself. Thus, in that regard, I've done extensive research on the topic, and most writers seem to favor the idea that women set the tone for sex in most relationships; if the atmosphere that the woman creates is not conducive to a loving, caring relationship; very little sex will be done in that relationship. A man wants a woman whom he likes and can trust: It all boils down to centripetal and centrifugal forces. Women who create centripetal forces in the relationship bind men to them, thus creating a strong bond. They study their men and understand how to love them; all men are not driven by sex and cannot be loved the same way: I love this man with all my heart.

Dr. Abeles: And how do you manage to love him that much without sex—how does that work: Isn't sex the binding glue in a relationship?

Vanetta: No, Dr. Abeles, it is the binding glue in relationships that don't work because it is the essence of those relationships; and like I've said before, a man wants a woman who is not only great entertainment in bed, but who also knows the foreplay lines to keep the sex going. And those are the centripetal forces about which I've spoken. They include great communication, being able to send messages without saying a word; being caring and loving; doing things that make the man laugh; treating sex as being last on the agenda; being kind and gentle to him, and putting his interests first. These things get a man's attention and make him think about you and want to be around you. You see, Dr. Abeles; this is how you preserve sex for a better time and force your man to see you as gold; and at the same time, you should not connect with men whom you already know are not your type.

Sex is a mental weight; if you concentrate on building a quality relationship, treating sex as the mere icing on the cake; not only will you build a better relationship: You will wind up having more sex with your feller because there will be less arguments. Building a relationship on exciting sex alone is a bad mistake that many women make; and when the sex gets stale and the going gets rough, because there is no solid foundation, on which the relationship is firmly entrenched; it fizzles out and fades away. As soon as a crisis develops, those feelings change really quickly, and all that sex just vanishes away. This is the reason that many women lament that they thought that they were in a solid relationship with their feller when, all of a sudden, it just wilted and faded away. The reality is that all that sex on which you depended to hold things together, when the going got tough, it did not work. It could not hold things together when the storms, that blow by ever so often, crashed upon it; and it collapsed—and that is too bad.

Dr. Abeles: If you don't have sex in the early part of the relationship, how would you know what time of day you prefer having sex and what sexual positions you really like and prefer?

Vanetta: Like I said, good relationships treat sex as a minor issue; in that regard, missionary style delivers the same level of excitement as the glide or doggy style. I have already studied all these different sex positions; and as exciting as they may be, they don't keep people married. In fact, you would not enjoy them if those centripetal forces are not there; at the end of the day, they are merely non-issues—they don't keep people married. There has never been a time when there has been more talk about sex and sex positions; and at the same time, there has never been a time when more marriages break up due to infidelity than today. In this regard, emphasis on sex positions is mere vanity and illusion; their virtue and value in marriage is marginal and relatively tiny. However, because human society is a fog and people are not concerned about truth and what works, but rather, what is popular; most people miss the substance of that on which they should be concentrating because they are so busy working on fads that are plain vanities.

The Sexual Cycle and Demon Transmission

Dr. Abeles: Now, that we've treated some of the lighter matters, I'd like us to do some of the heavier lifting at this point: Simeon, what, in your opinion, should married couples do in order to keep sex exciting. How would you go about keeping your wife sexually excited about you?

Simeon: There is only one way to keep sex exciting in a marriage, and that is to treat your wife with love and respect; for example, you should always insist on being your best around her and maintaining good, personal hygiene, that so easily slips away in so many marriages. Moreover, sex is a cycle, just like one's urinary cycle or eating cycle. Some people have rapid sexual cycles because they have a relatively high libido; others have an average or low libido: here is where centripetal forces enter the picture and play a great role in one's marriage. If you know that your wife's libido is high, then you should cater to it by gauging it and learning how often she becomes aroused, to the point where she really needs sex. You live with her; you should know her, and you should know her biorhythm.

Once you've nailed that down, you should then orient yourself to meeting her sexual needs: If she needs sex every day, you should do the best you can if your libido is not that high. And again, those centripetal forces would help things out. If you really love your husband, you won't force him to have sex with you beyond his capability; and you should have more respect for your marriage than that. That is why my wife insists that sex should only be viewed as the icing on the cake—and not the cake itself: Some people are demon possessed and have uncontrollable sexual desires. No one would ever be able to satisfy such people sexually because they are not normal; their sexual urges are driven by the devil; and if you try to meet their sexual needs, they would wear you out.

The solution to this crisis is to find an exorcist to clear your wife of these devilish forces and drives. This is one of the things that the Internet and pornography have done: Many people have caught demons from Internet pornography and from sexual partners that they've had in the past. This is why sex should be deferred for a later time when people have gotten to know each other better. In many ways, the world is a very naïve place; and fools rush where angels fail to tread. These things are real; people do become demonized and need exorcism. If you are married to one of them, and the need is sex; I'll tell you one thing: You have a Herculean job ahead of you. Careless sex is a very dangerous activity because it is one of the principal conduits through which demons are transferred or transmitted form one person to another. In many ways, demons are transmitted to people just like diseases. For example, if you have sex with a lesbian woman, whether you realize it or not; that lesbian demon is transmitted to you—and the same thing goes for a range of other situations. This explains why some people wake up one day and realize that they are gay—they never were before. It was when they had sex with that girl at the desk in the office that things changed forever.

And sometimes, it doesn't happen right away; however, at some point in time, that spirit was transferred to you when you had sex with that lesbian or bisexual girl, at the desk, in the office that you began to feel differently. The sexually perverted spirit began to let you know that it is there, in your body, and wants some action—and it does so by recalibrating and perverting your emotional system, throwing your life into upheavals. This discussion is not about demon transmission: It is about understanding your lover's sexual cycle; however, if you are out of control sexually, he will not be able to satisfy you—no matter what he does. In that case you are no longer a normal person, you are the devil and needs an exorcist. If your lover insists on trying to meet your sexual needs, you will merely wear him out—or kill him, for that matter!

People need to have more respect for sex and the risks associated with it; the world is driven by demon spirits; and they operate in every arena of world affairs. Under normal circumstances, your spouse's sexual cycle can be used to manage sex within your marriage; and the one thing that you do not want to do is to say no to your spouse when he or she insist on having sex. Think about it: If you don't give it to him, who will—the horny girl across the street, who has been batting her eyes at him ever since he was married to you?

Think about it: There is always a clean vagina somewhere else besides yours: If you don't give him access to yours, he'll find access somewhere else. And that is why sex should not be so greatly emphasized in the earlier part of a long-term, intimate relationship so that you two can get to know each other better and get to know what needs to be worked on before you jump into sex. Your partner's sexual cycle, use of tact, and good judgment should set the pattern of your marriage's sexual cycle. I will follow the flow and work with it; it's a good and reliable clock for any married couple.

Simeon: Centripetal Currents of Foreplay

In addition to gauging and working with my partner's sexual cycle, working with centripetal currents that bring me closer to my wife is a great sex regime aid; for example, not allowing my eyes to wander away from her when we go out, say to dinner or at the mall, reinforces my love and commitment to her. Nothing is more embarrassing than being out with a woman, and her eyes are wandering around; looking at other men. This is one red flag that she may be possessed by sex demons and is not the right fit for you. In addition, being playful and joking around with each other, as a matter of policy regarding your marriage, works wonders for a marriage.

It helps you to know when something is wrong, thus enabling you to jump on it right away and not allow it to fester and confuse your happy marriage. In this regard, success in my marriage is healthy teamwork, thus allowing both of us to work together, in a healthy way, on the same team.

Although working with my wife's sexual clock yields much valuable sexual frequency insight, that does not rule out setting up some kind of time system when sex is likely to occur and when it is definitely on the schedule. Working with these three gauges allows me to pace myself and to create a sexual system that works for both of us. Training ourselves to be both spontaneous; working with some kind Training ourselves to be spontaneous; working with some kind of love-making schedule; and being as playful as possible, as an ongoing form of foreplay; would definitely keep us right on target. Thus, we will apply a dualistic system of foreplay: ongoing foreplay and diversified foreplay, just before sex.

These would include things like use of games; taking a shower; applying sexy fragrances; staying in an attitude of romance with our words and action; touching each other in a sexy way, and especially each other's sexual zones; talking to each other about our hot zones and sexual fantasies; talking about sex; writing love notes to each other; watching a sexual movie that does not violate our Christian beliefs and values; reading clean, sexy Christian romance books; peeling off our clothes; and engaging in the kissing game. In sum, keeping marriage hot and full of sex is a bundle of teamwork in which couples need to engage in order to retain plenty action in the bedroom and not to allow the monstrosity of sexlessness to sour their marriage.

Other aspects of foreplay that we may apply in the pre-sex warm up is the kissing game, where we kiss each other differently every time, in view of producing maximum arousal: This includes applying ideas such as fifteen ways to kiss her brightly painted lips and to open the faucet downstairs. In addition, the use of amorous glances which we associate with sex, especially just before it happens, can add much fuel to the fire; we both love and use make up; and in my opinion, that is a splendid turn on. Moreover, soft rock music creates an environment that is ideal for foreplay; this is augmented by asking many questions about each other's hot zones.

Saying things such as, lead my hands where you want them to go, and show my mouth what it should do to you: These innocent words intensify the mood and passion built up in the hall of fire. Although I am the man, letting my wife know that it is okay for her to take the lead sometimes can greatly turn up the heat in the parlor of love. Letting her kiss my lips gently, firmly, and softly; whispering zany, erotic messages in my ear can work wonders in the bedroom. In addition, she would wear crotchless panties and do a lot touching and embracing when she is most sexually aroused, instead of always be waiting for me to initiate the sexual process.

Dr. Abeles: Simeon, I don't know if I'd would ever do this again with a feller like you; you've taught me some wonderful things to share with my husband. I must say that I'd greatly underestimated your level of skill and experience in romantic matters; I'm truly impressed with your skill and level of experience in erotic matters. I know that Vanetta is heartened and highly ravished by your no-nonsense romantic experience. Although you initially reflected a sour attitude about sex—because of your experience with unhappy women who've had devastating run ins with men—you are still quite a feller in the bedroom. You met these sorry women whose boyfriends impregnated, and left, them all by themselves; and they poisoned your jolly spirit. The pain and nightmares squeezed these sad women into a life of tears, meaninglessness, and suicide. Despite all that though, you scored high on the questions that I asked you; however, you still reflect a smattering of your original contact with these sad, sour women of your past.

Against that backdrop, Dr. Abeles took him back to the time when he was interacting with all these unhappy women who had killed their babies. These mental and emotional wounds, though sustained by the unhappy women with whom he interacted, affected him and needed to be cleansed and removed from his system. Though most women have the same hot zones, that is not a rule of thumb; it is amazing how widely the range differs. It is amazing to know how many women do not have any hot zones in their breasts; thus, men who use a one-size-fits-all approach to foreplay miss it by a thousand miles! However though, strangely enough, it is their breasts or; for most women, their vagina where the fire is located.

Thus, the list of hot zones that Simeon presented to Dr. Abeles included the mouth, the breasts, and the vagina—and that was great; but the range of a woman's hot zones is much more involved than that. Dozens of other areas were left out: these included the inside of the wrist, the side of the neck, the buttocks, the scalp, the nape of the neck, the bulge of the shoulder, the area behind the knee, the legs, the feet, the elbow, the armpit, inner arm, the bottom of the feet, the belly button, the hands, the inner thigh, the lower back, the pubic mound, the stomach, the crook of the arms, the space between your toes, the area inside the ankle, the lips, the perineum, the anterior vaginal wall, the brain, and the Achilles tendon. That is quite a list— wouldn't your say? Dr. Abeles purposefully left out the anus because of its association with sodomy and the Bible's negative response to that.

Dr. Abeles: Now, I'd like you to kiss your fiancée, Vanetta, as passionately as you can; and do it as if no one else was in the room with you two.

And to that prompt, Simeon got up, hugged Vanetta tightly, and kissed her as if they were alone on a fairyland. It was interesting to see where his hands automatically went, as if indeed, no one else was in the room but those two. As he dragged his hands against her vagina, Vanetta twitched like a hamster and began adjusting herself to his crotch: It was a shocking display of intimacy in a public setting. The kiss lasted three minutes, and even the sexologist blushed several times. From her reaction, it seemed as if she were trying to stir up some fire between them for later on that evening; however, they weren't too keen about sex later on that day; they'd already decided on that matter long before they'd met Dr. Abeles. Although they were very curious about, and appetent to have, sex; they had already decided not to do it outside the context of marriage; thus, to them; that was a foregone conclusion. Their moral value took precedence over their craving for sex.

Wrapping Things Up

Having thoroughly enjoyed the kiss with her fiancé whom they said could not do anything and could not get it up, she apprised Dr. Abeles that she is a sex maniacal virgin and that she thought about sex all the time but had learned to control her emotions. She told the sexologist that, though she liked talking about sex, she had seen the damage that unwise recreational sex does to young, directionless women; drifting on the raging sea of life, without a plan for their lives. Thus, she had learned to control herself and to put things in their proper perspective.

Dr. Abeles A sex maniacal virgin! I've never heard of that combination of words in my life—how does that work? How does one become a sex maniacal virgin?

Vanetta: Well, your see, I've had a few heartbreaks in my life, and they taught me to cross my legs and wait for the right time; currently, I believe I'm with the right man; but my father taught me, from a little infant, to wait for the time that God has specified in the Bible. So, God sent me a man who had been broken by past relationships himself; and so, we've decided to wait. Eating a fruit before it is ripe creates a tart and acrid taste in your mouth; but if you wait until that fruit is ripe and sweet; it is just delicious. Nonetheless, this does not mean that sex does not flood my mind almost every day. The world is full of sex—it is everywhere, but that same world is flooded with trouble caused by that same sex: After a while, you kind of get the message and learn to stay away from poisonous fruits that grow on almost every limb out there in the world. However, in the meantime, I fantasize about my favorite foreplay routine of choice: Long, pretty, poetic love notes; breathing bubbles in his face; hot, erotic whispers in his ears; massaging his legs, hands, and face; and scrubbing his back beneath the shower.

Dr. Abeles: So, Dr. Firne, I've heard much from your fiancé about his preferred time of day for sex; what are your thoughts on this matter?

Vanetta: Oh, that, sex at any time of the day is great; but early morning, when he is fresh and refreshed, is definitely preferred. I would keep sex exciting in our marriage by daily telling Simeon how much I love him and staying physically fit and in shape for him.

Dr. Abeles: Well, none of you have said anything about children: What are your thoughts on this matter? Children strongly affect a couple's life; how would you handle children, and how many do you want—have you given any thought to that?

Vanetta: Because of the damage that ill-timed pregnancies and children exert on married couples, we have already decided to have only two of the them and will not start having children until after five years of marriage. This is because children engender a certain level of sexual deformity in women; and the more you have, the wider and looser the vagina becomes. The silly child-generating mother develops stretch marks on her legs, and her skin becomes looser: She develops wrinkles on her skin and in her face; and without strenuous and extensive Kegel exercises, the vagina loses its tightness. Over time, her breasts fall down on her chest; her competitors increase by the day; they wax bolder and bolder.

The silly mother comes under immense pressure; and while all these unhappy things are happening to her, her husband has long walked out on her. She has been long divorced because she's older now and has lost her luster and bloom and is no longer seen in the same light: She is the older woman now; her breasts sag and have fallen down, and her vagina is looser now. All that youthful beauty and attention from the fellers, who used to wink at, and hound, her for a taste of her is gone now; they've all moved on to greener pastures and younger women. This is not to intimate that my dear lover boy, Simeon, would ever do any of those things to me; however, I do not want to fall into the trap up into which so many silly mothers wind: I wonder; why is the world so sick and sorry, Dr. Abeles?

Dr. Abeles: Oh, Vanetta, I wish I knew; it happened to my mother, Alona, and to my sister, too: My sister, Shift, had seven children for her husband, Doron, after which one day he got up and walked away. We haven't seen him since: That is the real price of beauty and youth; they last for a while and seem to be all yours; and then, they fade away!

Oh, my, why did such a professional sexological counselling session end on such a sour note? No, it did not end on a sour note; the truth about how the world really works could not remain in the bottle of human intellect and pretense forever. The hurt was on both sides; and Vanetta's seeming naivety, pertness, unwisdom, and weird sense of humor caused it to drain from the bottle. But eventually, they all cheered up and got ready for that magnificent upcoming wedding in Ajaccio, Corsica. They looked at each other and said, "Well, *c'est la vie*: Isn't it?" Suddenly, the umbral thought about the way the world works faded; and they brightened up about the wedding—that golden wedding that was about to take place in the charming enclave of Sargesse, Ajaccio, in Corsica, France. Several of these behavioral scientists were invited to this regal bash.

Final Comments

Well, all's well that ends well—isn't it? Many would prefer the world to be what they either want it to be or think it is; unfortunately, the world is neither of those; the world is what it is. We all wake up and find ourselves in a world that should make sense but doesn't; unhappily, not many dig into this strange, mysterious question: What are we doing here—why am I here, in this world? The truth is that, if more people would dig into their spiritual destiny and ask why they are here on this earth, the world would certainly make more sense. Each person who comes into this world is sent with a message for the world. The message is his reason for being here; and when that message is properly executed, he has no time to waste other people's time.

All the hurt in the world is caused by people who waste other people's time, and wasting other people's time is a jar filled with tears. Thus, the world would have been an entirely different place if people did not follow its lead; things would have been starkly different if people's focus was finding their purpose and executing it with integrity. All the happiness in the world is bound up in finding the reason that you are here—not in going to the best university but in finding your purpose. You see, that is what the world tells you happiness is: Going to the best university—that is a lie.

Happiness lies in finding your purpose for being in this world—and what is that? It is enjoying God's world with his approval, for no one can enjoy God's world without God. That is why the marriages break up; that is why the successful business did not bring you happiness—and that is why your daughter committed suicide. The man who walks away from his wife of twenty, thirty years is a fool because the fiddle gets sweeter with time. God created the world and sent you into it to enjoy the beauty of his presence while you are transmitting the message that you brought with you into the world to festoon and beautify it with your gifts and talents. That is what you should be doing every day of your life: Enjoying God's world in his presence—not in wasting people's time. Unhappily, though, the whole world is wrapped up in telling lies and wasting other people's time.

The Afterword

Historically, human society has reflected a peculiar pattern of growth, decline, destruction, and rebirth; somehow or other, society has been hamstrung by this mysterious weakness and inability to go on. This tenebrous pattern has, time and time again, been observed in society after society; reflecting a plain pattern of design. It almost seems as if each society has been wired to some mystical clock that stops working after a certain amount of time has elapsed; in many ways, human society reflects the normal biological program of human beings. The main difference is that people's psychobiological decline occurs much faster than society's: In almost every other way, they are similar. Just as how society's demise is hastened by moral decay, people's individual lifespans are reduced by their abuse of moral laws.

Whether the person has had any moral weaknesses or not, after a while; that decline sets in, suggesting some psychobiological clock at work in the person's life. Presumably, when Adam disobeyed God in the Garden of Eden, his immortal clock was recalibrated to work according the death law; thus, while no tangible reason exists for human mortality, it occurs regardless of the clear biological wiring and system that suggest that it ought not to happen. In a similar vein, human society should be able to continue functioning indefinitely, according to the laws that have been established in nature.

Despite that fact, though, human society weakens and disintegrates to nothing after a while; suggesting that, just as how man himself eventually fades away, society can only function effectively for so long. The facts seem to suggest that society is bounded by certain laws of design; and according to those laws, human systems are only allowed to last for so long. After a certain amount of time has elapsed, the system literally dies. And the fact that we see this obscure pattern, in virtually every major civilization of the past, tells us that human society functions according to some clearly defined system, with the Roman Empire lasting the longest. What is also peculiar here is that all human civilizations of the past faded away in the same clearly predictable pattern: They rejected their former religious foundation and embraced foreign, liberal ideas that were inherently detrimental to the society itself. As a result, they were devoured by the forces of liberalism and perversion of the natural order.

It is as if the society becomes cannibalistic and begins to eat its own self, by turning against the very religious principles that brought it into existence and made it great. In each instance of societal decay and fossilization, religious violation is involved. In the course of time, the society waxes increasingly corrupt; embracing falsehood and perversion of natural order. Eventually, the society becomes a nuisance to time and just fades out of view; turning into lifeless columns that just stand there in the storm of time. This has been the unfortunate pattern in society, after society, after society: Oh, how sad! It seems as if, once the pattern sets in, the destruction is irreversible.

It is rather interesting to note that these societies generally start out obeying natural order; and then, somewhere along the way; their leaders become corrupted by the devil; but secular historians don't see it that way. They put a secular spin on it, even though it is very obvious that these religious practices are connected to secret spiritual forces in the universe. However, many of these historians belong to secret societies, themselves; and because they do, they don't tell it like it is: They put a phony secular spin on things. For example, when Nebuchadnezzar was driven out into the field to eat grass, like an animal for seven years; secular historians do not record this incident in the King of Babylon's life. This suggests that historians are intentionally trying to cover up the supernatural, intimating that the world is driven by lies and that science is only a front that man uses to hide the work of the devil and the presence of God in the world. Here, we see that world is clearly false: It is a miracle of falsehood—an optical illusion.

More often than not, when a society dies, that society is supplanted by another society that follows it in that order and will go down in the same distinct manner as its predecessor. Thus, human history has been a parade of civilizations that appeared from the sea of mankind, grew and developed into regional or global powers, and then declined and disappeared back into the sea from which they arose. In this regard, the system in the world does not treat the entirety of the human experience. What you see in the world today is only partially connected to climate change. Its explanation is much more doomful and sinister than *the amorals* and *the iconoclasts* want you to believe. In other words, ordinary people in society are deceived by some very serpentine and clever folks who control the flow of information and the program of reality in the world. Thus, what they tell you about why things are the way they are is a lie. In this regard, life on the earth is one interminable stream of lies—and you need to know this in order to achieve your purpose for being here in this world.

Because these folks control the flow of information in the world, they determine right and wrong; therefore, they plan the destiny of the world. These societal engineers poisoned the Christian Church and tricked it into accepting and depending on phony, shallow psychology to solve society's problems. Using psychology as a substitute for the Bible, the world rapidly began to change and spin out of control. As man opens up more and more to the devil and his system of doing things; he will continue to lose control of law and order in the world, and things will get increasingly barbarous and lawless worldwide.

However, because of what Adam did in the Garden of Eden, man and the devil can only control the world for six thousand years; and that time has already elapsed; thus, mankind will no longer be able to rule this world as he did in the past. This explains why virtually every system in the world today is on life support: Man no longer has control of the earth, thus explaining why, all of a sudden, everything is in upheavals around the world. This explains the strange, peculiar changes and the rapidly deteriorating morals that we see in the world, with more and more women having sex with dogs and horses. They are insane; they've lost their minds—and it is going to get worse.

Bibliography

Behe, M. Darwin's Black Box: The Biochemical Challenge to Evolution, 1996, Free Press, New York, New York City.

Colson, C. How now Shall we Live, 2004, Tyndale House Publication, Carol Stream, Illinois.

Wakim, S. and Grewal, M. Chemical Reactions in Living Things, Butte College, Google Listing.

Google Listing with no formal contributors: One Billion Biochemical Reactions in a Cell per Second.

Bilson, J. 'Suicide and Youth Risk Factors'; 2018

2022, 'Increasing Suicide Rate Among French Young People,' *Le Monde*

Stoecklein, K. September 10, 2020. 'I was a Pastor's Wife: Suicide Made me a Pastor's Widow.'

Chamovitz, M. 'Dressed in Gold Bikinis: Sex Workers Solicit in Tel Barush,' August 10, 2018. *The Jerusalem Post.*

Feldstein, J. August 23, 2022 'Gilboa Ping-Pong Affair: Israel shouldn't See Prostitution as Normal.'

June 1, 2023, 'This Israel Nudist Beach in the Top of its Kind Worldwide.' The Jerusalem Post.

Wilkerson, J. August 19, 2020 'The Fetishization of Female Teachers in Sexual Misconduct Cases.' *The Leo Weekly News.*

Sheratt, A, May 23, 2017; Homeless Teacher: I wouldn't Talk about it; I was so. The UK Housing Crisis Hits Professionals. *The Guardian.*

Hall, S. October 7, 2022. 'Affordable Housing: Teachers Face Homelessness Across the Nation.'

The Streaming Library Bookshop

This rear section reflects the books that have already been written and are currently being polished and prepared for publication: If you enjoyed *Crashing Streams of Change: The Rise of World Government,* you will enjoy these upcoming, brand-new publications even more. They graphically capture the drama, the humor, and all the twists and turns of everyday life and the University of Later on down the Road. They poignantly depict the jarring tight corners and dead ends in which people find themselves and the difficulties that they face in extracting themselves from these gins and traps thrown in their way. Stuffed with a bellyful of laughs, a library of new information, and a boundless pool of wisdom; these books generate fresh insight and understanding about how the world really works and give you a unique tool set with which to conquer life's numerous issues and problems. The books are a new way of looking at the world, seeing it as being false, and giving you the heads up on how to deal with people in a false world. This approach is particularly useful, in view of the fact that most of the problems that people have are caused by lies that others have told them and led them to believe. The books are funny, electrifying, delightful and downright addictive; they will fry all your eggs and show you a new and productive way to live in this world.

New Books on their Way

1)Mysterious Connections: Weird Relationships

2)A Winding Blazing River of Fire

3)The Scarlet Flower of Beauty

4)The Poem of a Most Charming Honeymoon

5)Understanding the World: The Great Recession Crisis

6)A Strange Conversation: Divorce Averted

7)The Slut Gene and the Cheating Revolution

8)The World and Its People

9)A Shockingly Ugly Divorce Court Hearing

10)The Glorious Power of love

The book category is Women's Fiction and, or New Adult, set in Jerusalem and New Zealand. Its book's keywords are:

a) Relationship management

b) Finding love in a dark and difficult world

c) Managing sexual emotions

d) Societal Decay and Maniacal Virgins Lost in the Fog

e) Controlling the storm of sexual energy

f) Virgins' quaint craving for physical intimacy and their cross of sex

g) The virgin sex crisis: Old Virgins, the beating they take, and the Cross they bear in a sex-obsessed society

h) Pregnancy, abortion, and the plague of suicide--oh my

i) The golden beauty of love and marriage between a man and a woman

j) The awesome power of sex, the sex rush, and its grinding illusion

k) Sex's Devaluation and Destruction of Women

l) The Terrible Weapon of the Male Sperm

m) Pregnancy's cheapening of women's value

n) Abortion's ruin of women's value and the prison of their past

o) Abortion, a nasty prelude to suicide

p) Abortion, mental illness, depression, and suicide

q) Abortion and its damning side effects

r) Sex, pregnancy, single motherhood, and mother-son sex

s) Sex, Abortion, Depression, and suicide: Strapping lies, wrapped in invisible booby traps